READER COMMENTS:

On Shadow of Doubt

Finalist for RPLA Romance Novel of 2016

"Erwin writes with such a flow that one is compelled to turn
the page and stay absorbed in the story!"
--Ronald Woods

"Excellent book! It was a fast, evolving read."
--Isa Tanenbaum

"Modern day Downton Abbey."
--Nina Linkins

On Shadow of Silence

"I had a difficult time laying the book down."
--Shirley McCoy

"The kind of book that you're sad to see end because
it's so good!"
--Amy Tucker

"I couldn't put it down."
--Katherine Birnbaum

On Shadows from the Past

"Judith Erwin has become my absolutely favorite author. . ."
--Karen B.

"I love ALL of Judith Erwin's books but 'Shadows from the Past' is my absolute favorite?"
--Rhonda Hullender

The Ballroom

Judith Erwin

Emerald Cat Press
Jacksonville, Florida

Printed in the United States of America

Paperback - ISBN: 978-0-9863367-4-4
eBook -ISBN: 978-0-9863367-5-1

Library of Congress Cataloging–in-Publication Data has been applied for.

Second Printing

Editor: Julie Delegal
Literary Advisor: John C. Boles
Cover Photograph: Judith Erwin

THE BALLROOM book trailer

Choreographed and directed by Allison Erwin Norton
Dancers: Mattison Bedinghaus and Xander Chawi
Video: Stephen R. McFadden
Music: "Nocturne Op. 9, No. 2 in E Flat Major" by Frederic Chopin, performed by Akira Eguchi and Catherine Manoukian from the album: Catherine Manoukian: Classics on Violin, Courtesy of Marquis Classics, Toronto, Canada.

ALSO BY JUDITH ERWIN

Shadow of Silence

Shadow of Doubt

Shadows from the Past

The Ballet

Dedicated to

JUDSON M. NORTON

SARAH E. DOMINEY

TREVOR S. NORTON

H. BROOKS NORTON

MARY CAROLINE ERWIN

AMELIA I. ERWIN

CHAPTER ONE

The tortoiseshell Persian sprang—back arched, fur bristled—ready for attack. A reverberating sound of a diamond ring clanging against the bottom of the brass trash bin had brought about the cat's ire.

"Sorry, Gigi. Didn't mean to scare you." The petite, auburn-haired dancer's green eyes clouded over as she picked up the cat, trying to make amends. "Looking at that bloody thing has made me nauseous for two days."

Early morning sounds of traffic below signaled the beginning of another Monday in Los Angeles. As Holly put the cat down on her couch, Tchaikovsky blared from her cell.

Swan Lake was Holly's ringtone for her friend, Gabi Valera. Bolting for the phone, Holly stumbled over a corner of a large parcel covering most of the floor space in her small apartment. In trying to avoid a fall, she knocked over a mug. The remnants of her coffee formed a stream that cascaded over the edge of the table to the carpet below.

"Damn, damn, damn. This day is going great." With a dirty look and defiant kick to the offending box, she scrambled to catch the call.

Reaching her iPhone, Holly took a deep breath, allowing the muscles in her face to relax, and tapped the green circle. "Hey, sweet friend. What a surprise. Aren't you on tour with the new ballet company?"

"Next week. You sound out of breath."

"Don't ask."

"Okay. . . . If you say so. Just calling to wish you luck on the new season. Break a leg, gal."

Holly shifted the phone to her opposite ear and pushed her dance bag, bearing the official *Lights, Camera—Dance* logo, aside with her foot. "Thanks. I was about to leave for the studio. A little nervous. It's meet-new-partner day."

"That should be *exciting*."

Holly sighed. "Should be, could be, but maybe not. Say a prayer he's not another overweight, wandering-hands has-been with two left feet and bad breath." She wrinkled her nose as if sniffing a foul odor. "I'm not in a good mood, and if I have to dodge touchy-feely, I might slap the stuffing out of him."

Gabi chuckled. "It's your second season. Surely, the casting gods will show mercy. You've got to take home a gold medal before you retire—which, in my opinion, you're way too young to do."

"Too young to quit and too old to make it into a ballet company. Do you know how jealous I am of you?" Holly moved to the sofa and cleared a space to sit.

"Stop it. You have a great job—network TV."

"It's not ballet, and there's no chance I'll be given a winner. I'm a low pro on the pyramid. I doubt viewers even know my name."

"But, the camera loves you, kiddo."

"Says my friend and number one fan. Seriously, on the flight back to L.A. last night, I thought about where I'm going. Maybe, I should give this up and go to college for a teaching degree before I'm any older. Make Mom happy."

The edge to Holly's voice did not escape Gabi. "Whoa. Who am I talking to? What have you done with the girl who has dance in her DNA and music flowing through her veins?"

Holly took a deep breath without responding.

Gabi pressed forward. "Holly . . . what's wrong? You're on a national TV show. You've made it, kid. Even with Kermit the Frog for a partner, you should be happy."

Holly hesitated, trying to decide whether she wanted to share what was gnawing away at her. After several seconds, she gave in. "The dream bucket sprung a leak this weekend. My optimism drained out."

Gabi was silent for a moment. "That doesn't sound good. Want to talk about it?"

"Probably not, and I don't have time to give you chapter and verse, but in a nutshell, Dr. Don Barrett is getting married." She took a deep breath. "I'm not. He recast the role of bride."

"What? . . . He bloody did what?"

"Broke up. I knew there was trouble when I told him I was flying home for the weekend. He said, and I quote verbatim." She lowered her voice to sound masculine. "'We have to talk, Holly.' When we met at Cheesecake, he showed up with the wrong shade of lipstick on his collar. He freakin' broke up with me at Cheesecake."

"The dirty SOB. How long have you two been a couple?"

"Six years, leaving me with a six-thousand-dollar gown and no groom." She looked down at the box." Maybe I should wear it to his wedding. If anyone asks, I'll say I'm the understudy—the one who stayed faithful when she had the chance to date a megastar."

Gabi laughed. "I know it's not funny, but I can picture you crashing the nuptials. But, holy crap. . . . Six thousand?"

"Don't panic. I didn't pay that. I modeled it in that magazine shoot I did after the *LCD* tour. The designer offered it to me for her cost when she heard I was engaged. But, I still paid an obscene amount. Can't returned it because of the alterations." She stood up and kicked the box again.

"Got it. But, hey, there's always eBay."

Holly chuckled. "Good thought, but for some perverse reason, I think I want to keep it. Not that I want to even look at it for a while. Don't you think every gal should have one on hand in case a crown prince, riding a white horse and bearing a big diamond, drops by? One who can actually spell fidelity."

Gabi laughed. "I'm gazing into my crystal ball. He's headed your way."

"Bullshit. Tell him to put it in reverse. I'm not in the market for anything more serious than a one-night stand with Magic Mike. I'm keeping the gown to remind me not to be suckered in again."

"You are definitely not one-night-stand material. Changing the subject, if you're not coming back to Florida to get married, are you staying with the show?"

"Not sure. After work tonight, I'm going to eat a quart of Häagen Dazs and Google 'how to cure crushed self-esteem.' Then, I'll decide between masochistically chasing stardom or throwing in the towel and opening a studio in Jacksonville." She picked up the empty coffee cup and started for the kitchen.

"I vote for the chase. You can do it."

Holly grinned. "Too bad Amazon doesn't sell *big breaks* for wannabe stars with Kevlar-coated hearts and small cats."

"I think they're still working on that one. Kidding aside, Holly, you and Don were a couple for so long. Are you okay? Honest answer."

Holly pondered the thought before answering. "Wouldn't say I'm okay . . . exactly. More like numb and hollow inside. But I'll get through it. After being cut in about a thousand auditions, I'm on a first-name basis with rejection. . . . This one just blindsided me, because I believed I had the part."

"I have an idea. When the company tours the islands, I'll buy a pair of voodoo dolls you can stick hatpins in."

"Love it. I'll name them Don and Don's Darling." Holly glanced at the clock on her kitchen wall. "Listen, gal. I have to go—have to clean up a little spill before I join the smog brigade. Talk soon, and don't worry about me. Just enjoy your standing ovations on the road, while I try to turn a toad into a Derek Hough."

By eight-thirty, Holly was in the network studio, ready to work. Her discipline demanded she warm up before beginning a rehearsal. As she stretched, a production photographer, Sam Waring, walked in the studio to record the introductory meeting and day's rehearsal.

"Hey, beautiful. Ready to knock it out of the park this season?"

"Not sure about a homer, but hoping for at least a base hit. But, you know they'll probably give me an obese big-name from the past who doesn't know his ship sailed fifteen years ago and who couldn't pull off a two-step if he had five years of private lessons with Fred Astaire."

Sam chuckled, put down his equipment bag, and gave her a thumbs-up. "It's a job. What can I say?"

"I know. It's not like New York City Ballet is emailing me a principal dancer contract."

Sam drained the last of a Starbucks Venti as a knock came at the door. The videographer quickly grabbed a camera as the door opened.

Responding to the sound, Holly turned, froze, and released an involuntary shriek as a man walked in. Stunned by her own reaction, she covered her face for a second. "Oh, my God. . . . You're, you're Luke Damian."

The six-foot-two, sandy-haired British actor with the blue eyes of a Siberian husky nodded sheepishly. "Guilty. I hope that's not a problem."

Holly took a deep breath, forgetting about all else, including the rolling camera. "I hope not too." She walked over to him, extending her arms, and they embraced.

"I just hugged Luke Damian. How does life get better than that?" she said, backing away. "Are you really him?"

"Last time I checked my driver's license."

"This day just took a decided turn for the better."

"If you're talking about me, I hope I don't disappoint you." His British accent resonated, adding to his charisma.

"You *are* Luke Damian." Her green eyes were wide with awe.

"We've pretty much established that." He smiled, mischievously, exposing a dimple.

"You don't understand. I grew up with photos and posters of you all over my bedroom walls." She swung her arms around in a grand gesture. "When I was fourteen. I saved my allowance for weeks to order a *very* expensive, autographed headshot of you."

"I should reimburse you. I hope you came to your senses and trashed it all."

Shaking her head and rolling her eyes, she turned away. "I need a second." She walked across the room. On a side wall hung a larger-than-life poster of Holly and her former partner.

Luke stood where she left him, staring up at the picture, obviously puzzled as to what he should do.

As Holly reached one of the benches lining the wall, she stopped, turned around, and said, "Okay. Enough." She looked at Sam. "Can we reshoot that section? I'm sure I came across like a total dork." She held a palm up to the lens of the camera.

"Come on, Holly. You know the rules."

"Yeah, yeah. I know." Turning back toward her new partner, she said, "Well, now that I've made a *complete* fool of myself, let's get started. I'm Holly, and this is our photographer, Sam." She walked over and put an arm around Sam. "He'll be recording everything—and I mean *everything*. So, be nice to him."

"You'll either get sick of my mug or forget I'm around by the time we end the season," Sam said.

"Ready to get started?" Holly asked. "We have a lot of work ahead."

Luke grinned. "More than you know."

"Do you dance at all?"

He turned his head side-to-side, slowly.

"Have you ever taken a dance class?"

"Never."

"Not even one?"

"Nope. Modeling—Acting—all I know. You've got a real challenge."

"Do you at least like music?" Holly's face expressed a wide-eyed hope for the right response.

"I do—at least most of it."

Hearing a piece of positive information, Holly breathed a sigh of relief. "Do you sing?"

He shook his head. "Only if I want to clear a room."

She paused, distracted by the mental image of the Luke Damian she had rushed through homework to watch every week on TV. Back then, he was at the top of the A-List, on the cover of all the teen fan magazines, and even making the most-sexy-men edition of *People*. Five seasons in, the network canceled his amateur detective show, and Luke jumped into feature films. While remnants of his popularity hung on, his success on the big screen was limited.

Snapping into professional mode and wasting no time, Holly said, "Let's get started. I trust you can walk." She reached out and took his hand. "Our first dance is the waltz. We'll begin with a basic step— no music." She stood directly in front of him, close enough to smell the tantalizing fragrance he wore.

With an effort to forget who he was, Holly took charge. "I'm going to demonstrate from the man's position. Feet together, knees slightly bent. Lead with your left heel. Then step to the right on the ball of your other foot and close, shifting your weight. Watch me. . . . One, two, close and shift. Repeat, leading with the right foot. One, two, close and shift." Her heart pounded in double time as she avoided eye contact.

Luke watched her intently.

"Now, you do it."

He started forward, but then stumbled, confused as to where his weight should be. "I'm sorry. Show me again."

The morning proved Luke to be a hard worker, but it didn't come easy. They practiced the basic box step without music for about twenty minutes, and then Holly turned on the digital sound system. She took his left hand in her right and placed her other hand on his shoulder, praying he didn't noticed her slight shiver when they touched.

Luke looked down, his magnetic eyes locking with hers. "I'm trying to stay positive, but when I think of the routines I've seen others perform on this show, I have reservations as to whether I was insane to agree to this."

Holly felt as though she would melt but forced herself to appear cool. "You're going to be fine. Trust me. Listen to the music and follow my lead."

After going through three repetitions of the basic step, Holly stopped, removed her hands, and looked up at him. "Forgive me for asking, but why did you agree to come on the show?"

His eyes twinkled. "Not a secret. Exposure—no covert longing to twirl around the floor, I assure you. I said no at first, but my agent made a big fuss about it. He said, and not diplomatically, my career is one job short of county fairs and this gig could kick it back in gear."

"Well, if I can get over my awe at spending the next however-many-weeks-we-survive with you, then you can get over your fear of misfiring feet."

"I'd trade my place for yours in an instant. As to making a dancer out of me, you have my deepest sympathy."

"Relax. . . . You can't be worse than my last partner." She turned her head and blinked, the eye-contact becoming uncomfortable. "Let's look at your body placement. In the waltz, it's important you stand in the correct position. The judges call it your frame. Now, take me in the dance hold."

He raised his left arm in the air and put his right hand around to her shoulder blade.

"Good job. You apparently know the basic form."

"Just from watching this show."

CHAPTER TWO

Over and over, that morning, they did the same combination. Holly knew Luke was bored, but she had to be sure he truly absorbed the basics. Each time they touched, Holly felt a tingle but did her best to ignore it.

"Repetition will create muscle memory," she said. "That accomplished, you won't have to think about the steps, which will allow you to concentrate on your performance quality."

Stop thinking about who he is, Holly. He's just a dance partner— but, oh my gosh, how good he smells.

At ten-thirty, his phone buzzed. They were in the middle of working out a reverse turn. "Excuse me. I have to take this call." He looked at the caller ID as he took the cell out of his pocket. Without further comment, Luke walked out of the studio, leaving Holly in the center of the room.

She turned to the cameraman. "Double standard, Sam. We don't dare take a personal call unless there's blood or fire, but the celebs are free to do as they please."

Sam nodded.

When Luke came back in the room, there was a change in his demeanor. Holly fought the impulse to ask who had called.

His wife? Is he married?

"When do we break for lunch?" Luke asked at eleven-thirty.

"Actually, we usually don't break as in *leave the studio*. We can go to the commissary or the staff will have whatever you want brought in. I should have asked you. I'm sorry. What would you like?"

"How about Maine lobster?"

Holly looked at him, not sure whether he was serious.

"I'm kidding." His blue eyes sparkled. "A cheeseburger and fries will do just fine."

Holly relaxed. "I'm going to have to get used to your sense of humor. How do you want your burger?"

"Medium rare, all the way, but hold the onions. I'll spare you that. Would a beer be out of line?"

"Not as long as you're sober if you lift me higher than your waist."

"Yes, ma'am."

The first half of the day satisfied Holly's expectations, despite Luke's awkward execution and the multiple interruptions of his phone. She noticed his mood changed more and more with each call until he turned the cell off with a grand gesture, his blue eyes flashing.

"I'm sorry. That's the last distraction."

"Are you sure you should turn it off? You might miss an important call."

"I'll risk it."

Luke was a good student. What he lacked in skill, he compensated for with his commitment to learning. His self-deprecating sense of humor alleviated the tension when he failed to master even the basic steps.

"I probably should have told you that I'm dyslexic," he said as the day wore on, and he continually used the wrong foot.

"I'll forgive you, if you'll forgive me for being obsessive," Holly said, smiling and redoing her long ponytail.

He walked away from her and then circled back, grinning. "I *am* beginning to believe that you trained at Parris Island."

"How did you guess?" She laughed and put a hand on his shoulder. "I know I'm being tough on you, but repetition embeds the combinations into your brain. Now, show me the entire piece from the beginning."

"By myself?"

She nodded. "It's just ten seconds of choreography. We've got a long way to go before we have a complete routine." Holly kept conversation focused on their professional objective, even though she was dying to know Luke's marital status, who made the annoying phone calls, and why his mood changed each time he answered.

Luke leaned over and rubbed the back of his calves. "Damn—ten seconds is all we've done? I was hoping we were at least half done."

Holly shook her head. "It's day one. You've got a long journey to the finish line. We have two and a half weeks for this routine, but for the rest of the season, we only get a week at best—that is, *if* we survive the eliminations."

"How long is the entire number?"

"This one—ninety seconds. They'll get longer."

"We've done barely more than ten percent?"

"Afraid so."

He shook his head. "I don't know. I may have committed to more than this old body will do."

"I don't believe that. You're catching on faster than you realize. I've had the hopeless partner. I know the difference."

"After we do it one more time, can we go out for dinner?" He sounded almost pitiful.

"Sorry. No being seen together, yet. Also, eating a big meal while we're working . . . not a good idea." She shook her head. "Sam can call for snacks that will tide us over until we stop for the day."

"And that will be when?"

"Between eight and nine. The sooner we get the routine down, the more we can later relax. My goal is to have the entire number done by next Monday."

He looked down, a frown on his face. "I'm no math whiz, but that means doing twice as much choreography every day the rest of the week."

"Yeah," she said, nodding with a twinkle in her eye.

"You do remember that I'm not a kid."

"I don't want to hear that." She looked at his lean but muscular physique. "You're only about five years older than I am. What are you? Thirty?"

"Thirty-one, but you're a cross between the Energizer Bunny and the Road Runner. You don't even break a sweat." He walked to a bench, picked up a towel, and wiped his face and neck.

"I will. Give me time."

By eight thirty, Luke had the first ten seconds of choreography memorized and could execute it without Holly.

"Hey, now that I've got the steps nailed, shouldn't we work on cleaning up the technique? I see enough of myself in those mirrors to know how awkward I am."

Holly sat down on the studio bench. "There's quite a bit to polish, but I want you to have the entire dance firmly in your head before we start addressing the other three elements."

"Three?"

"Technique, musicality, and presentation. We do it one layer at the time."

"Damn. I know I can't do all of that."

She waved her right hand in a big circle, palm out, in front of her face. "No negativity. We don't use the word *can't* in this room."

Before he could respond, the door opened and his driver came in.

"Saved by the bell." Luke turned toward the door. "Be there in a second." He held up his index finger, and then turned back toward Holly. "Can I give you a lift home, or do you have your own car service?"

The vision of sitting in the backseat of the limo with him flashed across her brain, and she smiled. "No, but thanks for offering. I have my car."

He picked up his bag and sat down on the bench to change shoes. Holly rose, went over to her bag, and took out her jeans and athletic shoes. Kicking off her heels, she removed the dance skirt and slipped jeans over her leotard. Luke watched her with interest while he tied the laces of his sneakers.

When both were done, they stood. Luke took Holly by the shoulders and gave her a hug. "Thanks for your patience. I'll try to live up to your work ethic."

A tinge of excitement flowed through her, realizing again who he was, which she had tried to avoid thinking about for much of the day. "I have total confidence in you. See you tomorrow."

With Luke gone, Holly turned off the audio system and checked her bag to be sure that she had everything. Sam packed away his equipment.

"This was a day that I won't soon forget." She turned off the lights and started to leave the studio with Sam.

"Did you really have posters of him?"

"Oh, yes. I had a mammoth crush on him in my early teens. If he had walked into a room with me back then, paramedics would have been called."

"And now?"

"Don't ask. That damn camera is off, isn't it?"

Sam laughed. "You're cool. Nothing is recording."

Driving home, the realization of the day clicked in for her. *I'm going to be up close and personal with Luke Damian for weeks. Get a grip, Holly.* A warm glow of contentment spread over her. Any residual thoughts of her ex fiancé evaporated in the wake of her sexy partner with the mesmerizing eyes.

CHAPTER THREE

By Thursday, Luke and Holly had the ninety seconds of choreography completed, including two intermediate combinations, but it was far from polished. They were dancing to a Chopin nocturne."

He continued to stumble frequently, struggling to get his weight on the correct foot, which caused him to lose balance. On the positive side, he retained the combination of steps and had amazing strength, executing simple lifts as though she were light as Styrofoam. That afternoon, the couple sat down after Sam left for the day. With towels around their necks and sipping from water bottles, they reviewed their position.

"Tell me the truth. What would our score be if we danced for the judges tonight?" Luke asked.

"Sure you want the truth?"

He nodded.

"Between one-point-five and two."

"Ouch. You know how to hurt a guy."

"You asked for the truth. But—don't be discouraged. You're doing better than you realize. Surely, you didn't think you would have the whole thing mastered in one week?"

"To tell the truth, when I left here on Monday night, I never thought we'd make it this far in a month. I can work over the weekend if you like." He was looking straight into her green eyes. "We may lose rehearsal time when I go to New York the end of next week to shoot a commercial. I understand that you will make the trip with me."

She nodded. "One of the producers sent me an email about it. The staff will find us a studio to work in during any free time you have."

"What about the rule against being seen together?" he asked.

"Have you forgotten? We're on *Stars, Etc.* Saturday night for the announcement of the season's lineup."

"Right. I knew that. Would Mr. Holly mind his woman working a little extra this weekend?"

She looked up, startled that he had moved the conversation into personal territory. "Since, there is no Mr. Holly, no problem. But, even if there were, the job comes first."

He looked toward her left hand at an antique ring. She had worn it since tossing Don's in the trash, where it continued to reside.

"Oh," she said. "That's not an engagement ring." She looked up and caught him smiling. "What about Mrs. Luke?"

"Which one?"

"Pardon?"

"Sorry. That was too candid a response. The *ex-wives* would not care. In fact, they would be happy to hear that I'm earning gold they can try to mine."

"But, your phone calls?"

He didn't respond, and Holly hated herself for overstepping.

"Erase that, Luke. I was out of line."

He ran his fingers through his layered hair. "Considering how many times we've had to pause our progress for those calls, you're justified."

"No. I was wrong to intrude on your personal life."

"I breached yours. And, for the record, yes. Most of the calls I received were from a woman. Her name is Joy. Ironic, because at the moment, she is anything but a joy."

"I'm sorry. She doesn't like you dancing with me?"

"She wouldn't like me dancing with Queen Elizabeth."

"Is Joy an actress?"

"Model—Joycelyn Ambrose."

"Are you engaged? If you don't mind my asking."

"Having co-starred in two weddings and two divorces, I've proved beyond a reasonable doubt that I don't know how to choose a mate—or maybe that I'm not husband material." He made a face. "I'm not interested in strike three."

Holly felt a rush of pleasure, hearing that he sounded uncommitted. "Living together?"

"Hell, no." He picked up his bag. "Are you interested in working over the weekend?"

"Sure. I'll check to be sure the studio is available. If you'll give me your number and turn your phone back on, I'll let you know."

After Luke left, Holly was alone in the studio. She made a call to the production manager to see if the room was available over the weekend. It wasn't. Disappointed, she hung up. *Stop it Holly. If you can't afford the car, you'd better not take it for a test drive.*

Hesitating for a minute, she typed a text to Luke. "Sorry, no studio time available."

The next morning, Luke was in the rehearsal room when Holly arrived. "Got your text last night, but I might be able to work something out."

"Really?" She stifled the urge to show how much she liked the idea. "Let me know; but in case nothing turns up, we'd better put in some blood, sweat, and tears today."

Neither mentioned the extra rehearsal again. They put in a morning of hard work, pausing only for bathroom and water breaks, even skipping lunch. At three o'clock, Holly had to stop to attend a meeting with the director and the choreographer of production numbers, featuring the professional dancers. "I should be back by four-thirty," she said as she pulled on her jeans to leave.

"I'll likely be gone by then," Luke replied.

His comment caught Holly off-guard. They had worked every night until seven or later.

"You're leaving early today?"

"Sorry, but I have a prior commitment tonight."

"Oh." Holly fought it, but she couldn't hide her disappointment.

"Don't worry. I'll work on getting us space for the extra time.

Regardless, I'll definitely see you tomorrow evening for the announcement show."

"Just you and me, Gigi, again tonight," she whispered under her breath as she left the studio.

"Did you say something?" Luke called out.

"No. Just talking to myself. See you tomorrow."

Saturday morning, Holly forced herself out of bed at eight-thirty. The week's work had taken a toll. She felt every muscle threatening to strike and tried shaking them out, one limb at a time. After having a cup of tea, a boiled egg, and a piece of dry toast, she booted up her computer. Deciding against responding to emails, she googled "Luke Damian" instead.

A myriad of sites popped up with IMDB and Wikipedia heading the list. She scrolled down until hitting an article from the *A to Z Skinny* site titled: "Luke Damian and friend at the premiere." Clicking the link, an image of Luke popped up with a gorgeous blonde in a dress that plunged deeper than the Arizona canyon. The photo was captioned: "Luke Damian and model Joycelyn Ambrose pose for the cameras on the red carpet."

So, that's Joy. I've seen her on a dozen covers.

The article was short and did little more than recapitulate Luke's history as Alexander Holmes on the long-running series of the same name, but it put knots in Holly's stomach. Gazing at the photo for several minutes, she found herself looking for flaws in the woman. *What am I thinking? I'm out of my league. She's A-list.*

CHAPTER FOUR

The phone rang as she read the fifth article. It was her best friend from childhood, Dana Charles. Holly smiled as she answered. "Hey, Dana. What's happening in Florida?"

"What's this I hear about you and Don splitting up?"

"Good news travels fast, doesn't it? How'd you hear?" As she spoke, Holly moved to her couch, sat down, and put her feet up on the coffee table.

"I didn't. Claude and I went to a movie last night at Tinseltown, and there he was with a gal I don't know. When he saw me, he got a funny look on his face. Forgive me, kiddo, but I couldn't help but say something. Claude was furious, but I walked over to him and said, 'Don, how are you? Heard from Holly this week?'"

"You didn't."

"Yes, I did. He started to dodge, but then he looked me straight in the face and said, 'Apparently, you haven't heard that we broke up.' Holly, you couldn't have shocked me more if you told me Mother Teresa was sleeping with Brad Pitt. Is it true? Or was the cheater lying?"

"A little of both. We have broken up, but he was with Mystery Woman before."

"No! Are you okay?"

"I'm fine. It only hurts when I breathe."

"The son-of-a-bitch."

"Yeah. That sums it up. But, let's don't dwell on him. How are you and Claude?"

"We're great. I have some news."

"You're not?" Holly's face registered surprise.

"I am."

"Gosh, I'm jealous."

"Listen to you. A big-time career in Hollywood, meeting all kinds of really neat people, and you're jealous of a pregnant housewife."

"Dana Charles, you've got the ultimate—a loving husband, second baby on the way, a great house—don't be jealous of me living on rabbit food, dating a cat, and wondering where the next job is coming from."

"Speaking of your career, who is your new partner?"

Holly broke out in a big grin. "You know I can't tell you until the official announcements tonight."

"Not even a hint? Is it someone as cool as the tennis player who won last season?"

Holly hesitated. "Way cooler."

"Oh, my gosh. You have to tell me. Who is it?"

"I can't. Suffice it to say, it's a real trip working with him. Watch *Stars, Etc.* We'll all be on when the celebrities are introduced."

"You're killing me, girl."

"I know. I wish I could tell you."

"I know. I know. Contract, lawyers, and stuff. Well, I'll be watching, and you'd better call me afterward so I can get all the juicy details."

"Will call you the minute I can, but it might be tomorrow."

She had barely laid the phone down when it rang again. Expecting it to be her mother, Holly considered not answering but grabbed it on the last ring.

"Good morning, love. I hope you know that I can hardly walk. You put muscles I didn't know I had through hell this week."

His voice sent an involuntary surge of excitement through her, followed by a puzzled expression appearing on her face. "How'd you get my number?"

"You sent me a text, remember?"

The corners of her mouth turned up. "I did. I wasn't thinking."

"I have a place to practice, tomorrow. . . . That is, if you're free."

"Really." Her body relaxed, a happy feeling taking over. "How did you do that?"

"Sometimes, agents come in handy."

"You may be a little masochistic."

"Looks that way. So, what do you say?"

"What can I say? A dedicated student is not easy to come by. What time and where?"

"I'll pick you up."

She hesitated, mentally debating whether to ride with him. "I'll meet you there. I'm not sure where I'll be coming from."

"As you wish. I'll bring you written details this afternoon."

"Fair enough. See you then." She hung up, grinning.

Later in the day, the cast assembled in the green room of the network theater. The broadcast would originate on a portable stage set up in the street in front of the building. The order of introductions allegedly had no significance, but everyone knew that to keep the viewers watching, the biggest name would be last. As Holly looked around, she was impressed with the strength of the roster. Celebrities included an Olympic gymnast; an NBA player; a reality-show star; two adult children of top-rated celebrities; a talk show hostess; a network sportscaster; a *Sport's Illustrated* cover model; a recording artist; a former beauty queen; a TV courtroom judge, a writer, and a handsome celebrity chef.

As Holly circulated among her colleagues, introducing them to Luke, one of the male pros, a Russian, hugged her with lack of restraint on where his hands landed. Luke took notice.

When the dancer was out of earshot, he looked at her and rolled his eyes. "That blond guy was pretty familiar. I thought he might ravish you on the spot."

Holly laughed. "That's all an act. Trust me. If I responded affirmatively, he would run like a rabbit with a hungry fox on his tail. Wait until you see him on the floor. He moves like Magic Mike on Viagra, and so does the other Russian, Mika."

"Do they tour with the Chippendales during the off season?"

Holly looked at him for a second, smiling. He sounded slightly jealous. "Don't let them intimidate you. You're not competing with Andrei or Mika—just their partners."

"Assuming I manage to master this stuff, who do you see as the one to beat?"

Holly looked over the crowd and then down at a sheet of paper handed out earlier, naming the contestants. "Educated guess. I'll have my eyes on the gymnast and the singer. The gymnast has Andrei, one of the best choreographers on the show."

"The blond Russian, right?"

Holly nodded. "Working with Andrei, plus having the flexibility, balance, and grace of her sport, will make her tough to beat. The singer has musicality and showmanship in her favor."

"I've had fencing lessons. Think that'll help?"

"I didn't know that." She tipped her head sideways and pretended to think for a second. "But it certainly can't hurt. Just don't bring your foil to rehearsal."

There was no time for further conversation as the show was about to go live. Luke handed her a slip of paper with the address of the studio they would use on Sunday, and she slid it into her pocket.

"Is one o'clock okay with you?" he asked.

Holly nodded.

The show opened with two of the pros performing a short demonstration of the cha-cha, the waltz, the rhumba, the Argentine tango, and the paso-doble. Celebrity announcements followed. As the host called out each name, the camera moved in for a close-up. When finished, he promised the audience an opportunity to get to know each star better when interviews occurred throughout the program.

Holly scanned the gathered fans. Among the anonymous faces, one stopped her cold.

That's Joy Ambrose. Why didn't he mention she was coming?

Uncomfortable with the idea of eye contact with the model, Holly turned away quickly but glanced back several times throughout the rest of the broadcast. Each time, the model seemed to be staring directly at Holly. The expression on her face was undeniably hateful.

Nudging Luke, during a commercial break, she asked, "Did you tell Joy you are doing the show?"

He shook his head. "No, but she's here. I don't know how the hell she found out. I told her Jeff booked me for a brief taped interview to promote the DVD release of my last film—which, incidentally, went to DVD almost before it wrapped."

Holly's stomach turned, an invisible cloud dropping over her.

The celebrity interviews brought lively reactions from the spectators. Luke captured the coveted last spot and a thunderous round of applause. He handled the interview with all the poise and confidence that he lacked on the dance floor. Holly said little, primarily smiling and nodding. She was afraid to look in the direction of Joycelyn Ambrose.

At five-thirty, the telecast was over, and Luke left quickly, barely saying goodbye. Holly noticed Joy rush forward as the host bid farewell to the audience. She linked her arm through Luke's in a proprietary gesture. Holly tried not to let the scene dampen her spirits and went directly to the car that would take her home.

Her seatbelt was barely fastened when Dana called.

"Holly Dawson! Were you kissed by a Leprechaun? Luke Damian! Damn, girl, if I weren't pregnant and puking hourly, I'd get on a plane and fly out to watch rehearsals and drool. You can't be pining over dumb Don-the-dud when you've landed in the arms of *Alexander Holmes.*"

Holly grinned. "I thought you'd be impressed. Come on out for a visit. I'll introduce you."

"Yeah, I wish. What's he like—I mean really like?"

Looking at her driver, Holly hesitated. "Dana, I'm in the car on the way home from the show. Can I call you back later?"

CHAPTER FIVE

Between conversations with her mother, Gabi, and Dana, Holly was on the phone until nearly midnight. On the positive side, she enjoyed telling them about Luke. Dana had shared a crush on him along with Holly, while her mother remembered the posters and schoolgirl angst of her daughter's teen years. Gabi was impressed but was among the minority of adolescents who never watched his show. She was none the less enthusiastic.

"He is gorgeous. See, I told you the casting gods would bless you. The viewers won't give a fig whether he can dance. They'll be too busy drooling."

"He's *not* married," was Dana's first comment. "I looked him up."

"No, he's not. There might be a good reason. Don't go speculating about a relationship between us outside the show."

"Come on, Holly. If I was single, and in your position, I would sleep with him in a nanosecond."

Holly's face turned pink, even though there was no one to see. But the thought made her prickle in private places. "Dana Charles. What did you just say? What if Claude heard you?"

"He's sound asleep. Besides, he would know it's a fantasy. My chances of becoming Queen of England are better."

Holly laughed, picturing Dana with a crown, cape, and jeweled scepter. You're making me feel like we're fifteen again and having a sleepover at your house. The only thing missing is the Häagen-Dazs, potato chips, and Christina Aguilera on the CD player." Holly closed her eyes and let the image take over. She could almost smell the Stella McCartney fragrance she had once wore, with its soft aroma of rose, orange, and amber. "You know what? I think I'm going to treat myself to a new bottle of Stella."

"Seriously?"

"No. I'm just trying to recapture that fantastic feeling of raging hormones." Holly shook her head, a big smile on her face.

"Doesn't being with him reignite them? Be honest."

The phone was silent for several seconds. "Hell, yes."

The next day, she arrived at the appointed studio at the stroke of one. Two cars were parked in the lot. One was a Lexus SUV, the other a Black Ferrari convertible. Holly parked her Toyota Camry next to the sports car and got out, struggling to keep her eyes off the sleek vehicle. On her way, she had stopped at Neiman Marcus and purchased a bottle of Stella.

"Come in," a female voice said as Holly opened the door that led into the reception area. "I'm June Mattox, and I want to say I'm honored to have you and Lucas rehearsing in my studio." The middle-aged woman sat behind a small desk. Her salt-and-pepper hair swept back in a sleek ballet bun; her eyes highlighted with nicely applied, violet eyeshadow.

"Thank you for having us," Holly responded.

"If there's anything you need, don't hesitate to ask."

Luke was sitting on a wicker love seat adjacent to the desk. As usual, a stray lock of blond hair fell flirtatiously on his forehead.

"Your snazzy sports car?" she said, looking at him.

"If you mean the eight-year-old Ferrari—it's the last remnant of success." He smiled, seductively, his eyes bluer than ever.

"I guessed you weren't the SUV type."

A teenage girl sat on the other side of the room, next to an opening into one of two teaching rooms.

Turning back to June, Holly said, "I think we're good. You might show me your sound system to be sure it's one I know how to operate."

"Not a problem, and then my daughter and I will leave you alone to work. But, could I ask a favor?" She wrinkled her face, embarrassed to ask.

"Sure," Holly replied.

"Would you mind if we take a few photos of the two of you that I could hang for my students to see? Maybe one with each of us in the shot with you."

"It's fine with me, but I think it's Luke you want, not me. I'm nobody."

"We would disagree. Cynthia followed you all last season." She pointed to her daughter, who beamed at the mention of her name.

"You are so good. I wanted to see you dance more." It was the first sound from the young girl.

Holly smiled. "That's sweet of you. I think Luke and I will do better this season. He's doing very well."

"See. You're the celebrity here," Luke said. "I'm a dinosaur. I bet Cynthia was barely out of the playpen when Alec Holmes solved murders on the Oxford campus."

He no more had the words out of his mouth when his cell rang. Taking it out of his pocket, he made a face and then turned it off.

Joy, no doubt. Holly resisted the temptation to comment on the call.

"Where would you like to do the photos?" Holly asked as June stood up to lead them to their workspace.

"In the studio, I think. We can do the posed photos first, and then, if you don't mind, we'll stick around to take a couple of candid shots of the two of you."

Holly looked toward Luke and gestured to indicate it was his call.

"Fine with me. Just be merciful and avoid my awkward positions."

With June using her smart phone, the posing took five minutes or less.

"Thank you, guys. We'll let ourselves out after we take a picture or two. I've left a key on the desk for you to lock up with when you're done. Just turn out the lights and drop it back through the mail slot as you leave."

It was easy to see that the dance teacher was pleased to have celebrities in her place of business.

I wonder how good she was. Holly looked around the room for signs of a past career. There didn't appear to be any, only photos of recitals and group shots of students.

Putting her dance bag and purse on the floor, she wrapped and tied a short, jersey skirt around her waist, slid her loafers and jeans off, and put on rehearsal shoes. When dressed for practice, she went over to the bar opposite the mirrored wall and began stretching.

Luke didn't take his eyes off her.

"You might want to warm up a little," Holly called out to him.

"Right. Good idea." While she stretched, extended, and did a few plies, he stretched in the middle of the floor and did a few squats.

Cynthia snapped a dozen photos of Holly. Realizing that she was the subject du jour, Holly pushed her warmup further, doing 180-degree grand battements front and side, and a 135-degree arabesque to the back.

"Watch her, Cynthia," Mattox said. "See how she keeps her hips squared and her back up in arabesque? I've told you over and over that you have to watch that. You can't sacrifice technique for height. And didn't I tell you that the best ballroom dancers have ballet training?"

The girl made a face to indicate that she had heard it before. "I know that, Mother. Holly was on that other dance competition show before *Lights, Camera—Dance.*"

I hope she's not dreaming of a professional career. Legs that short will make it hard to succeed in this profession.

Holly was lucky. She had the right DNA for a dancer: legs like the blades of a pair of shears, a long neck, small head, narrow hips, and a naturally slender body.

Before leaving, the Mattox pair hung around long enough to snap a half-dozen photos of the rehearsal and printed a few copies for the couple to autograph.

As the door closed, Luke said, "Nice to have privacy for a change."

"Is that why you wanted to rehearse today?" she asked, putting her left hand on his shoulder and taking his hand with her right.

"It certainly added to the idea. All week, Sam and his camera hovered like a bee over an aster."

"Aster? You know that?"

"Of course, I know that. I'm more than just a pretty face." He winked, his eyes twinkling mischievously.

"I'm glad you told me that. All this time, I thought you were just another sex symbol."

"Touché, coach." He squeezed her waist. "Show me how this stuff is done."

For the next three hours, they went over and over the choreography. Each time, Holly either repeated an earlier correction that Luke had not applied or added a new point to enhance his performance.

By four-thirty, they were both growing tired. Without warning, Holly pulled away, walking to the opposite side of the room.

"What's wrong? Did I screw up?" he asked.

Her back to him, she shook her head.

"Are you okay?" He stood where she left him, obviously confused.

"I'm okay. It's just this music. . . . It's got bad voodoo for me." She kept her back toward him.

Luke walked over and put his hands on her shoulders, massaging them. "Old flame?"

"Only flame."

"Whoa. *Only* flame?"

She turned around, her eyes glazed with moisture. "Only one. We started dating in high school and broke up the weekend before these rehearsals began. I didn't think I cared, but I guess I was kidding myself."

"Wow. That's heavy. And this was your music."

She nodded. "It's a piece that I've always associated with him, because the orchestra was playing it at a symphony concert when he squeezed my hand and whispered 'I love you' for the first time. That year, I danced a solo to it in my studio recital."

"And this guy was the only one you've ever dated?"

"I don't know why I'm telling you all this. Let's get back to work."

"No, no. Let's clear the cobwebs away. Let me put the Damian magic to work." He rubbed his hands together and then made horizontal circles in the air, chanting, "Abracadabra, toil and trouble, out with—what's his name?"

"Donald."

"Out with Donald, in with Lucas; bad karma be gone."

"You're crazy."

"I hope so."

Holly relaxed, a smile crossing her face.

Luke snapped his fingers. "See. It worked. I made you smile."

"You did."

"And, by the way, you know that a song was created based on the nocturne, don't you?" he said.

"Really?"

"Indeed. It's titled 'To Love Again.' Google it." He winked.

"You are kidding me! Well, enough of my foolishness, let's rock and roll." She reset the music, and they resumed rehearsing.

By five-thirty, Luke's patience was wearing thin as he made more and more mistakes. "Damn it. I thought you got better with practice, not worse." After missing a step and getting his feet tangled in the process, he dropped Holly's hand, turned and walked away in a fit of obvious disgust.

"You're tired. We should call it a day."

He took a deep breath, walked over to a tall director's chair, and sat down, obviously trying to keep his temper in check.

"Come on, Luke. Let up on yourself. You are progressing."

"Yeah. I'm doing great. So great that I can't get through the damn routine one time without a freaking mistake."

"That's why we practice. By the time the show airs, you'll know it so well that you could do it upside down and backwards." She picked up her towel and wiped her forehead. "It's going on six o'clock. I think we should call it a day and start fresh tomorrow." She walked over and handed him his towel.

As he took it, he grabbed her hand. "Only if you'll have dinner with me."

Holly pulled her hand away. "I think Joy might have a problem with that."

He grabbed her hand back. "Do I look like I care if Joy has a problem? Do you see any handcuffs?" He held his left hand up. "Look, there's no ring. I can take a friend to dinner if I so choose."

"I don't know. I don't want to cause trouble."

"You're not. It's just dinner, not a randy romp at the Ramada."

She made a face. "Randy romp? What the heck kind of expression is that?"

"Damian special. Listen, ten hours a day together and I hardly know you. You keep telling me to think like we're a single machine on the floor. How do I do that when I know so little about the other half of the engine?"

"What you see is what there is." She took a sweeping bow. "Holly Dawson, one note wonder. Florida kid with failed aspirations of American Ballet Theatre. Sold out to pop culture for rent money. Nothing more to know."

He shook his head. "I don't believe that for a freaking minute. Behind those emerald eyes, there's an intriguing woman with a fascinating story."

"Hate to disappoint you, but twenty years of music, mirrors, sweat, and sore muscles sums it up. Like Olympic athletes, we dancers eat, sleep, and breathe our discipline."

He stood up. "All the more reason for a break. Gather up your things."

She looked at him for a second, mentally debating what to do next. Her heart screamed *accept*. Her head whispered *bad idea*. The heart prevailed. "It'll have to be super casual. I don't have anything but jeans."

His face lit up. "Brilliant!" He held up a hand to give her a high-five, and she matched it. "Jeans are fine. We'll pick up take-away and go to a little park where I like to hang out."

Slipping on her jeans and removing the skirt, she said. "Tell me where, and I'll meet you."

"No way. I'm driv—"

"But my car?"

"My auto club will pick it up and deliver it to your flat; or do you live in a house?"

"Apartment. Are you sure?"

"Absolutely."

An hour later, they were settled at a wrought-iron table in a small, out-of-the-way park with a box of Mexican food, a six-pack of Corona, a cold bottle of Evian, and a pair of limes. It was growing cooler as the sun dropped to the horizon. The sky was a mystical blend of water-color hues—pink, blue, lavender, and yellow.

"This is my favorite time of day," Holly said as she opened Styrofoam containers. One held a chimichanga dinner for Luke and the other, her chicken fajita.

He removed the caps from the water and a bottle of beer. "Sure you won't have a Corona?"

"Positive. And if you thought about how many times you're going to be lifting me, you wouldn't be encouraging me to eat or drink. But, I will have a few drops of lime in my water."

Luke handed her the water and then held up his beer for a toast. "Here's to team Dawson-Damian taking that ridiculous title."

She clanked her bottle against his. "And the handsome purse that goes along with it."

He took a swig and then looked at her as she took a bite of food. "Is the money important to you?"

Her eyes opened wide and she nodded, taking time to swallow before speaking. "Darn right it is."

"Aren't you paid well for being on the show?"

"Scale, unless I make the finals. Top three pros get a bonus."

"Judging from your car, you don't strike me as the extravagant type."

She laughed. "I guess my little Camry does pale in comparison with your Spider."

"Then, it looks as if a win will do well for us both." He stood up and extended his hand. "Let's go for a walk."

Taking his hand, she nodded toward the table. "What about our mess?"

"It will wait."

CHAPTER SIX

Night was falling and lamplights around the park began popping on. They walked along a white, gravel path toward a manmade lake, and Holly's mind raced as his fragrance mingled with the aroma of flowers and recently cut grass. Their hands had been interlocked in rehearsal for days, but this felt different, stirring thoughts that frightened her.

"So, tell me the rest of your story," Luke said, looking down at her, "and don't say there's nothing more. What are your plans for after the show?"

"Up until ten days ago, I thought this would be the end of my performing career." Traces of regret laced her words.

"No way. Why?"

"I had planned to go back to Florida, get married, and open a studio. That's why I needed the bonus. With wedding off, I need it to pay rent while I look for the next job—unless they renew my contract for the show."

He stopped and shook his head. "You're too good, too young, and too attractive to think of retiring."

She smiled. "You're an actor and don't understand. Old dancers don't fade away. They crash like crystal on concrete. One injury and it could be over. Actors evolve—take new roles."

"That fact presupposes they're offered new roles."

"But, you can always act. We're aberrations in the art world. Singers, actors, painters, writers, musicians—they all exercise their skills into old age. Our careers channel that of the athlete. Work like hell, torturing our bodies—all for a short shelf life."

"You could matriculate into acting."

"Yeah, right—without training or talent—I doubt it."

"Look at . . . what's her name? The little blonde that dated Seacrest."

"Julianne Hough?" She shook her head. "Luke, she's a triple threat—singer, dancer, actress, and gorgeous to boot."

"So? You've got the looks, certainly can dance, and I bet you can act, especially if given the right coach." He stepped in front of her and put his hands on her shoulders. "Trust me. You could do it." His blue eyes were mesmerizing—his touch, strong and warm.

A chill ran through her. "I'm flattered that you think so, but I'd best plan on opening a studio somewhere. Do something practical." Despite enjoying the touch of his hands, she removed them, squeezing a little before letting go. "Enough talk about Holly. Tell me about Lucas."

"It's all online. And don't tell me that you haven't Googled me. I'm sure you have. I've Googled you."

"You're kidding?" She spread her right arm out in a sweeping gesture directed at him. "Luke Damian Googled *me*?"

"Of course. It's what people do today. Surely you knew that I would want to know more about the beautiful woman I'm holding in my arms about ten hours a day for three months?"

"No, I didn't. Bet you didn't find much."

"Born in Florida. Your birthday is in May. You're twenty-five, performed on that jazzy dance series, and were in the chorus of a hit Broadway show. Did you sing?"

"Only in ensemble pieces where I couldn't be heard. What about the Lucas that the world doesn't know? You aren't at all like I would have thought you'd be."

His forehead wrinkled. "What exactly would that have been?"

She shrugged. "Honestly? I would have expected a little more ego—maybe even arrogance."

He smiled, nodding. "Been there, won the award for First Class Ass."

Holly shook her head. "I don't believe it."

"Trust me. I was *that* guy—not my grandest moment. Probably why my first marriage failed."

Holly looked at him without commenting.

"Ciara and I were both pretty high on ourselves—too young, too self-consumed with image, and too ignorant about who we really were. She was breaking out in modeling with impressive covers, and I was riding high on *Alexander Holmes*."

"The Luke I've come to know is certainly not self-consumed. You're as humble and self-deprecating as any one I know."

"God, I hope so. It only takes about three flops at the box office to deflate the ego balloon."

They stopped walking and stood looking at four swans gliding across the water. "If you don't mind me asking, what happened to your second marriage?"

"That demon ego, too much money, and too fast a slide down the ladder of success."

Holly frowned. "I read that she is an actress, but I'm not familiar with her name."

"Jeanne. . . . Jeanne Baldwin. She's hot in the UK. She does a little BBC but mostly West End work. She's currently playing Maggie in a revival of *Cat on a Hot Tin Roof*."

"Is she an Elizabeth Taylor or Barbara Bel Geddes type?"

"Taylor. Dark hair—but intense, blue eyes—not violet."

"Are you friends?" Holly couldn't help but notice that he kept up with his ex and felt a tinge of jealousy.

Luke smiled. "I don't think she has a contract out on me, but we don't exchange Valentines."

"So where is Joy, tonight?" Holly held her breath, unsure as to whether she should have brought up his current girlfriend.

"She flew to New York this morning to shoot a layout for one of the big fashion mags."

"Oh. . . . That explains why you were free."

Luke paused; his expression turning serious. "Not really, but forgive me for being rude. Joy is not a subject I want to discuss right now." He squeezed her hand. "Let's start back. I know you're going to work the hell out of me tomorrow."

Holly regretted asking.

They returned to the table, cleared up the remnants of dinner, and Luke drove her home. On the way, she wondered how he would handle the arrival at her apartment. More to the point, she wondered how she would handle any advances he might make.

Please God, give me the strength to keep my head.

On the freeway, the headlights of traffic twinkled like stars on a garland of highway as the city flashed by. Holly watched his hands on the steering wheel of the powerful car, methodically maneuvering between and around larger vehicles. He kept his eyes on the road. Watching him, she imagined what it would be like to have those hands taking her in his arms, removing her clothing, stroking her all over, making love to her. The thoughts brought changes to her body as desire surged, spreading heat to delicate areas.

Don't make a move on me, Luke Damian. My willpower is zero.

Reaching the apartment, Luke parked the car on the street. "May I walk you to the door?"

"No." It came out faster than she intended. "No. I'll be fine. Thanks for offering, and thanks for dinner. It was a nice evening." She didn't look at his face.

"It *was* nice. Nine, tomorrow?"

"Right. See you then." She got out and hurried up the walk to the entrance of her building, relieved that she had dodged what was likely a fatal bullet.

As she walked into the apartment, her landline was ringing.

Dashing to catch the call, she nearly tripped over Gigi. She glanced at the caller ID and smiled. "Dana! I can't believe you called. I just walked in."

"And where have you been to cause you to be so breathless?"

"Stop it. I'm not breathless, just out of breath from climbing two flights of stairs."

"Don't give me that, Holly Dawson. Stairs are nothing to you."

Holly's eyes twinkled. "When could I ever fool you?"

"How was your rehearsal with steamy Mr. Blue-Eyes? He's not there, is he? I didn't interrupt?"

Holly plopped down in her recliner. "Nooo. He's not here. Not that I would tell you if he were. But, I will admit that it was a nice day. After practice, we went to a quaint little park with a lake and had take-out food."

"Oh, my gosh. He is attracted to you."

"Stop it. There's no reason to believe that. He has a girlfriend." Gigi jumped on her lap.

"Must not be that serious, or he wouldn't be taking you to a park for dinner. Did he try to come in?"

"No. He didn't even get out of the car. He offered, but I said no."

"*Why?* For heaven's sake, girl, that was your chance."

"And don't you think that's why I said no? I was shaking. If he had touched me, I would have dissolved. I don't know how I'm going to work with him tomorrow." Holly shrugged her shoulders as if having a chill.

The next morning, Holly woke a half-hour before her alarm buzzed. As she anticipated the day ahead, feelings of dread alternated with feelings of excitement. "I've lost my mind, Gigi." She stroked the purring cat. "Letting myself become attracted to Luke is a guaranteed recipe for disaster." Easing Gigi off her lap, she started her morning ritual.

Arriving at the studio at eight-thirty, Holly was surprised to find Luke already there—talking to Sam. He wore khaki shorts and a sky-blue tee shirt, which not only enhanced his eyes and blond hair, but it also accentuated his lean and muscular physique. The shirt read, "A Man of Many Pieces." The slogan was encapsulated within the outline of a jigsaw puzzle shape.

Dropping her bag on the floor, she told herself to get a grip. *Act like a professional. He's just a fellow cast-member.*

"You're here early," she said. "Interesting tee shirt."

Grinning, he pulled slightly at the sides of the shirt to accentuate the design. "Birthday gift from Colm Bannister. We spent hours working jigsaws between takes on the set of *Alec Holmes.*"

Her face lit up. "No kidding? I love to work them but rarely do anymore."

"Why not?"

She thought for a minute before responding. "Two reasons: one, I'm so obsessive that once I start one, I can't stop until I finish it; and two, I live with a cat who is determined to be in the middle of whatever I'm doing. It's infuriating to have her jump on the table and destroy half my work."

He started laughing. "I might kill the cat."

Her face fell, his response striking a dissonant note.

Seeing her expression, he added. "Whoa, partner. I'm kidding. I wouldn't really hurt a cat. That was a figure of speech."

"Are you a pet person?"

He shook one of his legs as if he had a cramp. "I like them well enough. I've never had a cat. I take it that you're one of those cat devotees?"

"Guilty."

"I'm sure cats are nice enough," he said, rubbing his calves. "What's your puzzle piece record?"

She looked at him with a quizzical expression.

"The largest number of pieces in a puzzle that you worked."

"It's been a while, but I think I was up to fifteen-hundred. What about you?"

"Five thousand." He smiled, appearing proud of himself.

"You're kidding!" she said, kicking off her sneakers.

He shook his head. "It's true. Took me a month. I had the freaking thing framed when I finished."

"You make me feel like a wimp. What was the image?" she said, looking down to buckle her dance shoes.

"An old world map. It hangs in my TV room. I'll show it to you."

At the thought of going to his house, the nerve endings in her palms prickled. She felt her face flush and deliberately delayed a few seconds before looking up.

When he was ready to dance, he stood up and extended a hand to help her rise from the bench."

Holly's heart skipped a beat.

Stop thinking about him that way

"We'd better get to work. We have a short week with the trip to New York on Thursday."

"Yes, ma'am," Luke responded, giving her a salute, his eyes sparkling seductively.

"As soon as I do a quick warmup, we'll run through the choreography." Despite the tingle trickling through her nerve endings, Holly managed to keep her tone steady and unemotional. *I'm a professional. I will not allow my childish crush to interfere with my job.*

Luke nodded and sat down on the floor, while Holly stretched.

When done, she walked to the center of the room, extending her hand to beckon him to follow. "Hit the play button, Sam. I left our music in the system."

Luke took one of her hands in his and swept his free hand around her waist. "Let's rock and roll," he said, winking and giving her a slight squeeze.

The run -through was flawless. Luke didn't miss a step, even when they did a series of fast, sweeping turns that usually caused him to falter.

"Wow!" Holly said as the music ended. "You've got it down."

"Took me long enough." He leaned forward in a mock bow. "Guess we need to work on cleaning up my technique."

Holly grinned, her head bobbing up and down. "How adventurous do you feel?"

Luke tipped his head, raising one eyebrow. "What do you have in mind, coach?"

"Want to try a more complicated lift?"

"Pick you up?"

"I'm sure not going to pick you up." She gently shoved him on the shoulder with the heel of her hand.

Luke hopped around, pretending to lose balance. "I think the better question is: Are you willing to risk your career on the possibility that I might let you fall?"

"We're not starting with a death drop—just a simple, straight up and turn lift." She raised her hands up as if to demonstrate. "You'll have both hands on my waist."

"I've heard lifts aren't allowed in some dances."

Holly adjusted the straps of her camisole leotard. "In true competitions, that's true. But we're not bound by those rules. The producers want us to base our routines on a recognized dance but present an entertaining number to keep the audience interested—you *have* heard of ratings, haven't you?"

He nodded. "I think they were mentioned once or twice when I worked regularly."

"Well, our show is a hybrid between true ballroom dancing, cabaret, and theatrical dance."

"Lead the way."

Holly took his hand. "We'll come out of the swirling turns as before, but after we take the pose, I'll move around to face you as we rise. Take me by the waist and lift straight up as high as you can. Then travel in a circle, increasing your speed to make my costume flow." She paused for him to absorb her instructions. "Let's first try it without the music." She stood in front of him, bending her knees slightly. "On my count: five, six, seven, *eight*." She pushed off with a slight spring. He lifted her effortlessly, straightening his elbows until she was above his head.

As he eased her back to the floor, her body rubbed against his. Holly's eyes gleamed. The deft manner in which he had handled her was exhilarating. "Wow! You're stronger than I thought you'd be."

"Thought the skinny guy was a wimp, did you?"

Embarrassed, her cheeks flushed. "You're not skinny, but you certainly aren't a bulked-up, muscle-bound body-builder type."

"Not sure whether that's intended to be a compliment."

"I—" Holly caught herself as she was about to say that she preferred a body like his. "It *was* meant as a compliment. You must work out a lot."

He grinned. "A little."

Before she could respond, his phone rang.

"Damn. . . Sorry. I have to keep it on this morning."

"It's okay. We need a break to catch our breath." She turned to Sam and waved her hand in a circle to get his attention. "Can you cut the recording?"

He nodded and lowered his camera. "I'm going out for a quick cigarette. Don't do anything interesting while I'm gone."

Luke took several steps away from Holly and looked at his phone, his facial expression changing to annoyance. Studying the readout on the screen for a second, he punched the off key but continued to study the device for a few more seconds. "I'm sorry. My agent is supposed to call with the New York info."

"You don't owe me any apology. I know you have a life outside of this show."

"Truth be told, if we're to have any peace, I'd better deal with that call. I'll be back in a few minutes." Without waiting for her reply, he left the studio, closing the door as he went.

Holly walked over to the cooler and took out a bottle of water. Removing the cap, she sat down on a bench. Even with the door closed, she could hear Luke talking in the hallway as she sipped the cool liquid. Although the words were unclear, his tone was unmistakably one of anger. She wondered who was on the other end of the line. Was it Joy?

After a minute or two, she recapped the bottle, rose, and walked over to her bag. Taking out a leather notebook, she tried to concentrate on the page that listed the dance-styles and music assigned for the first four shows. Although her eyes scanned the page, her mind strayed to thoughts of Luke and how it had felt to have him lift her so masterfully.

As she looked down, the studio door opened, startling Holly. She dropped the notebook. Luke moved forward to pick it up for her. "Thanks. At least it wasn't the water," she said as he handed it to her.

"Is that a journal?"

"No, not exactly. It's my calendar, info on the show, and my notes. I was looking at the roster of numbers we're assigned."

"Planning ahead?" He took another bottle of water from the cooler and opened it. His demeanor did not expose the hostility Holly thought she had heard.

"Just thinking about the second piece. We're scheduled to do a jive number to Carrie Underwood's "Cowboy Casanova."

"Ouch. Is that supposed to imply my persona?" He grinned, a mischievous expression on his face.

Playing along, Holly replied, "If the shoe fits?"

"Not guilty. That's my story, and I'm sticking with it."

"Well, there have been rumors."

"Ah, and just rumors they are. I speak to a woman in public and the tabloids have me in a hot and heavy affair."

"Come on, Luke. You've been linked with some high-profile gals."

"Most of which were staged for mutual career convenience."

"Don't be modest. You were on enough *Tiger Beat* covers to wallpaper the average teenage girl's bedroom."

"Maybe in the day, but the sun went down on that one a long time ago. You're more likely to find me on late night cable, hawking a set of ninja carving knives that come with a bonus sharpener and cutting board at no extra charge."

Holly gave him a frown. "You haven't really done that, have you?"

He laughed. "Not yet, but it may happen if I don't land a good role soon."

CHAPTER SEVEN

Rehearsals were uneventful for the remainder of week two. Late on Thursday afternoon, Luke, Holly, and Sam boarded a private plane from LAX to New York. Filming for Luke's commercial for NYC & Company was scheduled to begin at eight a.m. on Friday. While packing for the trip, there had been a moment for Holly when thoughts of the intimacy associated with sharing a lengthy plane trip and three days in a hotel, albeit in separate rooms, had brought butterflies to her stomach.

After the flight attendant served a steak dinner, accompanied by a bottle of good wine, Sam moved to the back of the plane to watch a movie. Holly and Luke sat in side-by-side, luxurious leather recliners, watching videos of their rehearsals, along with films of professional dancers. She pointed out places in the choreography where Luke had lost his frame and where he failed to follow through a move to the tips of his fingers. She used the pro clips to illustrate her concerns. He took copious notes on her comments.

"You're amazing," she said, pausing the playback to allow him time to finish writing.

He looked at her quizzically. "How would that be?"

"You're the first partner I've had who wrote down my corrections."

"It sticks better for me if I write it down." He looked into her eyes, smiling. "I never realized how much detail was involved in this discipline."

"The devil is in the details," she said, returning his smile, "but you're doing great. Most of the novices are still working on remembering the combinations. I'm sure you're ahead of the pack, with the possible exception of the Olympians."

Watching the pros intimidates me. Just when I think I'm doing pretty well, I see how far I have to go."

Holly patted him on the leg. "You'll be fine. This is the first show. The judges don't expect perfection at this stage."

Looking apologetic, Luke closed his notepad and said, "Much as I would like to continue watching, I'd better go over my lines for tomorrow."

"No problem. I have a new book on this tablet."

Grinning, he said, "I should have known you would come prepared."

Within ten minutes of starting to read, Holly fell asleep, the iPad on her lap, her head resting on Luke's shoulder. Luke reached across, taking care not to disturb her, took the device, and shut it down. He then motioned for their flight attendant.

Whispering, he asked the young woman to bring a blanket.

"Would you like a pillow for Miss Dawson?" she whispered back.

Luke shook his head. "She's fine."

By the time they reached LaGuardia, the three passengers were all asleep. When the attendant woke them to announce the impending landing, Holly raised her head abruptly.

"Oh, my gosh. We're there?" She looked at Luke who was struggling to regain consciousness. "I'm sorry. I didn't mean to sleep on you. Your shoulder is probably numb."

He smiled. "Not a problem. I kind of liked it. I just hope you don't have a stiff neck."

Instinctively, she rubbed the back of her neck. "It's fine, but I can't believe I went out like that. It must have been the wine." She made a face. "I hope I didn't look dorky."

He shook his head. "Not at all. I would say more like angelic."

His comments gave her a warm feeling and the corners of her mouth turned up slightly. "What time is it?"

Luke looked at his watch. "If I'm doing the math right, it's ten minutes to six, New York time."

"And you have to be on the set in two hours. What's the plan?" she asked.

"Check into the hotel, grab a shower, and head to Central Park for the first leg of the shoot."

"Will there be time?"

"Should have no problem unless we hit a snag in traffic. We're staying at the Ritz Carlton on Central Park South."

A limousine was waiting at the airport to whisk them to the hotel and then to the location. The weather was beautiful in the city, and the work went well. Holly watched while Luke was filmed walking through the park, talking to a carriage driver, and observing art at the Metropolitan. Sam followed along, taking shots of Holly observing Luke work. At one o'clock, the crew took a lunch break.

"My hotel room is awesome. I could grow accustomed to the celebrity life," Holly said as she ate deli-sandwiches and fresh fruit in a private room at the museum with Luke and Sam.

"It has good points, I'll admit, but it's not all glitz and glory," Luke responded.

"I think I could tough out the rough spots to have a taste of the good life," Sam commented.

After lunch, they traveled to the United Nations Plaza and then to Rockefeller Center where they ended shooting for the day as the sun went down.

"We're free for the evening. What would you like to do? And please don't tell me we have to rehearse," Luke said as the limo took them up Avenue of the Americas.

"Aren't you tired?" Holly asked. "I can't believe how much work goes into a commercial that will air for only sixty seconds."

Luke grinned at her. "There are to be several sixty-second ads, along with a couple of thirty-second ones. They'll put it all together in editing."

"Just like what we do, Holly," Sam added from his seat across from them. "Overshoot to make sure we have enough good stuff to use in the weekly packages."

"Ever worked in commercials, Sam?" Luke asked.

Sam nodded. "I've covered the bases. Started in local TV, doing news gathering, moved up to the network, and ended up here after twenty-five years."

"Which do you like best?" Luke asked.

"News is good for the young, but this is the better gig for my old bones." He reached up, took off his baseball cap, and dropped it in his lap. "Working with Holly is a bonus."

"That's sweet of you to say," Holly said, looking at him with a smile. "I'm sure I'm no different than the others."

Sam shook his head. "Trust me, kiddo, some of the prima donnas on this show." He leaned forward, lowering his voice. "Not to mention any names but some, Lisa Cantrell for one, make life hell for the crew. You and Luke are a welcome relief."

"Back to the evening agenda," Luke said. "What about dinner in the hotel and a carriage ride around the park?"

Holly felt the pace of her heart quicken. Back in her time on Broadway, she had taken such an excursion with two other gypsies from the show. The trio had agreed that each needed the companionship of a lover to make the romantic ride complete. The thought of going with Luke was overwhelming. "I'd better pass on the carriage, but dinner would be great."

Intuitively, Luke responded. "I promise to behave. If you like, Sam can chaperone."

Holly's face turned pink. "I didn't mean to imply anything. I just thought it would be better if I got to bed early."

Luke looked at her with a you-can't-fool-me expression, waiting a minute before responding. "We'll make it an early night. I know you want to get rehearsal time in before I go back on location in the morning, plus, tomorrow night could run late at the club."

As part of the agreement between the producers of the commercial and the LCD show, Luke and Holly were scheduled to appear at one of Manhattan's popular nightclubs on Saturday night. Sam would do footage for *Lights, Camera--Dance* while the other crew focused on Luke to showcase New York nightlife.

Luke persisted. "Haven't you heard that to work better, you have to play?"

"You're a bad influence one me."

"I'll take that as a yes."

She shrugged, smiling.

They dined alone in the hotel dining room, Sam having excused himself in favor of room service. Holly avoided taking more than a couple of sips of wine for fear of losing control over her better judgment, which turned out to be a wise decision. As the horse-drawn carriage rolled through Central Park, the moon and stars presided over the scene like an inspiration for Van Gogh. A soft breeze gave Holly a slight chill as she soaked up the sight of moonlit trees and the soothing, clip-clop sound of horse hooves striking the road.

"Having fun?" Luke asked, sliding a little closer to Holly and taking her hand.

She nodded, cautioning herself to stay cool and not to allow the turbulence of her libido to betray her.

"Are you cold?" he probed.

She shook her head no, despite the chill bumps rising on her arms. *Think Joy. Think Joy. If only there weren't a Joy.*

Ignoring her response, Luke asked the driver if a blanket was available. The man said to open the door under the seat. Retrieving a throw, Luke draped it across their laps and once again took her hand.

Holly's conscience told her to pull her hand away as it was not professional to hold hands with your partner, but her emotions trumped her judgment. She felt like a schoolgirl on a first date with all the exciting sensations brought on by the slightest touch from that special boy.

The hour ride flew by and when it was over, the couple walked back to the hotel, still holding hands.

"I hope you enjoyed the ride," Luke said as they crossed 59th Street.

"I confess. I did. Thanks for insisting we go." She looked at him, thinking how sexy and attractive he was. It was only a block to the hotel, but Holly wished it were longer. She was enjoying her hand in his more and more. At the hotel, an elegantly uniformed doorman greeted them and held the door for the pair to enter the Ritz.

As they walked across the lobby toward the elevator, Luke said, "Our driver will pick us up at eight thirty. Want to meet me for breakfast in the dining room at eight, or would you prefer room service?"

"Eight will be fine. We're working at a studio on 7th Avenue, so it shouldn't take us long to get there."

When the elevator reached her floor, Holly turned to Luke and said goodnight. He responded likewise and gave her hand a squeeze as she exited. His suite was thirteen floors above with a view of the Park. Slipping the card into her door, she wondered what his rooms were like. If not for a fear of it being misinterpreted, she would have asked for a peek at the upscale luxury.

The next morning, Holly arrived in the dining room at eight sharp. She carried her dance bag, which contained her work clothes and the iPad with their music. Luke walked up as the hostess was about to show Holly to a table. His hair was wet.

"Just get out of the shower?" she asked.

"After my workout."

"You worked out already?"

"Got to stay in shape, so that I don't drop any dance partners." He winked at her and circled their table to take the seat opposite Holly.

"I'm impressed, Damian. Shows real discipline. I assume you used the hotel gym."

"I did. It's quite well equipped."

While she looked over the menu, Holly made a mental note to try the gym the next morning. As Luke read through the breakfast selections, she gazed at him for a several seconds. She could smell the fragrance of either his shampoo or cologne. She was daydreaming about being in his arms on the dance floor when he looked up, his pale-blue eyes sparkling.

"Something wrong?"

She shook her head. Her lips might have denied the question, but her mind did not agree. *God, you're so attractive, Luke Damian.*

CHAPTER EIGHT

They spent two hours that morning in the dance studio. After changing to street clothes, they went down to meet the limo. Sam followed.

"I'm going to play hooky and skip South Manhattan. I'll meet up with you guys at dinner," Sam said as they reached the sidewalk. I've got enough footage of the sights of the city."

"We'll never tell," Holly said, winking at the older man.

"If you're tired, the car can drop you at the hotel, too," Luke said to Holly.

Before she knew what she was saying, the words spewed out. "No. I'm fine. I'd like to see the 911 Memorial."

Luke smiled, standing aside to allow her to enter the limo first. "We'll leave you at the Ritz on our way, Sam."

The cameraman nodded. "I can take your bags. You won't need them the rest of the day."

As they settled into the limousine, Holly had second thoughts about her brazen action in accompanying Luke without justification. She thought about changing her mind and getting out with Sam, but something kept her from taking the step. In truth, she wanted to spend every available second with Luke and felt guilty because of it. It wasn't the lifestyle that she was becoming addicted to. It was the man. She was beginning to melt every time he looked at her with his incredible eyes.

I have to chill out. Three months from now, I won't be a blip on his radar.

Luke and Holly spent the rest of the day visiting the financial district, the Ground Zero site, and the Statue of Liberty, arriving back at the Ritz at five p.m. After stopping by Sam's room for their bags, they parted to rest and then get ready for the evening.

At seven, the couple met in the hotel dining room for a quick meal. They were both dressed for a night at the club. She wore a sassy mini-skirt with a strappy top and bare midriff. The emerald shade of the outfit brought out the green of her eyes and contrasted nicely with her long, auburn hair. Luke wore a button-down, Charvet shirt in an orange and blue madras plaid; black, Tom Ford pants; a bulky sweater; and a pair of Gucci loafers. Holly's shoes were Christian Louboutin, with the signature red soles and stiletto heels that accentuated her long, shapely legs. She carried a floral-print shawl.

"Nice outfit," he said.

Turning her head, coquettishly, she said, "Thank you, Mr. Damian. You clean up pretty well yourself."

When the waiter brought a bottle of wine to the table, Holly put her hand over her glass.

"You're not having even one glass?"

"Not tonight, thank you. With cameras rolling and heels that are six inches high, the last thing I need is an alcohol buzz."

"I see that you're wearing what I understand is *the* shoe for women."

"Only because the show stylist dressed me. You can be sure there are no red soles in my personal closet. I couldn't even afford a pair of the knockoffs."

"Well, regardless of who did the styling, you are stunning." He looked at her as if seeing her for the first time. "Every eye in the place is going to be on you—the men envying me—the women despising you."

She blushed. "Don't think flattery will give you a break in rehearsal."

"Never crossed my mind." He held up his glass of wine. "To a rising star—Holly Dawson."

Holly blushed, smiled, and raised her water glass to clink with his. "If only that was true, but thank you for the thought."

"Not going to argue with you. Just accept my words," he said, a twinkle in his eyes.

They took their time with dinner, finishing a little before eight-thirty. As Holly watched Luke take care of the tab, she said, "I think I'll run back up to my room and refresh my makeup before we leave for the club."

He looked up at her as he clicked the pen closed, the light catching his almost translucent eyes. "Things won't warm up until after nine, so you'll be fine." As he pushed the case to the side of the table, he asked, "Is Sam riding with us?"

Holly shook her head. "No. He's gone ahead to get a feel for the place and scope out his angles." She started to stand, and Luke instantly rose to assist with her chair.

"Probably best that I don't hang around the lobby. Call me when you're ready, and I'll meet you at the elevator on your floor." He picked up her shawl and draped it around her shoulders. "There'll be a couple of security guys with us tonight. You never know what to expect when you have a big group of people partying."

When the limo pulled up in front of the club, there was a block-long line of wannabe patrons, hoping for entry. Most were being turned away by two oversized bouncers. Like many of the hottest nightspots in the city, admittance was based on what the patron could bring to the establishment: money, branding, or publicity. Before Luke and Holly exited their limo, two security men met the car and took positions between the crowd and the celebrities. There had been no advance announcement of their appearance, but as they stepped out, a few women in the line recognized Luke and called out. Together with the club bouncers, the bodyguards immediately stretched out their arms to shield the couple.

"Your popularity is still alive and well," Holly said, looking up at Luke as they approached the door.

"More like struggling to survive, but with you at my side, it shows promise." He waved to the crowd and several women jumped up and down, blowing kisses.

Work on the commercial was first. The shoot called for footage of Luke on the dancefloor, paired with an unknown actress. With low visibility, loud music, and the dynamics of the crowd, they were able to move through the club unnoticed. With no script and only candid shots required, the director got what he wanted quickly. By nine forty-five Luke was done. He found Holly, and they went to the bar for a drink where they were met by the club manager.

"Sorry I didn't get to greet the both of you earlier, but I had a little internal fire to put out."

"Fire?" Holly said, her face registering alarm.

The manager smiled. "Figuratively speaking. Rocky, our DJ, doubles as emcee. He'll present you at ten-thirty, if that works for you."

Luke looked at his watch and he nodded. "Fine with me if it works for my partner."

"Sounds good," she said, smiling.

"Great. Enjoy your drinks and work your way over to the left side of the stage a few minutes early. The crowd hasn't seemed to notice that you're here, but if they do, and you need help, our bouncers are available."

"Appreciate that," Luke said. "But we've got a couple of guys here if a problem comes up." He nodded in the direction of the two bodyguards.

At the appointed time, Rocky Marco stepped to the center of the small, elevated stage and tapped his microphone. "Citizens, listen up." It took a few seconds for the loud clamor to die down. "I see you're all hot tonight—a lotta smooooth moves going on out there."

The audience started to clap, but he raised his hand. "We're gonna keep this party moving, but first, I want you all to give it up for our special guests from a show I know you all love, *Lights, Camera—Dance*. Luke Damian and his awesome partner, Holly Dawson!

Luke and Holly quickly walked up and onto the stage as Rocky began clapping, setting off a moderate amount of applause from the crowd.

As Luke and Holly met the DJ, they waved to the crowd. "Is

everyone having fun?" Luke called out enthusiastically.

The audience responded with louder applause, whistles, and a few shouts.

Holly stood by Luke, smiling, looking around the room, and making eye contact with a few patrons.

Rocky allowed the audience to quiet down and then said, "Luke and Holly are about to give you a sample of the dancing that's gonna make them this season's champs, so give it up one more time. He then resumed his place in the DJ booth and started a remix of Bruno Mars' "Uptown Funk." The music blared and as the high-tech lighting began flashing all around, matching the rhythm of the song.

Luke raised his hands over his head and began clapping to the beat, his arms sweeping in wide semicircles. Occasionally, he paused to beckon the crowd to participate. Holly joined in. When the patrons were fully immersed in the music, Luke took Holly's hand and they skipped down the four steps to the center of the roped off area. He resumed clapping and swaying with the rhythm. Periodically, he pumped the air above his head. Holly mirrored his actions. After a few counts, Luke stepped aside and pointed to Holly as if to say, "Take it." She went into a jazzy dance combination that brought the crowd to near frenzy as her hips gyrated and her sassy skirt swirled out. After twenty seconds of solo, she danced close to Luke, cocking her head flirtatiously. He grabbed her by the waist, and she responded by locking one arm around his. With their free arms in the air, he twirled her around the floor in rapid-fire turns.

As the couple performed, club staff moved through the crowd, tapping four couples on the shoulder and motioning them to the floor to join Luke and Holly. As each duo entered the space, the celebrities greeted them and interacted as if comparing steps, using only body language. Occasionally they changed off partners with a couple for a few counts. Although Luke appeared to be dancing, Holly was carrying their presentation. His movement was limited to shifting his weight from leg to leg and creating hip action, which he interspersed with bouncing to the beat. As the music came to a close, he reclaimed Holly and spun her into a deep dip, one leg extending high in the air.

The DJ stepped to the center of the platform. "And wasn't that something?"

The crowd roared.

"Think we could coax our celebrities into another number?"

Another roar burst forth.

Luke leaned over to Holly. "Most applause I've had in a long time."

"And you said you didn't know how to dance."

"Hell. All I did was clap and wiggle."

She shook her head. "You did a good job of making waltz turns fit into the funk."

He grinned.

"Okay, okay," the DJ said. "Let's give a few more of you the opportunity to show your stuff with our guests."

Luke looked around the crowd, nodding his head and smiling as if to affirm the comment. Rocky returned to the booth to start the music.

For the second piece, Andy Grammer's "Good to be Alive (Hallelujah)," six couples were chosen. As the song finished, a woman in the crowd screamed out, "Luke, will you sign an autograph?"

Quickly stepping forward, the DJ said, "I'm sorry, folks, Luke and Holly are on a tight schedule and—"

Luke held up his hand and the DJ leaned forward as if to listen. "I can work in a few autographs, Rocky."

Straightening back up, Rocky said, "Luke says he will sign a few autographs for you. Can our people set up a table over in the corner?"

A table and two chairs were quickly put in place, along with a ribbon cordoning off the area. A stack of advertisement-type postcards, containing the club's information and a headshot of Luke, were placed on the front of the table for autographing. They had just settled down, and Luke was signing for a young woman with excessive cleavage, when Holly glanced around the crowd. She froze. A tall blonde stood half-way down the line of autograph seekers.

Tapping Luke on the shoulder, Holly stretched her neck to speak to him as quietly as possible. "You might want to glance down the fans a little way."

He eyed her quizzically but followed her recommendation. Spotting Joy, his expression changed. Holding up his hand to the next person in line, he motioned to one of the security detail. Holly watched him intently as he spoke to the man.

The bodyguard immediately approached Joy. Holly wished that she could hear what was being said. Judging from the look on Joy's face, she wasn't happy. As Holly watched the exchange, a fan shoved one of the glossy cards in front of her to sign. Before responding to the woman, she glanced at Luke. He appeared undisturbed and carried on with greeting fans—most being female.

When Holly looked up from signing the autograph, Joy was gone, and the bodyguard was back in place. She looked back at Luke, but he was intent on what he was doing. Watching his hands as he signed the advertising cards, the thought of those masculine hands on her body flashed across her mind, filling her head with a feeling of desire—and jealousy of Joy. She couldn't help but wonder what message Luke had sent his girlfriend and what his evening held in store.

Later, when they were back in the limousine, Luke was quiet. Holly wasn't sure what to say. She wanted to ask him about Joy—about the message he sent—whether he knew Joy was coming, but she didn't think it was appropriate. The silence inside the car was deafening. Traffic was heavy, and the vehicle moved slowly.

Is she going to be at the hotel? Holly wanted to put Joy out of her mind, but she couldn't. *Will they sleep together tonight?* Her jealousy took control of her thoughts, and she cringed internally at the thought of Luke making love to Joy. Five minutes passed, and Holly could stand the silence no longer.

"Tonight was amazing. Did you enjoy it?"

He turned his face toward her. The corners of his mouth began to turn upward. "I enjoyed watching you on the dance floor."

Don't do that. Don't let me think I have any place in your life. "You weren't so bad yourself, Mr. Alec Holmes."

Shaking his head, he said, "I've got a long way to go. But, I think you'll get me there. We're going to take that damn trophy." He reached over and patted the exposed portion of her thigh, letting his hand rest there.

The touch caused chills to rise on her skin, contrasting with the internal temperature elsewhere. Holly's senses filled with the vision of his eyes looking into hers, the aroma of his fragrance, and the warm feel of his hand on her cool skin. Her breath quickened as she imagined his hand moving farther upward.

Luke's gaze lingered, and for a moment, Holly thought he might kiss her. She wanted him to—desperately. *God, I hate Joy Ambrose. I want to spend the night in his bed. Damn the consequences.*

Luke's cell rang, shattering the moment. Holly's heart sank, believing Joy to be the caller.

"Jeff. What can I do for you?" Luke said, as he answered. "From what I could tell, it went well."

Holly felt the tension in her body dissolve as she realized the person on Luke's phone was his agent.

"We'll be rehearsing for the show tomorrow and on Monday, doing a guest shot on *Morning with Monty and Marie.*"

By the time Luke hung up, the limo had stopped in front of the hotel. Holly half-expected Joy to be waiting with the doormen, or in the lobby, but she was nowhere in sight. Sam's cab pulled up to the curb behind the limo. As they walked into the Ritz, Luke and Sam engaged in a conversation about the filming. Halfway through the lobby, Luke stopped and looked at his watch.

"You guys go on up. I need to check for messages at reception."

Holly fought to mask her disappointment as she responded, "No problem. See you tomorrow."

Once the elevator doors closed, Sam said. "You like him, don't you?"

Wrinkling her brow, she looked at the older man. "Of course I like him. He's a great guy."

"That's not what I mean, and you know it. You *really* like him."

Holly frowned and shook her head. "Not in *that* way, if that's what you mean. He's a good friend."

"Un-huh." Sam raised an eyebrow. "I've come to know you, Holly

Dawson. You don't look at Luke in the same way that you looked at the last partner."

"That's totally ridiculous," she said as the elevator stopped at their floor.

Sam rolled his bag of equipment out as Holly held the door back for him. "Have it your way, but remember, I'm looking at you through my lens every day. The camera doesn't lie."

CHAPTER NINE

As Holly bolted all the locks on her hotel room door, Sam's words, together with the memory of Luke's hand on her thigh and the look in his eyes, spun circles in her head. Unfortunately, the warmth of Luke's touch and the promise in his eyes were chilled by the memory of Joy's expression at the club. *How can I compete with a super model? I'm a Broadway gypsy with a schoolgirl crush.*

She tossed her shawl across the desk chair, kicked off the designer shoes, and headed for the bathroom to shower and dress for bed. However, once in bed and settled deep in the sumptuous pillows, sleep refused to come. Over and over, Joy's glamorous image popped into Holly's head—first, as the cover model in high-fashion clothing ads and then in Luke's bed, minus her clothing. The latter vision, although imagined, caused Holly to turn her face into her pillow, trying to put the offensive picture out of her mind. For distraction, she turned on the TV and flicked through channels, hoping to find interest in a program that would erase thoughts of Luke and Joy.

I'm being ridiculous. He's my job—nothing more.

Holly was tempted to invade the minibar in a quest to induce sleep. She sat up, swung her feet over to the floor, and then stopped. *This is insane. My crazy infatuation will not drive me to drink.*

A little before one-thirty, she fell asleep, cozy and secure under the down comforter. Within ten minutes, her door opened and footsteps slowly approached her bed. Holly lay motionless, neither frightened nor curious about the identity of the intruder. The steps grew closer until she felt a wisp of cool air flow under the comforter, followed by the sinking of one side of the mattress from the weight of another body. The faint, fresh aroma of apple, cedar, and musk—mixed with the sun and salt smell of male skin after a day at the beach—filled her nostrils. Holly held her breath, not daring to move. A warm hand slid down the satin of her gown and then pulled it up, above her waist. With her body exposed, the hand began slowly exploring her peaks and valleys, from breast to bottom, gently caressing and stimulating every nerve ending. Holly trembled, her feminine fluid starting to flow as the stranger pressed himself against her. Her desire went far deeper than the boundary of flesh as she turned, hungry for more of him.

The dim light filtering through the sheer curtains caught the faded blue of his eyes and the sparkle of gold in his tousled hair, and Holly thought her heart would burst. He slipped one arm under her waist and pulled her to him—then leaned forward and lovingly took the back of her head into his free hand. Scooping her face close to his, he covered her lips with his, parting them with aroused passion. As her desire heightened, he worked his mouth down her neck and below.

"Yes," she whispered. "I've waited for this moment."

He gently eased her up just enough to slide off the gown and then tossed it to the floor, his mouth still hot on her skin. His chest was bare, revealing the definition of muscles in his arms and abdomen. Holly felt for his waist. Finding the button already unfastened, she deftly pulled the zipper down. He wriggled out of the jeans, while keeping one hand under her nude body.

It was happening. He had her heart, now she would give him the rest.

"Are you sure?" he whispered.

"Yes, yes. I'm sure. Do it. Take me."

As he was just about to complete his mission—without warning—it ended.

Her eyes popped open. Unfulfilled, nerve endings throbbing, and wet from perspiration, she whispered, "Damn it! Why did I have to wake up at that moment?" She gathered three of the pillows on the bed, propped up on two and clutched the third to her abdomen. "Damn, damn, damn. I'm fantasizing about a man that I have no better chance with than with one of the British princes. How do I continue working with him?"

It took her over an hour to get back to sleep, partly because she didn't want to give up the erotic feeling that lingered from the dream. When Holly finally lost consciousness, she slept until almost seven a.m.

Upon waking, the fantasy immediately flashed across her mind, and she lay basking in the details. Only a fleeting thought of Joy in Luke's bed, seven floors above, marred her illusions. After a few minutes, she looked at the clock and realized that she had to snap out of her dream state and get dressed. For better or for worse, they had to rehearse. Monday would be consumed by a TV appearance and travel. Tuesday, there would be rehearsals for the opening ensemble routine, final costume fittings, and a run-through on the stage in practice clothing for camera blocking. Wednesday was show day, which meant spray tanning, dress rehearsal, last minute fixes, plus hair and makeup. There was no time to waste.

As she put on eyeshadow, she studied her mirror reflection. "How are you going to look him in the face without feeling guilty after your imaginary tryst last night?" Applying eyeliner, she continued her soliloquy. "And how the heck are you supposed to act if *she* shows up at the studio with him?" With jealousy jostling her competitive streak, Holly took more pains with her grooming than she had for the camera.

As she walked out of the bathroom, her phone rang. She rushed to pick it up from the night table, holding her breath, her heart racing. She hoped it might be Luke. It was Sam. Deflated, she answered.

"Where have you been?" he asked. "Luke has been trying to reach you about breakfast."

"I didn't hear my phone. I had the bathroom door closed while I was getting ready and having a conversation with my reflection."

"You were what? Never mind. Just give him a call. He was worried about you and wanted me to come over to your room to be sure that you're okay."

"I'll take care of it." Clicking off the phone, she paused for a minute, psyching herself up to make the call. When she hit his name on her list of favorites, it hardly rang before he answered.

"Where have you been? You had us worried."

Would that be you and Joy or you and Sam? "I apologize. I was getting ready and didn't hear the phone." In her mind, Holly pictured Joy near him, combing her blond hair as Luke talked on the phone.

"As long as you're okay, I forgive you. Ready to go down for breakfast?"

"I'll just have some coffee in my room. I'm sure you and Joy want to have breakfast together—three's a crowd."

His response was instant. "What the hell makes you think I am having breakfast with Joy?"

"I assumed that since she was at the club last night, the two of you hooked up."

There was a pause at the other end of the line.

"Let me set the record straight for you." His tone was steady with a slight edge of annoyance. "I was with no one last night. Joy is not here—she was here last night, just long enough for me to tell her that she wasn't going to be here." His voice then softened. "Now, if I've made all that clear, will you have breakfast with me?"

"Ouch." Relief swept over Holly, instantly elevating her mood. "I stand corrected."

"I'll take that as a yes. I'll be at your door in fifteen minutes."

"You don't know my room number."

"Of course I know your room number. Be ready."

"Was that on Google, too?"

He laughed. "Beauty, talent, and quick wit, too. You are a triple threat."

Holly grinned. "Keep believing that and you'll go far in the competition." She breathed a silent sigh of relief. Joy had not spent the night in his bed. "I might need more than fifteen minutes."

"I don't think so. You told me that you were getting ready when I was trying to reach you."

"Whoops." She chucked. "Come on, Luke. You know women always have one more thing to do before they're ready. But, for you, I'll make it in fifteen." She hung up, crossed her arms across her chest, hugged herself, and took a deep breath. *Maybe they're not committed.*

Holly used the fifteen minutes to recheck her hair and makeup and to straighten her room. She managed to have everything stowed in either hotel drawers, her carryon, or the closet when he tapped on the door. As she opened it, he stood in front of her, looking like he stepped out of a magazine ad for upscale men's wear—the quintessential male model. Her pulse raced and a slight flush crept up her face. She forced herself to look him in the eye, fighting the memory of her dream. *Stop feeling embarrassed. It was a dream, and he can't read your mind.* She stifled an impulse to blurt out how handsome he looked.

"Good morning, coach. I trust you slept well, because you look beautiful."

"Makeup works wonders," she said, grinning, "but flattery will take you far."

As they walked to the elevator, Holly spoke first. "Luke, I'm sorry that I overstepped earlier about you and Joy. I was out of line."

He put an arm around her waist and gave her a squeeze. "Forget it. No apology necessary."

"That's kind of you, but your personal life is no business of mine, and I shouldn't have been prying."

"No harm . . . no foul. One of these days, I'll give you the whole story, if you don't get it on TMZ first." He winked at her as the elevator door opened.

After breakfast, Sam met them in the lobby. Luke had a hand on Holly's shoulder. She was smiling.

"You two appear refreshed and ready to rock and roll."

"We are," Luke said. "Have to get it right today."

Holly nodded. Sam gave her a sly look as if to say, "I told you so."

The large studio complex was dead with only a female dancer manning the reception desk. It was on the fourth floor of an old building on 7th Avenue, accessible via a shaky elevator. There was a vending machine in the lobby with fruit juices and water—no sodas. The walls were a dreary shade of light brown, but looked as though they had not been painted since WWII. Tacked to the wall were tee shirts decorated with the studio logo and poster-size photos of dancers in impressive poses scattered around in random fashion, together with autographed, 8x10, black and white glossies. A large, cardboard box in the corner held dozens of used shoes—tap, ballet, character, and jazz. The room reeked of rosin and musky age.

Holly's face lit up as they entered. "Chloe, is that you? How have you been, girl?"

"Ducks, honey, just ducks, but from what I hear, not half as good as you."

"Are you working here?" Holly asked, looking around the room and picking up a studio card with fond memories.

"Just working the desk to pay for classes. I'm busting the chorus in another redo of *Cabaret*. Don't have to ask about you—you've made the big time. When I heard you were coming here, today, I asked to work. You know, I DVR the show every week and brag about how we were in the same show a few years back."

"Don't know how big time I am, but it's a paying job." Turning to Luke, she said, "Chloe Santos, meet Luke Damian."

"Oh, honey. You don't have to tell me who this guy is. Me and every girl at Folsom High were loopy over him in the day." She stood up and walked around to shake hands with Luke.

He smiled and grasped her hand. "Nice to meet you, Chloe."

Taking her hand away, Chloe pointed to her cheek. "Plant one right here. I want to post on Facebook for all those snooty girls I went to school with to see that Luke Damian kissed yours truly."

"With pleasure," he said, grinning from ear to ear. "Got your phone, Holly?"

Holly nodded. "Of course."

"Take a photo to go with that post."

Sam had walked in behind Luke and Holly and had been silently standing by. "Hold it a second, Luke. Let me get my camera turned on, and we'll give her a video for You Tube."

Holly spoke up, directing her arm toward Sam. "I'm sorry. Chloe, that is Sam Waring, our cameraman."

Sam nodded as Chloe raised her hand in a little wave of acknowledgement and then turned her attention back to Luke.

As the cameras recorded, Luke kissed Chloe on the lips. Holly watched, smiling at Luke's good-natured gesture but was slightly envious of her colleague.

When the kiss was over, Chloe shook her fingers to the side of her face as if to cool off. "Wow! You are some kind of actor. If I didn't know better, I would have thought that was real." She turned toward Holly. "And you, my friend, better watch out for this guy. He'll tear your heart out by the roots."

Luke brushed it aside by shaking his head. "No worries about Holly. I think that scenario will go the opposite way."

"Okay, you two. All kidding aside, we'd better get to work. Time is not our friend," Holly said, still smiling. "Are you staying, Chloe?"

"I leave at one. Have to be in the dressing room by two for the Sunday matinee. There'll be someone coming in to relieve me. Do you mind if I watch you guys work for a while?"

"Not at all. You can probably help us out," Holly said.

"You bet. I'll lock the door and then show you to your studio. Dressing rooms are on the way. I assume you brought your music."

CHAPTER TEN

"You bet. I assume I can plug my iPad into your sound system." Holly said as the trio followed Chloe down a hall with multiple closed doors.

"No problem." As they made their way, Chloe pointed to rooms marked, "Men's Dressing Room" and "Women's Dressing Room."

The studio assigned to Holly and Luke was on the street side of the building. A wall of floor-to-ceiling glass provided a view of Manhattan traffic. Colorful, autographed handprints of famous and not-so-famous dancers, above permanently mounted ballet barres, decorated two walls. Mirrors covered the fourth. A grand piano anchored the room where glass met mirror, and a console holding the sound system stood in the opposite corner. "I hope this room is large enough for you," Chloe said as they entered the space.

Stepping inside, Holly said, "It's perfect." She walked to the sound system and connected her iPad.

"While you and Luke get ready, I can get everyone water or juice. What's your preference?" Chloe asked. The dancers and Sam all requested water.

After changing, Luke returned to the studio first, dressed in gray sweat pants and a plain, red tee shirt. Following Holly's training, he began warming up.

When Holly came in, she was wearing a long, white circular skirt of jersey over an emerald camisole that emphasized her absinthe eyes. Her auburn hair was loose and draped in a soft wave down the side of her face and over her shoulders. Chloe was behind her with the bottles of water.

Glancing at Luke, Chloe said, "I see Holly taught you well. Most singers and actors have no clue as to how to prepare."

Luke smiled. "She cracks a mean whip."

Ignoring the banter, Holly went to a barre and did a series of stretches, plies, and kicks before motioning for Luke to join her in the center. "Chloe, do you mind running the music for me? It's cued up."

"Got you covered."

Since waking that morning, Holly had dreaded the first physical encounter of rehearsal. When paired with her dream, face-to-face contact, touching, and acting as though they were indeed lovers for the waltz was intimidating. However, Chloe proved to be a neutralizing factor. Holly found herself more absorbed in impressing her colleague than dwelling on her errant feelings for Luke. The competitive performer overcame the lovesick woman.

Chloe was anything but a silent observer. As Luke glided Holly around the room in graceful waltz turns, Chloe shouted, "Great. . . . Way to go. . . . Stay on the music." At one point, when the couple opened to a single-hand hold, lunged in opposite directions, and swept their free hands in an over-the-head arc, Chloe jumped up, stopped the music, and trotted over to Luke. Taking his hand, she forced it into a large half-circle. "It's got to be a *big* rainbow. Let go of your inhibitions and let it flow. Stretch your extended leg, your arm, and your fingers to infinity." Turning to Holly, she said, "Sorry, girl. Hope I'm not stepping on toes."

Holly held her hands up. "No way. Thanks. He needs to hear it from someone other than me."

"Tell me to shut up anytime." Chloe made a gesture as though zipping her lips. "You know you can take the girl out of Brooklyn, but you can't take Brooklyn out of the girl."

"No problem. We need all the help we can get," Holly said.

"Weeell, there is one more thing."

They both looked at Chloe.

"This music oozes with romance. You guys have got to sell the audience on the fact that you're consumed with undying love for one another. Luke's got it down, but Holly, darling, you're holding back. Don't know how with this guy as your partner, but you're looking like your favorite cat just died. Give him that 'I'd like to be the melted butter on your biscuit' look."

"Yeah, Holly. Give me *that* look," Luke said, grinning.

Holly felt the color rising on her face. *Don't blush; don't blush.*

Chloe walked over and patted her on the shoulder. "You can do it, kiddo. I know you can."

Dear God, if you only knew.

Sam had been silently filming the entire proceeding. Holly turned away from Luke and Chloe, hoping neither saw the flush on her face. As she did, she caught Sam's eye, and he raised his eyebrow with another "told you so" look.

In her most professional voice, Holly said, "Start the music from the beginning. We'll do it again and apply Chloe's corrections." Turning back to Luke, she said, "Got it?"

He gave her a salute. "I serve at your pleasure."

They worked until noon. Chloe continued to make suggestions and several times adjusted Luke's placement manually, lifting his chin a little higher, pushing his shoulders down. Her corrections were minor but improved his lines. Holly watched, relieved that her old friend had stepped in. The only time that morning she reflected back to her fantasy was when Chloe put her hands on Luke.

Thirty minutes after Chloe left, Luke suggested they stop for lunch.

"Want me to call our driver?" Sam asked.

"Not unless Holly doesn't want to walk around. I'm thinking some New York pizza and a little sightseeing on foot. I could stand to flush out the cobwebs." He turned toward her. "You game?"

She did not hesitate. "I am. It's a beautiful day. Might as well take in the sights." She looked toward the street for a second. "I would also say fresh air but not sure there is any in Manhattan."

The outing cleared Holly's head. As they walked by shop windows, bistros, and office buildings, they chatted about Broadway shows, the strange people on the streets, and the electricity of the city. Only once was Luke recognized and asked for an autograph by a fan. He responded graciously.

While he signed the map of the city provided by the young woman, she turned to Holly and asked, "Are you anyone I should know?"

"No," Holly answered, which instantly caught Luke's attention.

"Apparently, you don't watch *Lights, Camera—Dance,* he said. This beautiful lady is one of the stars."

"Really?" the young woman said. "Will you sign the map, too?"

Holly wanted to protest, but Luke gave her a sharp look. Taking the pen from him, she wrote, "With kind regards, Holly Dawson."

After walking several blocks, they crossed 7th Avenue and bought slices of pizza from a quickie parlor, Luke's loaded and Holly's with veggies. He drank beer with his; she had a diet soda. It felt warm and natural to Holly to have him hold her hand. By the time they returned to the studio, reality had swept away the cloud left by the dream, and she felt totally at ease with Luke.

Back in their rehearsal space, she slipped into her dance shoes, but traded the skirt for black sweat pants. "I think we've covered the show number enough for today. The rest of the afternoon, we'll go over the basics of other dances you've learned to refresh your memory. Thursday, we'll be starting a whole new routine."

"Carrie's 'Cowboy Casanova,' right?"

"Right." *And my job is to make you look sexy without losing my head. I'm screwed.*

CHAPTER ELEVEN

Monday was hectic. Holly was up by six a.m. but still had to rush to have everything packed before the limo picked them up for the morning talk show. Normally, she would have skipped makeup, since the network team would prepare her for the camera, but her vanity kept her from allowing Luke to see her with a naked face. As she applied blush, she once again reflected on the weekend, including the dream sequence. Enough time had passed that the memory had lost most of its heat, but she still savored the fantasy and indulged the temptation to rekindle as much as her senses would permit. As she dusted her face with translucent powder, a knock on the door startled her. She dropped the brush, knocking over the container, which caused the silky substance to coat her navy-blue slacks. Not sure what to do, she froze for a moment.

A second knock, slightly harder than the first, occurred.

She was cornered. Hoping it was Sam, she went to the peephole. To her frustration, Luke stood, in all his glory, outside her room.

Darn it.

As she opened the door, she felt like a kid caught eating a chocolate bar before dinner. Not only was her clothing a mess, she bore the guilt of her erotic daydream.

"How does the other guy look?" Luke said, grinning.

Holly looked down at her outfit, then back up, and made a face. "I'm looking at him, and he seems to have fared a lot better."

He pointed to her slacks. "That's my fault?"

"Assuming it was you who unexpectedly pounded on my door, causing me to drop the box of powder."

He started laughing.

"It's not funny, my friend. Do you recall that we have a TV interview in less than two hours?"

He passed his hand down his face as if trying to wipe away the smile. "I'm sorry. Let's see what we can do to repair the damage."

"Sorry you caused it—or sorry you laughed?"

He couldn't help but smile again. "Both. Now, come on. Let's get the concierge on the phone. You take them off, and I'll make the call. I'm sure they can be dry-cleaned while we have breakfast." He moved close to her and put an arm around her shoulders. "It'll be fine. We have people to fix it."

Her frustration diminished as she enjoyed the feel of his arm around her. Looking up at him, she said, "I'm sorry for snapping at you. It really wasn't your fault."

He squeezed her shoulder and then bent over and kissed the top of her head. "Apology accepted."

The television spot went well—almost. The focus was on Luke. Holly felt like wallpaper. However, at one point, the hostess, Marie Martin, asked Holly what it was like to work with a former teenage heartthrob.

"I feel envy coming from a lot of women my age," she replied.

"Let's face it, Holly. Your job calls for you to be up close and *awfully* personal with a partner. Be honest. How do you handle that?"

The camera had moved in on Holly for a closeup of her face, an angle that always made a subject look guilty. Feeling like she had a wad of cotton in her mouth, she was at a loss for words.

Sensing her discomfort, Luke stepped up to the plate. "I can answer that for you, Marie. She treats me like a new puppy that needs to be trained. But, I love it."

"Well, you certainly make an attractive couple. Don't you think so, Monty?" Monty Rogers was the co-host of the show, but generally deferred to Marie.

"They certainly do."

"I know that I can't wait to see the two of you dance. Wednesday night is the first show of the new season, right?"

Holly nodded, while Luke responded. "It is, and we're excited. I only hope that I don't slip and fall, making a complete fool of myself."

"I'm sure that won't happen," Marie said.

He looked at Holly as he spoke. "If it does, it won't be this amazing lady's fault. She is a magician in the studio. I could never have done it with anyone else."

In the limousine, as they left the TV studio for the airport, Holly turned to Luke. "Thanks for coming to my rescue on camera. I drew a blank."

"You were fine."

"Talking is not in my job description." She had a wide-eyed expression on her face.

"We're going to work on that. They don't make many silent films these days."

"I'm not an actress."

He smiled and patted her hand.

She looked at him, internalizing his words. *"We're going to work on that." When is he thinking that will happen?*

"Well, today can only go up from here. Powder all over my clothes, losing my train of thought on the air. Maybe you should take a different plane. I feel like a jinx."

He shook his head. "Banish that thought. It all worked out. Your pants were cleaned within thirty minutes, and no one noticed your pause on the air."

The flight was smooth, and they landed in L.A. at six thirty. During the seven-hour trip, they watched a film, played cards, and reviewed some of Sam's footage from the Sunday rehearsal. As they deplaned, Luke asked if she would like to have dinner before going to her apartment.

"I'd better go home. I'm pretty tired, and I have to pick up my cat from a friend who has been taking care of her. Give me a raincheck?"

"Guaranteed."

After arriving home and retrieving Gigi, Holly settled into performing routine chores. As she addressed the cat's needs, Luke crossed her mind. Was he with Joy? His words, "She was here last night, just long enough for me to tell her that she wasn't going to be here," echoed in Holly's mind. *What did that mean?* The model had not been mentioned again. Holly's curiosity gnawed at her. *Is he or isn't he in a relationship with her?* She had barely finished giving the cat fresh food and water when the phone rang.

"I saw you on TV this morning with Mr. McSizzling Sexy. God, what a hunk he still is." It was Dana.

"Is he? I hadn't noticed," Holly said.

"Yeah, right. Don't BS me, girlfriend. I don't know how you stand it—being all close and snuggly with such a stud. It must be like being a diabetic in a fudge factory."

"It's a job—just a job."

"Like heck it is. You can't tell me those blue eyes don't make you melt. You've got to go for it, girl. When you're fifty, you don't want to look back and say, 'I could have had a steamy affair with a sexy, megastar.' Do you know how much I regret getting married before I had my share of thrills?"

"Dana, listen to me. Thinking of Luke that way is like swallowing a firecracker and counting down to the explosion. I just got over one breakup. I don't want an encore anytime soon."

"I'm just saying—you've got an opportunity thousands would kill for."

"Can't disagree with you there, but I'd better go. Tomorrow is a killer day."

"I'll be watching Wednesday night. Break a leg. And, think about what I said."

CHAPTER TWELVE

Tuesday offered no time for the couple to rehearse together. Holly arrived at the studio for spray-tanning at seven a.m. and then spent the rest of the morning with the other pros, fine-tuning the production number that would open the show. The choreographer, a Tony Award winning artist known for his quirky style, kept the troupe working until fifteen minutes before the call for camera blocking. No one complained because one of the bonuses of working on the show was the exposure to such prestigious names in dance. If a dancer was lucky enough to be noticed by the creative expert, it could lead to another job in a Broadway show, music video, Las Vegas gig, or even a feature film.

The night before, when Luke had expressed concern about not doing a run-through of their number before the blocking, Holly told him to relax; no judging would occur.

"They don't even film the run-through. Some of the pros let their partners mark the difficult combinations, but I want you to dance full-out," she told him.

"Why am I not surprised?" he said, grinning.

Blocking for the two-hour show began at three p.m. Holly barely had time to gulp down a container of yogurt and a half bottle of water. Luke was on the ballroom set with most of the other celebrities when she arrived.

"Ready for a touchdown?" she asked, smiling as she walked up to him.

"I'd like to be that optimistic. At this point, I think that I'm better off not interacting with the other competitors. The brunette in the tight, blue pants is so nervous that she had me shaking."

Holly chuckled. "With your on-camera experience, you're not going to let her get to you. She's a reality-show drama queen."

"I don't think that counts here. My best hope is having you to keep me on track."

"You can do it."

As they spoke, a production assistant approached with an envelope containing their assigned slot in the program.

"We're fourth to go on," Holly said as she took the card out.

"Is that good or bad?" Luke asked with a look of concern.

"Neither. It means that our piece is not a showstopper. Those get the first and last slots. It does give us a chance to see a few others dance without having to wait so long that our nerves feel like shredded carrots."

During the blocking, Luke was slightly stiff but otherwise got through the routine with no mishaps. When the practice run wrapped, somewhat out of character, he patted Holly on the shoulder and said, "See you tomorrow." He left without further comment.

She tried not to read anything into Luke's hasty retreat, nor to let it bother her, but it did.

Collecting her bag from the dressing room, Holly ran into Lisa Cantrell.

"Where's Luke?" Lisa asked. Her partner was the handsome TV chef.

Forcing an upbeat tone to her voice, Holly said, "Apparently, he had to leave."

"That's too bad. Most of the cast is going out for a *Hail Mary* party at Furore. You game?"

Holly hesitated and then plastered on a fake grin, struggling to hide her disappointment at Luke's departure. "Absolutely. We have to give this ship a worthy launch." *Luke Damian does not have an exclusive on the pin number for paradise.*

An hour later, all the pros and most of the celebrities were partying at the club. Several of the cast members brought along a spouse or a date. Few were hooked up with their show partners. When Holly walked in, the first person she ran into was Mika Dorofeyev.

"What? No handsome, how is it you say . . . stud biscuit with you?" he said as he leaned forward, took her hand, and kissed it.

"Muffin," Holly said, a smile on her face. "I'm sure you know that. You've been called it enough."

"No, no. I'm no stud muffin."

"Public opinion would refute that statement. If you're not, why is it that you are either shirtless or unbuttoned in nearly every number you perform?"

Shaking a hand in front of his chest, he said, "It's hot under studio lights."

"Right." She raised her eyebrow and tipped her head.

"You need something to drink, Holly Dawson. I'll get it for you, and then we'll dance. Vodka? Champagne?"

"How about Diet Coke?"

He made a face. "Soda? You don't drink soda. How will you have a good time on soda?"

"Good as I need to have, especially if I'm going to dance with you."

Mika shrugged his shoulders in mock surrender. "I'll be right back."

As he walked away, Kat Kenley, another pro, came over to Holly. "Looks like you won the queen for a night lottery, but be careful, it's a dangerous crown."

Holly laughed. "It'll be a brief reign. I'm leaving by eleven."

"Ah. But the question is: to whose home are you going?" Kat gave Holly a mischievous look.

"My home . . . *alone.*"

"Mika's not going to like that."

"It's not Mika's call. I'll dance with him because he's a great partner, but that doesn't get him a ticket to a private performance in my bedroom."

Kat chuckled. "You're going to hold the record for the gal who held out the longest with our sexy imports. By the way, where is that dreamboat you're teamed up with this season?"

"I have no idea. He left after the run-through." *Probably has a date.*

"You and Lisa got the best ones. I've got the middle-aged jock who has been enjoying way too much bubbly since he retired. We'll be kicked off by week three."

Before Holly could respond, Mika returned. Ignoring Kat, he said, "Holly, I have a drink for you at the table. Come."

Kat gave him a patronizing look. "Hello, Mika."

"Oh, Kat. Hello."

Shaking her head, Kat smiled and walked away.

Holly allowed Mika to lead her to a table where drinks were waiting. As he pulled a chair out for her, she asked, "Where is your partner?"

"She's here . . . with her husband." He shrugged his shoulders and made a slight face.

Settled at the table, Holly looked around the club and thought about Friday night in New York with Luke. The laser lights, loud music, and party people were universal. The L.A. club was smaller than the Manhattan hangout, but offered a similar ambiance.

"I took liberty of ordering appetizers," Mika said as a server, bearing a large platter of assorted meat, cheese, and seafood tidbits, arrived.

"They look delicious. Thanks," Holly said, picking up a chicken and waffle miniature. "I am hungry."

Mika's smile suggested that he was pleased with himself. "It's good that you came without your partner."

"Why would you expect me to come with him?"

"Single celebrities usually come with the pros." Mika picked up a small square of Ethiopian beef, skewered on a plastic sword. "Try this," he said and thrust the meat toward her mouth.

Her reflex was to take the appetizer before it reached her mouth. She did not want Mika feeding her. He watched as she chewed the tender meat.

After swallowing, she nodded and said, "That's very good."

He grinned. "I knew you would like."

They nibbled for a few minutes without talking. Conversation was too much effort between the noise and his accent. Several of the other cast members stopped by their table, including Mika's counterpart, Andrei Rodchenko, who made Holly promise to dance with him later.

This could be fun after all. I've been dying to dance with one of these guys. If I can't do it on camera, at least I have the chance here.

Of the two men, blond Rodchenko was probably the better dancer, but dark-haired Mika had a slight edge in the looks department. Both had great bodies, which they knew how to use to the pleasure of female fans.

Mika turned his glass up and chugged the vodka. Putting it down on the table with a flourish, he reached for Holly's hand. "We dance now." It was a mandate rather than an invitation.

She looked at him and pulled her hand away just before it connected with his.

Mika's face registered shock. "You don't dance tonight?"

She smiled and in a sweet voice said, "I'm sorry. I don't do well with commands from someone who is not signing my paychecks."

"Что такое?" He hesitated for a moment, and then the corners of his mouth turned up slightly. "I mean, pardon." With a grand sweep of an arm, he bent forward in a mock bow. "Would you like to dance, Ms. Dawson?"

"As a matter of fact, I would." She offered him her hand.

Mika took it, and as she stood, swung her around hard, which was indicative of his style. On the floor, he performed with razor-sharp precision and led with total confidence, in contrast to Luke, who was still unsure of himself and depended on Holly to lead.

For Holly, being on the floor with Mika was euphoric. She rose to the occasion, matching his moves with sass and style. The Latin music was hot, the dancers hotter. Couples around them began stopping to watch, and quickly a space cleared. Among the spectators was Andrei, who did not take his eyes off Holly. Although absorbed in the moment, she felt the intensity of his gaze and glanced around. For a second, their eyes locked. The attention brought out more and more exhibitionism in her. She was loving every minute. *This is who I am.*

When the music stopped, Mika jerked Holly close, wrapped his arms around her, and then kissed her on the mouth. She felt her knees weaken.

"My titian-haired vixen, I didn't know you are so good. I want to perform with you."

Holly was breathless and exhilarated. Thoughts of Luke vanished. "You're not so bad yourself." As she and Mika walked toward their table, Andrei stepped up from behind and put his hand on her shoulder.

"My turn, little fox. Magic Mika cannot have you to himself all alone."

It looks like Russia has discovered America.

Putting a hand on Andrei's chest, Mika gave a little push. "She needs to catch her breath. *You* may come back later."

Holly said nothing, looking from man to man.

"We let Holly decide for herself," Andrei said, looking down at her. Like lasers, his eyes focused on hers, penetrating all barriers.

"Here, here, boys. No fighting over the Southern belle." Kat had walked up with two drinks in her hand, one of which she extended toward Holly.

Her mouth dry, Holly accepted the drink and took a swallow. Making a face, she said, "Kat, this isn't my Diet Coke. What is it?"

"It's your soda, babe. I just added a pinch of rum."

Holly made a face.

"Trust me; it'll give your evening a little more sparkle."

"I think my evening has enough sparkle without firewater. I'll stick to plain Coke, thank you." Despite her protest, the drink spread a warm tingle through her as it went down. She turned to Andrei. "Give me five or so minutes to recover my breath, and I'd love to dance with you. Right now, I need to sit this one out."

"Do not let this Russian change your mind," Andrei said, pushing back on Mika's shoulder.

"I won't. I promise." She turned to Mika and thrust the drink toward him. "Can you take this to the table for me? I need to powder my nose."

He looked puzzled. "What powder?"

Kat laughed. "That's Southern speak for using the toilet." Looking back at Holly, she said, "Come on. I'll make the trip with you."

The quiet of the restroom was a welcome respite from the overwhelming noise of the club. Both women went straight for stalls, Kat leaving her drink on the vanity counter. By the time Holly reached the row of lavatory sinks, Kat was washing her hands.

"You're on a roll tonight, sweetie," Kat said.

"Is that what you call it?"

"Definitely. Take advantage of it but watch your back. Those two are dangerous, and I have the feeling that you've led a sheltered life." She reached for a paper towel. "Take it from someone who's older and has seen them operate for several seasons."

"I'm not a newbie, but I confess that my big-time dating experience is zero."

"I've wondered about that. I don't remember ever seeing you here and very little of you at the after-parties."

"I have made it a point to stay out of the fast lane. I was engaged to my high-school sweetheart until a few weeks ago."

"Breakup? That sucks. But all the more reason to tread softly. You're raw meat, prime for the lions to devour. Use them to help your career, but don't buy the bullshit. Love's got a whole different definition in their dictionary."

"Don't worry. I'm in no way interested in any relationship right now, but it sounds like you're the voice of experience."

"Observation *and* experience. I've been on this cruise ship since it first sailed seven years ago." Kat pumped hand lotion into her palm. "Yeah. When the pirates landed, I let the rush from Magic Mika play with my head. Nothing so dramatic as a broken heart—just a little rough mileage on the odometer. . . . But, I'm still here, watching him hit on a new girl every season. Pretty as you are, I'm surprised it took him this long."

Holly studied the older dancer's face in the mirror for several seconds. "Is Andrei no better?"

"Peas from the pod. They're cousins, you know."

Holly shook her head. "I didn't know. In fact, I know hardly anything about either of them, other than they are awesome dancers."

"That, they are." Kat took a tube of lipstick out of her pocket and leaned closer to the mirror to apply it. When done, she smiled at Holly. "I'm not saying abstain. Either, or both, can work magic on your career. They get to request partners for exhibition numbers, which is a great showcase. Just don't crawl out of bed in the morning thinking there'll be a ring in your cereal bowl."

"Right now, Kat, I have no plans or desire to change roommates. The one I live with weighs seven pounds, stays out of my fridge, wears her own fur coat, and never lies."

A smile spread across Kat's face. "Cat or dog?"

"Cat."

"Best voodoo you could have. Mika hates them."

"That would fit. Cat haters are control freaks—Hitler, Mussolini, Napoleon to name a few. It definitely keeps him off my list."

Kat pointed her finger at Holly. "You're my kind of gal. I hope you and Luke take the damn competition this season. God knows I don't have a chance with my partner." She then straightened the waistband of her mini-skirt and said, "Better get back to the warzone before someone sends a search party."

Holly nodded. "For a little while. I am still heading home by eleven. I don't see how anyone can be at the top of their game tomorrow if they stay here drinking until the wee hours." She stopped as if thinking. "Or, is that the game plan for crippling the competition?"

Kat laughed. "In this business, it could be, but probably not in your case."

When Holly got back to the table, Mika was on the dance floor with Lisa. Between them, they had taken the trophy eight times. Holly had barely sat down when Andrei slid into the chair opposite her.

"Are you stalking me?" she asked.

"Of course, I am. Why wouldn't I stalk a beautiful woman?" His eyes, the color of a lapis gemstone, were nearly as hypnotic as Luke's pale-blue ones.

He is so darn sure of himself that he could probably confess to murder with impunity.

"That's an honest answer."

"I am always honest."

"I'm sure you are." Holly grinned. *And Madonna is a man.*

"You are very good."

Holly tipped her head slightly sideways. "Good? In what way am I good?"

"You know. Your dance. It's very good. I notice you last season. You surprise everyone."

"Didn't help with winning."

"Can't make a bad partner win. Mika, he likes to win." He waived to a server, beckoning her to their table.

"And don't you?"

He shook his head. "Not so much as Mika. I like to dance good—win or lose, not so important."

The server arrived and Andrei ordered another drink for himself and asked Holly what she would like. She looked at the nearly full glass of rum and Coke and said she would like a ginger ale. As the girl left the table, Mika, with Lisa at his side, nearly ran into her.

"I see your admirer is back," Mika said to Holly as Lisa patted him on the back and walked toward the bar, giving Holly and Andrei a nod as she passed.

"You said five minutes and what do I find? You left the lovely lady to come to empty table. Shame on you, my friend," Andrei said.

Mika laughed. "And your mother is saying a prayer because her son would move on his cousin's woman."

Holly held up both hands in a mock reprimand. "I think you're both crazy." She then stood up and extended a hand to Andrei. "I think I hear our music starting."

He rose, took her hand, and gave Mika a sly smile before escorting her to the dance floor.

Andrei matched Mika as a partner, the only difference being that his hands took even more liberties. Holly told herself she should discourage his familiarity, but she did not. Truth be told, she was having a blast and liked the sensation that came over her with each touch. When the number was over, they returned to the table. Thirsty again, Holly grabbed her ginger ale and took a big swallow. She knew instantly that Mika had spiked it with vodka but took a second drink anyway.

"Okay. My soda is laced with alcohol?" She put the glass down. "I'm letting you get away with this one, but no more." She tipped her head and raised her eyebrows. "Do I make myself clear or do I need to say it in Russian?"

They both laughed.

It was a fun night for Holly. The alcohol she consumed erased her inhibitions, but she held true to her declaration and stayed with soft drinks the rest of the evening. Although she danced with Mika several times, Andrei dominated. The more she was on the floor with him, the more appealing he became with his shaggy blond hair and facial stubble. With all the attention from both men, she did not have time to think about Luke. At eleven-thirty, she looked down at her watch and gasped.

"Oh, my gosh. I've got to go home."

"No, no. It's early," Andrei protested.

"Not with the day we have tomorrow. You two stay. Have some more to drink, and when you have a massive hangover, Luke and I will outscore you both." Hearing herself say his name brought a knot to her stomach. She stood and started toward the door.

"I'll walk outside with you," Andrei said, standing up.

"I'll be fine."

"No, no. I'll go." He put his arm around her shoulders.

When they reached the sidewalk, Holly gave the attendant her valet check, and he went for her car.

"Would you like company tonight?"

CHAPTER THIRTEEN

Holly looked at him, thinking of how sexy he had been when they danced, and for the slightest fraction of a moment, temptation threatened, but prudence prevailed. "I have someone waiting."

"The pretty boy—what's his name, Damian?"

"No. Her name is Gigi. She's small, covered with fur, and the only one who'll share my bed tonight."

"Ohhh. That's too bad. But, you'll come to the after-party, tomorrow. Yes?" Andrei said, taking her hand and kissing the top of it.

Holly's eyes sparkled under the lights illuminating the front of the club. "Sure. I'll let you buy me a drink." *Why not? No show the day after, and Luke will likely bring Joy.*

As Holly attempted to withdraw her hand, Andrei tightened his grasp, pulled her closer, and, allowing no time for protest, kissed her. While not passionate, it was undeniably an invitation.

She took a step backward, uncertain whether she wanted to slap him or submit. She knew that taking one forward step would lead to his bed. The thought was titillating and tempting.

Andrei stared at her, a twinkle in his eye, a slight curl on his lips, and every inch of his sexy body exuding self-confidence and carnal magnetism.

Irritated with the part of her that enjoyed the fleeting brush with intimacy, she overrode the attraction and reclaimed control. Giving him a warning glare, she said, "That was bold. Did you learn that move before or after you came to America?"

He threw his head back and laughed. "I like you, Holly Dawson. You appear like delicate snow flower, but there is fire and steel beneath the icy exterior. I look forward to what may come between us."

"And I think it might be safer for me to take up sword swallowing." Before he could respond, she opened the car door, got in, and rolled her window down. As she started the engine, she turned toward him, smiled, and said, "See you tomorrow. Break a leg."

Pulling onto the street, Holly gripped the steering wheel so tight that her knuckles turned white. She needed the firm grasp to control her trembling. *How close did I come to sleeping with him?* She took a deep breath. *Am I going to regret that I didn't?*

Show day dawned. No matter how often she performed, the annoying stomach flutters always preceded the first step onto the stage or in front of a camera. Wednesday was no different. She spilled Gigi's dry food on the kitchen floor, sloshed hot water on her hand when making her tea, and almost tripped in the parking lot. *Sprain an ankle, Holly, and you are screwed.*

At eight a.m., she walked into the studio, ready for the first leg of the day—the final costume fitting. Disappointed that Luke was nowhere in sight, she took her bag to the girls' dressing room, stretched for a few minutes, and left for her fitting. As she grabbed an apple from the hall table set up by catering, she saw Luke dash in.

"Running a little late," he said, catching up with her. "My car was caught in massive traffic—a wreck on the freeway."

Happy to see him, she smiled. "You're fine."

"Actually . . . not fine. I haven't had this much stage fright since I auditioned for the *Holmes* role." He shifted the bag he was carrying to the opposite shoulder.

"Stop worrying. You're thoroughly rehearsed, and I'll be with you every second."

"Problem is live TV—*no* do-overs. How are you so calm?"

If you only knew.

"Got to drop this stuff in my dressing room. See you later." He grabbed her around the waist, pulled her close, and kissed the top of her head.

Holly stood watching as he rushed down the hall toward the row of celebrity dressing rooms. His hand on her waist had brought a familiar rush of sexual sensation but so had Andrei's kiss. And then, there was Mika.

Have I lost my freaking mind? How can I be simultaneously attracted to three men, all equipped with factory-installed trouble? Snapping back to reality, she quickened her pace toward the wardrobe department.

With no major alterations needed, the costume fitting took less than twenty minutes. Her demure dress for the waltz was pale-aqua. The capped-sleeve bodice consisted of lace over satin, embellished with mother-of-pearl sequins and rhinestones. The skirt was tea-length, of silk chiffon, which would billow and flow as they glided across the floor. In contrast, for the opening production number, her skimpy costume was metallic-gold with a glittery bra top and a mini-skirt that barely covered the attached, Lycra briefs. Two rows of thick fringe bordered the edge of the skirt, which would add a saucy flair when combined with the hip action of the cha-cha.

Her next stops were hair and then makeup. For Luke and Holly's first week, her makeup would be standard and her hair loose and flowing.

"I'll have you out of the chair in thirty minutes," the makeup artist promised and delivered.

Holly finished with preshow prep before eleven and went downstairs to the commissary to grab lunch. She thought about checking on Luke but changed her mind. The food bar was virtually empty. She picked up a yogurt, a bottle of water, and a package of dried fruit and nuts. Heading back to the dressing rooms, she bumped into Mika as he came down the stairs and into the hall.

"Whoa, pretty lady. What's the hurry?" He took her by the shoulders to steady her as she teetered slightly.

"I thought I would put my feet up and chill out." She caught a whiff of the fresh aroma of soap and surmised that he had just showered.

"Good idea. I'll join you. Give a minute to pick up sandwich."

Before she could respond, he darted into the cafe. Holly stood in the hall, feeling awkward, conflicted, and unable to convince herself to walk away. *Where has this interest in me come from? Did I step into a puddle of pheromones?*

It took Mika less than three minutes to obtain a club sandwich, chips, and a Mountain Dew. Coming out of the commissary, he put his hand on the small of her back and guided her toward the elevator.

"Where are we going?" she asked.

"To the roof. I like fresh air."

"This is Los Angeles. There is no fresh air."

"Maybe true, but it is quiet there. We can talk—get to know one another better."

Holly took a deep breath and entered the elevator. "This is against my better judgment in more than one way, but I'll give you twenty minutes."

"What is your rush? Rehearsal's not until twelve-thirty."

"I need to touch base with my partner . . . make sure he's okay."

"He's a big boy. Should take care of himself."

Holly didn't respond but noted that Mika's accent was not consistent.

The elevator door opened, and they walked onto the roof. Mika was right. There were several round tables, each with chairs and shaded by a large, striped umbrella. "Here, sit."

She did as she was told—immediately opening her container of yogurt.

"Is that all you eat?" he asked.

"That's all."

"How do you have strength to dance? You women. You never eat anything. There's no worry about the pounds with all the exercise."

"I think that only works for you men. If I ate that sandwich, I wouldn't fit into my costume this afternoon."

He shook his head while opening the drink. Taking a big swig and swallowing, he cocked his head slightly to the right and said, "Where is it that you are from?"

"Florida. On the other side of the country."

"I know Florida. Disney World, right?"

"Among other things—like a couple of oceans and a lot of hot weather."

He stared at her as she mixed the fruit and nuts into the yogurt and put a spoonful in her mouth. His gaze made Holly uncomfortable. Swallowing the food, she raised her eyebrows and said, "What?"

"No what. Just admiring a lovely woman with green eyes like the lime."

"I've never heard them described that way before. Why am I suddenly getting so much attention from you?"

"You should have attention. You are good dancer—sexy and beautiful. I told Mimi today that I choose you to dance with me when Carlos Santana appears on the show next week."

Oh, my God! Holly couldn't help but be excited. A duet with Mika Dorofeyev and a guest star was the next best thing to winning the competition. She remembered Kat's words, "Take advantage of it."

"Thank you. I'd love to dance with his band."

"And with me, no?"

"And you." *You are an egotist, aren't you Mika Dorofeyev?*

"Good. We need to do much rehearsing, alone."

Whistles and red flags went off in Holly's mind. *Who are you kidding, Holly? You knew this was coming.* "Are you sure they want me?"

"Sure? Of course, I'm sure. Mimi is director, and I always choose my partner."

Holly looked at him for a few seconds, trying to stifle the degree of her excitement. "I know that it'll take serious rehearsing to make a perfect routine, but I'm not going to cheat Luke out of any of my attention."

"Don't worry for him. He's celebrity—they come, they go." He flicked a hand in the air. "I'm always on show—every season."

How well I know you are. "I'll make it work, but, I've got to go now. I would think your partner, that country singer, would want you with her right now."

"Charlie? She'll be fine. She's done the big concert tours. Camera is old for her; what do you call it—old hat?"

Holly wadded up her paper napkin and crammed it into the empty yogurt cup. "Do you think she's good enough to win this season?"

Mika finished chewing the last of his sandwich and then said, "I make her good enough."

Of course, you think that.

Holly left Mika, draining his can of soda. As the elevator took her to the rehearsal studio level, her cell phone rang. Luke's name came up on the screen.

"Where are you?" His voice had an urgent edge.

"I'm on my way to the second floor. I'll meet you in our room."

He was pacing as she walked in.

"I couldn't find you. They said you left after your hair was done, which looks wonderful, by the way."

"Thank you, and I'm sorry. I got through early and decided to grab lunch. Have you eaten?" *He is so handsome.*

"No. Eating for me is not a good idea, today. Can we do a practice walk-through and a final check of the lift?"

"I think we can work one in; but remember, we've got to be in full costume and on the set by twelve-thirty."

"How could I forget? I've been asking myself all morning why I ever agreed to do this?"

"Luke, you're going to be fine. You've got it down."

His insecurity could not have been more obvious if he wore a peel-and-stick label on his lapel with the word "terrified."

Holly reached out and took his hands. "Once the music starts and you take the first step, you'll relax. Don't psych yourself out."

"I wouldn't say the day has gone well, so far. First, I'm late getting here, then my costume had to be altered, and finally I couldn't find you."

"I'm here. It's good. I won't leave you until the show is over." She squeezed his hands.

"I'll probably be eliminated tonight."

"Luke, no one is eliminated the first week, and we're going to the finals. Keep your head in the game."

He pulled his hands away, wrapped his arms around her in a hug, and said, "You are the best."

Feeling her body press against his, Holly wanted to remain in his embrace. The teacher in her felt protective, but the woman felt vulnerable. The Russians sparked her carnal appetite, but Luke's appeal surpassed sensuality. Life was growing more complicated by the minute. She wanted to tell Luke about Mika's announcement, but something held her back. Likewise, she wasn't interested in discussing the night before with him. *This is crazy. We're just friends. How can I be disloyal when there's no bond to betray?*

At twelve-twenty, Holly walked into the green room, dressed in costume for the opening number. Luke was ready and talking with Kat Kenley's partner, Roy Hobson, a former football star, turned network sports announcer. Luke's back was to her. Recognizing Holly, Hobson put his hand on Luke's shoulder, and pointed her out. Patting Hobson on the back, Luke turned and eagerly walked toward her with a mesmerized expression on his face. It was the first time he had seen Holly in such brief clothing, her long legs fully exposed and enhanced by strappy stiletto-heels. The costume accentuated her perfectly shaped and proportioned figure and left little to the imagination. Watching his eyes soaking up every inch of her, Holly felt more self-conscious than she ever had in provocative stage attire.

"You are stunning," he said as soon as he was within her earshot. "I'm speechless."

She smiled. "I'll take that as a compliment. Thank you. You wear your tux well."

"These wardrobe people are fantastic. It was too big this morning. I don't know how I changed sizes. . . . Well, maybe I do. You've worked the weight off me."

"Every pound counts when we have to wear tight-fitting costumes."

He looked her up and down with obvious admiration. "You're going to have to forgive me. I'm still in awe." His eyes sparkled, confirming his admiration. "You are *truly* beautiful. Why am I worried? I could trip, even keel over dead, and no one would notice. Every eye is going to be on you."

She shook her head. "Wait until you see the other girls. I'm just one of the pack."

A production assistant came in and shouted, "Five minutes to tape. Everyone take your places."

The pros in the room all moved toward the door, some with makeup people coming along for last minute touch-ups.

Luke followed the celebrity crowd out and went to the audience section of the main studio while the pros moved into their places. The musicians, singers, and hosts were already on the set. As the house lights went down and the theme music began, Holly felt the exhilaration of the theater, intensified by the fact that Luke would be watching. From her starting pose, she could see him, sitting ringside. As the band started to play "She's a Lady," Holly threw one arm in the air and began the sassy cha-cha walk, along with two other female dancers. The Tom Jones signature song provided all the impetus she needed to give it her all. She could feel Luke's eyes on her. Holly was sexy, and she knew it.

However, Luke wasn't the only one with eyes on her.

Whenever they were off the floor for a few counts, both Andrei and Mika followed Holly, but she didn't notice. She danced for Luke. With fourteen pros and six backup dancers in the production number, Holly did not actually partner with either one of the Russians.

When they struck the final pose, the celebrities joined their respective pros for the introductions. As Luke reached her side, he was grinning from ear to ear.

"You are something, Holly Dawson. I couldn't take my eyes off you."

"I'm nothing special."

"The hell you aren't. You stand out like the star of the show."

"Shh." She looked around, embarrassed at the thought any of the others had overheard, and then said, "We're next." Inside, she felt warm and fuzzy with the knowledge that she had impressed him.

CHAPTER FOURTEEN

As soon as the host completed the introductions, Holly went to change costumes, basking in the glow of Luke's approval as she scooted down the long hallway. There were three couples to perform ahead of them, but the rehearsal would move quickly without the interruption of commercial breaks and judges' comments.

Luke did well in the dress rehearsal. He remembered their choreography and, with her help, managed to stay on the music. What he lacked in artistry, he made up for with his infectious smile and intense effort. Holly was proud and relieved.

"I wish that had been the real deal," he said when they were alone. "Can't they just run the recording?" He took a towel from a production assistant and wiped his forehead.

"Stop it. You're going to do even better live. There's close to three hours until show time. Let's chill out."

Taking off his jacket, he said, "For that, I'll need hard drugs—or at least a triple Scotch."

"Sorry. Mind-altering substances are not on the menu. How about we go back to our studio and play cards or work on a puzzle—unless you'd rather be alone in your dressing room?"

His face lit up. "You've got a puzzle?"

"I do. As a matter of fact, I brought three—none as challenging as you're used to but, hopefully, good, time-killing distractions."

"I can't believe you thought of that. I expected that you'd keep me busy rehearsing."

"Nope. We might do one run-through, but it's more important

for you to relax now, clear your head."

"Then let's get out of these costumes and check out your puzzles."

They walked to the elevator with Luke's hand on Holly's shoulder. Once inside, he took her hand and squeezed it. "Thank god the producers gave me you. Anyone else and I would have quit the first week."

She turned. "No, you wouldn't. You're not a quitter, and you would have been happy with any of the others. Almost everyone thinks their pro is the best."

He pulled her close and hugged her. "I'll never believe that."

Holly hugged him back, fighting the desire to turn the hug into something more. The doors opened sooner than she would have liked. Looking up at him as they left the car, she chided herself.

I'm just a pal.

At four-forty-five, everyone was back in costume, hair and makeup refreshed. The celebrities paced the hallways while their pro partners did their best to be reassuring.

Luke reentered the zone of panic, deeper than before. His usual jovial demeanor was gone, replaced by a quiet tension. Holly, uncertain how much to push him, decided to give him space. When the show went live, he did not watch the opening production number, which surprised and disappointed her; however, he managed to mask his fear for the introductions with a big smile, which she recognized as fake.

As their names were announced and clips of their rehearsals shown, he ran in place off camera, shaking his hands in an attempt to loosen up.

"Luke. Focus. You're going to do great. Don't get in your own way."

He nodded, but it was obvious to Holly that he was not reassured.

The music began, the spotlight hit them, and they went into motion. Holly's butterflies disappeared, but she could feel the tension in Luke's hands. The first few measures went well.

He's got it! He's going to be okay.

As they were about to begin a series of turns—it happened. Luke missed a step. Although he tried to cover it, his expression registered disaster.

"I've got you, Luke. . . . Waltz turns. . . . Stay with me. . . . You've got it."

In less than four counts, he found his place, and the panic in his eyes subsided, but Holly could tell he was upset. His professionalism powered him through the routine without another blunder.

As he brought her up from the final pose, he said, "I'm sorry. I blew it. I'm so sorry."

Holly hugged him. "It's okay. Your recovery was fantastic. It will make up for the tiny flaw."

She was disappointed for Luke but tried to keep him from knowing. He had to let go of the mistake and not allow it to affect his future performances.

In the critique, the judges mentioned the faux pas but were not cruel with their comments.

Lorraine Gibson said, "I can tell that you've worked hard, and you did a good job of getting back on track when you missed your step. You haven't taken dance classes before now, have you?"

Luke shook his head.

Gibson continued, "Well, I would say that you are doing quite well. Up to the point that you had the unfortunate stumble, you were spot on. Don't let that discourage you. It's your first night. You've got a lot of potential."

When scores were revealed, each of the two female judges had given him a three out of a possible five. One male judge gave him a score of two, the other a two-point-five.

Luke smiled for their on-camera interview, but Holly felt the tension in his body.

I've got my work cut out.

When the show went off the air, Luke gave her a hug, thanked her for talking him through the mistake, and headed to his dressing room. Holly knew he was still upset. She debated whether to attempt to console him, but the prominent question in her mind was whether he would attend the after-party. They were expected to appear, because the entertainment media would be there doing interviews. Holly feared Luke would opt out even though their contracts required that they be available for publicity opportunities.

Do I try to connect with him or do my own thing?

Holly rushed through changing out of costume. They had not discussed the party. She had avoided the subject because of Joy. Family and famous friends of the celebrities, plus past contestants, were welcomed to attend, giving the press a broader range to cover. After debating the circumstances, Holly decided that a text was the best course of action.

"See you upstairs at the party," she typed. It was short, to the point, did not require an answer, and freed her to go up without him. She watched her phone for several minutes, hoping a reply would pop up, but it did not.

Giving her long hair a final comb-through, she left the dressing room at the same time Lisa Cantrell and Danique Janssen were walking out. Both scored well. Lisa's partner, the celebrity chef, was a season favorite. His cooking show was high in ratings, more because of his handsome face and sexy Swedish accent than his recipes. Danique's partner, an agile NBA player, was nimble on the court and rhythm in motion on the dance floor.

"Congratulations on your scores, tonight," Holly said.

"We got lucky," Danique responded in her heavy Dutch accent. "Sorry about Luke's mishap."

Putting a hand on Holly's arm, Lisa said, "Don't worry. I think it's better when they don't do well the first week. It keeps them humble and makes them realize the amount of hard work that it takes to win. My worst partner, *ever*, scored a four on the first week and never came close again."

"You mean you actually lost?" Danique said.

"Get out of here. I don't win every time. Especially since Andrei and Mika came on the show. Speaking of which, what's going on with you and the Russians, Holly? They were buzzing around you like two bees on a honeysuckle bud."

"If you find the answer to that question, tell me, and we'll both know."

"Watch out for those two, *lieveke*," Danique said. "They are good for the you-know-what, but never take their words to be so truthful."

Holly held her hands up as in surrender. "Advice taken. I have already determined for myself that juggling butcher knives would be safer than getting involved with Russia's gifts to American women."

Both dancers laughed. "Smart girl," Lisa said as the three got on the elevator.

Walking into the party, Holly couldn't help but look around to see if Luke was there. Not seeing him, she walked over to where Kat stood.

"Where's your drink?" Kat asked. "No worry about a hangover tomorrow. It's a free day."

"I'm thinking about it."

She was about to ask how Kat thought the show went when Luke walked in with Joy. Holly's heart sank. *No wonder he didn't respond to my text.* Taking a deep breath, she looked back at Kat and said, "You know. I think a glass of wine would be great right now."

Kat looked in the direction of Holly's last gaze and seeing Luke, said, "I'll go with you, honey. My glass needs refreshing."

As they reached the bar, Kat said, "You like him, don't you?"

Holly looked at her as if she had no idea what Kat meant. "Like who?"

"You know. You like Luke Damian."

"Of course, I like him. He's my partner. We've been working together eight or more hours a day."

Kat shook her head. "Don't give Mother Kat a bunch of bullshit. You have a real thing for him. The look on your face when he walked in with Miss *Sport's Illustrated* Swim Suit Cover gave you away."

"You are wrong. He's my partner, and I want him to do well. That's all."

Kat shook her head. "Have it your way, but tuck your heart back inside your chest. It's weeping on your sleeve."

Holly gave her a harsh look and then ordered a glass of Chardonnay. "Can you hold my place for a second, Kat? I need to run to the ladies' room."

"Sure, rosebud. I'll man the fort."

Holly walked quickly to the restroom and went into a stall. Taking tissue from the roll, she wiped her eyes and sat down on the toilet seat, fully clothed. *Get hold of yourself. How have you reached the point that you care about this man?* She sat for nearly five minutes, fighting the impulse to cry and silently admonishing herself for delusions of grandeur about Luke.

She had hardly returned to the bar and swallowed a substantial portion of her wine when a production assistant came for her.

"*E* wants a comment from you and Luke about the show."

Holly wanted to say, no, just let them talk to Luke, but then she remembered that he was not happy about the way the show went and would need her to keep the interview upbeat. "I'll be there as soon as I take another sip of wine."

Holly turned her wine glass up and drained it. *Okay. That should stiffen my backbone.* Turning to Kat, she said, "I'll be back."

Following the P.A. to the area where cameras were set up for celebrity interviews, she called up the breathing exercise she employed when auditioning. It consisted of inhaling through the nose, holding it for a count of three, and then exhaling slowly through the mouth for as long as she could. *I will not let anyone see how I'm feeling right now. I won't.*

Her greatest fear materialized when she reached the reporter, and Luke walked up, Joy holding his arm. Mustering all her strength, she put on a fake smile, tipped her head to the side, and said, "Hello, you must be Joy. I've heard so much about you."

Joy looked at her as if Holly had just exited from a UFO. "And you're Luke's instructor, Holly?" The model's voice was flat and devoid of interest.

"I am. Aren't you proud of him?"

Before Joy could respond, Luke interjected. "Certainly not on my performance tonight."

Joy put her slender index finger, with a blood-red, claw-like nail, on Luke's lips. "You're too hard on yourself, darling. You were one of the best."

Luke looked uncomfortable but said nothing.

Dear, God. Her personality is as fake as her nails and eyelashes.

Before anyone could say more, the P.A. stepped forward and guided Joy out of the camera's sightline as the TV reporter came up with a microphone.

The interview was little more than a soundbite and was over in three minutes. Luke and Holly went through the motions of complimenting one another and stressing how much fun they were having. Holly felt Joy's gaze burning through her skin.

She likes me about as much as I like her.

The second the interview was over, Holly darted back to the bar. She hardly spoke to Luke and Joy as she departed. Kat was where Holly left her, nursing the martini. "I'll have a refill, please," Holly said to the bartender.

"Careful, girlfriend," Kat said. "You might want to get a bite to eat. The buffet is great tonight."

"I'm not hungry. I just need to quench a little thirst. I'll be fine," Holly said, taking a swallow from the glass the barman handed her.

As Holly put the wine on the counter, someone grabbed her by the waist from behind. She stifled a squeal and turned to see that it was Andrei.

He leaned forward and kissed her on the cheek.

"Oh, my," said Kat. "Your knight in tarnished armor has arrived. I think I hear my mother calling." She took her cocktail glass and started to walk away.

"You don't have to leave, Kat," Holly said.

Kat paused. "You're in good hands. Right, Andrei?" She then leaned over and whispered in Holly's ear. "Just be sure when he puts those hands where I think he wants to put them that you're sure. *No* means the same in all languages."

"Of course, she is." Andrei tapped the bar. "I'll have the Chopin, straight up."

"Chopin?" Holly asked.

"It's the best vodka," Andrei said, taking the glass the bartender slid across the to him.

Holly tried to focus on Andrei and not look for Luke and Joy, but it was an exercise in futility. When she glanced around the room, they were dancing. Joy pressed against him tighter than peanut butter on bread. The image put a knot in Holly's stomach.

Why have I deluded myself? He is not available and not interested in me.

Ordering her third glass of wine, she looked at Andrei. *He is a hell of a handsome man—great body and fantastic dancer. Why do I need Mr. Right? Mr. Right-Now will do just fine.*

"I think that's our song playing," she said, tapping Andrei on the shoulder.

"Then let's show these people what we've got." He grabbed her by the waist and propelled her around. The Pointer Sisters' recording of "Slow Hand" played, giving Andrei a perfect beat for execution of a seductive rumba. Holly, aided by three glasses of Chardonnay, let herself go, matching every sultry move Andrei produced. Their hips moved in unison. He caressed her body, pushing the decency envelope to the limit. His face nuzzled her neck as they danced with her back to him, leaving room for no more than a sheet of paper between them.

In the crowd, Luke watched with a strange look on his face. Joy, at his side, stared at him with an almost vicious expression on hers.

When the music ended, Holly took Andrei's hand, leading him toward the bar. As they passed a couple of the show's backup dancers, one called out.

"You two thought about getting a room?"

Looking the speaker in the face, Holly said, "No. What I need is more wine. Beautiful wine."

Smiling, Andrei nodded.

CHAPTER FIFTEEN

Thursday morning, Holly woke with her head splitting. She opened her eyes and looked around an austere bedroom with sunlight streaming through the open louvers of mini-blinds. She had no idea where she was. A feeling of panic invaded her stomach. Her head throbbed and her brain felt scrambled. Struggling to piece the last ten hours together, she remembered being at the party, drinking more wine than she had ever drunk in her life, and dancing with Andrei Rodchenko.

Oh, my gosh! Where am I? Whose bed am I in? Not Andrei's. Oh, please, not Andrei's.

She turned over slowly, almost afraid to see who might be on the other side of the mattress.

Thank, God, there's no one there. But, where am I?

The décor in the room was neutral. She noted that there were no feminine items—no frills, no dressing table, and no mirror. She started to get up and realized that she was wearing only her bra and panties. Her dress lay draped across a nearby chair. She slipped out of bed, walked to the closet, and peeked in. Men's clothing filled the single rack. A robe hung on the inside of the door. She took it off the hook and put it on. It smelled of a familiar fragrance for men.

What have I done? Whose apartment is this? Holly rubbed her forehead. *How did I get here?* Her mind was blank. The last thing she remembered was dancing with Andrei. Tiptoeing over to the door, she eased it slightly open and looked through the crack. A body was on the sofa—a bare leg draped over the low back. It was definitely a male leg. *Who? Oh, my gosh. Don't tell me it's him.*

Gingerly walking over to the couch, she saw Bon Jovi hair and a spray-tanned McConaughey body. A sheet was mercifully draped across what Holly feared might be the bare private parts of Andrei Rodchenko. *Dear God, I didn't, did I? If I did, did he use protection?* She stood paralyzed, looking around the room, wondering what to do next. *Where is my car?* The last thing she wanted was to wake Andrei, but how would she get home without, first, knowing where she was?

Could I have had sex with him and not know it?

Andrei shifted his position, and Holly held her breath. She looked down the front of the robe to her bare feet with ten painted toenails, feeling like she had fallen down the rabbit hole. Her head continued to pound.

I need aspirin, something to drink, and then a way to get home—or back to the studio for my car, unless it's here.

Confused and trying to sort out the night before, she remained standing, rubbing her temples.

The apartment was amazingly neat for a bachelor pad. Other than Andrei's clothes scattered on the floor around the couch and over a nearby chair, everything appeared to be in its place. Three large, brass containers, holding huge houseplants, accented the white leather upholstery, ivory walls and carpet. Autographed and framed posters of Broadway shows hung on the walls, adding color. Holly looked around, trying to relate the décor to the sleeping Russian.

I don't know what I thought his home would look like, but I'm sure this is not it. He has good taste.

She was about to tiptoe to the kitchen when a door on the opposite side of the room opened. Holly flinched, shocked that someone else was in the apartment.

Out walked Kat Kenley in a silky, floral kimono. "Good morning, princess. Sleep well?"

"What are you doing here?" Holly's eyes were wide open, a look of surprise on her face.

"I live here."

Holly looked down at Andrei, who continued to sleep, despite the conversation. "You live with him?" she said, pointing at the couch.

"Good god, no."

"I don't understand. How did I, we, get here? Did I—" She looked down at Andrei. "Did we?"

Kat smiled. "Let's just say that if it's a girl, you can name her Kat."

"Oh, my, God." Holly put her hand over her mouth, close to tears.

Kat smiled, walked across the room, and gave Holly a hug. "No, no, kiddo. I'm giving you a hard time. Nothing happened between you and the Testosterone Czar. You had a little too much wine—maybe a lot too much—and passed out. We brought you here and put you to bed. Not that 'God's gift to women,' over there, didn't want to share it with you, but I kicked his ass out of your room. I wouldn't have brought him home, but I needed him to help me bring you up the stairs."

"How did we get here?"

"Taxi. We had no designated driver. I let him stay here on the sofa as long as he gave me his solemn word that he wouldn't sneak into your room. If you were going to do the nasty with him, I wanted you to know you were doing it—at least getting the full benefit. I told him that if he violated my rule, I would have no problem saying he raped you."

Holly put her hands in the prayer position. "Thank you."

"You're welcome. Now, let's get some coffee or tea in you. You look like a refugee from *The Spoon River Anthology*."

Kat started toward the kitchen. As she passed the couch, she gave Andrei's exposed leg a shove. "Wake up, Romeo. It's time for you to find your way home."

He turned over and groaned.

Holly looked at him as she followed Kat.

"Do you have any aspirin or Advil?"

"I've got it all. Even some Chardonnay if you want a little hair of the dog."

"I don't ever want to hear the word Chardonnay again in my life. How much did I drink?"

"At least one glass too many. Don't worry, honey. We all do it at least once. You're really not used to drinking, are you?"

"No. Thank goodness, we have today off."

Kat pulled out a box of tea bags and a can of coffee. She held both up. "Which will it be?"

"Tea, if you don't mind."

Kat nodded and filled a kettle. When it was on the burner, she reached up into a cabinet and took out three bottles of OTC pain medications. "Take your choice."

Holly chose the Bayer and said, "As much as I'm afraid to ask: How did I get undressed? I'm pretty sure that I didn't do it myself."

Kat smiled. "You didn't. We undressed you when we got you in there."

"We? You mean?" She pointed at the sofa.

Kat nodded. "Uh-huh."

"Oh, no. Now, I am really embarrassed."

"Holly—princess—you have on as much as we do when we perform. Just no rhinestones." Kat took a bottle of water out of her refrigerator and handed it to Holly. She then filled her Keurig with water and stuck in a pod.

"It's not the same." Holly opened the robe a few inches and looked down. "This is underwear."

"You haven't learned, yet, that the word modesty is not in our vocabulary? Changing the subject. Judging from the way you were acting last night, you needed to get something out of your system. Is it your partner? Or still carrying a torch for your hometown boy?"

"It's complicated." Holly shook three aspirin tablets out of the container and then washed them down her throat with the water.

The kettle whistled, Kat poured the hot water into a cup over a tea bag, and pushed the cup toward Holly, along with a holder of sugar substitutes. "Lemon or cream?"

Holly took the cup and shook her head. "No, thanks. If Andrei doesn't live here, whose robe am I wearing?"

Taking a carton of eggs out, Kat said, "Eddie Sinclair's."

"Eddie? You mean Eddie Sinclair from last season?"

"Yeah. He's on tour. Landed the role of Rum Tum Tugger in another revival of *Cats*. You'd think everyone would have seen that show, wouldn't you?"

"I love it. I grew up wanting to play Victoria, the white kitten, but never got the chance. I didn't know you and Eddie were a couple."

"We're not a couple—just roommates without benefits. Eddie and I go back a long way. We met auditioning for some box office flop. I can't even remember the name. We were both struggling to stay out here. It made sense to pool resources." Kat took out a skillet. "You were a ballerina, weren't you?"

"I don't know if you would call me a ballerina, but I trained for ballet."

"It shows. You have the grace and those fantastic lines, finishing every move."

"What about you?"

"Jazz and ballroom. Wish I had taken more ballet, but I was lazy—all that tedious work at the barre before you get to dance."

Andrei groaned again, causing both women to glance his way. Stretching, he threw the sheet off.

Holly shielded her eyes for fear of what he might expose.

Andrei stood up, wearing only his briefs. Holly cut her eyes around at Kat with a smirk on her face.

"Be glad he didn't go commando last night," Kat said.

Without saying anything, he walked into Kat's bedroom.

"Where's he going?" Holly whispered.

"Best guess? The bathroom."

"He knows where it is?"

Kat smiled. "He's been here before."

Holly's face registered comprehension. "He's part of the mileage you were talking about?"

Kat nodded. "He is." She leaned forward and in a stage whisper said, "If you're wild enough to risk it, he's worth the ride, if you know what I mean. Just be sure you have your eyes open and your head on straight if you decide to play the game."

"Did you care about him? Do you, now?"

"Hell, no. I knew what it was when I crawled into bed with him. I've seen him wreak havoc on the naïve. Guys like him are like a tart lemon pie: sweet cream on the top—sour underneath. As long as you stick with the cream, you're okay."

"I hear you. I know he's not take-home-to-meet-the-family material." Holly took a sip of her tea and then looked up at Kat. "Where is home for you?"

"Jersey."

"You don't have that accent."

"Had to get rid of it. Cost me a damn fortune, but dancing has an expiration date, and when the clock strikes, you either marry a man who can support you, open a dance school, or try acting. I hate kids, and I haven't met a man, yet, that I want to wake up next to every morning for a week, much less the rest of my life. *Voilá!* Trust me. Accent had to go. There aren't that many 'Snookie' roles around."

"Who's Snookie?" Andrei asked, ambling into the kitchen, still wearing only his briefs.

"A reality show character," Kat responded. "Don't you have some clothes somewhere? We all know you look like Adonis in the raw."

"Coffee first." He moved closer to Holly, put his arm around her shoulder and kissed her on the cheek. "Sleep well, my lovely?"

Holly pulled back, slightly. "I did."

"Would have been much better with company, but KGB officer," he pointed at Kat, "she made me sleep on sofa."

"And I'm grateful to her," Holly said, smiling.

"Next time. Maybe when you have one glass wine less?"

"No comment."

"You'll see. Would be good. You and I make a handsome couple. We burned up the floor last night."

"Cool it, lover boy. Too much charm this early in the morning is a little nauseating," Kat said.

He walked around, gave Kat a kiss on the cheek, and slapped her rear. "You might be jealous, no?"

"In your dreams," Kat snapped. "And for God's sake, put on some clothes."

CHAPTER SIXTEEN

After breakfast, the three dancers took a cab back to the network parking lot to retrieve their respective automobiles. Although better, Holly's headache refused to go away. Andrei continued to come on strong, but she deflected him, using her throbbing head as an excuse. No one mentioned Luke.

Holly reached her apartment shortly after eleven a.m. She fed Gigi and did laundry, checking her cell phone frequently for missed communications. There was a text from Dana, praising Holly and Luke's performance and a voice mail from her mother on her landline. Gabi was out of the country and would not have seen the show. She considered calling Dana but knew that Luke would be the topic of conversation. Holly was not in the mood to discuss him. Each time he crossed her mind, a feeling of dread accompanied her desire to see him.

Despite the lingering effects of her hangover, in the afternoon, Holly forced herself to pay bills and clean her apartment. Her phone remained silent. Each time she checked for missed calls and texts, the blank screen gave her a knot in her stomach. At seven-thirty, her disappointment in not having heard from Luke caused her to put the phone in a kitchen drawer with a pledge not to check again before morning.

On the way to the studio, Friday, Holly silently rehearsed the pep talk she would give Luke. Working through the weekend, they had only five practice days to create and perfect a new routine. There was no time to wallow in self-pity. When she entered their rehearsal room, Sam was sitting on one of the wooden benches, drinking from a Starbucks cup.

"How's it going? Luke get over his screw-up?"

Holly dropped her dance bag next to the wall, sat on the bench with him, and reached down to untie her shoelaces. "I wouldn't know."

Sam drained the last of his expresso, put the cup down, and looked toward her with a slight frown on his face. "What does that mean?"

She shrugged, avoiding eye-contact. "Just that. I don't know. I haven't heard from him."

"You guys went to the after-party, didn't you? How was he there?"

She raised her head, looking at Sam with a glimmer of sadness in her eyes. "Occupied. The girlfriend—Joy—came with him."

Sam nodded. "So, that's it."

"And what does *that* mean?"

"A little triangulating going on?"

"Why would you say that?" Holly's voice had an edge.

Sam smiled. "Like I said before: you've got a thing for the guy. Admit it. Your secret's safe with me."

Holly paused, stared at Sam, but did not respond.

He continued. "I like Luke. He's a cut above average—far as I can tell."

Holly nodded. "He is, but he's not exactly available on Match. com, Sam. Remember Joy? Not only that. It would be unprofessional to become involved with a partner."

Sam made a face. "As for professional conduct, in any other field, you would be right. But, hasn't your agent told you that in this business, any publicity other than an arrest for child abuse is good publicity? The producers would probably give you a raise if you landed a soundbite on *Extra* or a piece on *TMZ*. As for the girlfriend, I may not be his confidant, *but* I don't see signs of devotion. He flinches every time his phone rings, and, as I recall when we were in New York, he didn't give her the time of day. He may be in a relationship of some sort, but I think the love boat sailed *a long time* ago. He's attracted to you."

"Why would you say that? He hasn't given me a single sign."

"That's because he hasn't figu—"

The door opened, and Luke appeared, a solemn expression on his face. Silence fell over the room. Sam pretended to check his equipment while Holly fiddled with the zipper of her dance bag as Luke walked to another bench, dropped his gear, and sat down to change his shoes.

Holly knew she should say something. As the instructor, she was captain of the team, and the ball was in her court to break the ice, but words stuck in her throat.

Sam spoke up. "How's it going, Luke? Enjoy your day off?"

Luke looked up. "It was good but felt a little strange to not be here. My sore muscles thanked me for the break, but I can't say the same for my head. I'm really questioning whether I have what it takes to see this through." He shook his head. "I know that I made a fool of myself and embarrassed the hell out of Holly."

Hearing his comment prompted her to speak. "That's not true. You can't beat yourself up over one little misstep on the first week of competition. You weren't the only one to make a mistake. That high-fashion model messed up a lot worse than you did. And, I've seen turtles with more musicality than the football player you were talking to before the show."

Luke watched her intently as she spoke. When she finished, he raised an eyebrow and asked, "Does that mean I'll have to continue to humiliate myself for another three or four weeks?"

She stood up. "Stop it, Luke Damian. We're going to win the medal."

"You don't need to pretend to boost my morale. I know you were embarrassed. You blew me off at the after-party, and yesterday, you invoked radio silence."

His words stung Holly. Wrapped up in jealousy, it hadn't occurred to her that as his teacher, she might have been expected to call him. For a moment, she was speechless.

Sensing the awkwardness, Sam spoke. "While you lovebirds hash out your differences, I'm going to refill my cup with some of that miserable coffee they have here. Either of you want anything?"

Both shook their heads.

When the door closed behind Sam, Holly spoke. "Luke, I'm sorry. You misread me. I stayed away from you at the party, because I didn't want to interfere in your relationship with Joy. I have the sense that she doesn't like me."

He grinned. "That's a colossal understatement. She's *profoundly* jealous of you."

"I'm sorry. I know it happens because we spend so much up close and personal time together, but she has nothing to worry about."

He stood up and walked over to her. When he was within a foot, he stopped and stared down into her eyes, neither of them speaking for several seconds. Breaking the silence, he said, softly, "Don't be too sure." Pausing for another second, he took her hands, moved closer, and then leaned forward, pressing his lips against hers. When she did not resist, his arms went around her, pulling her against his chest.

Holly's attraction to him betrayed her. She could feel her breasts press against him as her desire rose. She wanted to return his embrace—to put her arms around him and crush her full body against his. But, she was afraid. When he pulled back, their eyes locked again.

The room remained silent until Holly whispered, "What did you just do?" She fought to quell the excitement ringing out from every pore.

Luke's expression changed. He raised a hand in the air as if to signal a halt. "I'm sorry. It was inappropriate." He took another step backward and shook his head. "I couldn't help myself. It won't happen again."

She wanted to scream "No. It's okay. Do it again." But she couldn't. Instead, she stared at him, her pupils dilated, her irises greener than usual. Her mind raced, searching for the right thing to say. Questions tumbled around in her brain like wet clothes in a dryer. Was he attracted to her? Was Joy a non-issue? Was the kiss an isolated moment of carnal attraction? Could Sam be right?

Her eyes searched his for answers to the questions that she was afraid to ask. After a few seconds, she spoke. "It's okay."

He didn't respond. He just looked at her.

A minute later, she broke the silence. "We'd better get started. You are going to blow America away next week."

He smiled and turned to go back to where he left his shoes. As he walked away, Holly called out.

"I drank too much at the party and had a horrible headache, yesterday. I'm sorry that I didn't call."

He turned, a smile on his face. "I forgive you."

When they both were ready to work, Holly put the music on. "Let's listen for a few minutes. Get into the mood and rhythm of the song. Forget that you're a London boy. In this piece, you're a Texas cowboy."

"And a jerk, right?"

Grinning, she said, "Right. You're cocky with a lot of attitude. Close your eyes and think arrogant swagger."

He lay back on the bench, eyes closed, one leg on the floor, and the other knee bent with his foot on the surface.

As Carrie Underwood sang "Cowboy Casanova," Holly spoke over the music, roughly explaining what they would be doing in each section of the song. "This is going to be entirely different from our waltz. Not only is the tempo faster, you're going to have to put in a lot of hip and shoulder action."

"Something like you and that Russian the other night?"

He noticed.

"I'm not sure what you're talking about, but this dance will be fairly sexy with a lot of spirit. It's more of a flirtation with overtones of seduction."

He sat up, eyes wide open. "Bring it on."

She looked at him, wondering how he could ignore what had happened earlier, but he seemed like the Luke of two days before. There did not appear to be any further remorse over the performance or acknowledgement of a change in their relationship.

Shortly after they began working on her choreography, a crew brought in a jukebox that Luke would lean against in the opening. A production assistant brought cowboy hats and boots for the two of them.

"What's wrong with the shoes I've been wearing for practice?" Luke asked, taking the boots out of the box.

"When was the last time you wore a two-inch heel?"

He looked at her with a puzzled expression.

"You have to get used to the feel of a higher heel. Dress rehearsal is not a good time to discover that your body placement has changed."

"Yes, ma'am."

They worked hard the rest of the day, and by six o'clock, exhaustion overcame them both.

"You've done great today. Better than I expected, because this is not easy choreography," Holly said as they changed into street shoes.

"Why do I have a feeling that there's more to come?"

Sam laughed, and both Holly and Luke turned around and looked at him.

"Is there something you want to say, Sam?" Holly asked.

"Not a thing. I'm just the cameraman."

"Give, Sam. You know her. What's she got in store for me?"

Sam hesitated as if reluctant to speak. "Well . . . if Holly follows her usual MO, the routine she gave you today is only the *basic* patterns."

Luke looked at Holly with an I-thought-so expression on his face. "What comes next, Sam?"

"Oh, she'll say something like, 'Why don't we kick up the volume with a little lift here. Something simple—like you twirling me around over your head for ten counts.'"

"Sam! I would do no such thing—at least not until Sunday."

They all three chuckled, and then Luke said, "Extra-Strength Tylenol, here I come." He then turned to Holly, a more serious look on his face. "How about we grab some dinner? Do you like Chinese?"

The invitation took Holly by surprise, given the events of the past few days. She turned and looked at her reflection in the mirrored wall, hesitated, and then said, "I'm all sweaty. I couldn't go into a restaurant."

"I was thinking of take-away. Pick it up and go back to the park."

"Aren't you tired?" Her heart was pounding. She wanted to take him up on the suggestion but did not want to appear too willing.

"Of course, but I have to eat, and I need to unwind." He wiped his face with a towel.

I should mention Joy, but I can't.

"Okay. Sounds good as long as there is no alcohol involved."

"We'll stick strictly to tea."

After picking up food, Luke drove them back to the park in Holly's car. It was as quiet as before. During the ride, Holly kept thinking of the kiss that morning, wondering if he would mention it—or repeat it. If he did, where would it lead?

But, he didn't mention the kiss. They ate, talked about the new number, and discussed the competition. No reference was made to Holly dancing with Andrei or Mika—or of Joy. She considered telling him about the Santana number she had agreed to perform with Mika, but the time never seemed right.

At seven-thirty, Luke said, "We'd better go home. I know you're going to work my British arse off tomorrow."

"You've got that right." She poked him in the chest with her index finger. "We are *going* to take first place. No excuses."

Holly had trouble sleeping Friday night. Her thoughts were haunted by the image of Luke looking into her eyes, leaning forward, and kissing her. Questions continued to plague her. How could he commit such an intimate act and then behave as though it never happened? She had managed to follow his lead during the day and ignore the elephant in the room. Could she continue to play the game? *What happens when we dance a tango or rumba? We're expected to look like we're all but making love.* She visualized him running his hands over her body as erotically as the FCC allowed, and the thought caused tremors in her erogenous zones.

Throughout the night, she tossed and turned, asking herself whether she should initiate a conversation about what happened. She wanted to explore its meaning, but her conscience told her that pressing the issue could damage the professional relationship that had eight weeks left to run. *I cannot make the situation any more awkward.*

CHAPTER SEVENTEEN

Sam had been right. On Saturday, Holly began inserting advanced lifts and tricks into their routine.

"You scare the hell out of me." Luke shook his head as Holly, with assistance from Lex Carson, a male dancer from the backup troupe, demonstrated a lift she wanted in the routine. "You think that I'm going to swing you around, over my head? Is your insurance paid up?"

"Don't be a scaredy-cat. You can do it. I know how strong you are. Just take my hands as I start to jump, raise them over and behind your head, swinging me like a lasso rope. My legs will be in a straddle split as I swing around you. I'll end the trick facing you with my legs wrapped around your waist."

Luke frowned. "Can I be charged with manslaughter if I drop you?"

"Hush. We will do it again, keeping it as slow as we can. Watch."

Holly and the young man did the trick again.

Luke put a hand over his eyes. "I can't watch this. You're insane."

"If it makes you feel better, Lex can spot us the first few times."

"First time is the hardest, Luke. After you do it several times, it'll be a piece of cake," Lex said.

"And how many years of training have you had? I'm the amateur here."

Holly put her hands on his shoulders, glaring into his eyes. "Tell you what. First time, I'll just come down without coming around you. That way, you'll get the feel of the lift without dealing with the dismount."

Defeated, he shrugged his shoulders, turned his back for a

moment, and then faced her. "It's your funeral, but don't say I didn't warn you."

It took Luke four tries to master the coordination but once he did, the lift went consistently well. When Holly was satisfied with his execution, she added another lift and a trick in which she did an aerial cartwheel in front of him as he held one of her hands and assisted with her rotation.

"Okay, madam, you've maxed out your allotment of tricks. One more and I'll demand a stuntman," Luke said, plopping down on a bench.

Lex smiled and looked toward Holly.

"Relax. I'm done. I like what we have. What do you think, Lex?"

"Looks good to me."

Holly turned toward Sam, "What do you think?"

He nodded and gave her a thumbs-up.

"Then, we'll call it a day. Tomorrow, we'll begin the polishing. I've got to run now because I have another rehearsal."

"Another rehearsal?" Luke asked, a puzzled look on his face.

"Yeah. I guess I forgot to mention that Mika Dorofeyev and I are doing a feature number with the guest artist, Carlos Santana, next week."

"That's a *coup de theatre*," Lex said, obviously impressed.

Luke looked at her, a peculiar expression on his face. "Mika. He's one of the Russian pros, right?"

Lex responded. "Mika's the sexy stud with dark hair who blows up Twitter every time he takes his shirt off."

"Not the one you danced with at the after-party?" Luke asked, looking at Holly.

"Well, I actually danced with both Mika and Andrei at the party, but I'm not sure you were there. Andrei is blond."

Luke didn't comment further. He changed to his street shoes, put his boots and hat on one of the benches, thanked Lex for his help, waved goodbye to Sam, and went over to Holly and gave her a hug. "See you tomorrow, boss. Don't work too hard and don't let that Russian Casanova steal you away from me."

Lex followed Luke out. As Sam put his equipment away, Holly pulled off her boots.

"He's not thrilled with you dancing with Mika and Andrei," Sam said as he clicked the latches on his camera case.

"You're imagining it, Sam. He's not interested in me." Her words belied her hopes.

He gave her a patronizing look. "Me thinks the lady doth protest too much."

Holly eyed him with a dubious expression but did not reply. Her heart beat a little faster. Whether it was caused by Sam's theory or excitement over starting the feature routine with Mika, she wasn't sure.

Holly and Mika worked with Antonio Marciano, a high-profile choreographer, until eight o'clock. Although the sultry Santana piece, "Smooth," was four minutes, fifty-six seconds long, the couple would dance in brief segments for a total of three minutes of choreography. Marciano was known for unique moves and sensual sequences. Neither the combinations, nor the hot interactions with Mika, caused Holly any problems, and the rehearsal time flew by.

As he raised her from the final pose, Mika said, "Why have you not been featured before, Holly Dawson? You are a real dancer's dream partner."

Holly looked at him and grinned. "I'll take that as a compliment."

"He's right, Holly. Even for a pro, you pick up extraordinarily fast," Marciano said.

With a grand sweep of his arm in her direction, Mika said, "Not only is she beautiful and talented, she's fearless. We tried that last lift with Daniella last season, and it never happened."

Holly picked up a towel from her bag. "The way I look at it, you know that the heat is on you. If I fall, the audience will believe you dropped me, and I'll walk away with the sympathy factor. Therefore, you're not going to attempt a trick you can't complete."

Both men chuckled. "Female logic! But, whatever works," Marciano said.

"It's all good. We make for a dream team." Mika put his arms around Holly and gave her a squeeze. "Maybe we go for a bit of dinner now?"

Kicking off her dance shoes, she smiled. "Raincheck? I'm beat."

Marciano closed his notebook and tucked it into his bag, along with a CD of their music. "I'm confident that we can polish this up in one more rehearsal. You've both got the choreography in the bag. Want to schedule for Sunday?"

"Good with me." Mika walked toward the bench his dance bag was stuffed under.

"Can we firm it up tomorrow?" Holly said. "I'd like to have another day with Luke to know how much cleaning up we have to accomplish before next week's show. I can make it work for Monday night."

Turning around to face Holly, Mika said, "Could you use help with Luke?"

Holly stopped what she was doing and looked at him. "Are you kidding? You would help your competition?"

"Why not? The better the show, the higher the ratings." He shrugged. "It's job security."

Holly thought for a second or two. "If you're serious, I might take you up on that offer."

"We Russians don't offer if we're not serious. How about Sunday afternoon? First, we get your boy on track, and then we put finishing touch on our dance of love." He turned toward Marciano. "Antonio, you good with that plan?"

The choreographer nodded. "I'll be here at five-thirty."

Holly was home before nine that night, having picked up a salad at a fast-food drive-thru on her way, which she put in the refrigerator while she showered and changed into sleepwear. The phone rang as she was about to sit down to eat. Her first thought was that it might be Luke. Pulling the phone out of her handbag, she glanced at the screen and groaned. *Why the heck is he calling me?*

She hesitated, giving serious consideration to ignoring the call, but as it rang for the last time before going to voice mail, she pressed the green circle.

"Why are you calling me, Don?"

"You don't even say, hello, anymore?"

"That depends on who the caller is. I repeat, why are you calling me?"

"Can't an old friend reach out to check on you?"

"Old friend? Is that what you would call us? Old friends."

"Of course."

"Sorry, Don. In my dictionary, friend is one you regard with affection and trust. Somehow, you just don't fit the profile." Holly's eyes filled with contempt as she contemplated hanging up on him.

"I know you're mad with me."

"You really think so? Don't flatter yourself. In my journal, I have you catalogued under the heading: 'colossal mistakes.' I don't think about you enough to be angry."

"Too busy thinking about Mr. Pretty-Boy TV Star?"

She thought for a second before responding. *Did he watch the show? He didn't even do that when we were together.* "If you're referring to Luke Damian, he is on my mind a lot more than you are." *Why don't I slam this phone down?* "Why are you calling me, Don? Is there trouble in paradise?"

"We were together a long time. I was just thinking about you and wondering if you're okay."

"Please, let me put your mind at ease. I'm doing great—more than great. Have a nice life." She pushed the red button, exhausted from the emotional impact of the call. *Why am I upset? He has hardly crossed my mind in the past two weeks. Like that TV therapist said, "Don't give the jerk permission to ruin your day."*

In spite of the call from Don, it had been a good day. Rehearsals with Luke progressed better than expected, and she had loved every second of dancing with Mika. It took only ten minutes of working with the Russian for Holly to understand why he had claimed so many of the show's trophies. Not only was he a technical and artistic talent, he was also creative, throwing in suggestions that enhanced Marciano's choreography. Last, but far from least, he was one hell of a handsome man.

CHAPTER EIGHTEEN

Holly and Luke began working early on Saturday morning. By lunchtime, he knew the choreography but frustrated Holly with his timing.

"You're rushing your steps. It's a fast routine, but you're ahead of the music."

"I'm not a musician." His tone indicated a loss of patience.

"Time for a break," she said, motioning for him to take a seat on the bench. She went to her bag and took out a bodhrán and tipper, a handheld Irish drum and stick. "Close your eyes, Luke, and listen as I count out the music." She started the CD. "One, two, three, four. One, two, three, four." Halfway through, she stopped. "Did you hear it?"

Opening his eyes, he nodded. "I think so, but what do I know?"

"Here try it." She handed him the hand drum and restarted the music. Holly counted as he struck the instrument. He was slightly awkward at first but quickly got into the swing of it and midway, she stopped counting.

When the music ended, she said, "That's good. Let's add feet."

He shrugged. "You're the boss."

"Focus on the count, but don't move your lips, or you might subconsciously do it during the performance."

As they began the routine, Holly knew from the expression on his face that he was concentrating. About two-thirds of the way through the song, his face relaxed, a grin spread, and she could see a breakthrough occurring.

Out of the blue, he shouted, "I've got it. Damn, I've got it." Grabbing her around the waist, he lifted her off the floor.

"Whoa, cowboy. Don't go crazy."

"You don't understand. I felt it. I was in the music," he said as he lowered her back to the floor.

Holly was all smiles. "You were. I'm *really* proud of you. I think you're going to be fine. Just don't overthink it. Start with the count and then relax. Let your natural rhythm take over."

"Want to do it again?" he asked, almost childlike.

Sam had caught the entire action and smiled at Holly as he lowered his camera.

"One more time and then we'll get a bite of lunch." She took a sip from a bottle of water. "Mika is coming in tomorrow to work with us."

Ignoring her comment about lunch, he looked at her with a puzzled expression. "Who is coming to our rehearsal?"

"Mika Dorofeyev. I'm sorry. I meant to tell you. He offered to coach us."

"You mean, coach me." Luke pointed to his chest.

"Whatever. Since he and I have a rehearsal tomorrow evening, we thought we'd kill two birds with one stone. Do you have a problem with that?"

Luke looked skeptical but shook his head. "No—no. I need all the help I can get, but I'm surprised that he is willing to work with me. Sure it's not a trick to sabotage the competition?"

"It crossed my mind, but he seems sincere. Trust me. I'll know if he pulls anything shady."

The afternoon went well, and they called it a day at five.

"Good progress, today." Holly pumped the air with a fist. "I think we can start a little later tomorrow."

"When is that, what's his name, coming?"

"Mika. He's coming at three." Holly sat down and began changing her shoes. "We should have a couple of hours to work with him before the choreographer comes in at five."

"Tell me again why we need him?" Luke pointed at Holly. "*You* are a great teacher, and it's going well."

Holly caught a trace of resistance in his voice. "You have done a good job, but there are still little things that can make the difference in getting that perfect score. It can't hurt to see what he can contribute. Let's start at ten. That should give you time to sleep a little later in case you're going out tonight."

To her chagrin, he did not take the bait and respond to her last comment.

"I guess I'll see you then," he said.

As he called for his driver, and then changed to street-footwear, Holly watched, wondering what his evening plans were and if they included Joy.

Sam picked up his gear and, in the process, accidentally dropped his keys, jolting Holly back into reality. She quickly walked to the audio equipment and removed the CD, trying to appear nonchalant.

"Sorry," Sam said and gave them a goodbye salute.

When Luke was ready to leave, he walked over to her and gave her a hug. "See you tomorrow."

Holly's eyes followed him for a few seconds and then she shook her head. *Sack those silly thoughts. That kiss was a fluke.*

At three o'clock on Sunday, Mika Dorofeyev burst into the room like a sudden gust of wind, filling it with his presence. Luke eyed him apprehensively.

"Thanks for helping out," Holly said, opening her arms to give him a hug.

"I am honored. Show me what you've got—jive, right?" He turned toward Luke and gave him a thumbs-up.

"You don't have to film this, Sam," Holly said. "It's kind of off-script."

"That often produces the best stuff. Just ignore me," Sam replied.

Holly smiled, went to the audio system, and turned on their music.

Taking his cue, Luke went to the phony jukebox and took his position, cutting his eyes around at Mika who stood with his hands on his hips, legs spread apart in a Russian soldier stance.

After only a few bars of the music, Holly sensed Luke was holding back. *Maybe this wasn't a good idea.*

Fifteen seconds into the routine, Mika shouted, "Stop." He turned off the CD and walked over to the couple. "Swing her hard. I'll show you." He grabbed Holly's hand, turned his back, and whipped her around his body. "See. Gives her momentum. Don't be afraid. She'll like it."

Luke's blue eyes moved between Holly and Mika.

"Now, you try," he said to Luke.

Holly turned the music back on and they started over. On the second pass, Luke swung her harder than he ever had.

Mika called out. "Better but you can still do harder."

Luke made a face.

"You're on the music," Holly hoped to soften the impact of the critique. "Good job."

As they started into a sequence of kicks and flicks, Mika's voice boomed again. "No, no, no, Luke. There's hot lava on the floor. Your toes—they'll burn." He stopped the music, again, and walked in front of Luke. "Watch." Mika's feet were like lightning, tapping the floor and fanning the air with precision.

Luke's head turned from side to side. "I thought I was in pretty good shape until I see you pros." He pointed to Mika. "I bet you could dance on ice without slipping."

"You can do it," Holly said. "You push a little harder each time we run through it."

The practice continued with Mika pointing out the smallest details. Holly agreed with every correction he gave.

Luke accepted the coaching, but Holly could tell he was not enjoying it. What Mika had in looks and talent, he lacked in diplomacy. Although he barked orders such as: "Sharper. Snap the head sharper. Attitude—more attitude. You know you're cool, and she's hot for you."

He is improving Luke's style and technique, but I wish he hadn't said that.

Shortly before five, Antonio Marciano opened the door. After introducing him to Luke, Holly walked over to change from her boots to high-heeled dance slippers. Luke followed her to the bench.

"Any problem with me hanging out for some of your rehearsal with Mika?"

She looked around, surprised that he asked. "I don't see why not." She turned to the others. "Do you guys have any problem with Luke watching?"

Both men shook their heads, slightly shrugging in assent.

Sam packed his gear and said goodnight to the group. Footage of the pros rehearsing without celebrity partners was never used on the show.

CHAPTER NINETEEN

Marciano took his place by the sound system while Luke made himself comfortable in a canvas director's chair near the mirrored wall. The dancers took positions on opposite sides of the room. As the recording of "Smooth" began, Mika winked at Holly before starting to cross the room in a slithering rumba walk, beckoning her to come forward. As they met, he took her hand and brought it to his face, his free arm encircling her waist. Every inch of him exuded raw sexuality. Luke's eyes were glued on the Russian.

He seems more interested in Mika than in me, Holly thought, glancing at Luke from the corner of her eye as she snuggled into Mika's embrace.

With hips in overdrive, the two moved seamlessly to the sultry Latin rhythm. Shortly into the routine, Mika's left hand traced the outline of Holly's body, barely touching her but unmistakably striving for seduction. As his caress slid down her leg, he reached under her thigh and lifted, stretching her legs in a one-eighty split—her foot resting on his shoulder. From the front of the room, Luke cleared his throat, causing Holly to wonder what he was thinking.

As the dance progressed, Holly felt an involuntary arousal taking over, causing her to emphasize each provocative step. It wasn't Mika drawing out her carnal side. Although undeniably handsome and over-endowed with sex appeal, the Russian wasn't inciting her passion. Luke was.

Throughout the beginning of the routine, Mika's eyes remained locked on Holly as though holding her under a spell. As the music gained momentum, he whisked her around in a series of rapid turns, their legs interlocked like the two parts of a set of precision gears.

When Marciano pushed stop on the CD player, Luke's chair squeaked as he shifted uncomfortably.

"You okay?" Holly asked.

Pulling himself up in the seat, he nodded. "Nothing a cold shower couldn't take care of."

Mika laughed. "The rumba, it's the dance of love, no?" Twirling a finger in the air, he said, "Maybe it cracks that icy exterior the British are famous for."

Luke tipped his head to one side and raised an eyebrow. "You might say that."

Mika held Holly's hand up, pointing it toward Luke. "Want to try?"

"No, no. I wouldn't intrude on your rehearsal time."

"Go ahead," Marciano said. "I was running late and didn't have time for a pit stop." He started to walk toward the door.

"Come on, Damian. Give it a try," Mika urged. "You're going to have to do rumba sooner or later on the show."

Holly's heart was beating faster. Between the music, the movement, and the conversation, her libido was on fast forward. She was afraid to speak for fear of exposing her desire to trade partners. *Get a grip, Holly.*

Luke stood up, his eyes on Holly. "Why not?" He moved toward her and extended his hand.

Holly smiled.

"You know basic box step?" Mika asked.

Luke nodded, his gaze still directed toward Holly.

"Remember, lead with balls of your feet. Transfer body weight with hip action."

"I think I've got it," Luke said, never losing his eye contact with Holly.

Mika turned on the music.

To Holly's surprise, Luke immediately fell into the rhythm of the music and executed the basic rumba steps as though he had done them before.

"Have you been holding out on me?" she asked, looking up at him. "You've had lessons."

He shook his head. "Never."

"But—"

"Shh. . . . With the right incentive, I'm a quick study."

She felt a ripple of excitement course through her body.

Although he ventured no further than the basic step, he held her so close that their bodies nearly rubbed together. Immersed in the moment, Holly relinquished her role as teacher and became his partner, caught up in a fantasy. And then, like the sudden waking from an erotic dream, Marciano's return interrupted the mood, returning Holly to reality.

"Looks like you're doing okay," the choreographer said to Luke.

"Maybe motivated by the irresistible charms of his partner," Mika interjected.

Luke dropped Holly's hand, grinned, and said, "Might be. But, on that note, I'd better leave and let you do your jobs." He blew Holly a kiss and walked over for his bag while the group began to prepare for another run-through.

Holly had trouble bringing herself back into the rehearsal, her mind racing with questions as to what Luke's behavior meant. *He is attracted to me?*

Week two of the show went exceptionally well. Luke performed without a flaw, garnering scores that put him tied for first place. Holly and Mika's routine brought a standing ovation, which could have been because of Santana, the dancers, or a combination. Luke had observed the couple intently throughout the number.

During the entire show, Holly scanned the audience as often as possible, looking for Joy. However, there was no sign of the super model. With all her heart, Holly wanted to believe that Joy was missing because of trouble between the couple, but her logical side said that career obligations could have caused Joy's absence.

As they left the set when the show went off the air, Luke said, "Going up for the party?"

That's a dumb question. He knows I have to make an appearance. She smiled and said, "I am."

"See you there. Save me a seat at your table."

She nodded, a little rush flowing through her. "You do the same if you get there first."

"You've got it."

Watching him walk away, she made a private pledge. *One glass of wine. No more.*

As she walked into the dressing room, she was showered with compliments.

"Good show, Dawson," Kat said.

Danique Janssen gave her a high-five and said, "Tied for first place—I knew you could do it."

Even Lisa Cantrell commented. "Your boy is looking like a contender."

Holly thanked them all. "Everyone improved this week," she added.

When she reached her station, there was an envelope with her name on it, lying on her chair. Having a suspicion as to its contents, she picked it up and held it for a few seconds before opening, guessing she knew the contents. *Decision time, but at least I have an option.*

As suspected, the document inside was a contract for the eight-week, national tour that would follow the final show of the season. Deep in thought, Holly didn't move for a minute or two. *Why would I even remotely think of not signing? What else have I got?*

Impulsively, she reached into her purse, took out a pen, and signed her name on the last page. *There. End of confusion.* She folded the original copy, returned it to the envelope, and then put the duplicate in her dance bag. *There are fourteen of us and only seven spots on the tour. I should be thankful.*

As she changed to street clothes and modified her makeup, her mind wandered. *You had to sign. When the season is over, you will never see him again. Stop engaging in delusions of a real future in his life. You are nothing but a brief encounter.*

Holly arrived at the after-party first and, shortly after obtaining a glass of red wine and claiming a table, was greeted by Andrei Rodchenko.

"Two impressive numbers tonight, sexy lady."

"Coming from you, that is a great compliment." She smiled. "You and Randy were only two points below us."

The blond Russian made a face. "Gymnasts! They are babies. She's only sixteen and like rubber. But the chemistry doesn't work so good—artistry is weak."

"She'll improve," Holly replied. "In her field, she works solo. It'll take a little while to get used to interacting with a partner."

"We'll see." He looked at the empty chair across from Holly. "You should not be alone. Come sit at my table."

"Thanks, but I promised Luke that I would save him a seat."

"Oh—your partner. Then, if you won't sit with me, at least dance with me." He extended a hand toward her.

Holly looked around. The room had not filled, so it was easy to check who was present.

"He's not here, yet," Rodchenko said. "Come."

Just as well that I'm not sitting alone, waiting for Luke. She nodded, stood, and followed him to the dance floor where two couples were engaged in a spirited salsa to Gloria Estefan's "Conga."

With the agility of a cat, Andrei spun Holly around, and put a hand on each side of her hips. His feet began to move as if they were on fire. She fell into the rhythm with him, matching his every step. Keeping up with him prevented her from thinking about Luke. She didn't see he had entered the room until the music stopped. When Andrei walked her back to the table, Luke caught her eye and she waved him over.

As he approached, Andrei extended his hand. "Well done, tonight. Keep improving and you'll leave the rest of us in—what is it that the Americans say—the dust?"

"Don't compliment *me*. It's all her work," Luke said, pointing at Holly. "She's awesome."

Andrei wore an I-know-that expression. "And, she's beautiful when she wakes up in the morning."

The look on Luke's face changed as Andrei's words came out.

How sneaky. He's trying to cause trouble. "Don't listen to him, Luke. It's not what he's implying."

Andrei grinned. "I think my partner is here. I'd better go do my duty."

As he walked away, Holly took a sip of the wine she had left on the table and then spoke. "It's a long story, but, trust me, Luke. I have not had an affair with Andrei Rodchenko."

"I doubt many women would pass up an opportunity with him. Have you noticed the crowd when he comes on the dance floor?"

"No more reaction than when you appear."

"Thanks, but you're being generous." He reached across the table and squeezed her hand. "Not to worry. I'm so high tonight that nothing can puncture my bubble. We tied for first place!"

"We did. . . . You did it." *What a difference a week makes.*

"I could be humble and insist that it was you, but you're always perfect. We scored at the top of the chart tonight because I didn't screw up." With that, he stood up. "I'm going to the bar for a drink. Can I get you another glass of wine?"

Holly looked down at her nearly empty glass. *One more glass can't hurt.* Looking up, she said, "That would be nice, thank you." As he left, she drained the remaining wine.

On his way, a TV interview team stopped Luke and asked for comments on the show and his performance. Before he could return to the table, Mika had induced Holly to dance a jive. Seeing her chair empty when he got back, Luke put the two glasses on the table and took his seat. Scanning the room, he caught sight of the couple and did not take his eyes off Holly throughout the dance.

When the song ended, Mika escorted her back to the table. Luke stood when they arrived and pulled Holly's chair out for her.

"Good show," Mika said to Luke, raising his hand in a high-five gesture.

"Thanks, and thank you for the coaching. It helped."

Mika leaned forward at the waist and tipped his hand to his forehead in a flip salute. Straightening up, he said, "Isn't our star beautiful tonight?" He pointed to Holly.

"She always beautiful," Luke answered, looking at Holly with obvious admiration. "And she seems to be the most popular lady in the room."

"Stop it, both of you. You're making me blush."

Mika leaned over and kissed her on the cheek. "We just tell the truth, but I'll leave you two to enjoy your drinks." He once again saluted Luke and then walked away.

"Can't leave you alone for a second before you're swept away by one of those macho playboys. What is the story on you and Rodchenko, if I may be so bold as to ask?"

Holly took a sip of her wine. "I'm embarrassed to tell you, but it's not as scandalous as it may sound."

"I'm intrigued."

"Last week, I had a little too much wine at the after-party. I am embarrassed to admit, I passed out. I have no recollection of leaving. Kat Kenley and Andrei took me to *her* apartment in a cab. We all slept there—separately. Her roommate is off on tour, and I had his room. Andrei slept on the living room couch."

Luke listened intently.

"I'm really ashamed of drinking that much. It's not my style."

He smiled, and Holly thought she saw a trace of relief on his face. "We've all had moments we regret. Don't beat yourself up over it."

"This is absolutely my final drink tonight."

The sound of Teddy Pendergrass's "If You Don't Know Me By Now" started to play. Luke stared at Holly for a few seconds before saying, "Let's dance." He extended his hand.

Without hesitating, Holly accepted his invitation and allowed him to lead her to the floor. As they began to dance, a warm and comforting feeling spread through her. She had danced with him almost daily for nearly four weeks, but this moment was different. They were no longer training or performing, they were man and woman bonding. His embrace made her feel secure and protected. As the love song played, he held her closer and closer. She yielded with pleasure.

As the song drew to a close, Luke whispered softly in her ear. "Let's get out of here."

CHAPTER TWENTY

Holly drew in a deep breath and nodded.

He took her hand and led her out of the party and into the hallway. They didn't speak. She didn't know where they were going, but it didn't matter. She would have followed him into hell at that moment. The elevator was deserted. As soon as the door closed, Luke took her in his arms and kissed her, his lips tasting of champagne. Holly dissolved against him, discarding all inhibitions and doubts. When the elevator stopped and the doors opened, they were on the floor of celebrity dressing rooms.

He broke the embrace but held her hand, leading her to the entry labeled, "Luke Damian." After punching a code into the panel, he opened the door to darkness. Feeling along the wall, his fingers found and flipped a switch, producing dim illumination no stronger than a night-light.

Luke pulled her to him, the scent of his fragrance blending with the aroma of his skin. He pressed his lips against hers, gently at first and then hungrily. His hands were everywhere, one cupping her breast, the other caressing her bottom and then easing up her dress. When his hand reached the bare skin of her thigh, she twitched but thrust her torso forward, pressing against him. Common sense screamed, "Stop before it's too late," but passion's cry of "Do it" obliterated the warning. Every stroke of his hand seared through her flesh, waking every nerve ending and taking her further and further into the state of total surrender. When his fingers slid under her panty line, he stopped. With one hand holding her around the waist and the other close to total intimacy, he whispered, "Are you sure?"

She couldn't speak for a second. Then nodding, she mouthed an almost silent "Yes."

Luke gazed into her eyes for several seconds before slowly easing the thin straps of her dress from her shoulders—leaving only brief panties to cover her nudity. As her clothing fell in a heap on the floor, he unfastened his belt and unzipped his pants, his eyes soaking in the vision before him. Empowered by her sexuality, she unbuttoned his shirt. Within seconds, they were prone on the plump sofa.

His hands caressed her with a light touch—her breasts, her hips—exploring her, teasing her, arousing her sensual desire to unbearable heights. His lips followed his hands, coming to rest on her mouth at the ultimate moment when he consummated their union—taking Holly on a magic journey to euphoria.

Later, lying in the wake of rapture, Luke stroked her hair, kissing her gently. "Tonight changes everything, you know," he whispered.

She gazed into his face, drawn even more to the man. Her chin moved slowly up and down.

He pulled her close. "I'm sorry. I should not have let it happen."

His words caused a tear to form in her eye. "Joy?"

He loosened his hold on her and shook his head. "Hell, no." Pausing for a second, he lifted her chin. "Joy is not what you think. She is nothing to me."

"Then why would you say this shouldn't have happened?"

"Many reasons. Most of all, because I care so much about you."

Holly was quiet as he once again stroked her hair and then brushed a tear from her cheek, his pale blue eyes glowing in the faint beam of light that barely illuminated the room. After a minute, she said, "I don't understand."

He rose on one elbow. "Holly. Sweet, unjaded Holly. My track record sucks. Two failed marriages. More ex-girlfriends than fans. I like you . . . treasure time with you. The last thing I want is to risk messing it up—to say nothing of the strain it will put on our professional relationship."

"Is this your way of saying that this was a disappointment?"

"Oh, my god, no. This was the perfect climax, in more ways than one, to a perfect night. If you only knew, love, how long I've wanted to do exactly what we did. But, *you* know we've crossed a line, and we can't check our feelings at the door to the rehearsal room. It's going to spill over."

"I've been checking mine since our first day together. I can continue." She sat up and reached for her clothes.

Luke rose and grabbed his shirt. When he had it on, he took her by the shoulders. "I don't want to just make love to you. I want to sleep with you—wake up next to you. Come home with me, tonight."

"I can't." She pulled her dress over her head and then slipped her panties back on. "I have a cat."

Standing and redressing himself from the waist down, he said, "How would you feel about me going home with you?"

Her mind raced. Luke Damian going home with her to the tiny apartment and the litter box? *Am I dreaming?*

"You don't live with someone, do you?"

She smiled, shaking her head negatively. "Just Gigi."

"Your cat?"

She nodded.

He stepped into his loafers and then pulled her to him. After kissing her again, he said, "Call Gigi and tell her you're bringing home a guest who wants to meet her."

"Do you like cats?"

"I've never been on a first name basis with one; but, if you like Gigi, I'm sure that I will, too. For now, I'm going back upstairs to pick up some food for us, while you finish dressing." He winked.

A thrill ran through Holly. She blushed and then watched him go out the door.

What have I done? There are no instruction books on what to do with the brass ring after you catch it.

The next morning, Holly refused to ride with Luke to the studio. "I'm not ready for questions," she said.

"I think it may be too late for that concern. I'm sure that our simultaneous departure from the party will bring those about."

"Maybe so. I can't change that, but I can keep from increasing the gossip."

"I want to be with you again—tonight."

"That's not a good idea. Whatever we've started, we need to take it slow—make sure we're thinking with clear heads, and you still haven't told me how Joy fits in your life."

"We don't have time for that story. Just suffice it to say that she is *not* a girlfriend, fiancée, or wife. If you want a classification, take your pick: Luke's typical exercise in poor judgment, a date gone bad, or a 'Fatal Attraction.'"

"Can't you just break up?"

"Holly, Holly, my sweet, slightly naïve Holly. I wish it were that simple. Let me come back tonight, and on my word of honor, I'll give you chapter and verse."

"Not tonight." *You have no idea how hard it is for me to say that.*

"If not tonight, then when?"

"Tomorrow or Saturday, but not both."

"It sounds like you're rationing me like Weight Watcher's calories."

She chuckled. "Yeah. You could say that, but if you're serious about this relationship, you'll be willing to move at a moderate speed."

"I would like to spend the entire weekend, but you're calling the plays." He grabbed her around the waist, pulled her to him, his eyes betraying his approval, and kissed her passionately. Before he finished, his phone buzzed, signaling the arrival of his car and driver.

Pulling away, he said, "I guess you're saved by the bell. See you at the studio and save my place in the other room." He pointed to the bedroom before reaching down to pet the cat that was stretched out on the back of the sofa. "Keep her thinking about me tonight, Gigi. I'm counting on you."

She walked him to the door and watched as he went down the stairs. *It wasn't a dream this time.*

Closing the door and walking to the kitchen to feed Gigi and wash the coffee pot, she reflected on the night before. He had been a tender and considerate lover. They had consummated the relationship again in her bed. Waking up next to him had been almost as good as making love. She was now far more vulnerable than she ever meant to be. When he walked away at the end of the season, Holly knew she was going to be devastated. While she wasn't ready to call it love, the limerence was powerful. *It's good I signed on for the tour. I'll need a distraction. To be dreaming of cottages and babies at this point is sheer folly.* She filled Gigi's water bowl.

It's nothing but a show business affair.

CHAPTER TWENTY-ONE

The drive to the studio usually gave Holly an opportunity to play the music for the next show and think through potential choreography. Becoming intimate with Luke had destroyed that plan. The CD played, but she wasn't hearing it. No matter how hard she tried, she could not get the night before out of her mind. As she pulled onto the freeway, she fought the impulse to call him and say she had changed her mind— that he would be welcomed to come to her apartment after work.

Get your head in the game, Holly. Listen to the music.

She dreaded seeing Sam. *Sam will take one look at me and know.* Even the thought of facing Luke in rehearsal made her nervous. *How can I look at him the same way?*

By the time she parked in the studio lot, it was beginning to rain. The cool, fall air smelled fresh as she climbed out and dashed to the door. Entering the studio, she felt as though a banner was draped across her body proclaiming what happened.

The room was quiet, with Luke already in his practice gear and stretching. Sam was sitting on the bench, drinking a Starbucks. The rain provided just enough distraction to divert attention from the guilty expression on her face. Putting her bag down, she avoided eye contact with either man by digging for a towel. Although she was not soaked, her knit shirt and hair were slightly wet.

"You're running late this morning," Sam said. "Didn't have an umbrella?"

"Left it at home," Holly lied.

Luke looked up and smiled at her. She wanted to scream, "Don't look at me that way." Instead, she said, "I'll be right back. I'm going to change to a dry top."

You're stalling. Your shirt isn't that wet. In the bathroom, she leaned against the counter and took a deep breath. *You can do this. You'll get absorbed in the work. At least, our new dance is not sensual.*

When she reentered the studio, Luke was drinking orange juice. "Ready?" he asked, tossing the empty bottle in a receptacle.

"Question is . . . are you?" she said with a coy smile and then sat on the floor next to her bag to change shoes.

Grinning, he responded, "Absolutely."

Sam had finished his coffee and picked up his camera to begin recording.

Don't start yet, Sam. I need a minute or two. She rose and, mustering the reserves necessary to keep her voice steady, said to Luke, "Let's do it—the *dance* of the matador." She made a sweeping arm gesture, clicked her heels together, and then walked over to the audio system. Without looking at him again, she turned on the familiar procession-of-the-bullfighters music, "España Cañi."

"Listen to the piece before we start choreography," she said. "Feel the flavor of the style. Paso doble is a dance of dramatic passion with an air of arrogance." She took a deep breath, pleased that she had maintained a relatively normal demeanor.

In the routine opening, the dancers faced off from opposite sides of the room. All went smoothly until the first time they made physical contact. At that point, Holly's composure came under threat. His hands had touched her countless times over the past weeks, occasionally producing a sexual exhilaration, but nothing compared to the sensation she felt the first time his arm went around her waist that morning. Instinctively, she looked around at Sam with his unforgiving camera, fearing either the man or his lens had penetrated her mind. Luke showed no outward sign of a change in their relationship. *Of course, he can pull this off. He's an actor.*

Although she glanced at Sam frequently during the morning rehearsal, looking for signs of suspicion, she avoided making eye contact. When Luke asked for a restroom break, she grabbed a towel to give him a head start, wiped her face, and then bolted from the room to avoid conversation with Sam. On the way to the ladies' room, she ran into Luke as he entered the empty hall, coming from the men's room.

Seeing her, a grin spread from ear to ear across his face. As they met, he blocked her way, backing her against the wall.

"Luke, someone will see us," she said as he held her by the waist and leaned forward to kiss her.

"We're not breaking any law," he whispered and pressed his lips to hers.

Her resistance compromised, she gave in to a brief moment of passion, putting her arms around him in an embrace. After a few seconds, discretion conquered desire, and Holly pulled away.

"Hold that thought until tomorrow night. I don't think we're ready to go public."

He brushed a loose tendril of hair gently off her forehead and with smiling eyes said, "I know. I'll try to behave." He then gave her a quick kiss on the lips. "See you back in the torture chamber."

As he started to walk away, Holly called out in a low voice, "Luke, wipe my lipstick off your face."

Without turning around, he raised his arm in the air and gave a thumbs-up signal.

Holly managed to settle comfortably back into their work pattern by lunch. Overall, the day went well. Luke seemed to enjoy playing the matador role, stomping his feet on the floor with gusto, exaggerating gestures, and taking appropriate stances. The actor stepped into the Spanish style with all the aplomb Holly could ask for. As they got ready to leave at six o'clock, Holly tossed her practice shoes in her bag and said, "I think you're beginning to like this job."

Luke zipped his bag, heisted it over his shoulder, and said, "I'd say that I'm *really* beginning to like the job." He smiled.

Holly cringed and instinctively turned to look at Sam, praying he had not caught the double entendre. To her relief, the cameraman's face was stoic as he packed up for the day.

"I'm craving sushi," Luke said. "Want to grab a bite before you call it a day?"

Darn him. Of course, I want to have dinner with him, but I shouldn't on so many counts. She paused before answering, engaged in a mental debate between her sensible and lovesick sides. Temptation won. "You're on. However, I don't do raw fish, so could we choose a Japanese restaurant that also has tempura?"

As they left the rehearsal room, Holly felt as though Sam was staring at them and seeing through their superficial act. *He knows. I know he does.*

The couple took Holly's car to a popular restaurant not too far from her apartment. It was off the tourist trail, thereby diminishing the threat of recognition. The trade-off was the noise factor of the busy establishment, which discouraged meaningful conversation. She was relieved to avoid a serious discussion. Being with Luke in a purely social setting was sufficient to satisfy Holly.

After dinner, Luke called for his car to pick him up at Holly's building. "I'm going to obey your rule and not press to stay, but tell Gigi to expect me tomorrow," he said as they pulled up to the apartment.

"Thank you." An intimate image of the two of them flashed across her mind, leaving a warm and fuzzy feeling.

Opening the door to the apartment, the space felt different. Luke had been there the night before and had left invisible traces of his presence. Gigi greeted Holly at the door as usual and rubbed against her legs. Holly dropped her dance bag and purse and then picked up the cat. Gigi pushed her face against her mistress's hand, purring.

"So, little bit, what do you think of him?" She scratched the Persian's chin for a minute and then said, "Pretty stupid to think you're going to answer, isn't it?" Putting the cat back on the floor, Holly went to the kitchen and filled the food and water bowls. As she went to her bedroom, she ran a checklist for what to do in preparation for Luke's return. *I need to call home tonight. Mom expects me to call on Friday, and I certainly don't want to talk to her with Luke here.*

Before making the call, Holly pulled down the bedspread. Picking up the pillow that Luke had slept on, she hugged it to her body, buried her face in it, and inhaled the remnants of his fragrance.

Gigi jumped on the bed.

"I am falling hard for him, Gigi." She squeezed the pillow and dropped it back in place. "I'm on a fast track to disaster and can't seem to help myself. There are a hundred reasons why I shouldn't be letting this hap—"

The ring of the landline interrupted her. Glancing at the caller ID, she recognized Dana's phone number and picked up the cordless.

"Dana. How are you?"

"Same as always, but you're sure hot, gal."

Holly paused for a second. *How could she have known? Oh, wait a minute. She's talking about the show.* "Thanks. It did go well—a lot better than last week."

"I'm not just talking about you and dreamboat. You were awesome in that sexy dance with the handsome Russian hunk. Tell me what *he's* like in person."

"Good looking, great dancer, not much more to tell."

"Holly Dawson. How can you be so casual? You're on national TV, doing erotic dances with two gorgeous, sexy men. Do you have any idea how many women in this country would kill to trade places with you? I hope that *a-s-s* of an ex is eating his heart out with what he gave up."

Don? He hardly crosses my mind. "That's a nice idea. Nothing beats Karma. You know he called me."

"No. . . . He didn't. Bet he's having second thoughts. I hope you told him what he could do."

"Don't worry. He was standing at the gate, without a ticket, when that flight flew."

"Good to hear. What I called for, besides congratulating you, was to ask if you're coming home for Thanksgiving?"

"Oh, my gosh. I haven't even thought about it. The show is preempted that week." Holly frowned. *Leave Luke?*

"Let me know if you are. I want to get together and hear all the down-and-dirty on Luke Damian and that Russian, whose name I can't pronounce."

"Mika Dorofeyev." *She would die if she knew that I slept with Luke.*
"Yeah. That's it."

"Listen, kiddo, I need to go now because I've got to call Mom before it gets too late, but I'll let you know as soon as I make Thanksgiving plans." *If only you knew how much I want to tell you about Luke. Maybe by Thanksgiving, I'll know whether to let anyone know about him and me—if there is still a "him and me."*

Hanging up with Dana, Holly immediately dialed home. Listening to the phone ring, she pictured her parents in the Jacksonville house. Her mother was most likely wrapping up kitchen chores, and her dad was watching TV. Life was so different there.

When Mary Lou Dawson answered, she was surprised that Holly had called on Thursday night but excited to share family news.

"Regina is pregnant."

"That's awesome news, Mom. Why didn't that brother of mine call and tell me?"

"You know Chris; he isn't one to talk on the phone, and Gina is superstitious. She wants to get further along before making a general announcement."

"I can understand. She was so devastated when she miscarried."

To Holly's relief, her mother did not mention Thanksgiving. *She probably assumes that I'm coming home like I've always done whenever I had time off.*

After hanging up, Holly sat on her bed, thinking about her status. *Chris is going to be a father, Dana is having her second baby, and I'm not even dating anyone. What am I doing in a dead-end affair with Luke Damian?*

Although her practical mind told her the affair was a mistake, it was no match against the power of hormonal attraction.

CHAPTER TWENTY-TWO

First thing, Friday morning, Holly stripped her bed to prepare for Luke's visit. She tossed all the linens in her washer, except the pillowcase he had slept on. She couldn't bring herself to destroy the traces of his scent. Her mind raced with preparations for his return visit. *Should I stop by Victoria's Secret? No. I'm not going to start that. He didn't need fancy lingerie to light his fire the other night.*

Although dinner plans had not been discussed, Holly decided to cook so they could avoid any chance of public recognition. Before leaving for the studio, she prepared a lasagna casserole and a fruit salad. To finish off her staging for the night, she scattered a half-dozen candles around the apartment and made a playlist for her iPod of music for lovers, including "With You I'm Born Again," by Billy Preston and Syreeta; "Woman," by John Lennon; and "Touch Me in the Morning," by Diana Ross.

Friday rehearsal was easier for Holly, despite her anticipation of the evening ahead. The awkwardness with Luke disappeared as they concentrated on the choreography. Sam gave no indication during the day of having any suspicions about the change in their relationship. When Sam left the room for a bathroom break, the couple discussed the evening itinerary.

"I wanted to take you to a good restaurant," Luke said.

"That's a sweet idea, but I think we want to stay under the radar. I'll cook at my apartment."

He thought about it for a minute and then agreed. "I'll bring my toothbrush, a bottle of good wine, and a big appetite." His blue eyes danced with mischief.

She laughed and then said, "I can't think of a more appropriate combination."

He grabbed her around the waist, but she put her hands against his chest, holding him back.

"Whoa. . . . Sam or someone else could walk in any minute."

"Yes, ma'am."

The doorbell rang at seven-thirty. Holly had been ready for forty-five minutes. She wore a pale-green, pull-on, jersey romper that displayed her long, tanned legs to full advantage. The combined aromas of Italian cuisine from the oven and English lavender from a Lampe Berger escaped when she opened the door.

Luke stood in the hall, breathtakingly handsome in a hydrangea-blue shirt with sleeves rolled up to reveal a cuff lined in the familiar Burberry plaid. His azure eyes sparkled even brighter than usual. Holly felt the thrill of a teenager on her first date. He held a bottle of wine in one hand and two dozen red roses in the other.

As he entered, Holly smelled the fresh scent of soap and his familiar Armani fragrance. "Thank you." She lowered her face to smell the flowers. "They're beautiful. Make yourself comfortable while I find a vase."

"Don't I get a kiss?" Luke said as she started toward the kitchen.

Holly stopped, laid the gifts down, and turned back around.

Luke pulled her close, pressed his lips against hers, lingered for several seconds, and then gave her a squeeze. "Something smells very good."

"I hope you like Italian."

"Italian is great."

The label on the wine caught her eye as she picked it back up. "My gosh, Luke. You shouldn't have been so extravagant. I've never tasted Dom Perignon."

"Then, it's about time you did. If I can't take you to a fine restaurant, the least I can do is bring a fine wine. Do you have an ice bucket?"

"I do." She went to a small pantry in her kitchen where she took out two vases and an ice bucket. Handing the latter to Luke, she said, "I hope the champagne isn't insulted by chilling in stainless steel."

He grinned, pointed to her refrigerator, and said, "Ice?"

While she arranged the roses, he filled the container, covering the cubes with water, and held up the bottle before nestling it in place. "Can I pour you a glass, now?" he asked. "It should still be cool."

"Let me take dinner out of the oven, first."

There was no dining room in the small apartment, only a bar between the kitchen and great room. For the occasion, Holly had set up a folding walnut table and covered it with an ecru linen cloth her grandmother had embroidered. She removed two of the roses from the bunch, put them in a bud vase, and placed them next to a candle burning in the center of her portable table. The remaining flowers went into a vase for the living room. When finished, Holly turned on the iPod, and they sat down.

Luke poured the champagne. After handing Holly hers, he raised his glass and said, "To Luke and Holly—the next *Lights, Camera— Dance* champs and to the beginning a very special journey together."

Holly said nothing but stared into his eyes. *This is not going to last, but carpe diem—to hell with the consequences.*

After dinner, Luke helped her clear away the dishes and load the dishwasher. When she put the leftovers in the refrigerator, he came up behind her and wrapped his arms around her waist, kissing her neck.

Holly turned. "Before we move forward, you promised to clear the air about Joy."

Luke stepped back, an indiscernible look on his face. "You're right. I did."

"I don't mean to be difficult, but I don't like the role of home wrecker—which, considering Wednesday night, may be like putting a chastity belt on your pregnant daughter."

"It's okay." He put his hand under her chin, lifting it slightly. "Although it's against my principles to kiss and tell, I owe you an expla- nation." He took her hand and led her to the sofa.

They sat down with Luke holding both of her hands in his.

"I met Joy at Fashion Week in New York a few months ago. I had done a print campaign for the designer who gave me my first break. It began with typical cocktail party conversation and ended up with me going home with her."

"Just like that?"

"Just like that. She was—is—a beautiful woman; I am a red-blooded man. The hookup led to three or four black-tie events, patronized by the paparazzi. Snaps of the two of us began popping up in the tabloids. A few images in print and in this town you're deemed a couple. Joy bought into what she read in the media." He took a breath and looked to the ceiling for a minute. "My gut told me I needed to back off, but Jeff was ecstatic. He is an agent first, last, and always. 'Any press is good, my boy,' he said, 'especially when fame is traveling in the wrong direction.' I should have listened to my instincts. When she started talking weddings, kids, and real estate, I knew I had to exit. But clearing Joy out of your life is like removing indelible ink from a white shirt."

"Did you tell her that you weren't on the same page?"

"Did I? You bet I did, and that's when all hell broke loose. She screamed, cried, and made threats while I stood dumbfounded. Two divorces, and more breakups than I want to claim, did not prepare me for her behavior. I managed to get away that night with a promise that I would rethink my position. I knew that it was dangerous to continue arguing. I could almost hear the sirens and feel the handcuffs in my future if I didn't placate her. She was capable of falsely accusing me of domestic violence or something equally dramatic. Images of Mel Gibson flashed before my eyes."

"When was that?"

"About a week before we began training for the show."

"I remember your phone ringing a lot the first day."

He nodded. "I had to buy a new phone. She still calls the old one and blows it up with messages."

"She sounds like a stalker."

"It's a strong term, but *Fatal Attraction* and dead rabbits have haunted me ever since I saw the look in her eye when I told her it was over."

"Why don't you get a restraining order?"

"And be the lead story on the six o'clock news? Joy is not playing with the same rule book that applies to the rest of us. I've conferred with a therapist and my lawyer. They all caution against confrontation, which could escalate her actions. If I were Joe Jones, working at the bank, and she was slinging fish and chips at the corner café, I would apply for an injunction." He paused, took a breath, and continued. "But, I'm not Jones, Holly. I'm an actor, and she's a super model. Even though my candle dimmed a long time ago, this sort of publicity is what sells papers. My advertising sponsors would drop me like Lance Armstrong. At the least, the press corps would paint me as a womanizing, thirty-one-year-old bastard who took advantage of a barely legal, twenty-year-old model. If she carried through on any one of her threats, it would be even worse."

"I'm so sorry."

Looking into her eyes, Luke tenderly caressed Holly's face—his expression, a cross between remorse and sincerity. "I'm not blameless. I could have bailed out and taken the heat in a timelier manner. But, Holly, I will swear to you, on as many Bibles as you care to produce, I never said anything to suggest I was interested in a serious relationship, much less a permanent one."

He paused, studying Holly's face as if expecting a reaction. "I didn't want to pull you into this mess. Shame on me for allowing desire to override good judgment."

She put two fingers across his lips. "Shh. I wanted it to happen as much as you did."

"Do you still want me to stay? I'm a poor investment, and you're someone I don't want to hurt."

Holly did not hesitate. "Do you have to ask?" She put her arms around his neck and whispered in his ear. "It's a relief to know that you aren't cheating." After hugging him for several minutes, she pulled away, her brow pinched in a frown. "Luke, what are you going to do?"

He took her hands back into his. "For the time being, hang tight, stay out of Dodge, and hope that some other poor bloke steps in the quicksand to distract her. Thank God, she lives in New York and works worldwide." He paused for a moment. "For your sake, we should keep our personal life on the down low." He stood up. "If you don't mind, let's drop the subject before it taints any more of our evening."

Holly looked up at him, her expression softening. "I am glad you're here." She stood up and hugged him again. "Thank you for telling me. I know you didn't want to—"

Before she could finish the sentence, his mouth covered hers, kissing her passionately. She responded in kind.

After several minutes of kissing and fondling, Luke pulled away and switched off the only illuminated lamp in the room, leaving only the soft glow of the candles. Holly restarted the playlist.

As John Lennon sang "Woman," Luke drew her to him and whispered in her ear. "The dance of love, right?"

Holly nodded and rubbed her body against his as they swayed to the music.

Holding her around the waist with one hand, he slipped the elasticized top of the romper off her shoulders and slid it down her body. Holly stepped out of the garment, wearing a pair of pink, bikini-cut, lace panties and matching bra. "That's better," he whispered. "Now, show me one of your sexy moves."

She broke the hold and did a rumba walk a few feet away from him, turned, and slowly shimmied down close to the floor. Rising, she repeated the walk back to him, turned her back, and raised her arms over her head, reaching backward around his neck. "You mean like this?" she whispered, turning her head to one side, her hips still swaying to the music.

"Exactly." He leaned forward and kissed her neck as his hands eased down both sides of her body, meeting in front at her panty line and then sliding under the lace.

His touch ignited erotic fires in her body. As the candles flickered and Lennon sang, they moved together with raw passion, hips moving in sync. Luke kissed and caressed her bare skin all over, shedding piece by piece of his clothing along the way. She surrendered to his every move, thrilling to each sensation and aching for him to take her while he deftly maneuvered her to the bedroom. As the carnal act moved slowly forward, Holly discarded control of body and mind. She willingly submitted to a euphoric state of nirvana and allowed audible sounds of rapture to escape as the electricity generated by the contact of their naked bodies sizzled.

Luke's climax closely followed hers. Lying on the bed, fully exposed, Holly could hardly remember moving the few feet from living room. Moonlight streamed through the second-floor window. Turning her head, she looked at him. His face glistened with moisture; his hair was damp—his eyes open.

Responding to her gaze, he said in a low voice, "And I thought you exhausted me in rehearsals." His words heated her blood.

"Don't blame me," she whispered. "Tonight was all Damian choreography."

He grabbed her and began tickling her ribs. She squirmed and squealed.

"Not complaining, are you?"

"No. No. Not complaining."

With her response, he stopped tickling and rolled over on top of her, kissing her as Joe Cocker and Jennifer Warnes echoed through the apartment, singing "Up Where We Belong."

Releasing her for a second, he gazed into her eyes, paused for several seconds, and then said, "I could become addicted to nights like this, Holly Dawson."

CHAPTER TWENTY-THREE

Love, lust, or star-struck fantasy? What am I feeling? As she took out a frying pan to make breakfast for Luke on Saturday morning, common sense told Holly that it could not be love. They had known one another only a few weeks; therefore, her sensible self said to strike that possibility. Of the remaining choices, she wasn't sure which would be worse.

He was sitting at the bar watching her. "Is there any chance that you've changed your mind about seeing me tonight?" he asked between sips of his coffee.

She thought for a moment or two. The night before had been nearly perfect. The revelation about Joy was unsettling, but she was relieved to know he was not cheating on a devoted girlfriend. Looking at him dressed in jeans with his shirt unbuttoned and sitting as though he belonged there, Holly's conscience said, "Don't take your foot off the brake." However, in matters of the heart, caution rides in the backseat.

"I should say no."

A smile broke across his face. "But, you're going to say yes."

She hesitated, dragging it out as long as she could. "I hope I don't live to regret it, but if you really want to . . . okay."

"I'll take that to mean the remainder of the weekend."

"Luke."

"You won't be sorry. After rehearsal, we can take a drive to the coast, spend the night, and have a brilliant day tomorrow, soaking up sun and surf."

"Spend the night there?"

He nodded. "I have access to a quiet place on the beach where there's both freedom and privacy."

"What kind of a place?"

"It's a beach house that belongs to Rex Folsom. He's in Costa Rica shooting."

"The Rex who was your nemesis on the Holmes show?"

"Right. We stay in touch."

Holly took a deep breath and mulled the idea over for several seconds before responding. A smile spread across her face. "I would love to." *I hope you know what you're doing, Holly.*

Saturday rehearsal went smoothly. By four-thirty, they were traveling toward the California coast in Luke's Spider. The small trunk held a cooler with potato salad and cold slaw from the deli and a package of chicken breasts to grill. Nature designed a perfect day for the road trip with clear skies and a late afternoon temperature in the mid-seventies.

"We should be there in ample time to enjoy the sunset," Luke said, reaching across the console to squeeze Holly's knee.

A torrent of passion passed through her like a tornado seeking its target.

They reached the beach at five-twenty. As Luke parked the car on the street side of the house, Holly stared in amazement. "My gosh, Luke. It's right on the water." Perched on stilts, the square building was only a few feet from the high-tide mark.

He led the way up the stairs, carrying their belongings and the bag of food. Putting the parcels down on the landing, he took out a key and opened the door. Although the architecture was basic, the inside of the building was perfection. An expansive bay of glass overlooked the Pacific with a long, ecru suede sofa positioned in the cove. Large occasional chairs in white linen with matching ottomans faced the window. The only touches of color in the room were provided by the backdrop of the ocean, the foliage of large plants, and four aqua pillows in several patterns scattered on the couch. The floor was Italian tiles.

"It's breathtaking, Luke. I imagined something far more rustic. It must be worth a fortune."

"Rex does well. Supporting players work a hell of a lot more than leads."

"I've heard that."

"Pick a bedroom while I put the food away and pour us a glass of wine. The sun will be setting in a few minutes."

The sky became a symphony of color as a quilt of clouds moved in to tuck the sun into bed below the horizon. Layers of gray-blue, amber, and persimmon covered the falling blaze of gold as it dropped from sight, leaving darkness and the sound of tons of water lashing the shore. Watching nature's performance from the enclosed deck created the perfect setting for Luke and Holly to consummate their union once more.

With the onset of darkness, they went inside, showered together, and then made dinner. He cooked the chicken on a gas grill on the deck while she put the rest of their meal together. Watching him through the glass of the kitchen door, Holly felt warm, fuzzy, and domestic. *I'll have this memory forever, no matter what happens.*

Sunday was a continuation of the nonpareil of the night before. They swam, chased one another around the beach, wrestled playfully, laughed together, and made love. Driving back to L.A., Holly said, "Thank you for a wonderful weekend."

He reached over for her hand and squeezed it. "I've never had a better time."

The tone of his voice sent a tremor through Holly. Nothing had been mentioned as to plans for the night.

As they reached L.A., Luke spoke. "I'm not going to give you a chance to tell me I can't stay with you tonight."

What does that mean?

"I'm going home and let you rest. I know the pressure of this week's show is going to close in on you, and I don't want to be a distraction."

For a moment, Holly's heart sank. *Does that mean he's losing interest?*

Continuing, Luke said, "However, I want your promise that Wednesday night you'll either come home with me or allow me to return to your apartment."

The tension dissipated immediately, as the corners of her mouth turned up. "You've got it."

*****

Their third week of competition went well. Holly managed to compartmentalize their personal life most of the time, focusing on perfecting their routine. Occasionally, her thoughts strayed with daydreams about the prior weekend and anticipation about the time they would spend together at the end of the week.

On broadcast night, Luke's scores for his paso doble put him in third place. He did not seem to mind having slipped a little from the week before.

"Not quite as good as last time, but I'll take it," he said as they left the performance area. "Maybe I'll score higher later tonight." He winked at her.

"Hush, Luke. Someone may hear you."

Thursday morning brought the beginning of new choreography. Their fourth dance of the season was to be a rumba. Holly anticipated working on the piece with mixed emotions. In past rumba routines, all the sexual tension had been manufactured for effect—even with Mika. This was brand-new territory. Holly agonized over how to perform seductively without betraying their private life. Luke had spent the night before with her as planned, and she could still feel his touch. Overtones of resistance moved in as she drove by herself to the studio.

Holly arrived first, even before Sam. By the time the cameraman sauntered in, she was dressed, warmed up, and working on choreography.

"Well, aren't you the early bird, this morning?" he said, putting his bag on one of the wooden benches. "Good show last night. Hope you slept well."

Is there a hidden meaning there? No. He's shown no sign of suspecting anything. "I slept great. How about you?"

"A shot of brandy at bedtime, and I always sleep great." He tipped his thumb and index finger toward his mouth to suggest having a drink. "What's on tap this week?"

"The rumba."

"Uh oh—the daaaance of luuve."

"Stop it." She punched him on the shoulder.

He laughed and started to say something else but was interrupted by Luke coming through the door.

"Hey, Luke. How's it going?" Sam said.

"Couldn't be better," Luke responded, dropping his bag on the floor. "Ready to take on a new challenge."

"Warm up, and we'll get started," Holly said. "Our music this week is 'How Deep is Your Love,' by the Bee Gees."

Luke grinned and did several squats, a few stretches, and then walked over to where she was standing.

"We'll begin with a basic rumba box. It's a quick, quick, slow; quick, quick, slow beat—starting with a side step to your left."

"Yeah. I think I got that from watching you and Mika." He took her hand and fell into the pattern easily.

For two hours, they worked on the patterns without regard for artistry. The execution was clinical. By eleven o'clock, Holly was ready to move forward. "Okay. I think you've got the combinations for the first minute of the music, let's add the feeling."

Although she had issued the instruction, Holly was tense as they began doing the routine to the music. She moved her hips as required, but she felt an awkwardness not felt since the first time she did the dance with a partner.

Thirty minutes into the phase, Sam abruptly said, "Cut!"

He turned off his camera, put it down, and stopped the music.

Holly and Luke froze, looked at each other and then at Sam with bewildered expressions on their faces.

"What's wrong?" Holly asked. "Are you okay?"

"I'm fine, but you guys aren't." He stood with his hands on his hips.

"What do you mean?"

"Come on, Holly. I may not be a dancer, but even I can see that the two of you are holding back. You had more chemistry the day you met than you're showing here. If you want to win this competition, that's not going to cut it. I know you're getting it on together in private, so put some of that passion into this number."

Holly's eyes popped open wide with astonishment. "What did you say?"

A smile crept across Luke's face, but he said nothing.

"You heard me. The two of you are sleeping together, so show it. I'm not one of your judges, but I've been around long enough to know that no chemistry equals no gold. Play it right, and the two of you have a real chance at winning this season."

"Why would you think we're sleeping together?" Holly's face was turning pink and looking as guilty as the dog that ate his master's steak.

"A man would have to be blind not to know. Ever since you showed up late last week and ran to the restroom, you've been holding back with Luke. And don't think I've missed the secret looks that have passed between you. You got away with it last week because the fire of the dance covered for you, but no passion in this routine is fatal."

"Does anyone else know?" Holly asked. Her heart was pounding and her hands trembling.

"If they do, nothing has been said. Of course, the other competitors have more to lose than to gain by outing you."

"What about the producers?" Holly asked.

Sam shook his head. "You'll know soon enough, but you have no worry there. A romance in the ranks is good for at least a ten-point boost in the ratings and will also translate into votes that keep you two in the running."

"Sam, you've got to promise me that you won't say anything," Holly said. "We have more than one reason to keep our private life under the radar."

"My lips are sealed. But, don't let it screw you out of points. I can hear Lorraine Gibson announcing that she deducted a full point, because she didn't feel any connection between the two of you."

"Was it really that bad?"

"Think Ugly Betty trying to seduce Sheldon Cooper."

"Ouch. Give us a break, Sam," Luke said.

Sam just nodded with one eyebrow raised.

Holly held her hands up in the surrender position. "Let's break for lunch. I need time to wrap my head around this." She turned toward Luke. "We need to talk."

"Want to go to my dressing room?"

Visions of their first time making love immediately flashed through Holly's mind. "Not a good idea. We can talk here and then grab lunch in the canteen."

"On second thought, would you pick up a bite to eat for us and bring it back here?" Holly said to Luke, her hand on her forehead. "I need a little time to focus."

Sam started for the door. "Back in an hour."

As soon as the door closed, Luke walked over to Holly and put his hands on her shoulders. "It's okay." Pulling her to him, he gave her a hug and then asked, "What would you like to eat?"

Holly relaxed and rested her head against his chest. "Chef salad, low-cal ranch, and unsweetened tea."

As Luke left the studio, she retrieved a bottle of water from the cooler and rubbed it across her face. Her hands were trembling. "Get a grip. You're acting like an amateur," she said, looking at her reflection in the mirror. "Figure it out."

CHAPTER TWENTY-FOUR

It took Luke ten minutes to get their food. By the time he returned to the studio, Holly had dabbed her face with cold water, re-combed her hair, and pulled herself together.

Unpacking their lunch, he said, "You're overthinking this. I know we both prefer to keep our personal lives between ourselves, but it's not a national disaster if we're found out."

"I know, and I know it was me that Sam was talking about. You're doing fine. I'm the one who feels awkward performing a seductive dance with you. It was so much easier when it was all acting, but every time I start a sexy move, I think of us at the beach, in your dressing room, in my apartment; and it feels like the whole world sees what's in my mind. You're an actor. You can make it work."

"You are an actress, whether you know it or not. You had to look like you were hot for Mr. Computer Geek, didn't you?"

A smile crossed her face. "That was different. When he touched me, it was with fat, clammy hands that were as sexy as being embraced by a giant lizard. When you touch me, I get chills."

Luke grinned. "Chills, huh?"

"Yes, damn it. As if you needed to know."

Luke reached over and lifted her chin so that they were eye to eye. "All you have to do is think Quasimodo. Don't see Luke Damian. Tell yourself I'm Mr. Silicon Valley, and it's your job to seduce me."

"How do I do that?"

"The same way I had to do it when playing a love scene with a woman who held no appeal for me. You just trick your brain."

"Let me get this straight. I have to pretend that you don't turn *me* on so that I can force myself to try to turn *you* on."

"In a nutshell."

"What if it does get out? What about Joy?"

"If it does, it does. I'll deal with it. Sam isn't going to tell anyone, and no one else is close enough to catch on—at least not for a while." He handed her a packet of dressing for her salad. "Now eat."

When they finished lunch, Holly gathered the trash and took it to the receptacle across the room. When she came back to the bench, Luke stood up and wrapped his arms around her, pulling her close he whispered, "We're going to be fine. Trust—"

"Whoops. I'm sorry. Didn't mean to interrupt," Sam said, coming into the rehearsal room.

"No, no. You're fine," Holly responded, pulling back from Luke. "We're ready to rehearse."

After the mini-breakdown, Holly applied Luke's suggestion and managed to improve the routine but never completely let go of her inhibitions. Nothing more was said. Even through dress rehearsal, she only gave about ninety percent. However, something happened when they took their places for the performance. Whether it was a competitive streak or a professional's adrenalin, Holly gave it her all. They took the top place on the scoreboard. Several judges commented on what great chemistry they had. Harry Fellows said that he needed a cold shower after watching the number.

The infamous Lorraine Gibson said, "Oh, my. That was *hot*. Do you two have something going on that we don't know about?" She fanned her face.

Holly struggled to maintain her composure, while Luke was as cool as a mint julep in July.

Sam flashed them a big grin as he filmed them walking down the corridor toward their dressing rooms after the show.

As they passed Kat, she gave them a thumbs-up. She and her partner, the sportscaster, had been eliminated at the end of the show, which came as no surprise. With ten couples left in the competition,

Luke and Holly were in the top three, along with Andrei Rodchenko and his partner, the gold-medal gymnast, and Lisa Cantrell and her partner, the sexy, Swedish chef.

Holly knew Luke was excited by the way he squeezed her hand.

It's going to be a good night.

After putting in a brief appearance at the after-party, Holly slipped away, basking in anticipation of the private celebration they planned for her apartment. Luke lingered long enough to dispel speculation that they were leaving together.

Thursday morning, Holly was in the kitchen, mixing waffle batter when Luke stumbled in, craving coffee. He walked toward the Keurig. "You pulled it off last night, partner." As he passed, he grabbed her around the waist and kissed her on the cheek. After filling a cup, he looked down his torso and said, "If you had been a hair sexier, I might have risen to the occasion and had an event worse than a costume malfunction with fifteen-million viewers watching."

Holly laughed. "I'm just *glad* that it's over. The only thing worse would be dancing that style if our relationship fell apart."

"Mark that possibility off your list." He took a big gulp of coffee. "So, what's the name of next week's torture?"

"We've got the cha cha."

Luke groaned. "Scratch the idea of first place. I'm not built for that one."

"Think positive. But we need to get moving. It's already eight. Sam will be in the studio, waiting."

"No rest for the weary. Since Sam knows about us, let's skip the dual transportation sham. That'll give us a few extra minutes."

"There are others who might see us arrive. Get your shower, and breakfast will be ready by the time you're dressed."

Taking his cup, Luke started back toward the bedroom, muttering under his breath, "I should have known it wouldn't work."

It was close to nine-thirty when Holly walked into the studio.

Sam was reviewing some of his footage.

"Slept in this morning?" he asked.

"One of us did, if you really need to know." Holly smiled. "You're not going to say anything—are you?"

"Not until you give the okay."

Luke ambled in at ten and dropped his bag on one of the benches. "Not looking forward to this."

"Don't give me that, Luke Damian." Holly held a palm up. "You can do whatever you put your mind to."

"My mind is not the weak spot. You've got to have hips connected with rubber bands and feet of fire to look good in that dance."

Holly shook her head. "One step at a time."

True to his prediction, Luke struggled with the choreography. By eleven-thirty, they had less than a minute completed and were using music for the first time. As Jennifer Lopez belted out "Let's Get Loud" on the audio system, Holly had just dropped into a backbend, supported by Luke, when the studio door opened abruptly. All eyes turned instantly toward the intruder as Luke pulled Holly upright.

Her heart stopped, while his face froze with disgust.

CHAPTER TWENTY-FIVE

"So this is what you're doing when you don't return my calls." The statuesque blonde towered over Holly as she walked up to the couple.

"What the hell are you doing here, Joy?" Venom saturated his tone. Hatred shot from his eyes.

Barely taking his eyes off the scene developing, Sam slipped his camera onto a tripod and opened the lens to a wide angle.

"Coming to see what has been keeping my boyfriend so busy that he doesn't have time for me. After seeing the two of you in that porn performance last night, disguised as a dance routine, it's pretty obvious that this bitch is out to seduce you."

"You need to leave," Luke said.

"I don't think so, love. I think that I'm right where I need to be." Turning to Holly, Joy said, "Has he told you that we're having a baby?"

Her legs turning to putty, it was all Holly could muster to remain standing. The color drained from her face.

Baby?

"I can see from your expression that he hasn't," Joy taunted.

"You need to leave before I have you taken away, Joy," Luke said, raising his voice.

Sam reached for his cell phone.

"I'm not leaving until we talk."

Sam motioned to Luke with the phone.

Getting the message, Luke nodded and then turned his flaring eyes, to Joy. "Leave."

The hostility in his voice frightened Holly. She was speechless. *Is she telling the truth? Is there a baby?* Watching Luke's expression and hearing his tone, fear that violence was possible overcame her concern with Joy's revelation.

"Security's on the way, Luke," Sam said, calmly.

Joy moved closer to Luke, balled up her fists and pounded him on the chest.

He jumped back with his hands in a surrender position as if to avoid physical contact.

"I'm not leaving until you talk to me," Joy screeched.

No one moved.

Instinct made Holly want to exit the room, but intuition told her that without witnesses, there was no guessing what Joy might do. Sam stood firm as well, staring at Joy as though seeking to stop her with a laser look.

Just as Holly feared she might vomit, two studio rent-a-cops came through the door.

"What's the problem?" the shorter one asked.

"This woman needs to leave the property," Luke said.

Sam silently nodded in agreement and then stepped forward. "If she won't leave voluntarily, you may need law enforcement backup. Mr. Damian and Ms. Dawson need to go somewhere else while we deal with the situation." With a hand gesture, he shooed Holly and Luke out. The guards inserted themselves between Joy and the couple.

Luke stood dormant for a second, but Holly took his arm and pulled him toward the door.

As they exited, Holly heard Joy screaming, "You can't do this. I have my rights. I'll call my lawyer. Do you know who I am?"

In the hall, she looked up at Luke, who was visibly shaken.

"My dressing room?" he asked.

She nodded.

Neither spoke as they approached the elevators. Burning questions polarized Holly's mind. *Is she pregnant? Why didn't he tell me?*

The hallway, lined with celebrity dressing rooms, was silent, in contrast to floors where rehearsals were taking place. Subconsciously, Holly walked on the balls of her feet to avoid the sound of her heels clicking on the tile.

When they reached his entry, Luke's fingers fumbled with the code.

He's nervous. Is he going to address Joy's declaration?

When the lock released, he held the door, allowing Holly to pass. It had not fully closed when he spoke. "I need a drink."

A drink? At noon?

He opened a built-in cabinet and lifted out a bottle of champagne. "A gift," he said, popping the cork. Picking up a glass from a tray on top of a console, he poured the warm wine, and offered it to Holly.

She shook her head.

Luke swigged down the contents in one gulp, put the glass down, and took Holly's hand, leading her to the couch where they had made love that first time. "You are entitled to an explanation. Ask whatever you need." His eyes, usually brilliant, were dulled by a film of frustration, tinged with remorse.

Holly's tongue was tied. *He knows my question. Why is he making me ask it?*

When she didn't speak, Luke took her hand in both of his, caressing it. "Okay. I'll take on the elephant. The answer to the question you won't ask is . . . I don't know. She spit the allegation at me in some of the hysterical phone calls."

Holly's heart stopped again. It wasn't what she hoped to hear. She wanted to run out of the room—perhaps out of his life. Because of the show, that option wasn't on the table. After a strained pause, she whispered, "Is it possible?"

He squeezed her hand. "I'm not proud to admit that there's a slight possibility, but I know she has the ability to lie. I didn't intend for a relationship to develop between you and me until I knew. . . . Damn, I wanted this resolved before I brought you into my life." He shook his head, clenching his jaw.

"You don't think it's true?"

"Does she look pregnant to you?"

"No, but her shirt was loose and some women don't show right away." Holly was trembling again.

"I haven't slept with Joy since weeks before I met you. I'm a sorry son-of-a-bitch but not quite that bad."

She stood up. "Maybe I will have a sip of that wine." She walked over to the tray, took a glass, and poured an inch of champagne. Standing for a moment, she watched the liquid settle and debated whether to follow through as she fought tears that were building. Suddenly, she put the rim to her lips, took a gulp, swallowed, and then put the glass down hard.

Luke rose and crossed over to Holly. He wrapped his arms around her, hugging her tight and pressing her head against his chest. "I hate myself for getting you mixed up in this mess, love. Believe me when I say that if I thought for certain she is carrying my child, I wouldn't have begun our relationship without telling you. She refuses to produce any proof, which intensifies my belief that it's a fabrication. However, all is takes is a whisper to the tabloids . . . and hello headlines."

"What if it is true, Luke? It would be your baby—your child."

"Holly, if Joy is pregnant, it isn't necessarily mine. You saw her. She's irrational. I would put nothing past her, from getting pregnant by someone else to artificial insemination. She's obsessed—maybe possessed."

"And if she *is* telling the truth?"

"She has a baby, and the DNA matches, I'll be there for the child. But, I'll have no relationship with Joy. I'm not an overly religious man, but I pray that there is no child, mine or otherwise. It would be doomed with Joy for a mother."

Holly lifted her head from his chest, turned, and looked him in the eye. "You would include the baby in your life?"

"Without question. I could never do what my father did to—"

The landline rang.

Pulling away, he answered. "Damian here." He looked toward Holly. "I understand. We'll be there."

"Who was that?"

"Jackson Forsythe."

"Oh, my gosh! Our executive producer?"

He nodded. "He wants to meet in the conference room upstairs at five-thirty."

"About Joy? How did he find out? Do you think that she'll be there?"

"I doubt it, but you know that with a scene like Joy made on the property, either the security team or Sam had to let the brass know what was happening."

Holly thought for a second. "You're right."

"I had better call Jeff before answering questions."

CHAPTER TWENTY-SIX

Although they managed to rehearse all afternoon, little was accomplished because of the emotional cloud blanketing the room.

Holly and Luke reached the top floor at the appointed time; the executive producer, two assistant producers, and the company attorney were already assembled.

Holly felt self-conscious as they entered the sleekly decorated conference room. Luke had insisted that she be present because of her position in the competition, and consequently her salary, was threatened by any adverse action against him.

As he shook hands with the executives, Luke announced that he would not discuss any business until his agent arrived. For approximately ten minutes, the group stood around, engaged in small talk. Holly smiled and accepted compliments on their last performance but, otherwise, remained silent and stared around the room at the rich mahogany paneling and built in cabinets displaying gleaming Emmys and autographed photographs.

When Jeff Corbett walked in, he was accompanied by Luke's attorney, Harvey Gold.

Holly felt awkward and wondered if she should be there at all. It wasn't really her issue, unless they knew about the personal relationship. *Could Sam have let the cat out of the bag?*

After introductions and handshakes all around, the group took their seats in the high-backed, swivel chairs. Sitting at the head of the table, Forsythe spoke first. "You know why I asked you to come up here, I'm sure."

From his place at the opposite end of the table, Holly seated on his right, Gold on his left, Luke nodded and said, "Before we begin, I have a question. How the hell did Joy Ambrose get through your security?"

Jackson Forsythe poured a glass of water and then answered. "She was cleared because she was on Art's calendar." He pointed to the assistant producer in charge of casting.

"On Art's calendar?" Luke looked puzzled.

"Her agent contacted my office," Forsythe continued, "and said that Ms. Ambrose was a huge fan of the show and would like a meeting to discuss becoming a contestant. Considering her current level of celebrity, I had Sally set up an interview with Art."

"Her agent was waiting in my office when word came in about the incident taking place in your rehearsal," Art interjected. "He immediately went down to help calm the situation."

To work out that elaborate a scheme, she certainly isn't just eye-candy, Holly thought.

Luke turned to Holly with an I-could-have-expected-as-much look on his face. Looking back toward Forsythe, he asked, "What do you want to know?"

"Luke, we respect that your personal life is your business, but I'm sure you understand that risk management requires that we take precautionary measures. Can you explain what's going on?"

Luke looked at Jeff, then his lawyer. Gold nodded and said, "Give him the facts, Luke."

It took Luke five minutes to recite the abridged version of his relationship with Joy, including her irrational behavior, the pregnancy allegation, and her acts of stalking. When he appeared finished, Forsythe spoke.

"First, understand, Luke, we have your back, but if there is potential threat of danger, or if it reflects negatively on the audience, the network, or our sponsors, we have to take action to contain the situation."

"Understood," Luke said.

"Do you believe she is dangerous?" the company attorney asked.

"I'm not qualified to make that call. I'm sure you've talked to your security people and to Sam. What was their take?"

"They all said that she behaved hysterically, but like you, they are reluctant to state a conclusion. Ms. Ambrose was escorted off the property by LAPD, assisted by her agent. I instructed our people to let the authorities take over." As he spoke, Forsythe twirled a Mont Blanc fountain pen between his gold-and-diamond adorned fingers. "I have to ask, Luke, why haven't you filed for a restraining order, if, like you say, she has been stalking you? And, why haven't you demanded a DNA test to see if she is carrying your child?"

"I can help you with the answers to those two questions, Jackson," Gold said. "Luke brought Jeff and me into the loop several weeks ago, and neither of us believe her story. As for a baby, California does not have a legal mechanism for requiring a woman to provide proof of a pregnancy outside of a defamation action. She cannot legally be required to undergo paternity testing until either a baby is born, or *she* opens a court case. On that point, Luke's hands are tied. As for a domestic violence restraining order, Luke has not wanted to enter into a he-said-she-said media fiasco."

"Can we cut to the chase here, Jackson?" Luke said. "Do you want me to withdraw from the competition?"

"Luke!" Jeff Corbett said, frowning.

Holly's stomach tensed, and she fought back tears. *Luke leave the competition?*

"Whoa." Jackson dropped his pen and held both hands up, palms outward. "We haven't said anything like that, Luke. The fans love you. The viewer response each week proves that you're an asset to us. As I said before, we've got your back. Unless you put the show in jeopardy of a lawsuit, we're behind you and will do whatever we can to help you with this mess."

Luke seemed to relax.

Carl Broadhurst, the production company attorney spoke. "In fact, we think we can help you with a restraining order."

"How's that?" Jeff interjected, his face showing interest.

"Sam has video of the entire incident, including Ms. Ambrose striking Luke. Should take it out of the he-said-she-said realm," Broadhurst said.

"You damned right it would," said Gold, his face registering instant satisfaction. "With that smoking gun, I can probably negotiate a consent order with Ms. Ambrose's attorney. It wouldn't help her career for that recording to go public."

"A copy is being made for you as we speak," Broadhurst said.

"I'll stay until it's ready," Gold replied.

Holly looked from speaker to speaker, relief sweeping over her.

"Then I think we're done here," said Forsythe as he started to rise.

"Wait a minute," Luke said.

All eyes turned toward him, including Holly's.

What now?

"I want to clear the air before speculation takes over."

What is he going to say? She wanted to stop him. *There's nothing he can add to improve the situation.*

"Holly and I are more than dance partners. It will get out sooner or later, and better you hear it from me. Regardless of what happens with Joy Ambrose, my loyalties are with Holly. If that's a problem, let's deal with it now."

Holly closed her eyes. *I don't believe he just did that.*

The room went quiet. No one moved or spoke for several seconds.

Breaking the silence, Forsythe spoke. "That's damned great news." He stood, looking from Luke to Holly and back to Luke. He then walked the length of the table, extended his hand, shook Luke's, and then patted Holly on the back.

Smiles broke out all around the production team.

"Hell, that's good for a ten-point-kick in the pants of old Nielsen. Right guys?" Forsythe looked at his assistant producers as he returned to his place at the head of the table.

Both raised a thumb affirming the declaration.

Sam was right. Thank you, God.

Without reclaiming his seat, Forsythe scooped up his cordovan portfolio and returned the fountain pen to his shirt pocket. "I think that about covers it, except to assure you, Luke, that our security people will be on high alert." He looked around the table. "Does anyone have more to add?"

The response from each of the group was negative.

Turning his attention toward Luke and Holly, Forsythe said, "Go home and get some rest. The two of you look drained."

Luke responded with an affirmative flick of his thumb.

Holly smiled.

Nice idea, but with Luke's struggle with the cha cha, we've got to work tonight.

The group disbursed, each shaking hands with Luke and nodding to Holly before departing. Several urged Luke to increase his personal security, commenting that it was difficult to assess the potential threat a stalker could present.

When the rest were gone, Luke took Holly's hand and led her to the elevators. Neither said anything until the doors glided closed.

"It's your call, captain. Want to work or follow Forsythe's suggestion?"

"I'd love to call it a day, but we're *going* to rehearse. I'll text Sam and tell him we'll be back in the studio at seven o'clock." Her tone had a slight edge.

As the elevator reached their floor, Luke put his finger on the stop button. "I know you're vexed. In my defense, my *protected* sexual encounters with Joy can be counted on one hand. The odds of her being pregnant are low." He paused, scrutinizing her face. "Holly, she did not make the claim until two months after our turn in the—"

She held her hand in the halt position. "Stop. Don't say it. I know what you mean."

"Holly, conventional wisdom says we men want to deny responsibility, but I promise you, that is not me. One of the reasons I was not interested in a long-term relationship with Joy was that her behavior struck me as dubious from the beginning." He shook his head, a negative expression forming on his face. "I don't think that I initiated a single date. I should have followed my instincts, but I told myself that I was being paranoid and went along when *she* made the plans for me to escort her to red carpet events."

He paused, staring at Holly as if expecting her to comment.

When she didn't, he said, "After the third date, I started to suspect that she might have a drug problem. If so, I wanted no part of it. That's when I began attempting to extricate myself." He took Holly's hand. "I did *not* sleep with her again."

She listened intently but still did not respond. *He cares. Forgive him. You don't want to lose him. But. . .*

Luke continued. "In hindsight, I should have finished the story when you asked about her."

"You should have. Coming from Joy, it blindsided me."

"Would it do any good to say that I'm sorry?" His expression was contrite.

"It wouldn't hurt, but it will still take me a little time to process the whole thing."

"Fair enough. Let me take you away from here for dinner—unless you would prefer to be alone."

Looking into his eyes, she hesitated and then shook her head slowly. "No. That's not what I want at all."

CHAPTER TWENTY-SEVEN

Rehearsals for their cha cha during the next few days did not go well. Holly wasn't sure whether it was Luke's mental block toward the style or the invisible residue that lingered from the Joy incident. Neither mentioned the model's name.

When Holly pushed him, Luke protested that he was trying his best to master the Latin dance style. She had hoped the beat of Jennifer Lopez's "Let's Get Loud" would loosen him up, but by Monday morning, it hadn't. She lost her patience.

"Two days until the show, and you're still not getting it."

"I'm not a hip-shaking kind of guy. I feel stupid."

"You're going to *look* stupid if you don't let go."

The expression on his face told Holly that she had been cruel.

"I'm sorry. That was mean."

"Forget it. You're right, but there's nothing I can do about it." He walked over to the cooler and took out a bottle of water.

Holly followed. "Do you remember what you said to me when I was having trouble putting out with the rumba?"

Luke turned and faced her but did not answer.

"*You* said that I had to psych myself out. You've got to do that now. Close your eyes and think Mika. You're an actor. Crawl into his skin. His hip-action is over the top, and it doesn't cost *that* sexy stud an ounce of masculinity." She turned toward Sam. "Isn't that right?"

The cameraman nodded.

"You can do it, Luke," she said.

He cocked an eyebrow. "Sexy stud, you say." His tone betrayed a trace of jealousy. "Mika is a Cossack Gumby. I'm a Brit—notoriously stiff—remember?"

Before she could argue further, Luke's cell rang. He put down the water and answered.

"Harvey. What's up?" A smile crossed his face and he walked toward the door, away from Sam and Holly but she could hear his comments.

"And the other?"

Ending the call, he returned to the bench and put the phone in his bag.

Holly watched—her curiosity piqued. *That must have been his lawyer. Judging from his expression, it was good news.*

Grinning at Holly, Luke said, "Let's get to work. I'm ready to kick cha cha arse."

Her eyebrows pinched together in a faux frown. "Oh, you are, are you? Care to share what changed your mood?"

Tipping his head and giving a tchick, he winked and said, "The restraining order is settled. Joy's lawyer, with the help of her agent, talked her into signing after Harvey provided a copy of the tape." His eyes danced as he spoke. "To decrease the risk of media exploitation, it'll be filed under her birth name, Joycelyn Armbruster, in Inyo County."

"Luke, that's phenomenal," Holly said, giving him a high-five.

Sam flashed Luke a thumbs-up.

"Any news about the baby?" she asked.

Luke shook his head. "Not yet."

Luke's style improved after his phone call from the lawyer but failed to duplicate Mika's. On Wednesday, their score put them in fourth place. Luke wasn't happy, but he did a good job of swallowing the disappointing performance and trying to look forward.

Leaving the studio after the show, Holly said, "The next few performances are critical. To make the finals, we can't afford any more slip-ups. Two couples are going home next week, and I don't want us to be one."

"As long as we don't have another wag-your-tail-feathers routine, I'll be fine."

"I'm going to hold you to that, Luke Damian. I think you'll like the new assignment. We're doing a fox trot to 'Stray Cat Strut.' Have you ever seen a Fred Astaire-Ginger Rogers movie?"

"England isn't a third world country, love. Of course, I've seen Astaire and Rogers."

"Then you know that the style is smooth and elegant. With our novelty music, we'll have to add a ton of personality."

He grimaced. "Tell me that we're not going to wear cat makeup and costumes, please."

"Relax. You're wearing a classic black tie. I'll be in a black camisole with sheer palazzo pants—no whiskers and no ears."

When they reached Holly's apartment, she picked up her mail from the gang of boxes inside the hallway. At the door to her apartment, she handed Luke the stack and her dance bag to hold while she fished her key from the depths of her purse. "I think that I'll have a key made for you so that I don't have to dig for mine," she said.

"Wow! You have that much trust in me."

She gave him a look that said, "As if you didn't know."

Once they entered her living room, he handed the mail back. As she accepted, two envelopes slipped to the floor. One caught Holly's eye. She stared at it for a moment, frowning. "That's weird."

Luke had started toward the bedroom but stopped and turned back toward her. "What?"

Holly held up a pink envelope, addressed in longhand. There was no return address, but on the back side was a crudely drawn sketch of a baby in a circle with an X drawn through it. The word *killer* was printed below the image. Her hand began to shake. As Luke reached for it, she looked at him, sending a silent message of fear.

"Damn her." Fire raged in his eyes.

"How did she find where I live?" Holly's voice shook.

He shook his head. "I don't know, but I'm calling Harvey Gold tomorrow morning and telling him to get you a restraining order against her, and I'm ordering security for you."

Although Luke and Harvey Gold were certain the unsigned letter to Holly was created and sent by Joy, obtaining a civil harassment restraining order for Holly would not be simple. The text only accused Holly of being responsible for the death of an unidentified baby. No explanation was provided as to how the alleged baby died.

"I don't understand the problem," Luke said to Gold on the telephone with Holly listening via speaker. "No one else would have sent such a despicable letter to Holly. I'm sure the handwriting can be matched, and there should be fingerprints on the stationery and envelope."

"Even if we can prove Joy Ambrose wrote the letter and mailed it to Holly, there is no explicit threat of harm. If she repeats the behavior, harassment should apply, but with only the one act, it's not likely."

Luke was frustrated. "You mean there's nothing we can do?"

"I can look into a potential defamation action, but there's no proof that she disseminated the information to others. And again, we would face a problem with proof that connected Ambrose to the letter. If we failed, she could turn the tables and sue Holly."

"So, what are you telling us to do?"

"Sit tight and wait for the next move."

Luke threw his phone on the bed. "I knew that I shouldn't let you become involved in my life until I resolved this nightmare."

Holly walked over and put her arms around him. "It's okay. I can handle it. We can handle it together."

He took her gently by the shoulders and held her at arm's length. Looking into her eyes, he said, "You are very special. I hope you know that." He then pulled her back and kissed her.

Holly dissolved in his arms, and they were late reaching the studio.

Despite the disappointing legal news, the morning rehearsal

went well. Holly breezed through the choreography, and Luke took on the style with ease.

"Well, this is a sharp contrast to work last week," she said as they took a break. "How does it look to you, Sam?"

"Looking good. Want to review the playback?"

"That would be great."

As the video played on the large screen TV, Holly watched intently, her chin resting on her folded hands, her expression revealing how pleased she was with the piece. When the screen went black, she said exuberantly, "It's even better than I thought. You're doing fantastic, Luke. And we're halfway through choreography on our first morning of rehearsal. I can't believe it."

With a slight grin, he said, "At the risk of sounding narcissistic, I do look pretty good."

"You're far more than good. Your frame is perfect; your lines are extended; your feet are working properly; and your personality is a showstopper. I couldn't ask for more."

He beamed.

At five o'clock, Holly called the rehearsal. As they changed to street shoes, Luke asked, "Do you want me to come home with you tonight?"

"Do you think she's sent another letter?"

"I hope not, but I don't want you to be alone if there is one."

Holly looked at the floor, thinking, for a few moments before speaking. *He's trying to be protective.* "Thanks for the concern, but Joy Ambrose is not going to dictate my life. I'll be fine." She looked him in the eye. "If it makes you feel better, I won't pick up my mail tonight. I'm not expecting anything that can't wait a day."

"Promise."

"I promise."

After assuring Luke that she would call him immediately if she felt uneasy, Holly left the studio and headed home. However, the model and the letter plagued her thoughts. *Should I have let him come with me?*

Delays caused by the rush hour gave Holly too much time to think. *Why is she claiming I killed a baby? Did she miscarry or have an abortion? What will she do next?*

For distraction, Holly turned on the radio. Carrie Underwood was singing "Casanova Cowboy." The image of Luke in their jive, wearing the ten-gallon hat, cocked over one eye, and tight jeans, flashed across Holly's mind, bringing a smile to her face and causing her heart to beat a little faster. *May the saints have mercy—that man turns me on.*

Reaching the complex, she parked in her assigned slot. Her pleasant mood continued as she entered the building hallway. Pausing in front of the mailboxes, a magnetic pull to open number 204 came over her, like the compulsion to scratch an insect bite.

Her finger was on the combination pad when Luke's voice echoed in her mind. *I promised I wouldn't.* She dropped her hand and walked briskly up the stairs to her apartment.

Since Luke had begun spending weekends with Holly, she used Thursday nights for laundry and housekeeping. As she walked into the apartment, the image of the anonymous letter resurfaced, causing her to shudder.

Maybe I should have let him come tonight.

As usual, Gigi had been waiting in front of the door. The cat mysteriously knew when her mistress arrived home. Following her usual pattern, the Persian came forward and rubbed against Holly's legs.

"We're okay, aren't we, girl? There's no reason to be afraid."

As she went to the kitchen to give Gigi fresh water, her landline rang. Holly flinched. *Stop it. You're letting this thing get out of hand. It's Mom or Dana.* Before lifting the receiver, she glanced at the caller ID. It read "Caller Unknown." A chill went down her spine.

Should I answer? Don't be silly. Calls from home come up that way—sometimes. And, Gabi's on tour out of the country. She could be calling.

She put the instrument slowly to her ear, listening for any familiar sounds. The only thing she heard was heavy breathing.

"Hello."

There was no response.

Whoever it is wants me to know they are there. Holly slammed the phone down, her hand shaking.

Frightened by the crash of plastic, Gigi scooted away.

I will not give in to this. That call could be totally unrelated—an obscene caller or a wrong number. Feed Gigi and get your work done.

Back in the kitchen, Holly put a low-cal, frozen dinner in the microwave and finished caring for the cat. While the food cooked, she stripped her bed and gathered dirty clothing. After starting the first load, she retrieved her meal and began eating.

An offensive ring pierced the silence. For a second or two, Holly sat motionless, dreading what might be in store. Taking a deep breath, she put her fork down, went to the phone, and found, to her relief, that it was a familiar number.

"Hey, Mom. How is everyone?"

"Healthy and dry, thank you, honey. I don't know if you heard that we have been having torrential rains."

"I'm sorry. I guess I didn't know that."

Abruptly switching subjects, Mary Lou said, "I thought you and Luke should have gotten higher scores last night."

"It is what it is," Holly responded. "We'll try to do better next week."

"I know you will, but that's not why I called. You haven't mentioned your plans for Thanksgiving."

Holly paused before answering. "Dana asked me the same thing. We are preempted by holiday specials that week, but I have no idea whether Luke plans to stay in L.A. If he stays, we need to put in extra work to redeem ourselves. You know that the last dances have to be worthy of a standing ovation."

"I understand. But, honey, Dad and I would like you to come home. We see so little—"

"No!" Holly shouted, dropping the phone.

"Holly, honey, what is it?"

There was no response from Holly.

Raising her voice, Mary Lou called out, "Holly? Can you hear me?"

CHAPTER TWENTY-EIGHT

Picking up the receiver, Holly said, "Sorry, Mom. I dropped the phone. Gigi was about to sample my tuna casserole. Listen, can I call you back in a day or two and let you know about Thanksgiving?"

After hanging up, Holly finished eating, cleaned up the kitchen, and was switching laundry to the dryer when the phone rang again. Absorbed in thoughts about Thanksgiving, she absentmindedly answered without checking the ID.

"Did you forget something?" Holly said into the phone, assuming it was her mother.

There was silence on the line for several seconds before an instrumental version of "Rock-a-bye Baby" played.

She slammed the phone down so hard that it fell off the table. Crying, Holly jerked the cord out of the wall socket. *How could I have been so stupid?* For a minute, she stared at the disconnected instrument, and then, pulling herself together, she plugged it back in and called Luke.

He picked up on the third ring.

Her voice breaking, she said, "I shouldn't have called you, but I'm upset."

"Of course, you should have called me, love. Did you get another letter?"

"No—at least not that I know. I did what you said and didn't look at my mail."

"Tell me what's happened?"

"Anonymous phone calls. What will she do next?"

"I'm on my way. Close your curtains. Do not answer the phone or the door for anyone but me. I'll call your cell when I'm in the stairwell. I don't think she would come to your apartment, but I don't really know what she's capable of doing."

"Am I in danger?"

"You should be safe, love, because I have surveillance on your building."

"Really?"

"I said last night that I planned to order security for you."

"I didn't know you had. Luke, she may be doing this to lure you into an ambush. Be careful."

It took him less than an hour to reach Holly's apartment. During that time, she sat locked in her bedroom with Gigi. He arrived, accompanied by a security agent, whose muscles threatened to rupture the seams of his sharply tailored suit. Opening the door, Holly collapsed in a torrent of tears as Luke grasped her in his arms.

"We're going to move you to my place tonight. It's more secure—no offense, Ken."

"I can't do that, Luke. I can't leave Gigi." She wiped her face with the shirttail of her blouse. "Remember what happened to the rabbit in *Fatal Attraction*."

"You're not going to leave her. She's coming." He motioned toward the bodyguard. "Ken and I will help you pack."

The agent responded, "Just tell me what to do."

"I don't know where to start," Holly said, obviously confounded.

"Just bring the essentials," Luke said. "If we can't resolve this, I'll have you relocated to a new apartment."

"You can't do that."

"I can, and I will." His tone was resolute—his jaw clenched.

"I could never let you do that."

"I got you into this, and it's my responsibility to protect you." Luke took her gently by the shoulders and looked eye to eye with her. "I would, even if it weren't my responsibility." He turned loose of her left shoulder and brushed a tear from her cheek. "I will *not* let anything happen to you—or Gigi."

By the time Holly and her cat were in Luke's home, it was after midnight. The events were surreal to Holly. Despite how much time they had spent together, it was her first time at his condominium; however, she was too disturbed by the circumstances to make much of an assessment at first. They decided that Gigi needed the comfort of being with her mistress in the strange environment. Holly needed the assurance that the cat would not try to escape and attempt to return to their home. Luke put the litter box in his bathroom and made a bed in the corner of his room with a spare quilt. Of course, the cat ignored his effort and chose to nest in his closet.

As he hung Holly's clothes next to his, he pointed to the rack and said, "They look very comfortable together, don't you think?"

She couldn't help but smile.

When the unpacking was finished, Luke went to a console in his dining room and took out a bottle of wine. "I think you need something to relax you."

"I'm okay. I'm beginning to think that I may have overreacted."

"No. After the way Joy broke into our rehearsal, the letter she sent, and the brazen calls, we have every reason to be apprehensive about what she will do next. She may be just a spoiled, immature kid who can't accept not having her way, or, she may be totally deranged."

As he poured two glasses of the wine, Holly looked around the tastefully decorated space. The blend of furniture styles—plump upholstered pieces with period cabinetry and tables—was eclectic. Framed magazine covers from his modeling and teen-idol days hung on one wall. Holly recognized some of the latter as duplicates of ones she had in her youth. She crossed the room to take a closer look.

"Homage to my past," he said, coming up behind her.

"I had those three," she said, pointing to the wall. "That was my favorite." She referred to an image of Luke by the deer park fence at Magdalen College, Oxford. His blond hair was tousled and his pastel-blue eyes sparkled. He wore a dark-blue plaid shirt, under a light-tan, crew neck sweater. "I had the poster, too."

"I wish I had known you then," he said. "Platonically, of course."

She laughed. "Not half as much as I wished, *then*, that I knew you—and *not* platonically."

He grinned. "Think you're relaxed enough for bed?"

She put her glass down. "I think so. Is it okay if I take a shower? I didn't have a chance before everything exploded."

"Of course. Take your time. I'll try to stay awake."

When Holly finished her shower and got into bed, Luke was dozing. As she slipped under the sheet, he awoke, reached over, and pulled her close. She expected him to make love to her, but he didn't. Instead, he wrapped her in his arms, cocoon fashion, and held her for most of the night. All her fears melted away in his embrace.

The tranquility of the night disappeared in the cold light of day when they had to confront what had happened. Despite not getting to sleep until one-thirty, they were both up by seven. Luke put on a kettle to make a pot of tea. "Would you prefer coffee?" he asked.

"No. Tea is good, but you never ask for it at my house."

"I don't drink anything made from those little American bags, love."

"You wouldn't be a snob, would you?"

"Where my tea is concerned, I confess. Watch, and I'll show you how it should be made."

"Raincheck. I need to text Sam and warn him that we'll be late today." She started back toward the bedroom but turned. "Are you sure you don't mind Gigi staying here?"

"Positive. As long as she's here, I know you'll return."

Luke and Holly arrived at Harvey Gold's office at eight o'clock. Luke had called his home and scheduled the appointment.

After being filled in about the anonymous phone calls, the lawyer said, "If Ms. Ambrose is the caller, she is escalating."

"It couldn't be anyone else, Harvey." Luke said. "Can't we get Holly's phone records and prove it was Joy?"

Tapping his pen on the legal pad, where he had been making notes, Gold nodded, frowning simultaneously. "In an ideal world, yes, but she likely used a disposable phone. From what I've seen of the woman so far, she's not stupid." He turned to Holly. "Have you checked your voice mail for messages, today?"

Holly shook her head. "I didn't want to hear any more. I unplugged the phone after calling Luke and never plugged it back in."

"Harvey, I hope you're not saying that we're no better off than yesterday." Luke's expression exposed his frustration.

"Patience, Luke. Catching anonymous stalkers is difficult. If Holly's voice-mail service is through a carrier, it captures calls without an instrument connected. Shall we check?" He punched the speaker button on his phone and turned it toward Holly to dial.

She turned to Luke, a look of panic on her face.

"Go ahead, love. We need to know."

Holly closed her eyes for a second, took a deep breath, and made the call. As the trio sat motionless, six messages with the same "Rock-a-bye Baby" music played. According to the service, one call came on each hour, starting at nine p.m. and ending at one a.m. The sixth came in only minutes before Holly dialed.

"She must have been calling between TV shows," Luke said, staring at the phone.

"It's definitely harassment," Gold said. "Could also be characterized as intentional infliction of emotional distress—a civil cause of action—but a hard case to make."

"What about the police? Should we file a report?" Luke said, leaning forward and putting his palms down on Gold's desk.

"I would definitely advise Holly to talk to LAPD's Threat Management Unit, even though the woman has not made an overt threat. Ms. Ambrose doesn't have to be named in the initial report, since the contacts have been anonymous." He turned toward Holly and, in a sympathetic tone, said, "If questioned by a detective, report your suspicions."

"What is she hoping to accomplish?" Holly asked.

"The bit— witch is barmy," Luke said, taking her hand in an attempt to comfort her.

"Maybe," Gold said and turned back to Holly. "She either wants Luke—or wants to hurt him. Either way, she wants you out of the picture."

"Why would anyone believe that harassment would engender a positive result?" Luke rubbed his temples as though he had a headache. "So, what do you suggest we do next?"

"Make the report and, as a precaution, keep a security detail on the two of you at all times. If she continues, she'll likely slip up—maybe lose interest. I'll make a call to a contact at LAPD and set up an appointment for you.

As Luke drove them to the studio after leaving Gold's office, he held Holly's hand. "I'm sorry that your freedom is going to be clouded by constant security."

"I don't see that happening. Bodyguards would be way above my pay grade."

He squeezed her hand. "Not your problem. I obviously need protection. You and Gigi will stay with me. As long as we're together, my team is your team."

She looked at him. *Do I dare take him up on that?* "Twenty-four-seven?"

"All times we're not at the studio. After Joy's intrusion last week, Forsythe will make certain we're safe on the property." He chuckled.

"What the hell do you think is funny?"

"The irony of it all. In trying to break us up, Joy has brought us closer together. I couldn't have talked you into moving in with me, otherwise."

"I wouldn't call it moving in." Holly smiled for the first time that morning. "You didn't set this up, did you?"

"I'm not that devious, or that smart, love."

Sam was drinking his morning Starbucks when the two walked into the studio. "Late night?"

"You could say that," Luke said.

"But, not what you're thinking," Holly added.

"Cameramen aren't paid to think. We're invisible robots, recording history. I could set up equipment all around this room and stay at home, but don't tell anyone, or I'll be out of a job."

"You could always join the vulture club, torturing celebrities for the shots the tabloids pay big bucks to publish," Luke said.

"Not my style. I'm way too old and too lazy for that frenzy. I'd probably have to go back to weddings and bar mitzvahs."

They all laughed.

"Okay, guys. Cut the comedy. We have work to do." Holly was stretching at the barre. "Warm up, Luke. You know the drill. Just because you looked good, yesterday, doesn't mean you can slack off today. We're going to nail this one."

"Yes, ma'am."

Watching Holly in action, an observer would never have thought that she was going through emotional hell. For the next three hours, she pushed Luke hard, demanding that, despite his good lines, he could be even better. "Lengthen your leg in that lunge. . . . Deeper. Plie deeper, Luke—deeper. . . . More shoulder action."

"Are you sure you were never in the military?" he asked at noon, his shirt wet with perspiration. "I hear the Green Berets are missing a drill sergeant."

"Very funny, Kimmel." Smiling, she got up in his face, pointing her finger at his nose, her eyes blazing. "I am going to make you a champion."

He grabbed her around the waist, pulled her against his chest, and kissed her on the mouth.

Despite an overwhelming desire to melt into his embrace, Holly pulled away. "Luke! We're not alone."

"He knows," Luke said, pointing to Sam, who was nodding—a grin on his face.

"Okay. It's time to break for lunch," Holly said. "Back here at one-thirty, Sam."

"Make it two," Luke said. "We have an errand to run."

"Copy that," Sam said.

When Sam was out of the room, Holly turned to Luke. "What errand?"

"I had a text from Harvey. We need to be at the LAPD station on 1st Street at one. We can grab a sandwich from the commissary and eat on the way."

CHAPTER TWENTY-NINE

The detective taking the information from Holly and Luke confirmed Harvey Gold's reservations concerning what action could be taken to stop the harassment. He listened to the telephone messages, agreed to dust the letter for fingerprints, and promised to trace the phone that had called Holly. However, he warned them that it was likely a burner.

"We take these situations seriously, Mr. Damian. Unfortunately, the lack of evidence often frustrates our ability to act. I don't have to tell you to save any further voice-mail messages, text messages, emails, or letters."

The detective pulled apart the copies of the completed incident report and placed each in a folder. "Fortunately, the majority of alleged stalkers are harmless. It's the ones suffering from mental illness that we need to fear. I'll touch base with you when we obtain information about the phone used to harass Ms. Dawson." He stood and took two cards from a holder on his desk, handing one to Holly and another to Luke. "Call me if anything further occurs."

"We're not going to let Joy compromise our place in the competition," Holly said as Luke drove them back to the studio.

"Absolutely right." He reached over and gave her thigh a squeeze. "On the *bright* side—at the risk of repeating myself—I could not have gotten you to move in with me if this had not happened."

Turning slightly, she cut her eyes toward him, her brows pinched together. "At the risk of repeating *myself*—I have not moved in with you. We are *not* living together. I am simply your guest until this is resolved."

Luke glanced around at her, a grin on his face. "A rose by any other . . . you know the rest."

The weekend passed without trauma. Holly found it easy to relax in Luke's home. However, Gigi wasn't so quick to adapt. She refused to eat, drink, or use her box, hiding away in the corner of the closet.

"Should you take her to a cat doctor or something?" Luke asked on Saturday evening when they arrived home after rehearsing all day.

"I will, if she doesn't give in by Monday or Tuesday. Cats don't like change. She stayed under my bed for five days when we moved to L.A. On the fifth night, she jumped on me, demanding attention at three a.m."

He shook his head as in disbelief. "I guess that I'm still on the feline learning curve."

"And being a good sport about it, too." She walked toward the bedroom, pulling the elastic band off her ponytail. "Mind if I take my shower, first?"

"Be my guest. I'm going to have a cup of tea and relax—maybe make a dinner reservation."

Fifteen minutes later, Holly came out of the bathroom, her hair wet, wearing a terry robe. Luke was stretched out on the sofa.

"You checked my voice mail, didn't you?" she asked, making eye contact.

"Sure you want to know?"

"Yes. I don't want to listen, but I want to know about them. Give."

"More of the same—the recording and heavy breathing."

"How many?"

"I didn't count, but I'd guess about ten." He broke eye contact with her as he spoke.

"There's something you're not telling me. I can tell."

"Don't push it, love. Don't let her ruin our weekend. You are good at putting it aside when we work. Hey, why don't we take a holiday out of the city, tomorrow? We can afford the day off—don't you think?"

"You're not going to tell me, are you?"

"No."

After a leisurely Sunday breakfast, Holly and Luke took off in his Spider, top down—destination unknown.

"We'll just drive up the Pacific Coast Highway for several hours, stop for lunch, and turn back for home," he said as he cranked the car.

"And forget the competition and everything else except what a beautiful day it is."

"That's my girl. Good attitude."

They were barely twenty miles out of Los Angeles, when Holly turned toward him. "You know we have the week of Thanksgiving off?"

"I remember it being mentioned somewhere along the way."

"My family wants me to come home, but I told Mom that if you stayed in L.A., we needed to use the time for extra work to improve our chance of winning. Have you made plans?"

"None that don't include you."

"Be serious. Are you planning to leave the city?"

"Why do you *not* believe that I was serious? But, to answer your question, I have no plans. We can work, but I don't want *you* to miss a chance to spend time with your family." Reaching up to adjust the rearview mirror, he continued, "It would do you good to bury the stress of the past couple of weeks and to escape the necessity of the security detail in that car behind us."

Holly listened but did not respond.

Glancing at the dashboard, Luke said, "Excuse me, love." Punching in a number on his phone, he called the bodyguard. "I better fill up. I'm pulling off at the next exit."

When Luke turned off the road and into a service station, the trailing SUV followed, pulling in behind him at the pump."

Holly watched as he got out, swiped his Platinum AmEx card, and then filled the tank.

As he sat back in the driver's seat, she said, "I've been thinking. Would you consider going home with me for Thanksgiving?"

He looked at her. "You mean Florida?"

"Uh-huh. No one would have to know where we are, so no need for security." The more she talked, the more enthusiastic she became. "My parents have plenty of space. You could sleep in my brother's old room."

A smile crept across his face. "I couldn't impose on your family. I doubt they want a stranger at their holiday table, especially the foreign chap who made their daughter the target of a stalker."

"My parents know nothing about Joy, and they would *not* mind. Mom loves to cook for a crowd. She's in her glory." Her eyes sparkled. "We could rehearse at my old dance studio." And then her expression changed. "But if you don't want to, I understand."

"Wait a minute. I didn't say that I don't want to. I just don't want to intrude." He turned his attention back to starting the car. "You haven't told them about the letter and the calls?"

"No, and I'm not going to. If Mom knew, she would decide that the Son of Sam, the Boston Strangler, and Charles Manson were all after me."

"Now, I feel even worse."

"It's not your fault."

The car was silent for several moments before Luke responded. "Okay. But, I want you to discuss the invitation with your mom before I accept."

"Does that mean you'll go?"

He pulled the car away from the pump and headed back to the highway. "It means that I'd be delighted to go home with you, Ms. Dawson, if your parents are onboard."

Yes, yes, yes. They will be. The thought of Luke in Jacksonville gave Holly an adrenaline rush.

Spending Sunday away from L.A. gave both Holly and Luke a welcomed respite. The stress of phone calls and the competition were temporarily put on hold as they exchanged stories of their respective childhoods, took in the sights, and enjoyed a quiet lunch in an out-of-the-way café.

Driving back into the city at sunset, a veil of gloom, brought on by returning to reality, blanketed Holly's thoughts.

"Don't go there," Luke said, noticing her pursed lips and the lines that had formed on her brow when he stopped for a traffic light.

"You're right." She forced a smile and gave him a thumbs-up. "The day has been too nice to let anything spoil it."

"And I know just how to end it," he said, giving her a devilish look.

Holly tipped her head to the side, looking him up and down flirtatiously. "I'll just bet you do."

When they reached Luke's condo, Holly took a shower while he ordered Chinese food. When she came out of the bathroom, he was propped up on the bed in his stocking feet, watching a video of their latest rehearsal. "Come here, beautiful. Look at this. We are bloody *brilliant.*" He gave her a high-five. "If I can avoid making a stupid blunder, we've got this week in the bag." Taking her hand, he pulled her down on the bed next to him. "Can't wait to get back in the studio, tomorrow."

"Have I created a monster?"

"No. You tamed a monster." He leaned over, kissed her, and then looked back at the screen. "Look. I'm dancing—and jolly-well fine."

"You've been dancing for weeks."

"No. No. I'm *really* dancing. Look." He pointed to the iPad. "That's Luke Damian."

Holly smiled, shaking her head. *He's like a little boy who just learned to ride a bike without training wheels.* "Why don't you take your shower? After dinner, we'll restart the video and watch together."

"Splendid." He stood up and peeled off his shirt, exposing his tanned torso with its washboard abs.

As he walked toward the bathroom, tossing the shirt over the back of a chair and unfastening his jeans, Holly's eyes followed. *Oh, my gosh. I am so, so . . . no, no, not in love . . . in heat.*

Rehearsals progressed smoothly on Monday and Tuesday. Mysteriously, after Sunday night no messages were left on Holly's voice mail. She wanted to believe that Joy was losing interest, but Luke warned her against making premature assumptions. A call from the LAPD detective was disappointing. The caller's phone could not be traced, and the lab was unable to lift an identifiable print from the letter.

The couple had made a pact that where Joy and the anonymous communications were concerned, a moratorium would be in effect on show day. Neither would check Holly's mail or telephone messages. Regardless of what was going on in their personal lives, it would not be allowed to affect their performance.

When the last bar of "Stray Cat Strut" played on Wednesday night, the audience went wild. Even the judges rose, applauding the couple.

"Holly, where have you been hiding this dancer? His footwork and frame were perfection," Lorraine Gibson commented, pinching her thumb and forefinger together in the a-okay sign.

Harry Fellows was even more complimentary. "Superb, my friend," he said, addressing Luke. "Absolutely superb. You will most definitely be in the finals this season." He then pointed to Holly. "And very nice choreography, my lady."

Kikki Donavan slapped her palms on the desk in front of her. "Not only were you spot-on in that routine, Luke, you rock that tux." She then made a gesture like a cat slapping her paw, claws extended. "Meow."

"Sounds like you two are going to like the numbers, tonight," Ted Serianni, the host, said.

Serianni was right. The tally mirrored the comments, putting Luke and Holly once again in first place with a perfect score.

Hearing the total, Luke grabbed Holly by the waist, lifted her up, and spun around. Letting her down, he pointed to the top of her head and mouthed the words to the audience, "It is all because of her." Turning back toward Serianni, he said, "I'm loving this show and this lady."

A chill came over Holly.

As they ran off the set, Luke held her by the waist. When out of camera range, he pulled her around and kissed her. Kat and Lisa saw and gave one another aha looks, their eyebrows raised.

"Anything you two want to tell us?" Kat asked.

Holly brushed her off with a not-going-there look.

When they reached an area where they were alone, Holly stopped and faced Luke. "Have you lost your mind? Lisa and Kat are going to tell everyone."

"Do I look like I care?"

"Well, you should. You know it's better to keep our relationship private, at least until the competition is over. Neither of us wants to be this week's couple-of-the-hour and then next week's split du jour—to say nothing of adding fuel to Joy's fire."

"My but you're pretty when agitated; however, I'll tell you what. I'll behave if you'll not assume our relationship has an expiration date."

His declaration made her heart beat a little faster. *Slow down, Holly. It's too soon for long-range ideas.*

The week after Holly and Luke's big win with the foxtrot, they did an Argentine tango that earned a tie for the top score and a place in the semi-finals. The harassing calls seemed to have stopped. Assuming Joy had lost interest, Holly began planning a return to her apartment. However, on Friday, the bubble burst when Luke received a phone call from his agent.

"Forget moving back to your apartment." Luke stuffed his cell back in his pocket. "Jeff just found out Joy has been in Italy, working on a campaign for an Italian designer. At least that decreases the likelihood that she's pregnant. But, there's no way to know what will happen when she returns to the States."

"You don't think she would have done something from there if she were still in revenge mode?"

He shrugged. "What could she do from Europe? I think she

would be afraid a call from Italy might show the country of origin, which would implicate her. Anything mailed would bear all the international stamps."

Holly looked down, a defeated expression on her face. "Then, I'll pray she finds an irresistible Italian and forgets about you." She then lifted her chin with an air of confidence.

"Now that would be jolly good."

"No matter what, next Wednesday we escape to Florida." She raised her arm with a fist-pump.

He nodded and bumped his fist with hers.

CHAPTER THIRTY

"Hey, Mom, it's me. We just landed. With rush-hour traffic, it could take us an hour or more to get there." Holly put her phone back in her purse and began gathering her personal items. Turning to Luke, she said, "Welcome to Jacksonville."

"Thank you." He grinned.

True to Holly's prediction, their taxi reached the two-story, brick house in the San Marco area a few minutes after five p.m. Mary Lou Dawson greeted them, wearing a light-blue polo, khaki slacks, and loafers. Her light-brown hair, cut in short layers, sparkled with threads of silver.

"Luke, it's so nice to meet you." Mary Lou started to offer him her hand and then, in a change of mind, put her arms around him and gave him a quick hug. "The family is thrilled that you're spending the holiday with us. Come on in."

"I appreciate your generous hospitality, Mrs. Dawson. I've been looking forward to meeting Holly's family."

Holly watched, holding Gigi's carrier and analyzing her mother's interaction with Luke. *She's nervous with him.*

Mary Lou turned to Holly and gave her a hug. "So good to have you home, honey." Releasing her daughter, Mary Lou stepped aside to allow them to enter. "I'm sure the two of you are exhausted. How long did the trip take?"

"We took off from L.A. at six a.m., California time," Holly responded.

Mary Lou made a face. "I'm not a good traveler, so that would be brutal for me, but Holly's used to it after all her touring. I'm sure you are too, Luke."

He nodded, still holding the handles of his and Holly's roller boards. "True."

"Luke, Holly's dad and I are indebted to you for agreeing to come here. Otherwise, she would have insisted on staying in California to work."

"It's entirely my pleasure, Mrs. Dawson."

"Turning to Holly, Mary Lou said, "Why don't you show Luke to Chris's old room? The two of you can freshen up and recoup for a while before dinner. Your dad won't be home for at least an hour."

As Mary Lou spoke, a small Havanese came running into the entry hall, her claws clicking on the hardwood floor. Seeing Luke, the dog skidded to a stop, her frantic barking causing her little body to flutter.

"Hush, Cindy. Luke's a friend," Holly said as her mother picked up the seven-pound canine.

"Offer her your hand slowly, Luke. It'll take her a minute or two, and she'll be fine," Mary Lou said.

Leaning back, he looked skeptical. "Does she bite?"

Holly grinned. "Not yet, but you could be the first." She found it amusing that the six-foot-two man was intimidated by the little bubble of fur.

Luke gave Holly a sharp look, raising one eyebrow.

"I'm kidding. Go ahead. She's a typical female. You'll charm her."

Narrowing his eyes, he lowered his chin and then slowly extended his hand. "How does the dog and cat thing work?"

"No problem," Holly said, watching the dog sniff his fingers and then begin licking them. "Cindy knows better than to cross the DCZ line."

"DCZ line?"

"Danger! Cat Zone" She made a circle with her free hand. "Four-feet around Gigi."

Looking up at Mary Lou, he smiled. "You'll have to forgive me, Mrs. Dawson. I didn't grow up with pets, but I'm learning. The cat actually allows me to feed her."

"Please call me Mary Lou, Luke. And I know you have Gigi's

stamp of approval, otherwise, Holly wouldn't give you the time of day."

He smiled and glanced at Holly. "I got that early on."

As Mary Lou put Cindy down, the phone rang. She excused herself, waving the couple toward the staircase.

Luke carried their luggage as Holly led the way up the steps. On the second-floor landing, she pointed to the right. "Your room is at the end of the hall."

"And yours?"

"The opposite end. Leave your suitcase here and follow me. I'll show you."

"A safety zone between us, I see."

"Something like that. The other two are Mom's art studio and a small exercise room. I'm sure Mom considers them the morality zone. She can tell her friends that Holly's celebrity friend stayed with us, but they had separate rooms at opposite ends of the house. My parents know we're adults, but they are old fashioned. If we're sleeping together, they don't want to know about it or appear to approve."

"I understand and respect that. Where is their room?"

"Downstairs." Reaching her room, she opened the door. "This is mine. As you can see, Mom is sentimental and keeps everything like it was when I left. Chris's room is the same. You'll be sleeping with basketball trophies and surfboards."

Walking in, Luke looked around the feminine décor—ruffled curtains, painted furniture, and a canopy bed. A corner étagère displayed porcelain ballerinas and cats, along with a pair of satin pointe shoes and photos of Holly in ballet costumes at different ages.

"Where are the posters?" he asked as Holly put the cat carrier on her bed and unlatched the door.

"What posters?" Then she realized what he meant. "Oh! My god, Luke. That was over ten years ago. I grew up."

"You didn't keep them?" His eyes twinkled, mischievously.

She gave him a reproving look but did not answer. Walking to her closet, she opened the door, dug through the contents for a second, and then pulled out three rolled-up posters.

"Voila! . . . Satisfied?"

A huge grin spread across his face as she unrolled them. "I'll be damned. You weren't kidding."

"I most certainly wasn't. I'll have you know that I lay on that bed, every Friday night, for two years, glued to *Alexander Holmes* on my little TV screen. The fourteen-year-old me dreamed of what it would be like to be held and kissed by you."

"Well . . . do allow me to demonstrate." He took her in his arms and their lips met in a passionate kiss.

Holly felt her body heat rising. Then, she caught herself and tried to pull away, putting her fists against his chest. "Whoa. Save that thought, cowboy."

As they separated, he whispered, "Maybe I'll get to finish that dream for you before we leave."

"Maybe." Her eyes sparkled. "But in the meantime, put your libido in park."

He squeezed her and then reached down to pet Gigi. Accepting the attention for a moment, the cat then jumped down and ran toward the bathroom.

"Where's she going in such a hurry?" he asked.

"Litter box. She knows where it is, and she's been in that carrier all day."

"On that note, if you'll show me to my quarters, I'll shower and change."

Les Dawson ran late, arriving home at seven-thirty. "Sorry I couldn't get here earlier," he said, shaking hands with Luke and then giving Holly a hug. "With holiday shopping kicking off Friday, there were things that had to be lined up before I could leave."

"No problem. We've been catching up on everything Jacksonville with Mom."

Mary Lou turned to Luke. "When you're married to a business owner, you get used to unpredictable hours. That's why I plan forgiving meals. Go wash up for dinner, Les, while Holly and I put dinner on the table."

A few minutes later, Mary Lou positioned a large tureen of sirloin tips and gravy on the table, while Holly brought in a crystal bowl filled with rice. A wooden bowl of garden salad was already in place. "Honey, if you'll take the rolls out of the oven, I'll bring in the squash casserole, and we'll be ready to eat."

"It looks and smells delicious," Luke said, standing next to the fruitwood table.

"It's simple comfort food, not fancy gourmet. I'm sure that you're accustomed to dining in some of the best restaurants," Mary Lou responded.

"The best restaurants don't always have the best food. I've found that nothing compares to home cooking."

When Les arrived in the dining room, they all sat down, joined hands, and he said grace.

Dinner conversation centered on Luke and Holly's TV routines. Mary Lou knew every dance and how they had scored. She had her own opinions about the judging. Les had watched each segment, but didn't know a tango from a mambo. His comments were limited to either the music or the costumes.

"Dad hates my abbreviated costumes," Holly said.

"I know better than to comment on that," Luke responded.

"Guilty as charged," Les said and wiped his mouth with a cloth napkin. "I can't understand why they have to be so . . . so—"

"Risqué?" Holly said.

"To say the least, not to mention the risk of, what do they call it . . . costume malfunction? If you ever have a daughter, Luke, you'll know what I mean."

Luke moved his head up and down, his facial expression indicating he agreed with Les.

"Are you enjoying doing the show, Luke?" Mary Lou asked.

Gazing affectionately at Holly for a moment before responding, Luke said, "It's one of the hardest things that I've ever done, but having Holly as my instructor has made it one of the best."

"We're proud of her. I want you to know that I vote every week," Mary Lou said. "I think you have a great chance of winning."

"Shh. Don't jinx us, Mom," Holly said.

"What's for dessert, Mary Lou?" Les asked.

"Boston cream pie—Holly's favorite."

"With all the lifts coming up in our routines, Luke's going to hate you when I gain ten pounds this weekend, Mom."

As Mary Lou stood and went to the buffet for the after-dinner treat, Les looked at Luke. "I have to say, you're not the typical type I'm used to seeing Holly dance with," Les said.

"That's because Luke is not a dancer, Dad. He's an actor."

"Right. I knew that. He was the one on that TV show you liked when you were in your teens."

Holly's face flushed. "Let's skip that subject. Luke knows all about my adolescent crush on him."

Turning around, Mary Lou gave her husband a dirty look.

Les shrugged his shoulders. "I didn't mean to ruffle feathers. Forget I brought it up."

"It's okay." Holly put her hand on her father's arm. "But let's talk about your new store."

After dinner, Luke joined Les in the family room for a snifter of brandy while Holly and her mother cleaned the kitchen.

"How many are coming for dinner tomorrow?" Holly asked Mary Lou as they hung their dish towels to dry.

"Just our family, Aunt Susan, Uncle Len, and the Carters."

"That's ten with Chris and Regina. Are you and Dad still playing bridge every week with the Carters?"

"Over twenty years. They're looking forward to seeing you and meeting Luke."

"They're familiar with Luke?"

"Honey, Lorna watches *Lights, Camera—Dance* as religiously as I do. She thinks Luke is a dreamboat."

Holly smiled. "He is."

"He seems like a nice young man, sweetheart. But you do know that he's been married and divorced—twice."

"I know that, Mother. We spend a lot of time together. How do you know it?"

Mary Lou looked around as if she feared someone listening. "I Googled him. It said that he is dating a supermodel. Is he? I couldn't believe that he would come home with you if he's dating someone else."

Holly tipped her head quizzically. "He's not dating her any longer. When did you start using a computer?"

"Well, that's good to know." Mary Lou took her apron off and hung it on a hook in the pantry. "I *am* using the computer and loving it. I signed up for classes, along with three of the girls from the garden club and one of the other docents from the museum. I even made a Facebook page last weekend."

Holly smiled at her mother. "I'm proud of you. A real, twenty-first-century woman."

"Do you think Luke would mind if I took a picture and posted it on my page?"

Holly frowned. "Mother. Do you really want to do that? It might send the wrong message."

"Phooey. Who's going to see my page other than a few friends? He doesn't seem like he would mind."

"He probably wouldn't, but don't go overboard with your post."

CHAPTER THIRTY-ONE

Thanksgiving Day started early. By the time Holly and Luke came downstairs at eight-thirty, Mary Lou had been up several hours, and the kitchen was filled with aromas of turkey roasting, pumpkin pies baking, and yeast dough rising.

"There's fresh coffee in the pot," Mary Lou said when the couple appeared. "I can make tea if you prefer, Luke. I know you British like your tea."

Holly chuckled. "Don't even think about it, Mom."

He gave her a dirty look as if daring her to expose his tea obsession. "Coffee is fine. Thank you, Mary Lou."

"There are ham biscuits and fresh fruit in the refrigerator, and you know where everything else is, Holly."

"We're good, Mom. When is Chris coming?"

Mary Lou finished kneading the dough and began breaking off pieces for cloverleaf rolls. "Regina said they would be here about twelve-thirty. She's still battling morning sickness. Chris is making the cranberry salad."

"My brother, cooking?" Holly looked at Luke with a puzzled expression. "Will wonders never cease?"

"Chris has become quite domestic. I'm proud of him," Mary Lou said.

Holly turned to Luke. "Let's get you squared away with breakfast, and you can go sit on the patio with Dad. I know you won't enjoy our hen-talk."

He smiled, looking relieved to have an escape.

Holly prepared a tray and led him outside where her father was relaxing on a chaise lounge with his coffee and a book.

"Have a seat, my boy. Make yourself comfortable. We have good weather, today."

"It's a grand day," Luke said as he swung one leg across the companion chaise and lowered himself into place while Holly placed his food on a table.

"I'll leave you two to solve the world's problems," Holly said as she left them.

By the time guests began arriving, everything was ready. Holly greeted her brother, a six-foot-four, brown-haired man with green eyes like hers, at the door. She gave her petite sister-in-law a hug, congratulating her on the pregnancy, and then led them into the family room where Luke was sitting with her father.

"So, you are the movie star," Chris said, shaking Luke's hand.

Holly punched him on the arm.

"What did I do? You are a movie star, aren't you, Luke? I know she was gaga over you when she was a kid."

Holly's face turned red. "You shouldn't be let out of your cage without a gag."

Chris grabbed her around the shoulders and pulled her close in a bear hug. "Just giving you a hard time, sis. Sorry, Luke. If I embarrassed you, it's probably because I'm jealous. My wife was pretty taken with you as well."

Regina nodded. "He's right, Luke. I loved your show."

Luke smiled. "I appreciate the flattery, but let me set the record straight. As much as I would love to be the chap you're talking about, he was totally fictitious—the product of good writers and great directing. I'm not him."

As Chris was about to respond, Cindy came running into the room, jumping up on everyone she passed.

"Saved by the dog," Chris said, picking her up when she got to him and scratching her jowls.

At one o'clock, the family and guests stood in the dining room with bowed heads while Les Dawson said the blessing. It was a scene that Holly had taken for granted her entire life, but with Luke present, she saw her family and the details of their traditions from a new perspective. The comforting aromas of Thanksgiving food and fresh flowers, along with the beauty of Limoges china, sterling flatware, and Waterford crystal, combined to produce an unexpected feeling of pride.

He's a stranger among us, but he blends in so well. She glanced up at Luke. He stood easy in his Tom Ford, blue-gingham shirt with sleeves rolled back, tan chinos, and burnished-brown Ferragamo loafers. As he put a hand on her shoulder, he was just close enough for Holly to catch a whiff of Armani Acqua Di Gio. She relished the feeling his touch generated.

As Les began carving the huge turkey that dominated the antique sideboard, Mary Lou crossed the room to take Luke's hand. "You are our honored guest, today, Luke," she said, leading him to the front of the buffet line. "You must go first."

"Being here with your family is my privilege," he said, obviously uncomfortable with the attention.

"There are place cards on the tables set up in the family room and on the patio," Mary Lou said, looking around at the others.

"Assigned seats, Mom?" Chris commented.

"I thought you young people would enjoy one another's company, so I put the four of you together at the table outside."

As Regina lowered her plate and took her place, she looked across at Luke. "I watch you and Holly every week. It's getting exciting. You guys have to win."

"If we do, it's all Holly," he replied. "On my own, I don't know my right from my left foot."

Regina unfolded her napkin and spread it across her lap. "I used to watch *Alexander Holmes* every week. I actually cried when it was canceled."

Luke smiled. "So did I."

Chris chuckled. "It must be a real bummer for you guys when

a show is dropped. What are your plans for after *Lights, Camera—Dance?*" He reached across the table for the silver salt shaker. "Will you stay in the States?"

"I live here. I have a green card."

"Really," Regina said. "Are you going to do more TV or another film?"

Luke swallowed a bite of turkey and then said, "Thanks to this show, I've been offered a couple of promising projects. We're working on details."

"And you, Hol. What's next?" Chris asked.

"I've been too busy to think ahead." She hesitated and then looked toward Luke with an apprehensive expression on her face. "But, I have signed for the national tour of *LCD.*"

Although he tried to hide it, Holly could see that the revelation surprised Luke. Looking at him, she said, "I had forgotten about it."

An awkward silence blanketed the table.

Apparently picking up on the whisper of tension between Holly and Luke, Regina redirected conversation to her pregnancy.

By five o'clock, all the guests had departed and the dinner remnants had been cleared away. Luke was relaxing in the den with Les as Holly and Mary Lou emerged from the kitchen.

"I know you're exhausted, Mom, and we need to squeeze in some rehearsal time. If you'll let us use your car and tell me where to find the key that Sandy dropped off, we'll leave you and Dad to rest."

"I'd argue with you, honey, if I had the strength." Mary Lou leaned back on the sofa and put her feet up on the large, oak coffee table. "My keys and the studio key are hanging on the rack over my desk in the kitchen. Sandy's has a ballet shoe charm attached. The alarm code is thumbtacked onto my board. It has 'Dance' printed at the top."

Turning to Luke, Holly said, "While I get the keys, can you go up for our bags? Mine is by the door in my room."

He nodded, stood up, and started for the staircase.

A few minutes later, Holly settled into the driver's seat of the Lexis SUV, which was parked in her parent's garage. Before starting the engine, she turned toward Luke. "You had a funny look on your face when I mentioned the tour."

"You caught me off guard."

"I honestly forgot that I signed the contract. It was the first night of the season—before we—"

He grabbed her hand. "It's all right. You have to take care of your career. I just wondered why you never mentioned it."

She shook her head. "No ulterior motive."

He leaned across, kissed her, and afterward said, "I'm a bit disappointed about the separation and maybe a little jealous of you traveling with Mika and Andrei."

"Perish the thought. I don't speak Russian." She grinned, enjoying the idea that he could be jealous. "I probably didn't think of it because I expected you would be moving on with one of your projects."

"Maybe we should talk about that. How long is the tour?"

"Only eight weeks."

He shook his head, a small smile on his face. "Not a chance that I'll let two months go by without you." He caressed her face and then kissed her again. "As for my projects, the one I'm seriously considering might include you—that is, if you're interested."

Holly gave him a puzzled look. "What would that be?"

"A pilot for a TV series. Let me work some things out, and then we'll talk about it. But right now, if we don't leave, your parents are going to wonder what's going on in their garage."

She grinned. "Yeah, and we're wasting rehearsal time."

Sandra Benton's studio was in the San Jose area of town—a fifteen-minute drive from the Dawson home. By the time they arrived, it was growing dark. Luke held their bags while Holly unlocked the door, turned on the lights, and disarmed the security system.

"So this is where you trained."

"A lot of memories here. I started with Sandy when I was in first grade."

He walked over to a photograph on the wall of a dancer in a white tutu and pointe shoes. "You?"

"Yeah. It was from *Nutcracker* my last year here. I danced 'Snow Queen.'"

"And the autographed one next to it?"

"The official photo from my first season on *LCD*." Pointing to a narrow hallway, she said, "We can change in the dressing room."

When they were both in rehearsal clothing, Holly dimmed the lights and started the fervid "Feeling Good." Her purpose was to set the mood for their contemporary piece while they warmed up.

"Let's mark the first run-through to refresh our memory of the choreography," Holly said as she finished stretching and walked to the right side of the room.

"You think I've forgotten it after one day off?"

"No, but I want to be sure that when I jump, you know to catch."

She restarted the Bublé song, and Luke took his place across the room. They walked through the number. The routine was based on the theme of Luke playing a handsome ladies' man, with a cool and controlling demeanor, while Holly was a sophisticated, street gal intent on seducing and conquering him. The setting was to be a steamy-hot, New Orleans night. For practice, she wore a camisole, black trunks, and a below-the-knee, jersey wrap-skirt. Her feet were bare. Although marking the steps, both gave the drama their all.

"Okay. This time—full out," she said, restarting the music.

Again, they each put all the passion possible into each look, each move. At one point in the music, Holly jumped onto Luke, wrapping her legs around his waist and dropping her upper body to near the floor. As she came out of the lift, Luke held her skirt at the waist. She spun away with the skirt peeling off in his grasp as she turned. When she reached the edge of the room, her back was to him—her head turned to the side, looking down. He tossed the skirt and followed. When so close, she could feel his breath on her neck, he ran a hand slowly down her body, caressing her hip.

"That's not where your hand is supposed to be," she whispered.

"I know." With that, he jerked her around, as choreographed, but instead of moving into the next step, he pulled her tight against his torso with one hand, while the other slid the strap of her camisole off her shoulder.

Their eyes locked.

"Let's get this over if we're to rehearse tonight," he whispered.

A smile creeping across her face, she responded in a low, sultry voice, "Good idea."

His lips immediately covered hers as Holly undulated within his embrace, rubbing tantalizingly against his manhood.

Afterward, they lay on tumbling mats near the wall of the studio, holding hands. "I can't say that I ever made love on the floor of a dance studio before tonight," Luke said, not moving.

"I certainly haven't."

"It had to happen."

"I know, but it can't happen again."

"Might get us some votes." He squeezed her hand.

She pulled her hand from his and slapped his shoulder. "More likely get us arrested."

"Maybe we should check with the chemist to see if there's a drug to treat erectile hyper-function." He raised up, leaned over and kissed her, and then began gathering their clothes. After dropping Holly's on her stomach, he said, "Let's do it!"

"Wasn't that what we just did?" she said, pulling on her trunks.

CHAPTER THIRTY-TWO

Early Friday morning, Luke and Holly were having coffee on the patio. Her parents were not yet up.

"The family is going to St. Augustine for dinner this evening. I told Mom that we would pass because we have a full day between going over to Dana's house and rehearsing at the studio." At the mention of the studio, they exchanged knowing glances. "Yeah. Not there again. But, we'll have the house to ourselves for several hours."

Luke's eyes sparkled. "I like the way you think."

"I thought you would. You were a good sport, yesterday, letting my family show you off like a prize pig at the county fair."

He made a face. "*Pig*? That's your best analogy?"

"It could have been worse; I could have said prize rooster. Kidding aside, I really appreciate your patience with my relatives and friends—even letting Mom take all those photos."

"Being here has been a pleasure. Your parents are phenomenally gracious. You have a perfect family, love—the kind of family I wish my brother and I could have had."

Holly frowned. "Why do you say that?"

He shook his head. "My childhood wasn't like yours. Mum did her best as a single parent, but she always worked two jobs—sometimes, three."

"What hapened to her?"

"Breast cancer." His expression grew cloudy. "She would have liked you."

"Did she like your wives?"

"She never met Jeanne and probably wasn't too crazy about Ciara."

His expression relaxed with a smug smile of reflection. "However, she gave me hell when we broke up. I think she was afraid I had inherited my father's proclivity for desertion."

The mention of his father reminded Holly of the statement he made that he would never do what his father did. "What about your father?"

The muscles in his face tightened. "What about him?"

"What is—or was—he like?"

"Absent."

"Absent?" She looked at him, puzzled by his statement.

He paused. Holly wondered what he was thinking and if he would say more.

"He left for work three months before Marc was born. That's all I know, and all I need to know."

Holly was curious but afraid to pry.

"Like you, I had a dream at fourteen—of having a family like yours. One where I wasn't mother and father to a ten-year-old, didn't have to cook dinner, clean the flat, do the laundry. I dreamed of living in a house—maybe having a cat." He winked.

Holly returned his smile but instinctively knew his wink terminated the subject.

Later that morning, Holly drove Luke to Dana Charles' house in Mandarin, not far from the dance school.

"Thank you for letting me drag you to Dana's. If I didn't bring you by, she might not speak to me again. I promise we won't stay long."

Luke yawned. "No problem. I like meeting the people in your life.

When Dana opened her front door, there was no need for her to speak. Her wide-eyed expression said it all. After taking a second to gain her composure, she invited Luke and Holly in with a sweep of her hand. As the couple passed by, Dana grabbed Holly's arm, holding her back for an instant. Making a face, she mouthed, "Wow!"

Holly nodded, a huge grin on her face.

"Luke Damian in my house," Dana said. "If our friends from high school could see us now." Looking toward Holly, she covered her mouth with her hand. "Whoops! They do see you every week on TV." She did a little dance twist. "Don't mind me. I'm a little celebrity struck."

"Don't feel bad. I made a complete fool of myself the day we met," Holly said as she walked into the living room and sat down on a sofa.

"Ladies, could we forget about Luke Damian, actor, and settle for just plain Luke, the guy who is happy to meet Holly's best friend?" he said as he took a seat next to Holly.

"Done," Dana said as she made a circle in front of her face with one hand, snapping her fingers Heidi Klum fashion. "So, tell me just plain Luke, how do you like our town?"

"I haven't seen much of it, but so far, I like it. The weather couldn't be better."

"Dana, where is my precious goddaughter?" Holly asked, looking around.

"She's watching TV in the den. I'll get her." Grinning at Luke, Dana left the room.

Luke turned to Holly. "I like Dana, but you didn't tell me that she is expecting a baby."

Holly made a face. "I forgot. Probably Freudian. I'm a little jealous."

"Really?" Before he could say more, a curly-haired three-year-old burst into the living room.

"Aunt Holly," Brittany Charles shrieked, running to Holly.

Hugging the preschooler and giving her a kiss on the cheek, Holly then reached for her bag. "You grow taller and taller every time I go away." Taking a package out of her tote, she handed it to the child.

Brittany tore away the ribbon and opened the box. "A princess crown, a princess crown. I can be a real princess."

"You are a princess, but this makes it official," Holly said, taking the rhinestone tiara from the child and placing it on her head. "I dub you Princess Brittany of the Kingdom of Charles."

"Tell her thank you," Dana said, "and say hello to Mr. Damian. You've seen him dancing on TV with Aunt Holly."

The child looked at Luke. She turned, smiled, and reached out to give him a hug.

He reciprocated, grinning. "Now, I can say that I've been hugged by a princess."

Ginning at Luke, Brittany said, "Mommy says you and Aunt Holly are going to win."

"That's right, honey. They make a perfect couple," Dana added.

"You'll get no argument from me about that." Luke reached over and took Holly's hand.

Holly shivered.

By the expression on Dana's face, it was clear that she caught the gesture. "Can I get the two of you anything to drink? Coke? Coffee?"

"None for me," Holly said.

Luke shook his head.

"We have a lot of rehearsing to do, Dana. The pressure is on. You watch the show. You've seen who is left in the competition: Mika and that singer, Lisa and the Swedish chef, and Andrei and the gymnast. We've got our work cut out. Sandy is letting us use her studio while we're here."

"I can't believe that she's still teaching. She must be seventy." Turning to Luke, Dana said, "Holly and I started taking classes with Sandy when we were in kindergarten."

"You two took dance classes together in kindergarten?" Luke asked.

"We did, but Holly had talent. I was a klutz and dropped out in middle school."

"You weren't a klutz. It just wasn't your passion." Holly looked down at her watch. "I'm sorry, but we can't stay. We've got a lot of work if we are to perfect our piece. Sandy is coming in today to look at it and offer suggestions." She stood up. "I just wanted to squeeze in a chance for you to meet Luke and for me to see Brittany." She took Luke's hand, inducing him to stand.

Dana accompanied them to the door, giving both a hug as they left. "Thanks for taking the time to come by." As they walked down to the car, Dana called out, "Break a leg Wednesday night."

As Luke climbed in the passenger side of the car, he asked, "Did you mention a hometown friend who dances in a ballet company?"

"That's Gabi. She is awesome, but she didn't move here until my sophomore year in high school. Gabi is a little different. Ballet is the beginning and end of her world. Like Dana said, she and I go back to kindergarten."

Sandra Billings was already at the studio when Holly and Luke arrived. After introductions, they changed into rehearsal clothing and did a quick warmup.

"Please point out where we can improve," Holly said as she walked toward her dance bag to retrieve their music.

"From what I've been seeing on the show, you don't need help, honey, but I'd love to offer what I can."

Holly took out her iPad and started the Michael Bublé song. *Okay Holly, put last night out of your mind.*

When they finished the first run-through, Sandra clapped. "It's good, very good. Holly, you've made great use of Luke's acting skills. I'm impressed with his lines and the lifts are breathtaking. For a non-dancer, you're outstanding, Luke."

"So, where can we improve?" Holly asked. "And don't say it can't be any better."

"Honey, it's a winner the way it is—but if you want to add a little more drama, I have one idea."

"And?"

"Remember the trick you did in your last recital here?"

"The one in 'Remember Me' where I crossed the stage and did a saut de chat with Joseph catching me in the split and raising me over his head?"

"That's the one. You were the only student I ever had who could pull that off."

"Yeah, and I was only 50-50."

"But, you made it when it counted. I had parents tell me that when you left the floor, they stopped breathing, afraid you would fly through the ceiling. You got a standing ovation."

"But, that was a recital, Sandy. If I had missed, only family and friends would have seen the disaster. We're on network TV. Millions could be watching. Plus, Luke is taller than Joseph. That will put me even higher."

"You people are making me nervous," Luke interjected. "What is a saut de chat?"

"It's a big, ballet jump," Holly responded. "I leap in the air by pushing off from my back leg and straightening my front until I arrive in a split."

"And I'm supposed to catch you in the air?"

Holly nodded.

"If you pull it off, I promise the hair on the arms of the judges and the audience will stand on end," Sandra said.

"And if we miss, we're toast," Holly said.

"I say you should try."

Holly turned to Luke. "What do you think?"

"You're the boss. I'll try anything you think I can do. You've already had me do things that I would have bet my life could never happen. I'm in, if you are."

"Just keep your hips square, think ballet, and you can do it, Holly," Sandra said.

"Ooo. . . kay. But I'd better lose five pounds before next Wednesday."

"Can I ask another question?" Luke said.

"Sure," Holly and Sandra answered simultaneously.

"If I succeed in getting you over my head, how the hell do I get you down?"

Sandra and Holly chuckled at his naiveté. "You just bend your elbows enough to be able to give me a boost upward, and then let me fall into your arms."

"My arms?"

"Yeah. You'll make a cradle to catch me."

He shook his head. "Is your insurance current?"

The first seven attempts ended in disaster, ually with Holly's split collapsing and her derriere ending up on Luke's chest. After the seventh try, he turned his back and walked away, shaking his head.

"This isn't going to work. Shouldn't we move on?"

"One more try," Sandra said. "I know you can do it."

Holly looked back and forth between Luke and her teacher. "I'm game if you are," she said to him.

"One more try and we admit defeat," he replied.

"I've got a feeling that we can do this—we can!" She pumped both fists in the air, nodding her affirmation.

They backed up to their respective starting positions. As Sandra counted, Holly ran toward Luke. She sailed into the air, almost pausing in defiance of gravity. He caught her. Up she went, high above his head. Holding her there for four counts, he then dropped her dramatically into his arms and then gave a little thrust, tossing her to a standing position on the floor, her back to him. She turned back to face Luke, and then threw one leg around him while he formed a circle with his arms around her waist, allowing her to drop into a backbend.

As she came out of the ending pose, she shouted, "We did it! We nailed it, Luke." She gave him a high-five.

"One out of eight. Are those good odds?" he asked.

Sandra spoke up. "Did you feel the center of your balance directly below Holly's the last time?"

"Maybe," he replied. "Still, eight tries before success?"

"The first three were throwaways. Holly didn't keep her hips square."

Holly spoke up. "I had to find my groove. It's been a long time."

"I believe that the two of you can make it work. But, you've got to believe you can," Sandra said. "Do another run through, with music.

My money is on a victory."
They did it.

CHAPTER THIRTY-THREE

By five-fifteen they were on the way back to the Dawson house. The pair had executed the breathtaking trick consistently for a total of five times. Holly was ecstatic. "This has been a fantastic day. We're going to rub the Russian noses in it. They move like cats on the floor, but as good as they are, they don't have as much strength in their arms as you do. They can't compete with our lifts, even with Miss Olympic-Gold-Medalist. Thanks to Sandra, we've put on the finishing touches. Now, all we have to do is rehearse a little every day to keep our muscle memory solid."

"I hope you know that you're killing me with all the tossing and twirling you in the air."

"If you want to win, we've got to make the audience gasp." She turned onto Arbor Lane. "Want to eat leftovers or swing by the square for take-out?"

"Leftovers and a hot shower sounds like a winning combination."

When they reached the house, it was empty. Holly went to the kitchen to make their light dinner, while Luke went upstairs for a shower.

When he came down, she had the sandwiches made. It was dark outside.

"What time do you expect your parents?"

"Their reservations are for eight o'clock. Mom wanted to shop a little first. It should be ten or after before they are back." She put two plates with turkey sandwiches, chips, and pickles on the table.

Luke smiled as he sat down. "Do you have any plans for after dinner?"

Holly gave him a mischievous look. "I was thinking that I might like to have a date with Alec Holmes. I found a box of old VHS tapes in my closet."

"Oh, no." He made a face. "You're not going to make me endure my ancient self?"

Her chin bobbed up and down. "My house, my game."

"Doesn't this country have a law against cruel and unusual punishment?"

"Indulge a girl's fantasy." She winked. "I'll make it worth your while."

"You're darn right you will."

When they finished dinner, Holly asked Luke to clean up the few dishes while she took a shower.

"I'll see you upstairs in about ten minutes," she said, winking at him as she started out of the breakfast room.

Twenty minutes later, Holly stood in her bedroom, fresh from her shower and dressed in a silky, powder-blue gown. Her auburn hair was loose, flowing over her shoulders in soft waves. She scanned the room, smiling at the three posters of Luke she had rehung on the wall. Candles burning atop the étagère gave off a soft glow, contributing to the romantic ambiance. As she took a bottle of Stella cologne from her dressing table, a soft knock came at the door. Her heart fluttered with anticipation as she quickly pressed the pump, emitting a spray of fragrance, and then said, "Come in."

Luke entered. A draft closed the door behind him as he paused, looking her up and down. The backlight coming from the moon outside her windows revealed the silhouette of her figure through the gossamer gown.

"Nice." He extended a hand, beckoning her to come closer. When she did, he grasped her around the waist, pulled her close, and kissed her.

Holly felt herself dissolving in his embrace but was determined the evening would hold more than just sex. She wanted all the elements of romance she had fantasized about years before. "Humor me," she whispered, easing backward. "I have a plan."

"I hope it includes finishing what you've done a damned good job of starting." He countered her attempt to escape with a tight squeeze and then released her with a playful slap on her rear.

"Keep to the script, and you might find it has a powerful conclusion." She winked, flirtatiously.

"I think I'm more interested in the climax than the conclusion." Glancing around the room, a bottle of 20-year-old tawny port, between two stemmed glasses on her night table, caught his eye. Nodding toward the wine, he said, "If that was included when you watched my show, no wonder I looked good."

She raised an eyebrow in faux disgust. "Think you're smart, don't you?"

He reached out, grabbed her hand, and pulled her back to him. "I don't need to be smart. All I need is a little TLC." His glanced around. "We're not in jeopardy of your parents coming home early, are we?"

"The alarm is on. It'll warn us if an outside door opens. Of course, you may have to crawl under the bed."

He cocked an eyebrow. "Now, who's the smart ass?"

She grinned mischievously. "Don't worry. They don't want to catch us."

"I feel like a teenager, sneaking in my girlfriend's room." He drew her close, lifted her chin, and kissed her, hungrily, while allowing one hand the liberty to wander.

The sensation of his body rubbing hers through the thin veil of her lingerie caused erotic sparks hard to resist. Pulling away, she put her hands flat against his chest and said, "Slow down, tiger. We have a show to watch." She motioned to the bed. "Shall we?"

Giving her a sly look, Luke kicked off his loafers, moved onto the bed, and made himself comfortable against the array of ruffled pillows. Holly walked to the opposite side, poured wine into the stemware and handed one glass to him before stepping out of her slippers and climbing up beside him. His eyes followed her every move. As his free arm circled her shoulders, she clinked her glass against his.

"To us winning."

"Here, here," he responded and gulped the liquid.

Taking a sip, she then put her glass back on the table, picked up the remote, and started a VHS tape.

"This is my favorite episode," she said.

"Oh, my God." He rolled his eyes. "We are *really* going to watch this?"

Her chin bobbed up and down as she snuggled under his arm, wrapping one of hers around his chest.

Shortly into the show, a younger, blonder version of the man next to her appeared on the screen. The camera took full advantage of his piercing-blue eyes, sending chills through Holly. As the scene unfolded, she wriggled against him. "Oh, yes. I remember this."

He groaned. "I can't believe you're making me watch."

Less than fifteen minutes into the show, Luke reached across her, took the remote, and flicked off the TV. "I'm done. No more competing with Alec Holmes. We're putting this show on fast forward." With a devilish, come-hither look, he unzipped his jeans.

The sound of the slider moving down the metal teeth sent a bolt of desire coursing through Holly's erogenous zones.

Oh, my God, how I want him.

He sat upright, turned, and swung a leg across her as she scrambled to unbutton his shirt and tear it away.

A moonbeam streamed through the lace curtains, spotlighting Luke's bare chest and rippling abs as he gingerly slid the straps of her gown down, exposing her breasts. For a moment, his eyes drank in her body with a gaze that tortured her with desire. Slowly, gently, his hands caressed her, teasing her sexual hunger.

Yes, yes.

As he removed her gown, she arced to assist. With her last remnant of clothing discarded, he gently stroked her body as though it were a fragile porcelain.

His touch was hot, inciting, and Holly responded by thrusting her lower torso against his, inviting him in. All the while, her hands explored his body, flirting with forbidden territory.

As the passion escalated, Luke released his grasp and pushed up to remove his jeans.

Holly moaned. She ached to merge her body, her soul, with his—starved for the fulfillment.

Luke moved over her again, staring at her naked body as though he wanted to devour it. "There are no words to express how beautiful you are."

Dear God, he could be a Greek God—Apollo.

He leaned forward as if to kiss her. But before pressing his lips to hers, he paused. Staring into her eyes, he whispered, "I'm falling in love with you, Holly Dawson."

Her heart pounded so hard that she was sure he could hear it.

Falling in love with me?

For several moments, both remained motionless, frozen in silence. Luke then spoke again in a tone slightly above a whisper. "That wasn't right. . . . I *am* in love with you, my very dearest angel."

Holly wanted to scream, "I love you, too." She wanted him inside her, consummating all the feelings she had been afraid to acknowledge. Before she could respond, his mouth covered hers, and then—he took her.

The act surpassed the bounds of sex. Holly was lost in a nirvana she never knew existed before Luke. His words, his touch, robbed her of autonomy. For the moment, he owned her. She was his to do with as he wished.

After the climax, when her body began to settle and the tingling of nerve endings calmed, she looked over at him. He was lying on his back, his face turned toward her, staring.

"I can't find words. I don't know what to say," she said.

"There's only one thing I want to hear." He reached over to caress her cheek. "I want to hear you're in love with *me*—not that character from the ancient TV show—but me, Luke Damian." He rolled onto his side and brushed damp hair off her forehead.

"I can—I can say it." A tear sneaked down her cheek.

He took her chin and gingerly raised it. "Let me hear it."

"I'm in love with *you*, Luke Damian." Her eyes squeezed shut. "I am. God, help me. I am *so* in love with you."

He grasped her to him—naked body against naked body.

At ten o'clock, Luke returned to his room.

As she closed her bedroom door behind him, Holly knew she was lost in lust and love for Luke. Their love-making had surpassed carnal indulgence. She wanted to spend every night with him.

He's in love with me.

She walked toward the window. As she passed the posters, she kissed the tips of her fingers and then touched them to Luke's image. Gigi lay on the sill, purring. Picking the cat up, Holly rubbed her face against the soft fur. "I want to hold on to this magic moment forever."

CHAPTER THIRTY-FOUR

Holly woke the next morning, feeling like a ten-year-old who found that Santa had brought everything on her list.

It wasn't a dream? Luke said he is in love with me?

She glanced at the clock on her night table. *My gosh. It's nearly nine o'clock. I never sleep this late.*

She sat up, looked at the posters, and felt her blood churn.

Luke Damian is in love with me.

She was about to get out of bed when her cell phone rang.

"Good morning, Sleeping Beauty. Coming down today?"

At the sound of his voice, Holly's face glowed. "Where are you?"

"By the pool, having coffee all alone. Were you planning to sleep all day?"

"I hadn't planned to, but it looks as if I did a good job trying."

"Well, put your beautiful little ass in gear and let's get to the studio. We have work to do, and your mum asked me to find out what you want for breakfast."

"Whoa. Who died and left you in charge?"

"Sometimes, a man has got to be a man. Besides, I'm anxious to see the woman I'm in love with."

"Give me fifteen minutes, and I'll be down. Tell Mom coffee and toast will be fine."

"I'll tell her coffee, toast, eggs and bacon. You need your strength."

"You might want to rethink that when you remember what doing five lifts in our number is like."

"I'll handle it. I lived with an anorexic model. You're not going to starve yourself on my watch."

"You've certainly become bossy. Don't think you can get away with that just because you said you're in love with me."

"Hey, hey. Cut me some slack, love. I've been taking orders from you for two months. Let a poor lad flex some authority for a minute or two."

"We'll discuss that later. I'm hanging up."

"Love you."

Her face beamed like a happy emoji. "Back at you."

After breakfast, Holly and Luke returned to the studio, rehearsed until lunch, and then spent the afternoon driving around Jacksonville. Holly pointed out the private schools she and Dana attended, St. John's Episcopal Cathedral where she sang in the children's choir, and the theaters where she had performed.

"We better head home. Mom made reservations for all of us to have dinner tonight at San Jose."

"Formal or informal?"

"It's a country club, but we usually eat in the Vista Room, which is less formal. You don't need a tie." She turned onto her parents' street. "Trust me. Neither Dad nor my brother will have one on. Mom does well to get them into a jacket."

That evening, Les Dawson drove the foursome to the club for their last dinner together. "I hope you've enjoyed your stay in Jacksonville, Luke." He turned into the parking lot. "It's not L.A. or London, but we have our share of things to offer."

Luke reached for Holly's hand. "The visit exceeded my expectations." He looked at her and winked. "I hope you and Mary Lou will consider inviting me again."

Luke's response brought a warm sense of satisfaction to Holly.

"Most certainly," Mary Lou said. "We'd love to have you."

Les pulled the car under the porte-cochere, stopping to let the passengers out before parking. They waited in the alcove until he joined them.

As the family entered the reception hall, a female employee of the club looked up from her desk. Her expression revealed that she recognized Luke, but protocol forced her to remain nonchalant.

Chris and Regina were already seated when Luke and the Dawsons arrived at the table.

"Nice to see you, again," Chris said, standing up to shake Luke's hand. As Chris hugged his mother and Holly, Les patted Regina on the back, leaned over to give her a kiss on the cheek, and then took a seat.

"So, you head back to L.A., tomorrow?" Chris said.

Luke nodded. "Early. Our flight leaves at seven. I hope we can get Holly up in time to make it."

"Very funny," Holly said. "He's giving me a hard time because I overslept today."

"Holly. How are you?" The question came from an attractive woman, accompanied by a short man, who had walked up behind Holly's chair.

"Jenny Conseulas! It's been forever. You look wonderful!"

"It's Danvers now. You're beautiful, as always. I see you every week on TV. I tell Walter" she motioned to the man with her, "I know her." Looking over at Luke, she continued, "This must be Luke Damian."

The corners of Holly's mouth turned up. "It is." She turned toward him. "Luke, this is an old friend from school, Jenny Danvers," Holly pointed to Jenny's escort, "and her husband, Walter."

"I don't want to interrupt your dinner but I just had to say *hi*. Stay in touch, okay? It was nice to meet you, Luke."

With that, the couple moved on to a table across the room. When they were out of earshot, Holly said, "She only came over to our table to meet Luke. We were never friends."

Chris laughed and then looking over Holly's shoulder said, "Don't lose your cool—but guess who's heading this way?"

"Who?" Holly said, under her breath, leaning closer to Chris with her eyebrows coming together in a frown.

Before Chris could answer, a nice-looking man, wearing khakis, a navy blazer, and a University of Florida baseball cap, stood next to their table. "Holly, I thought I recognized your family pass by the dining room." The man took stock of the table, his gaze lingering a few extra seconds on Luke. "Hello, Mr. and Mrs. Dawson, Chris, Regina."

Most nodded. Les Dawson, spoke. "Hello, Don. Haven't seen you in a while."

Holly thought she would choke but forced a smile instead. *Why would he dare come over to my table?* "Hello, Don. How are you?" *If he has the unmitigated gall to approach me, I have the nerve to respond.* She turned toward Luke. "Luke, I'd like you to meet Donald Barrett—my ex. Don, meet Luke Damian." Each word dripped from her lips, coated in southern sugar and tainted by icy sarcasm.

Luke glanced at Holly, a smug glimmer in his eyes, which turned to a twinkle when he stood and shook Don's hand. "Happy to meet you."

"The pleasure is mine," Don responded and then turned his attention to Holly. "How long are you in town for? I'd like to get together with you."

Has he lost his freaking mind? "Gee, sorry, Don, but we leave for L.A. first thing tomorrow."

That felt so good!

Speaking as though he had not been brushed off, Don said, "That's too bad. Well, best of luck with the show. I'll give you a call." With that, he walked away.

Holly looked around at her family, rolling her eyes, and shrugging her shoulders. "I'm not believing that."

"I think he's sorry he broke up with you, honey," Mary Lou said.

"You know what, Mom? Best thing that happened to me this year."

"The best?" Luke said, an amused expression on his face.

"I stand corrected. Second best."

No one said anything, but Regina gave Chris a did-you-get-that look.

The remainder of the dinner went well, despite being approached by other friends of various members of the Dawson clan.

"I'm sorry we had so many interruptions, Luke," Mary Lou said as they were riding back to the house.

"Just about every one of them wanted to meet him," Holly said. "Although no one would admit it."

"No need to apologize. I enjoyed the evening, and thank you for your hospitality. I would like to reciprocate if you'll consider coming out to L.A."

"You know, I have been thinking that we might come out for the finale. What do you think, Les?"

Holly felt her stomach clench. *Do I want them in L.A. with the stalking thing hanging over us?*

"You can get us tickets, can't you, honey?" Mary Lou asked.

Holly didn't respond.

"Of course we can," Luke said. "You let us know when you're coming, and I'll make arrangements for your stay and tickets for the show. Bring Chris and Regina as well."

Holly wanted to kick him. *They can't know that I'm living with you, much less why.*

Not long after arriving at the Dawson home, Luke and Holly went upstairs to finish packing. On the second floor, they paused before going to their separate rooms.

"Would you like help with getting ready for the flight?" Luke asked, taking her hand.

"I can manage." She stood on tiptoe, gave him a quick kiss, and then put her index finger to his chest, her head shaking. "You in my room tonight? Too risky."

"Don't trust me?"

"Let's say I don't trust myself."

He chuckled. "So, tell me. Is the torch extinguished?"

"The torch?" She wrinkled her face as if confused.

"The one that gave you trouble when we danced to Chopin." He tipped his chin, raising his eyebrows.

"If you are referring to Don, what do you think?"

He leaned forward, putting a hand behind her head and the other around her waist. Drawing her tight against his body, he kissed her passionately. When they parted, he stared into her eyes. "What I think is that it better be extinguished, or else I have my work cut out for me."

Holly's eyes danced. "I think you might have a jealous streak, Mr. Damian."

"Impossible. . . . But, just in case I do, how about putting me out of my misery?

"That's doable." She put both of her hands around his neck, pulled his face to hers, and then kissed him fervently. Pulling away, Holly gave him a sassy look. "Convinced?"

"I'm not sure. Mind showing me again?"

Glancing down the front of his slacks and then back up, she said, "If I show you any more, we are going to have to get a hotel room. Now, take a cold shower, go to bed, and dream about tomorrow night in L.A."

He threw his hands up in mock exasperation and turned toward his room. "Someone hear me. This woman is killing me. First, she makes me dance like a maniac, tossing her around until my arms feel like they will fall off." His arms flailed around in the air and then crossed his chest in repose, a soulful expression appearing on his face. "Now, she's a *sadistic* temptress—seducing me . . . deflecting my desire . . . leaving me to suffer in solitude."

"Shh. They'll hear you downstairs. Don't think you're going to win an Oscar for that performance."

He turned, a big grin on his face. "You don't think so? I thought it was stellar."

"You're incorrigible."

"Guilty." He held up his hands in surrender. "But I love you."

"Good—really good," she said, moving to where he could put his arms around her again.

"You liked that, huh?"

"I did, and I'm not even going to ask if it was impromptu or scripted."

He leaned forward and kissed her, again. "Impromptu and every syllable true. I love you, Holly Dawson—so much that I feel like taking a full-page ad in *Variety*."

"That is a commendable thought. But first, I think we'd better pack. I'm going to my room now. See you in the morning."

"One more kiss."

"One."

A half-hour later, as Holly closed the zipper of her carry-on, she sneezed. Reaching into the bottom drawer of her night table for a tissue, she noticed a framed photo of Don Barrett next to the packet of Kleenex. She had put it there the night they broke up. Picking up the picture, she stared at the image for a minute. "Thank God, you dumped me, Donald." She took the picture out of the frame, tore it into pieces, and tossed the bits into her trash basket. "You bet the torch is out. The king is dead; long live the king."

CHAPTER THIRTY-FIVE

Monday morning, Holly and Luke were exhausted from a frustrating trip back to L.A. They departed Jacksonville on time, but a five-hour delay in Houston turned the trip into an ordeal. Luke had been on the cusp of arranging for a charter when their flight was finally cleared for take-off.

"Our clocks might have said we got home at eleven, but my body knows it was two a.m.," Holly said, between sips from a Starbucks cup on the way to rehearsal.

"We could cut out early this afternoon. I feel comfortable with the choreography, even with the trick from hell you added."

"Maybe. But, why don't we treat ourselves to a massage after the camera blocking?"

"I like your thinking."

The car stopped at the rear door of the studio. Luke got out first and walked around to retrieve their bags from the driver, standing at the back of the studio SUV. As Holly stepped from the vehicle, her foot went wrong. She fell, emitting a gasp as she plopped onto the concrete.

Both men rushed to her aid.

"Let me help you up," Luke said, reaching for her elbow.

"No. No. I can't stand on it." Holly's face became instantly devoid of color—her eyes filled with panic. "This can't be happening. I can't be injured." She fought back tears.

"My God, it's already swelling," Luke said.

"Ice. Can someone get me some ice?"

Luke motioned to the driver. "Go. Find Sam Waring. He'll know what to do."

Taking his cue, the driver hurried into the building.

"Let me carry you. We need to get you inside," Luke said.

Holly held on to his arm, squeezing so hard that her nails nearly broke his skin.

"You're going to be all right. We'll get a doctor. It's okay, darling."

"No. It's not okay. The semi-finals are two days away. What if I can't dance?"

Luke put his hand to the side of her face. "It will be fine. If you can't dance, you can't. It's not the end of the world."

"But, we stand—stood—a good chance of winning."

"Holly, it's not important. We have a lot more going on than winning a title no one will remember in two weeks. It's okay."

He scooped her up and started into the building. As he reached the door, the driver and Sam emerged from the other side.

"What happened?" Sam said.

Holly's chin quivered as she shook her head, afraid to speak for fear of breaking down completely.

"She somehow missed her step exiting the vehicle and fell. Her ankle is swelling fast. Let's get her inside," Luke said.

Sam turned to the driver. "Go to the commissary and tell them you need a plastic bag filled with ice."

"Fourth floor, right?"

Sam nodded. "Hurry."

With Sam leading, they made their way into the studio. After holding the door open for the couple to enter, Sam pulled out his cell and made a call. Luke carried Holly to one of the director's chairs.

Noticing Sam on the phone, Holly asked, "Are you calling Bruce?"

He nodded, then turned his attention to the call. "Hey, buddy. We've got an ankle injury in room 2-J. Get down here STAT."

Bruce Grainger, the in-house physical therapist, was in the rehearsal room before the driver was back. "What happened?"

Holly extended her injured foot.

"Uh-oh. Let me check." Kneeling, he gently took her ankle in hand, unlaced her shoe, and removed it.

"Fix it. I have to dance Wednesday." Holly's voice quivered.

He shook his head. "Slow down. Let's see what's going on." He twisted her foot slightly to the right.

Holly gasped, reflexively jerking it away. "Sorry."

"How did it happen?"

"I was getting out of the car, and the next thing I knew, I was on the ground. I guess my feet got tangled up with one another, and I tripped myself. It was stupid."

He pushed upward on her heel. "Does this hurt?"

Holly shook her head in the negative and did likewise when he pulled downward on the injured foot.

"There's quite a bit of swelling, but I doubt any bones are broken. Hopefully no connective tissue tears. Imaging is the only way to know."

"That means the hospital. No, Bruce. We've got to rehearse." Tears began forming, again, despite her best effort to suppress them.

Luke moved closer, putting his hand on her shoulder.

"Dawson. You're injured," Grainger said. "You pros are a determined lot, but you're not rehearsing today—likely not this week."

Holly looked up at Luke, who had not spoken since the therapist arrived, her eyes pleading for support.

"Listen, love. He knows what he's talking about." Luke stroked her hair. "Your body is your instrument, the number one priority. You can't gamble your entire career on one performance."

Stepping closer to Holly's chair, Sam spoke. "Honey, there are alternatives."

Holly turned toward the cameraman, a quizzical expression on her face. "What are you talking about?"

"A stand-in. This far into the season, there are several eliminated pros. One could step in. You can choose a sub."

Luke perked up. "That's a capital idea, love."

Creases formed on Holly's brow as she turned her attention to Luke. "Wrong. You're totally accustomed to me—how I move, my height, weight. Plus, I choreographed the dance based on our strong points. It wouldn't be the same."

"Of course, it wouldn't be the same, Holly," Sam said. "But, it would work. All you need is to cover Wednesday night. Luke will capture the sympathy vote from viewers. I've never seen a couple eliminated because a pro was injured. Take care of that foot, and you can probably hit the floor next week."

"Unless she has a tear," Grainger said.

"Don't say that," Holly said.

"Did you feel or hear a pop when you fell?" the therapist asked.

Holly shook her head. "It happened so fast, but I don't remember hearing anything. I just felt a stab in my ankle and knew it was trouble."

"Let's get you to an ER for the MRI and X-rays—only way to know how long you'll be out of the game," Grainger said as he wrapped the ankle with an ace bandage and applied a flexible cold pack. "Do you want me to call for an ambulance?"

Holly shook her head, but Sam immediately disagreed. "Holly, footage of you getting into an ambulance will play well for the camera. Let Bruce call for the medical transport."

"This is unbelievable. I practice dangerous tricks with Luke all weekend without a scratch and then step out of a car and sideline myself." She looked around at the three men, wanting any one of them to produce a miracle. Silence sucked the air out of the room. "Call the ambulance."

Shortly after lunch, Holly, on crutches, was back in the studio. Tests had revealed no breaks or tears, but she had a bad sprain. To her dismay, the orthopedic surgeon advised against her returning to dance for ten days to two weeks and only after a follow-up exam.

With a long face, she sat down, handing the crutches to Luke. "I guess we have no choice but to bring in a sub. I might be able to dance by Wednesday, but you need to rehearse today."

"You're not dancing this week."

Holly's face snapped up toward him. "Excuse me. I will if I feel okay."

"If you try, I'll walk." Sparks flying from his eyes affirmed his position.

"You wouldn't."

"Don't test me. I will not be part of aggravating your injury. Either I dance with an understudy—or not at all."

Sam cut his eyes back and forth between the couple but kept his camera rolling.

Holly stared at Luke, disbelief written on her face. After several seconds of silence, she broke the deadlock by looking down at her lap and whispering, "You win."

Moving closer to her, Luke put an arm around her shoulders and squeezed. "That's my girl."

She raised her chin; her lips had a slight upward curl. "Well, at least it's better I'm the one who's lame. I'm replaceable."

"I would argue that point with you," Luke said. "But I know how stubborn you are."

"Sam, who's available?"

"Among the pros, you have Danique, Kat, Ulyana, and Maggie to choose from, plus all the female backups."

"Not Ulyana or Danique. Both are too tall, which would put more strain on Luke. Maggie's a little weak. Of those four, Kat Kenley would be the best to take my place."

"So, it's Kat?" Sam said.

"Call her."

It took Kenley less than fifty minutes to reach the studio. Dropping her dance bag on the closest bench, the pro walked to where Holly sat with her foot elevated on a wooden bar stool. She wrapped her arms around Holly and gave her a hug. "Bad break, hon. No pun intended."

"How did you get here so fast?" Holly said.

"Sam put me on notice earlier. I made sure I would be ready if you needed me." Turning to Luke, she said, "You ready to kick ass, handsome?"

The corners of his mouth turned up for the first time since Holly was hurt. "I am, if you are."

"I'm not this amazing, beautiful gal." She squeezed Holly's shoulders. "But I'll give it all this ol' hoofer's got."

A tear slipped out of Holly's right eye, which she quickly wiped away. "Luke, can you take the iPad out of my bag. I'll show Kat the video Sandy shot of our rehearsal on Friday."

"I've got plenty of video, hon," Sam said.

Holly shook her head. "We made a change in Jacksonville you don't have."

Luke brought her the device, which she propped up in her lap with Kat standing behind, looking over her shoulder.

As the video played, Kat watched intently, oohing and aahing appropriately. "Nice. . . . Sexy, girl. . . . Fantastic. . . . I got that." When Michael Buble's voice built to a dramatic climax on the video, Holly flew off the floor to Luke in a grand saut de chat.

Kat gasped. "SHIT! . . . Whoops. Sorry for the language. Erase that, Sam." She circled Holly's chair with her hands on her hips. "Girl-friend, I can't do that." She pointed to the device.

"That's what I said when she added it to the routine, but she refused to hear," Luke said.

"No freaking way. Less than two days to show-time. Holly, Holly, Holly. I couldn't do that if we had two months to air."

"It's not as difficult as it appears."

"Don't let her kid you, Kat," Luke said. "It's as hard as it looks."

"Could you at least try?"

Kat leaned forward, put her hands on Holly's shoulders, and stared her in the eye. "I'm all about helping you, babe. I want to see you beat the crap out of those pompous frontrunners, but no way am I doing that lift. It would be wasting valuable rehearsal time for me to try. We have to rework the choreography." She glanced Luke's way. "Be fair to lover boy, over there. Giving him such a challenge would equal torture."

Holly cut her eyes around to Luke at Kat's last remark and then back to her stand-in.

Reading Holly's reaction, Kat said, "We all know, sweetie. Those of us who aren't green with jealously are thrilled for the two of you. You make a handsome couple."

"I agree," Luke said.

"But, let's face facts about the number. It's going to be tough enough for him to adapt to the style, timing, and feel of a new partner," Kat continued. "Cut us some slack."

Looking back to Kat, Holly's face betrayed her disappointment. "We worked so hard to master it, and then I make a stupid mistake and ruin it."

Luke walked up behind Holly, his hands replacing Kat's on her shoulders. "You haven't ruined anything, and it wasn't your fault. Freak accidents happen, sweetheart." He leaned forward and kissed the top of her head. "Concentrate on getting better, relax, and enjoy bossing us around."

"Believe me. I know your pain and wish I could do the lift. I'd love to see the look on Cantrell's face. She couldn't pull the trick off with an NFL wide-receiver catching her." Kat turned and walked over to the barre to warm up.

When Kenley finished her warmup, she reviewed the video once more by herself. "Let's take it eight counts at a time," she said to Holly.

Holly's stomach churned. I can do this.

The first half hour, watching Kat Kenley with Luke, was emotionally the hardest for Holly. She couldn't lose her self-pity.

The substitute was a quick study and had no trouble with the combinations but the nuances of Kenley's moves differed from Holly's. Luke messed up a couple of the lifts on the first few attempts. As the couple made errors, the pro came out in Holly. She became more and more absorbed in perfecting their performance, which redirected her focus from depression to determination. The trio rehearsed until nearly nine p.m.

CHAPTER THIRTY-SIX

As the studio car drove them to Luke's condo that evening, Holly wore a solemn expression and was uncharacteristically quiet.

Luke broke the silence. "Kat is a quick study. She learned in an hour what it took me days to master."

"All pros pick up quickly."

Luke could tell by the flat tone of Holly's voice she was lapsing into a morose state. All afternoon, she had managed to concentrate on coaching the new partnership. In the calm of the SUV, the reality of not performing on Wednesday tore at her heart. Tears filled her eyes, and she gazed out the window, hoping he wouldn't notice.

"I know what you're doing, and you need to stop it. Kat and I will pull this off Wednesday. You'll be back next week."

She wiped her face with the hem of her shirt and turned toward him. He pulled her close, pressing her face against his chest. "Go ahead and cry, angel. Get it out of your system. It's okay."

For several seconds, she cried softly as he stroked her hair. "I was so excited. We did the impossible in Jacksonville. I felt we couldn't lose this week."

"Sweetheart, I never expected to stay past the second or third week. Because of you, I'm in the semi-finals. The real prize for me is meeting and falling in love with you. Compared to that, the first-place title is insignificant."

"But the money? You would get a big bonus for winning."

"Not important to me. I want to win for you."

"But you've been struggling with your career."

"My career. I never said my budget."

She looked at him for a moment, her face still wet.

Wiping the tears from her cheeks with his fingertips, he said, "I am far more concerned with winning this competition for your professional and financial benefit than mine. I've received needed exposure, and, my bank statement is quite healthy, thanks to my mum."

"Your mum?"

He nodded, a wistful look on his face. How many times she said, 'Save, invest, avoid foolish luxuries, my boy. It may not last.'"

Holly tipped her chin, looking up at him, dubiously. "A Ferrari qualifies as a necessity?"

He chuckled as the vehicle stopped at his door. "Give me a break. A boy has to have at least one toy."

"This has been a long day," Holly said as she hobbled through his front door. "I am going to plop on the couch for a few minutes before I give Gigi her food and water."

"Got that covered." He dropped their bags, next to the hallway that led to the bedrooms, and started toward the kitchen.

Holly called out. "We haven't checked my voice mail since before we left for Florida."

"I know."

"Well? Shouldn't we?"

Turning around, he said, "I think we've had enough drama for one day. I'll check it tomorrow." As he disappeared around the corner, Holly watched, a frown forming on her face.

He knows something. Why else would he say we don't need more drama? She's back. That's it.

She wanted to go after Luke, press him for information, but the injury suppressed her motivation. Despite being elevated on the coffee table, her ankle was throbbing.

From the corner of the sofa where she was curled up, Gigi heard the rattle of her cat food bag, stood, stretched, and scampered across Holly's lap. Sailing to the floor, the cat trotted to the kitchen, while Holly leaned forward and massaged her foot.

"Can I bring you something to drink," Luke called out, "glass of wine or a soft drink?"

"I'm good." She picked up the remote control and flicked on the TV.

When he returned, in one hand he held a plastic bag of ice, wrapped in a dish towel—a glass of wine in the other. Handing her the cold pack, he said, "Put this on your ankle for now. I put a couple of zip-locks with the water and alcohol mixture in the freezer." Sitting down next to her, he leaned back, put his feet up next to hers, and offered her a drink of his wine. She accepted.

"Thought you didn't want any."

"I didn't . . . but on second thought."

He smiled and put his arm around her shoulder as she returned the glass to him.

"Luke."

"Yes."

"Is Joy back in town?"

His answer was quick. "Why do you ask?"

"Why are you answering a question with a question?" She turned her head to look him in the eye. "You're dodging. She is back—isn't she?"

He shook his head. "Can we let that dog sleep until tomorrow? I'm exhausted, and I know you must be."

"You've checked. There's another message."

He paused as though calculating his response. "No. I haven't checked. Yes. She's stateside. Satisfied?"

She took note of his abrupt tone. "Don't be mad. I just want to know what is going on."

He sat upright, putting his feet on the floor. After taking a large swallow of wine, he put the glass down, flicked off the TV, and turned toward Holly. "I'm not mad, but I don't want to cause you any further anxiety. Jeff texted me she's back. That's all I know. We'll check your messages tomorrow. . . . I promise. For now, let's put Joy and the show on hold." He stood, took the cold pack from her ankle and handed it to her. Scooping her up in his arms, he carried her toward the bedroom.

"If you don't check, I will."

"I don't doubt that for a second."

Tuesday morning, Holly was awake before Luke. She eased out of bed and limped to the kitchen for a cup of coffee and one of the cold therapy bags he made the night before. When he came into the kitchen, she was sitting on a bar stool with her injured foot, covered with the ice pack, propped up on another stool.

"Why didn't you wake me? I would have gotten your crutches and made the coffee." Leaning over, he kissed her on the cheek.

"I'm fine." She reached up and took his hand, giving it a squeeze.

Pointing to her foot, he said, "How is it, today?"

"Better. It's tender but not throbbing." She took a sip of coffee and held up a cell phone. "Check now."

"Whoa, Sherlock. You don't waste any time, do you? Have you been thinking about that all night?"

"Make the call." With knots in her stomach, she slid his phone down the counter toward him

"Let me clear my head with a little coffee. Okay?"

After taking a couple of swallows, he picked up the phone, hit Holly's home number on the favorites list, and waited. As Luke listened to the messages, Holly watched him like a cat stalking prey. His face registered no concern, and at moments, he seemed amused. Only once did he raise an eyebrow but did not appear alarmed. Clicking off, he said, "No anonymous calls."

"What were you listening to? I saw you punch a button four times."

"Let's see. There was a request to talk to you about your web presence, an offer of a three-day complimentary stay in a timeshare in Arizona, a message from your ex, wanting to talk to you—he sounded a little desperate. And, oh, yes, a call from your friend, Dana, telling you that Luke Damian is a sizzling-hot stud, and you better hang on to him." A grin broke across his face as he repeated the latter.

Holly rolled her eyes, blushing. "She didn't?"

"She did. Want me to call back so you can hear her yourself?"

"No."

"I knew I liked her." He moved closer to Holly and gave her a hug. "Satisfied now? May I go shower and let you return Don's call?"

Holly made a face. "Yeah. Like that's going to happen in this lifetime." She then tipped her head in thought. "That's good news, isn't it? She's back but there's been no call. I can return to my apartment—since you were so gracious as to invite my parents out here for the finale."

"Screwed up, did I?"

"What do you think? But never mind that. You can call off the Perrington watchdogs."

He shook his head. "No, on both counts. You're not going anywhere until we have proof the harassment has ended."

"But—"

He took her by the shoulders and kissed her. "Discussion closed. See you when I'm dressed—unless you'd rather like to join me." He gave her a devilish expression.

"I'll pass on that generous invitation, but this conversation is not over."

"It is until Thursday. You want me to drop Kenley on camera because I'm distracted by concern for your safety?"

She twisted her mouth to the right and cut her eyes to the left in a semi-frown. "Checkmate."

He gave her a high-five and left the kitchen, coffee mug in hand.

Rehearsals on Tuesday were intense but productive. Holly adjusted more and more to her new role, falling into the rhythm of coaching.

"You're a godsend, Kat," Holly said as they wrapped up for the day. "I don't think anyone else could have stepped into my shoes and picked up so fast."

"I second that," Luke said.

"Having a blast working with this guy. You hit the jackpot with him, babe. I think everyone is shocked at how well he performs—with no dance background."

"I know." Holly looked at Luke. "You're going to kill it tomorrow night."

"Should I leave the room while you two sing my praises?"

Holly punched him on the shoulder. "His talent is overshadowed only by his modesty."

They all chuckled.

CHAPTER THIRTY-SEVEN

Show-day dawned with Holly awake first. She sat on the side of the bed, wiggling her injured foot in circles.

Maybe I can dance.

Luke opened his eyes and watched her curiously. "What are you doing?"

"Oh. I'm sorry. I didn't mean to wake you."

"I repeat, what are you doing?"

She extended her leg up for him to see, continuing to make circles in the air. "I think I can dance tonight."

His facial muscles contracted in a harsh frown. "I think, you will not."

"Luke . . . it's hardly hurting. If I dance, we can put the trick back in the choreography. Dancers are accustomed to performing through pain. Kat told me she danced on Broadway with two cracked ribs."

"You're not listening, Holly. Do you remember what I said?"

She looked at him for a few seconds. "What you told me?"

"Don't play dumb. You know. You try to dance, and I walk."

"You wouldn't."

He reached over, grabbed her by the arm, and pulled her to him, wrapping a leg around her. After kissing her, he said, "Trust me. I will walk out of that studio, even if you try to change places with Kat in the wings. I'm not letting you risk more damage to the ankle. Am I clear?"

"You're being controlling."

"I call it protective. If you want to take us out of the competition, try me. It doesn't require a medical degree to know that two days after a sprain you would be taking a chance of exacerbating the damage.

You're letting your emotions trump your common sense."

She lay silent.

"If for no other reason, look at it this way, love. You dance tonight and something goes wrong, then you're out for the final round." He raised his eyebrows in an unspoken sign of confirmation.

Holly took a deep breath and let it out. Shaking her head, she said, "You win, again."

"I can trust when the music begins tonight, it will be Kat on the other side of the stage? No sneaky switch ups?"

She nodded. "You know your contract says I'm supposed to be the boss."

"And you are. But, the fine print says I can't be forced to do anything potentially harmful."

"You looked that up?"

He grinned. "No, I made it up. But, I'm sure it's in there, somewhere."

Wednesday was hectic. Last minute alterations were necessary to Kat's costume. While she and Holly appeared the same in height and weight, Holly's legs were longer and her torso shorter, making the length of the over-skirt too long for Kat. The dress rehearsal went smoothly with Holly taking her place on the sidelines in stride.

"It wasn't until they went on the air, and Kat stood next to Luke during the introductions, that the full thrust hit Holly.

He's performing without me.

In twenty years of recitals, concerts, Broadway, and TV, she had never missed a show. She had danced with bleeding blisters on both heels and all her toes, strep throat, temperature of 103 degrees, headaches, cramps, lack of sleep—but she had always performed.

How did this happen? The most important show of my career, and I can't dance. . . . Or, can I?

She worked her ankle. *Is it possible? Our number doesn't go on for forty-five minutes. Would Luke walk off the stage? No. He wouldn't dare. He's a pro. He would be angry, but he would perform.*

Her heart started beating faster. She could hear Serianni explaining why Kat was on stage with Luke. A video clip of Holly leaving for the hospital went up for both the studio audience and the viewers at home.

Who am I kidding? There's no way I can step in. The costume's been adjusted. The camera shots of me watching them perform are set. Everyone would be furious—even Kat.

For Holly, the time between the opening and Luke's turn on the floor went by in a flash. As the house lights dimmed, she slipped into place on the sidelines, aware that the camera would cut briefly to her several times during his performance. If giving Luke and Kat each a send-off hug before their entrance had been hard, it did not compare to her anxiety when they took their marks.

As the orchestra struck the first note of the intro, a follow spot hit Luke, his shoulder leaning against the black post of a gaslight. He wore all white—suit, shirt, shoes, and hat. Gazing down, his face was in three-quarter profile, his left hand in his pants pocket, and his right leg crossed in front of the other.

"Five … six … seven … eight … *go*," resonated silently in Holly's ear.

"As if he heard her count, Luke straightened, stepped forward, and assumed a two-legged stance as the camera panned in to capture the roguish eyes of a man on the make. Adjusting his tie and skimming the brim of his cocked Panama, he exuded an air of supercilious sensuality, tinged with danger. Aware of the electricity his presence generated in the room, Holly took a deep breath as envy, desire, and depression swept over her in equal portions.

Every woman in this room must be imaging what making love with him would be like.

Like a lightning streak, the image of passion in Sandy's studio flashed before Holly eyes but was chilled when the spotlight switched to Kat. Watching her stand-in slither toward him, Holly was overcome by a force of nausea that made her want to run. She had sworn not to cry, but when Luke grabbed Kat and she wrapped her leg around his waist, Holly's emotions prevailed. At the same moment, the camera zoomed in for a close-up of Holly and caught her glassy eyes.

Get a grip. It's a four-minute dance. You're the one going home with him.

When the music built to where the sensational trick would have been, another dagger sliced through Holly's heart. Although the substitution went well and invoked a round of applause, Holly grieved.

If we could have done our lift, the audience would have gone crazy.

When the music ended, Holly breathed a sigh of relief. It was over. While Kat, a consummate pro, danced beautifully, their chemistry was off at times.

The judges profusely complimented the couple on the difficulty of switching partners with abbreviated rehearsal time and acknowledged Holly for her choreography. However, the scores were lower than Luke had become accustomed to receiving.

As the couple left the floor, Kat paused to embrace Holly as they passed. "Don't worry, hon. You only have to stay in the competition."

Holly quickly praised the performance and thanked Kat.

Luke grabbed her in a bear hug. "It's all good."

Hugs and kisses were traditionally distributed generously among performers. However, anyone paying attention would have recognized Luke's embrace of Holly was more than perfunctory.

"I should have been out there with you," Holly said, trying not to lose it with Sam recording every move. "I let you down."

He lifted her chin. "You couldn't if you tried."

When the judges' scores for the night, which would be applied to the following week's elimination, were tabulated, Luke and Kat were tied with Lisa Cantrell and the handsome chef for third place. Andrei Rodchenko and the gymnast were on the top of the chart, with Mika Dorofeyev and the singer coming in second.

Following Luke and Kat, there was a production number by a guest dance troupe and a solo performance by a pop singer. As the latter neared completion, a production assistant called for the four couples to be ready to lineup on stage for the elimination. Holly would stand with Luke and Kat.

"Who do *you* think is going home?" Holly asked Kat.

"Good money is on Mika. Andrei and his bouncing bundle of Olympic bubbly are the ones to beat. His old-country training with the Moiseyev is cosmic. The bastard is almost as good as he thinks he is."

"You're probably right. Their freestyle next week will be nonstop flips and tricks. We have to do the lift."

"Hold up," Luke said. "You may be able to dance but forget the suicide step."

"I will be ready."

He cocked his head to one side and pointed to her foot, "How does it feel right now?"

"It's fine."

"Holly . . . Look at me. How does it feel—the truth?"

"It's okay. Maybe a little twinge here and there, but it's much better."

"I'll take that as excruciating."

Ignoring his comment, Holly asked Kat, "What about Lisa? Where do you think she and Chef Theo will come in?"

"She'll be in the top. She has—"

Before Kat could finish, the signal came for them to take their places.

The room went dark. As specials from above popped on, bathing each couple in a circle of light, the band played suspenseful music. Following three minutes of orchestrated tension, Mika and his partner were eliminated.

After hugs, high-fives, and the usual condolences to the exiting couple, Luke and Holly went to his dressing room. She sat on the couch with an ice pack on her ankle, watching him strip off the costume. Her mind wandered to the night of their first act of intimacy in the spot where she was sitting.

Luke pulled on a pair of jeans but remained shirtless as he sat in front of the large mirror and began removing his makeup.

So, I didn't dance tonight. I've got—

Luke turned around, cosmetic remover on his face. "Think we

could skip the after-party?"

She chuckled. "Cold cream becomes you, but no, we can't."

Eleven weeks ago—strangers. Now—lovers.

Rehearsal was not scheduled to start until eleven on Thursday morning, so Luke and Holly slept later than usual even though they left the after-party early. He was up first and had coffee made when she limped into the kitchen.

"How's the ankle?"

"Good. The swelling is down. I'll dance in the finals."

"We'll see." He handed her a cup of coffee and then picked up his cell.

She took a sip. "Can we leave early? I want to stop by my apartment."

He straddled a barstool and scanned email on his phone. "Any special reason?"

"Mostly to check my mail, but I also want to pick up a jacket. It's getting cooler at night."

Closing out the phone, he looked up at her. "We should be able to fit it in."

An hour later, they reached her building. Luke and Jimmy Cox, the security guard driving them, accompanied her up to the unit, stopping on the way at the postal box.

Arriving at her door, she handed Luke the mail and then dug through her handbag for the key. "I hate these large purses. I'm always digging for my keys."

While she fumbled with her search and Jimmy stood by, Luke flipped through the stack of envelopes and circulars. "No suspicious envelopes."

When the door swung open, Holly started to step in—then froze.

CHAPTER THIRTY-EIGHT

A blank envelope stood, propped up against a cat figurine on her coffee table. "What's that?"

Luke frowned. "You didn't leave it there?"

Jimmy moved in front of Luke and Holly, motioning them to hold back.

"No. I've never seen it before." She turned and looked at him, panic in her eyes." How did it get there?"

"Don't touch it. Don't touch anything." Luke whipped out his phone and wallet. "I'm calling Montgomery."

"Stay here," Jimmy said, drawing his weapon. "I check out the rest of the apartment."

Holly moved closer to Luke. As soon as he keyed in a number from the detective's card, he shoved the card and wallet in his pant pocket and put his arm around her shoulders.

"Detective, Luke Damian. We're at Holly Dawson's apartment. Someone broke in and left an envelope for her to find."

Holly was trembling but trying not to give entirely into her emotions.

"No. She wasn't here and hasn't been for several days." Luke squeezed her shoulders. "Right. We'll wait." After providing Holly's address, he terminated the call with one hand and dropped the cell back in his pocket. Putting his other arm around her, Luke wrapped Holly in a protective hug. "He's in the field but not far away. Said not to touch anything and for the sake of caution, we should get out of the apartment. He's on his way and is calling for specialists to handle the envelope and collect any evidence the intruder left."

"Get out of the apartment, clear the envelope? What is he thinking is in it?" Her eyes reflected her stress.

"Sweetheart, no one knows. But better to err on the side of caution."

Jimmy walked back in the room, sheathing his gun. "All clear in the rest of the apartment. Did you reach the cops?"

"They're on their way."

"Luke, how did this monster get in? The door was locked."

The body guard went to the entrance and visually examined it. "No sign of forced entry. Probably had a key."

"That's impossible." Holly said, pulling back from Luke.

"Either that or you—or someone—left it unlocked. Does your landlord access the unit when you're not here?"

Holly thought for several seconds. "Maybe. The pest control people come in. I've always been hyper about that because of Gigi. Maybe maintenance if there's a problem."

"The police will check that out."

"Let's get out of the apartment and get you to where you can sit down, honey." He pointed down, tipping his head toward her ankle. "You need to get off that foot."

Leaving the apartment door open, they went downstairs and out of the building. While waiting in the car, Holly massaged her ankle and tried to steady her nerves.

The bomb squad, including an explosive sniffing dog, arrived within five minutes, attracting a small group of curiosity seekers. Luke wore a baseball cap and sunglasses to allay recognition while he directed the team leader to Holly's unit. Within three minutes, two patrol cars pulled up and took charge of the bystanders.

When he returned to the car, Holly's hand covered her mouth and her eyes were glassy.

"This is scary, Luke. They look like they're going to war." She referred to the team heavily covered in armor who had climbed out of the tank-like van.

Montgomery was only minutes behind the first wave of police. While they waited, Holly called Sam to warn him they would be late.

When the detective and his partner arrived, the envelope had been placed in the van for inspection.

"Can we go back in?" Holly asked.

"I'd prefer that we not do that. I want a clean sweep of the unit to be certain nothing has been planted out of sight before you go back in, plus the evidence techs will be here shortly."

By the time Montgomery had questioned Luke, Holly, and Jimmy, the envelope had been cleared and turned over to the detective. With gloved hands, he carefully slid out the contents, a single sheet of standard paper. Unfolding it, he held the communication, which consisted of words crudely cut from print media and attached with clear tape, for Luke and Holly to read along with him.

WARNING

DANGER IN L.A.

GIGI IS HANDSOME CAT

SAD FOR ANYTHING HAPPEN TO HIM OR YOU

Holly's heart raced. She could barely breathe as her knees went weak, and her face lost color. Seeing her distress, Luke grabbed her around the waist.

"That has to be interpreted as a threat." Luke's body was tense as he held Holly.

Montgomery nodded. "Uh, huh. That it is."

"She's been in my *home*. What if Gigi had been there?" Holly's eyes were filled with panic. "How does she know about my cat?"

"She can't know much to refer to Gigi as male," Luke said. "Even the name is female."

Holly's stomach tightened, panic taking over. "What are we going to do?"

"Gigi is safe at my flat." He pulled her to his chest. "But, the woman has to be stopped." He looked Montgomery in the eye.

Like Luke, Holly cast her gaze at Montgomery. "She can't know about Gigi unless she's been in my apartment before."

"Maybe. Have you ever posted a comment about your cat on social media?"

"No. I don't do Twitter or Instagram. I have a Facebook page but don't even look at it more than twice a month. I never posted anything about Gigi or Luke."

"Just to cover the bases, mind taking a look?"

She shrugged. "Sure."

He went to his car and retrieved an electronic tablet. Bringing up the site, he turned the device to Holly. "Open your page."

Holly shook her head. "We won't find anything there."

"Humor me."

Luke stood behind her, his hands on her shoulders as she typed in her password and scanned down the multitude of posts.

"Oh, my god. Oh, my god."

Luke bent over to see what had caught her attention. A smile crept across his face.

"What did you find, Ms. Dawson?"

"My mother posted a photo of Luke, me, and Gigi from our Thanksgiving holiday. Regina, my sister-in-law, shared it." She turned to Luke. "I knew I shouldn't have let her take pictures. She has no idea about the traps with social media."

"She meant no harm," Luke said.

"Of course, she meant no harm. She just wanted to show off." Holly handed the tablet back to the detective.

"Anyone might have seen that. Our techs can probably check on who has accessed your page, but given your celebrity status, that could be a significant pool of people."

"What else can you do?" Luke asked.

"We'll start with the obvious. Looking at the grammar, it's possible the sender is either poorly educated, or English is not his or her first language." The detective eased the note back into the envelope and put it into a plastic evidence bag. "The lab will try to lift fingerprints and DNA from the note, and around the apartment. We'll do the usual interviews of neighbors. If the complex has security cameras, we'll ask to review footage, beginning with the last time Ms. Dawson was in the unit through this morning. If nothing turns up, I'll request a canvas of all the cameras in the neighborhood. You'd be surprised how many people have them."

Holly looked down at her watch. "How much longer do we have to stay?" she asked, looking at the detective. "We are under pressure to rehearse for next week's show."

"Go ahead for now. We'll secure the apartment, but I advise you to arrange to have your lock changed. When can the two of you stop by the station? We'll need samples of your prints and DNA."

Luke looked at Holly. "What do you think? Early tomorrow morning?"

She nodded.

Midway through the ride to the TV studio, Luke's cell rang. It was Harvey Gold.

After filling the lawyer in on the latest development, Luke's expression turned angry as he listened.

"How the hell can that be?"

Holly studied his face, alarmed at what information the lawyer was delivering. She could see Luke's muscles tightening under the snug tee shirt.

Ending the call, Luke turned to her. "Joy's lawyer filed a petition to dissolve the injunction."

"No."

"Harvey says not to worry. Filing a pleading and winning in court are not the same. He thinks she may be hoping to divert suspicion if she is the stalker

"That's easy for Harvey to say.

Kat and Sam were waiting when Luke and Holly arrived. In her brief call to the pair, Holly had not given a reason for their delay.

Kat immediately looked down at Holly's foot. "Was your ankle acting up?"

Before Holly could respond, Luke took the lead. "I wanted her to have it looked at to be sure it's safe for her to work."

"And?"

Relieved that he covered for their absence, Holly said, "It's much better, but I'm going to set the choreography on you, if you don't mind."

"No problem." Kat smiled. "I love your music. 'This is the Moment' is one kick-ass piece —flow, emotion, power." She pointed to the cameraman. "Sam played it for me."

"I thought it would work well for us. I'm convinced that lyrical is our best bet. We're not going to go head-to-head with Andrei's pyrotechnics or Lisa's one-wardrobe-malfunction-short-of-a-centerfold."

Kat nodded. "Good choice. I watched the two of you rock that waltz the first week. Even with the little snafu, it was a class act."

Luke made a face and rolled his eyes toward the ceiling. "I'm trying to erase the memory of that blunder."

Kat pointed her index finger at his chest. "Don't give me that look, buddy. You know it was good and your foxtrot was a showstopper."

"So, let's get this party going," Holly said. "We've got work to do."

The next morning, Luke and Holly met with Montgomery as promised. After a technician took DNA samples and fingerprints they sat at the detective's desk.

"I don't have any results to share with you, yet," Montgomery said, circling his desk and taking a seat. "Have the two of you given anymore thought to potential suspects?"

"Have you ruled out Joy Ambrose?" Holly asked.

"No one has been ruled out, but it's not wise to assume any specific person is responsible without more evidence." The detective manipulated a pencil through his fingers as though it were a majorette's baton.

"I hate to think it, but what about Sam?" Luke said. "He's been working with you for two seasons and certainly knows how much you care about Gigi. He also knew about Joy's ludicrous claim about being pregnant."

Holly shook her head, her face scrunched up in a frown. "You'll never convince me Sam would do anything like this. He's been nothing but a wonderful friend."

"Maybe he would like to be more," Montgomery said.

"No way. Also, Sam knows Gigi is female."

"Would any of your neighbors have reason to do something like this? Any male neighbors show an interest in you? Have you had any unusual attention on social media?"

"No, as far as neighbors. I'm not home much and only interact with the girl in the apartment below me. She's a makeup artist on a TV series and is engaged to an actor. She has no reason to hurt me. She has fed Gigi for me a couple of times when I went on a short trip, but Gigi goes to my parents' home in Florida when I'm on tour."

"What about your ex I met when we had dinner at your parents' club?" Luke asked.

"Don? How could it be him? He's three-thousand miles away. Also, he may be a jerk, but he would never hurt Gigi—or me."

"Planes fly every day. He could be here without you knowing it." Luke's brows went up. "He certainly appeared interested in you when he came over to our table Saturday night, plus he seemed passionate about reaching you in the message left on your voice mail."

Holly made a face and a thumbs-down gesture. "He snuck out the back door of our relationship. Why would he want to come back in?"

"Your mother thinks he might."

"Don't rule anyone out, yet," Montgomery said. "What I need from the two of you is to go over again a list of every possible suspect. From the first phone calls, we know this stalker had knowledge about an alleged baby. I'm assuming that's not common knowledge."

"True," Luke said.

"Who has that information?"

Luke thought for a few seconds. "I haven't told anyone. Have you, Holly?"

"No. No one."

Luke counted on his fingers. "Only the pool of people in the meeting the afternoon Joy invaded our rehearsal, the security guards who responded, and Sam."

"Don't overlook the possibility of someone in that group spreading the word," said Montgomery.

"But, it couldn't have spread to Florida for Don to find out. So that takes him off the list of suspects." Holly took a deep breath. "We'll try to think of anyone else, but we need to get to the studio now."

CHAPTER THIRTY-NINE

For the remainder of the week, Kat did the dancing while Holly coached. Erring on the side of caution, Holly forced herself to be patient and pamper her ankle. Every day, she spent an hour in physical therapy with Bruce and followed his directions to the letter. She soaked the ankle every night, applied cold packs afterward, and wore a tight brace from the time she woke in the morning until she went to bed at night. To keep herself in shape, she worked out at the barre, avoiding weight on the damaged joint. The following Monday morning, she announced she would mark the first run-through, which meant she would not do any difficult steps.

"Are you sure?" Kat asked.

"No doubt, *whatsoever*. Look. I'm walking without a problem." She did a waltz turn to demonstrate. "Trust me, I'm not going to take a risk."

Luke raised an eyebrow, shrugged, and gave Kat a what-can-we-do look.

As he walked toward the opposite side of the studio to take his entry position, Holly called out, "Tomorrow, I'm planning on doing our big trick at the end."

He stopped abruptly and turned around. "*Damn* it, Holly." His eyes shot darts across the room. "You can't do that. We can't do it."

"Of course, we can. We've got twenty seconds on the last note. I'll jump, you'll catch me, lift me over your head, and then promenade in a backward circle, dropping me down for the finish."

"You're insane."

"Holly," Kat interrupted. "He can't possibly catch you in the split, much less find your balance, with that long skirt flapping in his face."

"It's detachable."

"She's demented, Kat. We're going to crash and burn in living color on national TV."

Holly walked over to Luke and took his hands. "Let's don't argue about it now. We have two days. I'm not going to try it today. Tomorrow, I'll dance full out. We'll decide then. If it makes you feel better, we'll rehearse the ending both ways. The final decision can even be made when we're on the floor."

"Oh, god. You plan to surprise me on camera?"

"Something like that." She grinned, impishly.

Nothing more was said about the special lift. As Holly participated in the rehearsal with Luke, she engaged more and more in the choreography but resisted the temptation to dance full out. After several run-throughs, she conceded to a break and let Kat take over.

"I'm fine. I just don't want to overdo it."

Luke grinned. "It's refreshing to see you exercise a little caution."

At twelve-thirty, the dancers broke and went to the studio commissary. When they passed through the archway into the dining area, Lisa Cantrell and her partner were leaving. Cantrell acknowledged Kat, but when Holly started to speak, the dancer turned away.

Was that intentional?

Luke gave no indication of noticing Cantrell's action and exchanged a handshake and pat on the upper arm with her partner, Theo Svendsen. As they neared the salad bar, Luke asked, "Either of you want something from the grill?"

Kat shook her head. "Rabbit food for me."

Holly nodded. "Same here." Luke walked toward the hot food section, while the two women grabbed plates from the salad bar.

"Did you notice how Lisa avoided me?" Holly asked Kat as they circled the array of fruits and vegetables.

"She's jealous."

Holly made a face. "Of me? How so? I'm the rookie; she's the thousand-time champ."

"And she wants to remain so. You're younger, prettier, and have the best partner. Believe me. She's royally pissed she screwed up by choosing the pretty-boy kitchen stud over Luke." Kat reached for the low-cal dressing.

"Choosing Theo? I don't understand. We don't get to choose our partners."

Kat put a knife, fork, and napkin on her tray and then looked at Holly with a you're-so-naïve expression that turned into a mock frown. "Of course, she chose Theo. Her royal highness has first pick of partners."

Holly was bewildered. "How does she get to do that?"

Kat glanced around to choose a table. "You really don't know?"

"Apparently, I don't."

"Connections, babe. How do you think she wins so often? She's no better a dancer than the rest of us—probably not as talented as you."

Holly stared at Kat, astonished.

"You are so precious, Snow White. I bet you still believe in the Easter Bunny. Everyone knows Lisa is Art's play pal." Kat put her tray down on a table by the windows.

Holly took a place adjacent to Kat. "Apparently not everyone. I didn't. Are we talking Assistant Producer in Charge of Casting Art? Married Art?"

"Married on weekends only. With her pick of partners, the queen rides the inside track—if you get my meaning. Hell, Dawson, she's pee-green Luke is a gladiator. She chose the crock-pot-jock because he's gorgeous and currently hot as hell on the tube. If she'd had any idea Luke would turn into a winner, he would have been her—"

Luke arrived at the table with a tray of drinks, causing Kat to abruptly stop talking.

"What are you ladies discussing so seriously?"

Holly said nothing, waiting to see what Kat would say.

"Feminine hygiene. Boring as crap to you guys," Kat said.

Holly's face flushed at Kat's comment, but she kept her mouth shut.

Kat did most of the dancing after they returned from lunch but cut out early for an appointment. At five-thirty, Luke and Holly were waiting for their car to arrive. Sam, in a hurry to get home for his wife's birthday, left a few minutes before. As she finished a bottle of water and was about to toss the container, Holly's cell phone rang. She glanced at the caller ID. "I think it's Detective Montgomery."

Luke put down his bottle of Gatorade and paid close attention as she answered.

Holly listened intently, a frown on her face. "We are under a lot of stress between now and the Wednesday show. I know it's important, but we can't afford to lose any rehearsal time." It was a short conversation, ending with Holly telling the detective she and Luke would come into the station on Thursday morning. Trembling, she slid her phone back in her bag.

Luke took her hand. "What did he say?"

Holly cleared her throat. "They found two security cameras in my neighborhood with footage that shows a person, wearing a black hoodie and carrying a slim briefcase, going into my building."

"Did he say when?"

"Four-thirty a.m., last Tuesday. He wants both of us to come in and review the film."

"Was it a man or woman?"

"He didn't say." Holly made a face and slapped the heel of her hand against her temple. "I was so nervous I didn't think to ask."

"Did he mention fingerprints?"

She shook her head. "You want to call him back?"

Luke put his arms around her, trying to calm her. "Maybe we should take the time to go in tomorrow."

"No. It has to wait until after the show. We have to focus on the dance."

"But, can *you* do that?"

"I can—as long as Gigi is safe."

He tightened his hold on her.

During the drive home, Holly was quiet. The lunch conversation with Kat played over in her head, but she didn't mention it to Luke.

I'm being paranoid. There's no reason to suspect Lisa.

Despite feeling guilty, she continued to inventory her memory of interactions with Lisa Cantrell, concentrating on the time the harassment began.

Tuesday morning, Holly alternated run-throughs of the dance with Kat.

"How's the ankle?" Luke asked after her third turn.

"It's fine. It feels a little weak, but I have no doubts about performing. Let's try the other lift at the end."

Alarm crossed Luke's face. "You're *not* talking about the one we've been rehearsing all morning, are you?"

"I'm not."

"You really haven't given up on that?" He stood with his hands on his hips.

Kat and Sam watched the contentious exchange escalate.

"Why would you think I had?"

He sighed. "Not think—hoped." He threw his hands in the air. "Talk to her, Kat. See if you can persuade her to be reasonable."

Kat shrugged her shoulders. "Don't put me in the middle of your lovers' squabble. This is your dance, and the two of you have to work it out."

Holly walked over and positioned herself in front of him. He turned his face away.

"Luke, look at me."

He shook his head, refusing to face her.

"All right. Then, listen. It's all mental. If you *believe* we can do it, we can. We've done it. I know I'm up to it. I push off on my healthy foot—no risk there."

He turned to face her but declined to answer. She reached around him and gave him a hug, and then walked over and started the music.

During the first eight seconds of the intro, Luke stood his ground and refused to move. Then, with an annoyed expression on his face, he gave in. Holly danced full out. By the second repetition of the signature lyric, Luke was relaxed, smiling at her, and fully immersed in the moment. When the vocalist neared the end of the song, Holly was in position. She left the floor with complete abandon as the baritone hit the final note, which he held for approximately fifteen, breathtaking seconds. Luke caught her and pressed her up above his head. Kat gasped. But, just as the lift reached its peak, Holly's balance shifted, and she crumbled. Luke kept her from crashing to the floor, but the trick was destroyed.

He eased her to her feet and said, "See. We can't do it."

"We can." She turned toward Kat, who, overwhelmed by the piece, had tears in her eyes. "Tell him. We had it. I'm the one who messed up. I was a little nervous from lack of rehearsal and lost my square. Let's do it again. I won't repeat that mistake."

Luke looked like a child whose lollipop had been stolen. "You're relentless."

Kat stood up from where she had been sitting. "We're all crazy. . . . It's what makes us good."

"One more time—no music—just the lift," Holly said.

"I don't know."

"Come on. We won't have another chance. We have camera blocking and spray tanning after lunch. Give it one last shot."

He shook his head. "Play the damn music from the beginning. I need the three minutes to psyche up for the kill."

On the second attempt, the lift was perfect.

"See!" Holly was ecstatic. She grabbed Luke and hugged him. Kat and Sam were clapping.

"She's right, handsome. It's a spectacular ending to a damn awesome piece," Kat said, walking up to them and putting her arm around Holly's shoulders. "I wish I had the skill to pull it off."

Luke smiled. "I'll probably live to regret feeding the monster."

Holly hugged him again. "It's not written in stone. If we don't have the right vibes tomorrow night, we'll go with the easy version."

Luke gave Kat a nod. "Like that's going to happen."

"I'm serious, Luke. If either one of us doesn't feel confident about it, we don't do it."

After lunch, Holly accompanied Luke and Kat to the camera blocking but did not dance. Lisa Cantrell and the Swedish chef were going through their routine when the trio reached the performing area. True to Holly's prediction, Cantrell and partner were dancing a sultry rumba. Holly watched the pair with the question looming in her mind as to whether the dancer could be responsible for the harassment, and if so, was she dangerous? By the time the music entered the final phase, the sight of Cantrell had begun to make Holly nervous. Quietly, she slipped back into the audience section of the room.

When Luke and Kat moved into the dance area, Lisa spoke to Kat. "You filling in again tomorrow night?"

"Jury's out. Minute to minute."

With a hand shielding her eyes, Cantrell scanned the room. Spotting Holly, she smiled, and waved.

What's that all about? Snub me one minute, friendly the next?

Out of the corner of Holly's eye, she caught a glimpse of Svendsen and for a second thought he was scowling.

CHAPTER FORTY

Show day dawned with Holly feeling as bright as the sun, which admirably attempted to burn through the L.A. smog. She made a pot of coffee before a barefoot Luke stumbled into the kitchen.

"Today's the day," she said, standing on tiptoe to reach around his neck.

He grabbed her around her waist. "Good morning, sunshine. Did I sleep through the show and we won?"

"Very funny. That comes next week."

Still groggy, he smiled, pulled her tight, and gave her a kiss.

"Are you ready to take gold?" she asked.

"It's on my list. But coffee first, please." He took a mug from the rack on the counter. "How's the ankle? Any trouble after working it, yesterday?"

"Ankle is good, but to be safe, I'm having acupuncture this afternoon."

After filling his mug, he took a sip. "Acupuncture? Does Bruce know?"

"It was his idea. He said it can't hurt." She opened the pantry door and took out the cat food. "As soon as I feed Gigi, I'm taking a shower. We should be at the studio no later than eight." She poured the dry food into the cat's bowl, put away the bag, and started toward the bedroom side of the condo. Luke stopped her.

With a serious expression on his face, he set his mug on the counter. "Holly, I've been thinking about the last lift." She turned around but said nothing. "I think we ought to play it safe. I know you have your heart set on the big ending, but we don't have it under control. I haven't felt this nervous since our first number."

She walked back over to the bar where he was sitting. "Look at me." She used two fingers to point towards her wide-opened eyes.

He smiled. "Yes, ma'am."

"Do you trust me?"

"Not a fair question."

"Absolutely fair. I'm the pro, who is presumed to know what she's doing. Either you trust me, or you don't."

He studied her face for a minute. "I am well aware that you know your art, but you don't know how I feel. My gut is telling me to run the hell away from the ticking bomb."

She reached up and ran her fingers through his sleep-disheveled hair. "I'll make a deal with you. No more talk. If you are willing to go through with it tonight, when we separate before the final lift, discard your tailcoat. That'll be my cue, and I'll rip off my skirt."

Holly opted out of dress rehearsal, taking the time to have her acupuncture treatment while Kat filled in. The costume department had made duplicates so that both dancers would be in makeup, dressed, and ready to perform. No one, other than Sam and the three dancers, knew about the special lift.

Shortly before going on the air, Lisa Cantrell saw Holly in costume for the first time. The expression on her face changed quickly from pleasant to surprised, ending in sour.

If looks could kill, I'd be dead.

When Kat walked into the warmup area, Cantrell's expression relaxed. "Are you guys dancing a *pas de trois*?"

"No. We thought we would tag-team it tonight. Keep everyone on their toes," Kat said.

Holly smiled but felt uneasy.

"I'm surprised you would risk further injury," Cantrell said, pointing to the bound ankle.

"Kat is ready to step in if needed."

"I would certainly hope you value your career enough to protect your instrument." Without waiting for a response, Cantrell gave each dancer a perfunctory hug and wished them good luck, which is a superstitious curse to dancers who prefer to hear *break a leg*. As she walked away, Kat gave her the finger.

"Kat—the *cameras,*" Holly said, her eyebrows scrunched together but her mouth grinning.

"Bullshit! They'll edit it out. I hope you and Luke stick it to her ass."

"Ooh?" Holly jumped as a pair of cold hands grabbed her shoulders. Turning around, she saw it was Andrei. "You almost gave me a heart attack."

"Sorry. Not my intention. Just want to tell you to break a leg—and give you a kiss for luck." Although not quite as handsome as Luke, the Russian was raw sex appeal from hair follicle to dancing toes.

"Not a kiss of death, I hope," Kat said.

"Go away, Kenley. You know I want the best for my girl. She's good." He leaned over, kissed Holly on the cheek and then moved on toward his partner, who was glaring at the trio.

"I doubt he meant that," Holly said, rubbing the spot on her face where his lips had touched.

"Oh, he means it all right." Kat nodded. "Andrei Rodchenko competes only with Andrei—and maybe Mika. He knows he's good and audiences love him. He can work wherever and whenever he chooses."

"I'll take your word for that. You certainly know the guy better than I do." Holly smiled coquettishly.

"Touché. But, all things considered . . . I *might* take him home after the party, tonight."

Holly grinned at Kat and then gave her the thumbs-up sign.

Luke appeared in the archway leading to the pre-show room. Holly's heart stopped. Her breath caught in her throat.

"Oh, my god, how well you clean up," Kat said. "If I weren't afraid this one would put a tack in my slipper, I would take *you* home tonight."

Kat did not exaggerate. In his white tie and tails, he was extraordinarily handsome. His eyes sparkled like aquamarine crystals, accented by his tanned face and blond hair, which had been enhanced with highlights. The cut of the suit fit his trim frame like a custom-tailored Armani.

"And, if I were not hopelessly in love with this stunning lady," he said, thrusting an arm toward Holly, "I would take you up on that." He walked over and kissed her on the cheek.

Entranced by the sight of him and the aroma of his fragrance, Holly was speechless. Everyone else disappeared from the room.

"Well, at least give the understudy a consolation kiss," Kat said.

"My pleasure." He crossed the short distance to Kat and leaned down to kiss her. She took hold of his head and whispered something in his ear. He smiled and then returned to Holly.

"What did she say to you?"

"Un-uh. That's on a-need-to-know basis." He raised his eyebrows, a slight smirk on his face.

"Luke . . ."

"Shh. The show's starting." He squeezed her waist.

Following the opening production number, Andrei and his partner performed to the Queen sports anthem "We Will Rock You," leading into "We Are the Champions." As Holly predicted, the routine was fast and furious with crowd-pleasing gymnastics blended with the Russian's forceful aplomb and attack. When the couple finished, applause rocked the room. Holly looked up at Luke, as he clapped vigorously, seeing tension creeping across his brow. He turned his face toward her and said, "They were good."

"They were. Don't let it psych you out."

Lisa Cantrell and Theo Svendsen took their places. Keeping an eye on the competitors, Luke put his arm around Holly as "Slow Hand," the Pointer Sisters' classic, began.

Cantrell wore a draped, beige gown that was open all the way down one side, with the front and back connected only by three, narrow strips of fabric. It created an illusion of nudity when the gap faced the audience. She would not have looked more provocative had she been totally naked.

"It looks like you called this one, too," Luke said as Cantrell slithered across to her partner and wrapped a leg around his waist.

"Choreographers play to their strong suit, and Lisa's is definitely sensual." As she spoke, Holly could feel Luke was tight. She, too, was edgier than usual.

For the remainder of the Cantrell-Svendsen performance, neither Luke nor Holly spoke. Luke stared at the erotic moves being made by the dancers as if he were hypnotized. Fearing a camera might be spying, Holly forced herself to watch but tried to block the transmission of the images to her brain by thinking about Thanksgiving dinner in Florida. She wanted to shake her arms and legs to loosen up but feared showing any sign of stress to Luke. He appeared to have enough of his own.

Three minutes and fifty-two seconds of Cantrell rubbing against Svendsen, and his hands wandering over her body, flirting with the forbidden, had the audience mesmerized.

As the couple fell into their final pose, Luke said, "Another minute of that and half the men in this room would have embarrassed themselves."

Holly smiled at him. "Time for us. Ready?"

"All good. Let's rock and roll."

He sounded confident, but Holly knew it was false bravado. She took his hand and gave it a squeeze. "See you on the other side."

As she walked around to take her place on the set, she heard the judges gushing over Cantrell and Svendsen.

"My darling, I was afraid we would have to call the fire department. The two of you were too hot to handle," Harry Fellows said.

Lorraine Gibson broke the choreography down technically, complimenting each section. "Captivating, courageous, and carnal," she called the piece.

When the accounting was revealed, the two performing couples were tied with perfect scores.

As the crew changed the set for their number, Holly's nerves threatened to get the best of her. The show had cut to commercial, and they would be on immediately after the break. An overhead special would illuminate Holly shortly before the first bar of music. Her hair was down, pulled back on both sides and caught with flowers. Her costume was a simple white-satin camisole sprinkled with rhinestones and edged with tiny pink rosebuds. The detachable skirt was comprised of two, circular layers of white chiffon with a scrunched, pink satin cummerbund at the waist.

Holly took her place, seated on an old-fashioned park bench, flanked by fake shrubbery and a garden statute. She closed her eyes and took a deep breath. *Please God, give us strength.*

The light came on slowly, capturing her in a pensive profile. The music began and Luke appeared. Holly's heart pounded. She looked up. He extended his hand. At first, his expression was serious, bordering on stern—his body tense. But as their eyes met and their hands joined, his face began to soften and his body loosened, washing away her anxiety.

In turn, Holly's face relaxed as she was captured by his tender and loving gaze. Magically, the music absorbed them as they moved across the floor in gracefully sweeping steps. For the pair, all—the room, the audience, the judges—ceased to exist. They floated in their own private realm—free and fearless. It was their moment. Rather than dancers, Holly and Luke were skaters gliding across invisible ice with her skirt swirling and her long hair cascading. As the dramatic music swelled, Luke lifted her as though she were weightless. They turned flawlessly—her costume spiraling in ripples like water assaulted by a pebble. Neither heard the thunderous applause they were generating. The lovers were one with the music and with one another.

At that moment, thoughts of choreography or technique vanished. The dancers were aware only of their love for one another. As the final seconds approached, Luke released Holly for a series of traveling turns away from him. Reaching her destination, she turned to face him as he discarded the tailcoat. Smiling, she tore her skirt away as he silently mouthed, "I've got you."

CHAPTER FORTY-ONE

Taking a deep breath, her smile larger than life, Holly started toward him. She didn't jump; she flew. Gravity dissolved, and she was in the air, high above Luke's head.

They had done it.

The room shook with a standing ovation. The judges were all on their feet. It was more than applause, it was awe and adoration. Whistles and shouts of "bravo" abounded.

As Luke dropped her to the cradle position and then gently to her feet, she threw her arms around him, tears slipping down her cheeks. He hugged her and kissed the top of her head. Neither spoke. The audience continued to applaud as the couple walked to the where Ted Serianni stood. The emcee attempted unsuccessfully to quiet the house.

After more than a minute of the eardrum-bursting clamor, Serianni, holding a hand up, shouted, "It's a live show, folks. We have to get moving."

The judges were profuse with compliments, exhausting most of the superlatives in the dictionary.

"I'm speechless," Lorraine Gibson said, putting a hand to her neck. "You brought us all into the music and the moment with you. If that was acting, Luke, every producer in this town should be calling before the night is over."

"If the two of you don't have something going off stage, I think you better reexamine your priorities," Kikki Donavan said. "You danced with your feet but sang with your eyes. Every woman here wanted you, Luke. And every man wanted to be you."

Jamie Bradshaw said, "Enchanting. Absolutely enchanting. How does one presume to judge perfection?"

And Harry Bellows sat back in his chair. Throwing up his hands, he said, "I have nothing to say. Words would only desecrate the sacred moment. The two of you have brought this show to a new level and set a bar I cannot fathom being matched."

Serianni took the floor. "So, tell me, Luke. How does it feel? That final lift was beyond belief."

Luke shook his head. "Good and good to be over." He looked down at Holly, smiled and gave her a squeeze. Then, glancing around, he swept his arm in the air. "I hope you fellows got the end on film because that was the one and only time it's ever going to happen."

The couple was met with mass confusion backstage after the show. Congratulations, combined with interrogations, stalled their passage to the dressing rooms, giving Holly no opportunity to express her personal emotions to Luke. Kat led the pack with Sam right behind her.

Giving Luke a high-five and hugging Holly, a grinning Kat said, "Way to go, champs. The queen is dead; long live the queen." The veteran dancer had tears in her eyes.

"We haven't won, yet," Holly said. "The viewers still vote."

"After that performance, a viewer would be blind or ignorant to pass you over."

"Agreed," said Mika, slapping Luke on the back. "What is the word? . . . *Gutsy*? Gutsy move, English. I am great dancer, but even I have no such *храбрость*."

"No clue what that is, but if I've got it, I hope it's good," Luke said.

"It is," Andrei said, pushing in to offer his congratulations. "It means courage. What you and Holly did there took much of it. If you win, I will concede with honor."

"I appreciate that." Luke patted the Russian on his shoulder.

While the cast continued to bombard them with kudos, Holly noticed two members were conspicuously absent.

Everyone's here but Lisa and Theo. A knot formed in her stomach.

When they finally made it to the dressing room, Luke and Holly stood for a moment, gazing into one another's eyes without speaking. She moved first, throwing her arms around him. "We did it! I am so proud of you. Thank you."

He hugged her, holding her tight for several seconds. "You did it. I just stood there and caught you." He lifted her chin and kissed her. Afterward, he said, "Want to open a bottle of champagne?"

"No." She smiled. "Let's save our celebrating for next week. I want to put in the obligatory appearance at the after-party and then go home."

When they arrived at the condo, Luke attended to Gigi while Holly prepared for bed. He had showered at the studio while she changed in the group dressing room. By the time she came out of the bathroom, he was propped up on pillows, waiting—wearing only pajama bottoms, the top draped over the back of a nearby chair.

"I saved you a place," he said, patting the sheet.

"I bet you did. After tonight, I'm sure the applications for space in bed with the heartthrob of the hour are pouring in."

"Let's be accurate. *Has-been* heartthrob."

"Oh . . . I think you moved back up in the ranks."

He beckoned her with his index finger. "There's only one applicant I care about, and she needs to bring her pretty little bum to bed right now before this randy has-been dies of deprivation."

She crawled onto the mattress on her knees, leaned over, and kissed him. Pulling back, she said, "Not a fatal affliction, sweetheart. You get the cure when you tell me what Kat whispered to you."

He pulled an arm out from under her, causing her to collapse, and then rolled on top, pinning her down. Raising his torso up, with his elbows locked, he stared her in the eye. "*That,* my love, is classified."

"Then, you need to move back on your side of the bed, because my shop is closed for the night, and I'm going to sleep."

He started tickling her ribs. "I don't think so, but *if* you must know, she simply told me my private after-party would be a lot more fun if I gave the final trick a go—assuring me she believed I could do it."

Holly tensed, frowning. "Is that what prompted you to try?" She pressed her hands against his shoulders, attempting to push him away, but he held fast.

"Simmer down. . . . No—you *know* that. I did it because of how much it meant to you. As we moved across the floor, I could see the love and trust in your eyes. No way could I disappoint you."

A tear slid down her cheek. "Were you afraid we'd fail?"

His head turned from side to side. "Are you kidding? At that moment, I was invincible. You were right—it's all mental." He cocked an eyebrow. "But, don't even think about including anything as difficult in next week. I was dead serious when I said last night was my one and only go at it."

"You're safe. No pressure in the finale." Holly's hands moved from his shoulders to around his neck. She pulled his face to hers and whispered. "It's time you claimed your reward."

At four a.m., Luke turned over and reached for Holly, but she wasn't there. He ran his hand around her side of the bed before opening his eyes. Not finding her, he glanced at the clock and then rose. The bathroom door was ajar, allowing a sliver of light to escape. He walked over and listened.

"Holly? Are you okay?"

From inside, she gasped. "Oh, my gosh. You scared me. . . . I'm fine. Do you need the bathroom? I can come out."

"Not really." Pushing the door open, he found her on her knees, wearing his pajama top with sleeves rolled up—a sponge in her hand and a can of cleaner on the floor beside her.

"*What* are you doing?"

"Cleaning the tub."

"Holly . . . darling . . . it's four a.m. I have people who do that."

"I know, but I couldn't sleep, and I need to keep my hands busy so my brain relaxes."

"Is it the Montgomery appointment, today?"

She nodded. "I think so."

"Hand me the other sponge."

She looked at him. "Why?"

"It's a huge tub. If you're going to scrub it, I'm going to help."

She laughed. "You're going to clean a bathtub?"

"I am."

"You wouldn't know how."

"Give me the damn sponge. I'll show you who knows how. You have no idea how much time I spent cleaning when I was a kid. Remember, my mum worked two jobs. I'm betting you are the one who lived the charmed life with a stay-at-home mother, maybe a housekeeper."

"Okay. You got me."

After five minutes of spraying, wiping, and rinsing, Holly broke out in spontaneous laughter.

"What's so funny?"

She sat back on her heels. "Just picturing what we must look like. Ten years ago, I would have never dreamed one day I would be sitting on a bathroom floor with Luke Damian at four in the morning, cleaning a garden tub with Scrubbing Bubbles."

He chuckled. "Especially since said tub has not been used since the cleaning crew was here on Monday . . . unless Gigi has a secret life." Laying down the sponge, he said, "Maybe we should take a selfie."

"Uh . . . I don't think so. It might end up on the Internet."

He sat back. "Tell you what. Let's either fill this swimming-pool wannabe with warm, sexy water and get naked—or go back to bed. I can probably think of a way to keep your hands occupied."

"Can you now?" She grinned at him.

"Indeed, I can."

Luke's intervention resolved Holly's stress-induced insomnia. When the alarm rang at six-thirty, both were asleep. She crawled out of bed and stood for a few seconds, waiting for the cobwebs to clear her mind. As the veil of slumber lifted, she remembered the morning mission and took a deep breath.

Will either of us recognize the person on the tape?

Sitting back down, she leaned over and rubbed her injured ankle. The ache reminded her of the performance the night before and evoked a smile. She glanced over at Luke, but he was sleeping like a baby. Taking her cell from the night table, she tip-toed out of the bedroom. Gigi followed.

Once the cat was given fresh food and the coffee made, Holly texted Sam and Kat. "Ankle a bit aggravated, so Luke and I taking the morning off. Will start work on next week's number at one p.m. Enjoy!"

"Why didn't you wake me?" Luke asked, stumbling into the kitchen. He walked over to Holly and gave her a hug and kiss.

"You didn't need to get up this early. We aren't due at the police station until nine-thirty. What would you like for breakfast?"

He took a cup and filled it with coffee. "Forget cooking. I think you and I deserve a treat. Get dressed, and I'll take you to Huckleberry for green eggs and ham."

He's trying to distract me. "How could I refuse that offer?"

CHAPTER FORTY-TWO

At nine-twenty, Luke and Holly walked into the station. The officer on duty at the visitor's desk recognized them and immediately issued visitor badges. "Detective Montgomery is expecting you. I'll let him know you're here."

When Montgomery arrived, another detective accompanied him and was introduced to the couple.

"Detective Samuels is working the case with me. He's the expert on electronics. We old-timers know only enough to tangle the system up."

"Holly told me there is a video of a suspicious person entering her building," Luke said.

"We have footage from two cameras, capturing the person entering and leaving. Unfortunately, the face is obscured in all the views. Hopefully, one of you will notice something to help identify the subject."

"Is it a man or woman?" Holly asked.

Montgomery shook his head. "We can't really tell for certain."

Holly and Luke followed Detective Samuels, with Montgomery trailing, to a bank of computers and monitors where the younger man sat down in front of one. He inserted a DVD. Holly's hands went cold and her knees weak as the black-and-white image came on the screen. Luke had his hands around her waist.

"If you see anything you want enlarged or rerun, let me know," Samuels said.

The person on the screen was dressed in all black, a hood masking the face. Although still dark, streetlights and outdoor lighting on the building allowed for a reasonably clear image of the physique.

"See anything familiar?" Montgomery asked.

"The only thing I can tell is it's not Joy Ambrose," Luke said. "Joy is taller with a totally different body shape."

"Ms. Dawson, do you recognize anything about the subject?"

"I have no idea who that is." Holly trembled as she spoke.

"I was afraid you wouldn't be able to tell much, but we are working on another lead," Montgomery said. "Do you know Theodore Svendsen?"

Holly felt a cold chill course through her body. "Who?" *Theodore Svendsen?*

"The owner of the Swedish Wayfarer restaurant chain."

"Yes. He's one of the celebrity contestants on our show."

"Has he shown any interest in you?"

Bewildered, Holly said, "No. Absolutely none."

Luke turned his head, obviously puzzled by Montgomery's inquiry. "What would Svendsen have to do with what's going on?"

"I'm not at liberty to say. I can only tell you we've received some information we're looking into."

Luke frowned. "What kind of information?"

"Please, be patient. I'll let you know when the time is right. In the meantime, Ms. Dawson, I'd like you to tell me everything you know about Mr. Svendsen."

Holly paused. She turned to Luke, wanting to speak but hesitant.

"What is it, love? Is there something you haven't told me about the man?"

She curled her lips inward, her eyes blinking nervously.

Luke lowered his voice. "You need to tell anything you know."

Holly folded her hands together, clenching tight. "I don't want to make a false accusation. I might just be paranoid."

All eyes turned toward her. She looked to Luke as if seeking the courage to release her covert information.

He nodded, taking her hand.

Turning back toward Montgomery, she took a deep breath. "I

don't know anything about Theo Svendsen, but there is something about Lisa."

"Lisa?" the detective asked.

"Lisa Cantrell. She's Theo's pro partner on the show."

"What about her?" Montgomery took a small notepad out of his pocket.

Luke squeezed her hand as she spelled out the details of Cantrell's attitude and the information Kat Kenley had given about the dancer. He stared with intense interest as she spoke.

"Please don't tell anyone I've said she could be stalking me. If I'm wrong, it would be awful."

"We'll be as discreet as we can." He clicked his pen closed. "I appreciate your candor. We'll certainly follow up and look for a connection to what we have. Give us a few days and feel free to check in or to add to what you've told us."

Holly was quiet as she and Luke left the station and entered their waiting SUV.

"Since you canceled rehearsal for the morning, do you have any plans in mind?"

"Not really. We both need a break after all the stress of the past ten days. Next week should be a piece of cake—a simple waltz—no pyrotechnics, no judging."

He leaned back, his hands behind his head. "I've seen what you call a piece of cake, love, but a little time off isn't all bad. By the way, why didn't you mention your suspicions about Lisa to me?"

"I wanted to, but I kept thinking how bad I would look if wrong. Lisa and I will be on tour together. I don't need to make an enemy."

"But, if you're right, she should be arrested."

"As if I don't know that." She slid across the seat, leaning against him as he put an arm around her shoulder. "I wonder what brought Theo Svendsen to the attention of the police. I hardly know him."

"Same with me. I bet I have exchanged less than thirty words with either one."

Holly was quiet for a minute or two. "There's something else we need to talk about."

"What would that be?"

"My parents. Have you forgotten you invited them to come out for the finale?"

"I did, didn't I?"

"You did. Got any ideas as to how that's going to work?"

He turned and kissed the top of her head. "As a matter of fact, I do."

She tapped him, playfully, on his thigh with her fist. "I should have known. Please share."

"I reserved a suite at the Beverly Hilton. Your dad is making the travel arrangements and your mum will pass details along to you. They plan to fly in on Wednesday and out on Saturday. I invited them to stay longer, but your dad said December is a bad time for him to be away."

She snuggled against him. "Thank you, but the idea of having them here makes me nervous with this stalker thing. Mom is hyper about my safety. She hates me in living in New York or L.A. And, they don't know I'm staying in your condo. That reminds me. I should go by my place. I'm sure there are bills in the mailbox."

"Got it."

When the SUV pulled up to the curb in front of her building, Holly started to get out.

"Stay," Luke said, putting a hand in front of her. "Jimmy, you don't mind going in and picking up Ms. Dawson's mail, do you?"

"Certainly, Mr. Damian." The driver put the transmission in park and turned off the motor.

"I can do it," Holly said. "I'm not helpless."

"After what we found the last time? Stop giving me a hard time and hand the key over," Luke said, extending his open palm.

"No use arguing with you." She dropped the key in his palm, and he passed it forward. "It's box number 204, Jimmy."

The security guard exited the car, as Luke's cell vibrated. Holly sat up straight and moved to give him wiggle room.

Turning his face toward the window to talk, Luke said, "Not a problem. I can work that in today." He shifted the phone to his opposite ear. "Holly cancelled our morning rehearsal."

As Luke disconnected the call, Jimmy arrived back with a substantial stack of mail. Luke slipped the cell into the pocket of his jeans and turned toward Holly with a big smile on his face. "That was Jeff. He's got the final paperwork for me to sign for the pilot I told you about."

"Luke, that's awesome. It sounds like a great series."

Jimmy climbed into the vehicle and handed the mail over the seat to Holly.

She flipped through the stack of mostly junk as the vehicle pulled away from the curb. Halfway through, she gasped. "No!"

Luke instantly turned his attention to her. "What is it?"

Holly pointed to a plain envelope on top of the remaining circulars.

"Damn it. Turn around, Jimmy, we're going back to the police station."

"We don't know it's from the stalker unless we open it," Holly said.

Luke's eyes flashed. "Same type of envelope, no return address— it's him—or her. Don't touch it." He reached for his wallet and pulled out Detective Montgomery's card. Not taking his eyes off the envelope, he tapped in the number on his cell.

"Holly's received what looks like another piece of mail from the stalker. This one came through the postal service. We're under a tight schedule, so we're bringing it to you."

Fifteen minutes later, they were met outside the LAPD building by Montgomery and the bomb squad. "Leave the envelope in the vehicle and all of you get out," the Detective said, motioning to them to clear the area.

A black Labrador immediately approached the SUV and sniffed around. The Squad moved in behind him.

"You took a risk bringing it here and in using your cell phone," Montgomery said.

"I think we had the tiger by the tail. We were in the middle of a heavily populated area and on a busy street."

Standing next to Luke, his hand on her shoulder, Holly frowned. "This is terrifying."

The detective shook his head. "Do you want to wait or just let me call you? The dog doesn't seem to have detected dangerous materials."

Her heart pounding, Holly dreaded finding out what the message contained but at the same time, needed to know. Before she could respond, Luke spoke up.

"As I told you on the phone, we've on a running clock. We'll come back around eleven-thirty."

"Why don't—" Holly caught herself. "Never mind."

The ride to Jeff Corbett's office was silent. Luke kept his hand over Holly's in a wordless attempt to calm her anxiety.

When they walked in, a pretty, young receptionist greeted Luke with a big smile.

"Jeff is expecting you, Luke. I'll buzz him."

Luke turned to Holly. Her face was nearly colorless. "Try to get your mind off the envelope, love."

In a matter of seconds, Corbett appeared. "Come on back, man." The agent extended his hand to shake Luke's and then took Holly's and kissed the top, continental style. "Good to see you again, Ms. Dawson. Congratulations on a spectacular performance last night."

She smiled. "Call me Holly, please. And thank you." She looked up at Luke. "I can wait here while the two of you take care of business."

Luke shook his head.

Corbett said, "Absolutely not. This won't take long. Would you like a cup of coffee or glass of wine?"

"I'm good," she responded.

"I'll take a coffee," Luke said.

Corbett nodded to the receptionist and then led the way to his office.

"Luke, you'll be happy to hear they gave on all your conditions."

"Including the one I said was non-negotiable?"

"Including all." A look passed between the two men, which eluded Holly.

Files, assorted documents, and 8x10 headshots with resumes stapled to the backs littered Corbett's office—on his desk, chair seats, and much of the floor. The walls were covered with memorabilia, including, five, full-page *Variety* articles, multiple photos of the agent with various celebrities, and eight magazine covers. Holly quickly spotted Luke's images.

As Jeff rummaged through the mess on his desk, Luke asked, "Any updates on the status of my least favorite model?"

Without looking up, Corbett said, "As a matter of fact, I heard she *is* likely to be offered the spokesperson role for that French cosmetic outfit. I had two clients vying for the spot. Word on the street says it's a multi-million-dollar package."

"Being pregnant would likely interfere, right?"

The comment caught Holly's attention.

Corbett looked up, one eyebrow cocked. "She's no more fucking pregnant than I am."

Luke laughed.

"She hasn't made any contact, has she?" the agent asked.

Holly's eyes grew wide.

"That's a long story, but the short answer is: We don't know."

Paying little attention to Luke's answer, Corbett said, "Here it is." He handed Luke a thick packet of paper. "Do you have time to read it, now? I'd like to button up the deal today."

"Hand it over."

The receptionist came in with Luke's coffee. "Are you sure I can't get you something, Ms. Dawson? We have soft drinks, Perrier, and Evian."

"Actually, an Evian would be great."

When she returned with the water, the girl had a handful of magazines for Holly to look at while Luke read the contract.

CHAPTER FORTY-THREE

It was noon by the time Luke and Holly returned to the police station. They had not had lunch, but Holly's stomach was so tight from nervous tension that anything she swallowed would have bounced back. When they checked in at the reception desk, they were told Detective Montgomery was in a meeting.

"I know this is not his most important case, but the anticipation is killing me," Holly said as they sat down on a bench in the lobby.

"Here he comes," Luke said.

Holly breathed a sigh of relief, but it lasted less than five seconds.

Montgomery waved them back. When they reached him, he shook Luke's hand and said, "Follow me."

As they walked down the hall, Luke asked, "Did you open the envelope?"

"I did and have copies for you at my desk. We have the originals marked and sealed in evidence bags. Forensics are following up on finger prints."

Holly felt a wave of nausea.

"What makes this case difficult is that unless it turns out to be Ms. Ambrose, we have no motive for the harassment. The communications have been threatening, but up to this point, no demand has been included."

"I am less and less inclined to believe it's Joy," Luke said. "She's crazy, but she's also fixated on her career."

Reaching his desk, Montgomery motioned for them to sit. Taking documents out of a file on his desk, he handed the papers to Holly.

Luke stood and moved behind her to look over her shoulder. The items appeared to be copies of newspaper and Internet articles. The top one was a *New York Times* piece describing the attack on Olympic ice-skater Nancy Kerrigan in 1994. The next described Wanda Holloway, the Texas mother who attempted to hire a killer to murder the mother of her teenage daughter's cheerleading rival. Holly's hands quaked as she read, causing the papers to waver. As the third article was about to come into view, Luke reached over Holly and snatched away the stack.

It was too late. Holly had caught a glimpse of the headline. She immediately burst into tears, her body shaking. Luke tossed the papers on Montgomery's desk and moved in front of Holly as she stood up. He wrapped his arms around her and held her tight against his body, pressing her face to his chest.

"She doesn't need to see that fucking trash."

"Why is he or she doing this?" Her tears made wet spots on Luke's shirt.

Montgomery picked up the scattered papers, straightened them, and pulled the last one out. "Take note of this one. It constitutes a demand."

Holding the document up, the veteran detective looked from Luke to Holly and back, his expression suggesting Holly's reaction had pierced his objectivity.

"Let *me* see it," Luke said with one arm still around Holly.

While he read the brief text, Holly pulled away, searching his face for a hint as to what the message said.

"Tell me." She reached for the piece of paper.

"Are you sure you want to know?" Luke asked, holding it out of her reach briefly.

She nodded and took the document from his hand.

GET OUT OF LUKE'S LIFE
OR <u>YOU</u> WILL BE THE NEXT HEADLINE.

"It's Joy! She's going to do something horrible." She dropped the paper as though it burned her fingers.

Luke hugged her close. "No, she's not."

"Gigi. You saw that article—I can't even read anything so cruel."

"Put it out of your mind, love."

"Ms. Dawson, your reaction is what this person wants. We're going to take every precaution to insure your safety, which includes your pet, but it's still possible this threat is a paper tiger."

Holly tried to compose herself. "The woman is crazy, and crazy people do atrocious things every day."

"You can't assume Ms. Ambrose is the stalker."

"Who else would want me out of Luke's life?"

"An obsessed fan, anyone wanting to impact your performance in the competition, ex paramours—yours or Mr. Damian's. I am correct that the winners on your show stand to take home a substantial bonus?"

"Yes. But, that doesn't fit. It's too late now to affect the outcome. The competition ended last night. We only have the finale and awards left," Luke said.

"Notice the postmark. This envelope was mailed Friday. Under normal circumstances, Ms. Dawson would have received it before you performed last night."

Holly sat down, leaned forward, and rested her head against the palms of her hands. "What are we going to do?"

"Whatever it takes," Luke said. "If necessary, we'll withdraw. The winner hasn't been announced."

"I don't think you need to go that far," Montgomery said. "Increase your security and change up your routine—maybe avoid the studio as much as possible and have heightened security whenever you're there. Consider staying in a hotel for a few days. Put my numbers in both your phones. I can't give you twenty-four-hour protection, but I can step up police presence in your neighborhood and put studio security on alert."

"How are we supposed to avoid the studio and rehearse?" Holly said.

"Surely there are other locations in L.A.," Montgomery said.

"What about that dance school we rehearsed in before the first show?" Luke asked.

Holly hesitated, searching her memory before responding. "Maybe. If the owner can clear enough time. What was her name? Judy? June? That's it. June Mattox."

"For the right price, I'm sure she can find the time." Luke brushed a tendril of hair from Holly's forehead. "We'll make it work."

It took most of Thursday afternoon to put everything in place. June Mattox was all too happy to accommodate the rehearsals. A story was fabricated as to why Luke and Holly were not rehearsing at the studio, but no one seemed to have a problem with the idea. It wasn't unusual for celebrities to use alternative space to accommodate other commitments. Focusing on choreography gave Holly the distraction she needed to cope with her mounting fear. A few minutes past five p.m., Luke received a call from Harvey Gold. He put his phone on speaker.

"I thought lawyers kept banker's hours. What are you doing at your office this late?"

"I was about to leave when I got a call from Joy Ambrose's attorney. The court has ordered mediation in our case, and he is pushing to schedule it. He said our mediator has a cancellation and can do the conference on Monday afternoon. Otherwise, it will be two months out. Can you make it?"

"How long will it take?"

"Not an easy answer to that one. However, we can give notice you only have a certain amount of time. If not settled, we go back to finish up on another day. It's up to you, buddy."

"Let Holly and I talk, and I'll ring you back."

After hanging up. He filled her in. "What do you think?"

"It's up to you. I think we can knock out our choreography over the weekend. You have a group rehearsal Monday morning and then costume fittings, but you should be able to get away no later than three."

"What about you? Can you leave then?"

She shrugged her shoulders. "It's your mediation. I wouldn't be going, would I?"

"I'd like you there. I know it's between me and Joy, but you're implicated as well—especially if there's any chance she is the stalker."

Holly shuddered. "That thought gives me chills."

He walked over to where she was sitting on a barstool in his kitchen and put his hands on the top of her shoulders. "I like the idea of confronting her. We may get a clue as to whether she is behind the harassment."

"Speak for yourself. But since the detective believes it could be someone in the cast as much as it could be Joy—I may as well face it."

"That's my girl." He leaned forward and kissed the top of her head. "I'll make the call."

CHAPTER FORTY-FOUR

Costume fittings were done by two o'clock on Monday. Holly and Luke were alone in the studio, preparing to leave when she dropped her bottle of water. It spewed liquid down the front of her warmup pants and made a puddle on the floor.

"I don't believe I did that."

"Hey, it's okay. You didn't drop your iPad. Maintenance will mop it up." Luke put his towel down, walked over to her, and took her hands in his. "You're like ice. You're letting it get to you. Harvey said we'll be in separate rooms."

"It's not just the mediation. It's everything. Having to hide from a ghost. Not knowing who it is or how dangerous the person is. Every time I looked at Lisa during the group rehearsal this morning, I couldn't help but think: is it her? Now, we are going to the mediation. What if it is Joy? She might have a gun."

"Joy Ambrose wouldn't know the grip of a gun from the barrel. If she had one, she'd be as likely to shoot herself as someone else. Second, she would be totally insane to try anything with her lawyer, Harvey, the mediator, and an armed security guard present. Do you think I would let you be there if I thought there was a risk?"

"No."

"Then give me a smile, and let's get it over with."

Holly closed her eyes, took a deep breath, and forced a smile.

"Come on, angel. You can do better. You look like the beauty-pageant runner-up right after crowning of the winner."

"I'm practicing for Wednesday night."

"I have breaking news for you. We're going to win."

She titled her head to one side. "Really? And, when did you arrive at that conclusion?"

A smug grin crept across his face. "When I didn't screw up last week. I've always known you are a winner."

Nodding, a tight-lipped grin on her face, she said, "You are good. Always ready with a great line."

"Not a line. And who was it who preached the power of positive thinking?"

She rolled her eyes. "I thought you didn't care about winning."

"I don't. But, you do, so that makes it matter to me. That said, we'd better get going."

For the mediation, two bodyguards accompanied Luke and Holly. When Holly saw the men waiting by the SUV, she turned to Luke. "Is that a bulletproof vehicle?"

He laughed. "Could be. I didn't ask."

During the drive to the mediation, Holly didn't say two words. Her stomach was in knots, remembering the vicious look on Joy's face when she crashed their rehearsal. Luke held her hand but did not try to force her to talk. Instead, he carried on trivial conversation with the guards about soccer, David Beckham, and American football.

The mediator's office was on the tenth floor of a high-rise building. They entered the lobby through a revolving door. Holly's pumps clicked as she walked across the marble floor. Subconsciously, she counted out the cadence of her pace. Walking into the mirrored elevator, a smirk came across her face as she noticed the contrast in her size compared with the three men surrounding her. Luke kept his hands on her shoulders.

When they reached the appointed suite, one bodyguard entered the office while the other remained with the couple. The long hallway was deserted and silence prevailed.

A gunshot would echo in this place.

The guard came out and gave a go-ahead sign.

Harvey Gold was sitting in the reception area. "All set?"

"As set as I will ever be. Is she here?"

Gold nodded. "Yes. She and her attorney are with the mediator. He has a litany he's required to give. In most mediations, it's done with both present, but when there have been allegations of domestic violence, it's best to keep the parties separated."

"I am not sure what this will accomplish. With what has been going on, I can't agree to dissolve the protective order."

"Showing up is all you had to do. You aren't required to resolve the issue. The mediator will push you to settle, but he *cannot* compel you. He is a facilitator, not a judge. However, it would keep you from having to work a court appearance into your schedule down the road. I know you are going to be starting a new series, which could create a conflict."

"I'm filming a pilot. It's not a series until it's sold."

"I read your contract, and Jeff tells me it's a hot property—maybe a bidding war."

"Music to my—"

"Harvey, hello." The mediator came from a hallway on the left, holding a hand out to shake Gold's. Turning to Luke, he said, "And this would be Mr. Damian—and Ms. Dawson. George Blackfoot, here. I'm your mediator." He nodded to Holly and shook Luke's hand. "Come into my conference room. I've already met with Ms. Ambrose and her attorney. They will remain on the other side of the suite. No contact unless you authorize it. Your security people can either join us and sit on the side or wait here."

"We'll have them join us," Luke said and nodded to the guards.

After informing Luke of the purpose of mediation, the confidentiality component, and benefits of settlement, he had Luke explain his position in the case. Holly sat quietly between the security men. Luke concluded his explanation with a description of the harassment Holly had experienced since the day Joy invaded their rehearsal.

"Joy is a prime suspect. It all began after she confronted me in the studio and accused me of fathering her unborn child. Her eyes were almost red with rage as she refused to leave. She physically attacked me. If she is responsible for the mental anguish Holly is going through, then there is no way I will consider giving up the injunction. Frankly, I don't see how she can convince me she is not the demon."

"Can you give me a list of dates, times, and the actions you suspect she committed? She says she has not made any contact with you and has no desire to do so. It seems she has moved on, is in a new relationship, and her career is exploding. To quote Ms. Ambrose, 'Luke Damian is old news.' She said a little more that doesn't bear repeating."

Luke smiled at the last remark. "She's in a new relationship?"

Blackfoot nodded. "She says she has been out of the country most of the time since the unfortunate incident. She spent the last two weeks in Costa Rica, ziplining and skinny-dipping with Rocky Boyd."

Luke glanced at Holly, shrugging his shoulders, a bewildered expression on his face. "Rocky Boyd, boy wonder of rock? What is he, fourteen?"

"That's the one. Only looks like a kid. He's actually in his early twenties."

"Can she back it up? And, what about her pregnancy?"

"Creative thinking. She admitted it was a stupid move. Said it infuriated her that you brushed her off. I suspect she was embarrassed in front of Ms. Dawson."

Harvey Gold spoke up. "You said she has evidence to support her claim of not being in the country. Did you see it?"

"Not yet. She has a briefcase, supposedly containing the proof. She wants to know Mr. Damian will agree to dissolve the injunction if she produces the documentation."

"Since when does she call all the shots? Her behavior is what got us here in the first place."

Holly cringed.

"You're right, Luke. But, I would like to know *why* she came prepared to prove her whereabouts," Gold said. "How would she know she was under suspicion, unless she is the one harassing Holly?"

Holly didn't say anything, but her mind raced with the same question. Neither she, nor Luke, had told anyone other than Gold, Corbett, the security people, and the police about the calls and letters. No one at the studio had been told. *It must be Joy.*

"I don't know, but I'll find out. Can I tell them Mr. Damian will consider her request?" Blackfoot said.

"Tell her I *won't* consider it unless she produces her so called evidence—and tells us how she knew she would need it." He turned to Gold. "Do you agree, Harvey?"

Gold nodded. "Absolutely."

When the mediator left the room, Luke turned to Holly. "Are you okay, love?"

Her face was pale. "I'm fine."

He pushed his chair away from the conference table, stood up, and then sat beside her. The two agents moved to the other side of the room. "You want something to drink?"

"No. I'm good." She clutched the purse in her lap as though it were a life preserver. "What do you think?"

He shook his head. "Who knows? She hallucinated about her relationship with me and fabricated a pregnancy, which she apparently admitted today. Why wouldn't she lie about anything else to get what she wants?"

"If she is in a relationship with that rock star, I would think a tabloid, TMZ, or one of the entertainment shows on TV would have exposed it as hot as he is right now."

"What do you think, Harvey?" Luke said.

"I'm a lawyer. We don't believe anything until we see concrete proof. However, you must be relieved to know you're not going to be a father."

Luke made a face. "I don't think it has sunk in. I was ninety-nine per cent certain it wasn't true, but I admit it was good to hear."

"Think you might become the poster boy for safe-sex?" Gold chuckled.

Holly stared at the floor, uncomfortable with the subject of conversation. *What would I have done if it had been true?*

The twenty-eight minutes between Blackfoot leaving the room and returning seemed an eternity to Holly. She could not concentrate on either the talk show playing on the mediator's TV, or the available magazines. Luke appeared relaxed with a copy of *Fortune*. Harvey

Gold stepped out to check in with his office.

When the door opened, Holly jumped. Luke put his hand on her knee and then stood to resume his seat at the conference table as the mediator and lawyer entered.

Blackfoot tossed his portfolio on the table and eased into his seat at the end.

"Well, George, what do you have for us?" Gold asked.

The mediator reached for the pitcher of ice water in the center of the table and poured some into a crystal glass.

Can he hurry up and let us know?

"Harvey, it appears our gal is not responsible for the recent harassment of Ms. Dawson." He took a small green item from inside the portfolio and handed it to Gold. "As you can see from her passport, she was out of the country for all but a couple of days at Thanksgiving. That includes all the dates you've provided related to the phone calls and anonymous correspondence."

Gold opened the document, glanced through it, and then handed it to Luke. "Very convenient. Passports have been known to be forged, and how did she know to bring it with her?"

"There's a simple explanation. Ms. Ambrose was questioned over the weekend by an LAPD detective. He had her account for her whereabouts on the subject dates and was satisfied to eliminate her as a suspect when she produced the passport." He opened the leather folder and spread the contents out. There were images of Joy on her photo shoot in Italy and Costa Rica with the boyfriend, plus travel documentation. "She asked me to be sure to show this one to Mr. Damian, which I find a little awkward."

Luke took the photo, and then quickly turned it over. "How asinine of her." He turned around toward Holly. "It's a photo of her and wonder boy skinny dipping."

"She said to tell you she knew you would recognize her in that one, plus a few other things I don't find productive to mention."

"How childish. The woman's a nut case. I should take the damn thing and sell it to the tabloids. How would her fancy sponsor like her then?"

Gold snickered. "Probably just fine. Remember, it's a French company."

Blackfoot interrupted. "This is all digression from our purpose. I'm sure you all have better things to do, so what's Mr. Damian's answer?"

"Hell, no. Why should I?"

Gold reached over and patted Luke on the arm. "I know how you feel, Luke."

"Do you want to jeopardize her career?" Blackfoot asked.

"Why should I care? Her actions back in October set this ball in motion. Now, two months later, she wants to waltz in here and have it all go away? Not happening."

"I get that. But, maybe there's an alternative," Blackfoot said.

Holly tensed. *If he doesn't give her what she wants, what will she do? She was out of control that day in our rehearsal.*

"Luke, could I talk to you for a second?" Holly said, reaching forward to touch his arm.

He turned around, still angry, looked at her, and then turned back to Blackfoot. "Excuse us a second."

"Certainly. I'll be in reception when you're ready." Blackfoot closed his portfolio and left the room.

"What is it?" Luke asked, turning his chair around to face Holly.

"Maybe you should let her off the hook. If you don't, she is going to be an enemy. It's never good to make an enemy."

"Holly, you're too soft. She needs to know there are consequences."

"What she did was wrong, but if she's not responsible for the phone calls and letters, the person who is would have done it anyway. Joy didn't create that person's motive."

He shook his head.

Gold held up an index finger. "Hold on, Luke. There might be other ways to handle this. You're right in that you're holding all the cards and her behavior has cost you a lot of grief. But, do you want to perpetuate the animosity?"

"You, too?"

"We're both on your side. But let's hear if Blackfoot has a suggestion. You're paying him to think outside the box."

"I'll listen, but I'm warning you, I'm not inclined to think there is a solution."

Gold motioned for one of the security guards to bring Blackfoot back in.

As the mediator sat down, Gold said, "I'm sure you can tell my client is justifiably angry with Ms. Ambrose, but he is willing to hear you out. Do you have an alternative solution?"

Blackfoot looked Luke in the eye. "What if the OP is left intact but sealed? You execute a consent order that says the Clerk of Court will seal the file, and it can only be opened if Ms. Ambrose commits any act in violation of its terms."

Gold glanced at Luke, who was still frowning. "What do you think?"

He turned his head from side to side, but more in the nature of pondering the matter rather than rejecting it.

"That's a small compromise, but not a risky one," Gold added.

Luke's eyes went to Holly. She shrugged.

"It's up to you. But it seems reasonable." She turned to Blackfoot. "Do you think she will accept that?"

"She doesn't have much to bargain with, which her attorney recognizes. I think there's a good chance she will."

"That's not enough." Luke's voice was resolute.

All eyes were on him.

"What else, Mr. Damian?"

"She comes in here and apologizes in front of everyone for the lie about her pregnancy, and she pays for this mediation. I will not accept the deal under any other circumstances."

Blackfoot flipped his portfolio closed. "I'll present it."

When the mediator returned, the model and her attorney were with him.

Holly felt a cold chill course over her at the sight of the woman.

"Ms. Ambrose has agreed to your terms," Blackfoot said.

Luke was silent as was Joy.

She's not going to do it. She's too stubborn.

Following a few seconds of uncomfortable silence in the room, Joy took a deep breath, glared at Luke, and spoke in a monotone. "For the record, I apologize for accusing you of fathering a child with me."

He stared, venom boiling in his eyes. "For the record, were you ever pregnant?"

Joy glared back at him. "That's not part of the deal."

Holly clenched her fists, afraid of what might come next. *She's not going to let him tell her what to say.*

"You want my cooperation, you'll say it."

"No. I was not." With that, Joy turned and walked out, leaving her attorney standing alone. He raised his hand in a farewell gesture and followed. Before the door closed, everyone heard her say, "Go to hell."

"Good luck, wonder boy," Luke said under his breath. "You're going to need it."

"Who are you talking to?" Holly asked.

"No one." He turned to Blackfoot. "Are we free to go?"

"I'll have my secretary prepare the consent order for both of you to review. Once you sign, you're done."

CHAPTER FORTY-FIVE

After the mediation, the ride to Luke's condo was quiet. He faced straight ahead, his jaw clenched. He was obviously struggling to unwind his hostility, but Luke's anger was not the cause of Holly's silence.

As she internalized the notion Joy was not her stalker, she discovered eliminating a suspect left more confusion than satisfaction. Joy had been a quintessential suspect with her can't-let-go complex.

If not Joy, who? Lisa? One of the other cast members? A deranged stranger?

Holly's mind was a jumble of questions and fears. The thought of cordial interaction with Cantrell over the next two days ignited panic.

Gazing at Luke, her mind wandered. While withdrawing from the competition would be a relief, she wanted to win. Winning would at least provide a financial foundation in the event all else failed.

This fairy tale could end.

He had said he loved her, but so had Don. When the aura of the competition faded, her magnetism could disappear with it.

Before they left Florida, Mary Lou Dawson cautioned Holly to be aware of fickle feelings.

"He's an easy man to be attracted to, honey; but never forget, Luke is as appealing to an army of other women as he is to you. Ordinary guys wrestle with loyalty. For men like him, fidelity is an aspiration, rarely an accomplishment."

Her mother's words echoed in Holly's mind as her eyes traced the contours of his face, his trim body, and his strong hands—the hands that embraced her, lifted her, and set her on fire with the slightest touch. A desire to run, fueled by doubt, spread through her as if intravenously injected.

Sure. He believes he loves me—now.

As the vehicle turned onto Luke's street, Holly diverted her gaze to her window, wondering what would come next. Absorbed in thought, a warm hand sliding onto her lap startled her. He pried her folded hands apart and took one in his. She turned. His eyes were filled with warmth as he squeezed. His body language, louder than words, said, "I've got you. It's okay."

Holly smiled, her tension evaporating.

"We're here, Mr. Damian." It was Jimmy who spoke.

"So, I see," Luke responded. "Thank you, fellows. Are you two off for the day?"

"Roy's off. After I see the two of you in safely, I'll be stationed out here until eleven, unless you plan to go out tonight."

Luke glanced Holly's way. "I think we'll stay in."

"Good idea."

Monday evening passed with little discussion about what had happened. Luke made a simple meal of steak and salad, but neither ate much. Holly wondered if any contacts from the stalker had come over the phone or mail during the day but did not bring up the subject.

It's best I don't know. Focus on the show until Thursday.

They watched a TV program and went to bed early. Luke kissed her goodnight but made no further physical contact.

It was pouring rain when they woke up Tuesday morning. Holly groaned at the thought of the hectic day ahead. *Where is sunny California when you need it?*

Luke seemed back to his normal disposition as they rode to work. He traded jokes with the bodyguards and treated Holly with affection. She used the time to review the day's schedule.

The finale had a two-hour time slot and would include several high-profile guest performers and video recaps of the season. Even though Holly was comfortable with their final choreography, she wanted to work in rehearsal time. She tried not to think of winning or losing the competition.

"Use my dressing room for the rest of the week—just in case the stalker is a member of the cast," Luke said as their driver pulled up to the rear entrance of the studio. "Everyone knows we're a couple."

"That will work."

Shortly before the scheduled run-through of the pros' production number, Holly excused herself for a trip to the restroom. She nearly collided with Lisa Cantrell, who was exiting.

"I'm sorry," Holly backed up to let the dancer exit.

"No problem. By the way, you and Luke stopped the show last week. Congratulations."

Wow! She's friendly.

Holly could hardly mask her surprise. "We got lucky, but thank you for saying that. You guys, break a leg tomorrow night."

"Back atcha."

With that, Cantrell walked away, leaving Holly puzzled. *Was she sincere? Or playing with my head?*

To Holly's relief, there were two other cast members in the ladies' room. Although not interested in conversation, she was happy to avoid the vulnerability of being caught alone. The dancers wished her well and complimented her on the previous performance.

In addition to rehearsals and camera blocking, costume fittings and consultations for hair and makeup swallowed the rest of the day. By the time they arrived at the condo, Luke and Holly were exhausted.

"Okay with you if we order a pizza?" he asked as they unloaded their gear.

"Anything delivered sounds great. Right now, all I want is a hot shower and a good night's sleep."

"You sure that's all?" He tipped his head with a mischievous smile creeping across his face.

Exhilarated by the implication, she grinned. "Ask me again after my shower and a few minutes of R and R."

"Count on it."

As she turned to head for the bedroom, he said, "I'll order. Want your usual veggies?"

She nodded without looking back.

Later that night, after they made love, Luke fell asleep. Holly found herself marshalling her worries. Detective Montgomery had not called with any news on his investigation. Her parents would arrive the next afternoon. With security shadowing her, they were bound to find out about the stalker, which would make her mother's paranoia a nightmare. Holly didn't need the added stress. Although the finale would be the climatic end of a mad rollercoaster ride, what would be the shape of their relationship without the common goal? She turned her head toward him. The sight of his bare shoulders, his thick, blond hair, and the memory of minutes before sent a cold chill coursing through her veins.

No guarantees in life. You can't control the tide, but you can chart your course. Sometimes, you have to take a chance.

Despite her fatigue, it was nearly two a.m. before she slept.

Wednesday was the longest day of the season for Holly. Considering how much was crammed into the hours before the show aired, it should have sped by. But, it seemed to drag, causing her anxiety to grow with each passing minute. When the time to get into full makeup and costumes arrived, Holly craved relief from the butterflies homesteading in her stomach. True to her personality, anxiety brought forth silence. Other than an "excuse me" when she bumped into Luke in the dressing room, she said nothing. Whether he was experiencing a similar status or simply honoring hers, he said almost as little.

Holly's parents had arrived in L.A. shortly after lunch. Her mother called to let her know they made it and would see her after the show

When the production assistant gave the call to come to the floor at five minutes to five, a twinge of exhilaration flowed through Holly. She stood up from the dressing table as Luke came behind her and put his hands on her shoulders. They both looked at the reflection in the mirror.

"This is it. You ready?" he said.

Holly's head moved up and down. "Our last dance."

He squeezed her shoulders and then used his grasp to turn her to face him. "Not a chance. You created a monster, and now you are going to have to feed it." He pulled her close, causing her to pull her head back to avoid getting makeup on his white coat. He then took her hand, leading her to the door. "Let's rock and roll."

Two hours later, the three remaining couples stood in their individual pools of light as the ominous music drummed the countdown.

"And the winner of this season's *Lights, Camera—Dance* gold medal is Luke Da—"

Applause, whistles, and cheers drowned out the rest as Luke broke into a wide-eyed grin, raising his hands—one holding Holly's and the other balled up in a fist, punching the air. Although inaudible, it was clear he was shouting, "Yes, yes, yes."

She threw her arms around his neck. "You did it!"

"We did it," he responded hugging her and kissing her on the cheek.

The other cast members began to converge onto the couple, hugging and congratulating them.

"I know you're thrilled for them, but clear a path so they can come over here," Serianni said.

As the couple walked down from the riser to receive their trophies, the host held up a hand to quiet the crowd.

"Quiet, please, folks. We have one more thing to address and don't have much time."

As the previous celebrity winner hung gold medals, embossed with a pair of dancers, around the necks of Luke, first, and then Holly, the roar of the crowd subsided. Reaching into his coat pocket, Serianni said, "Bear with me. I have to interrupt this victorious scene." He pulled a small box out. "Before the show, Luke gave me something to hold and asked that I give it to him on the air, if he and Holly were to win the competition. Well, you won, Luke, and here it is." With that, the host handed Luke the box and stepped aside.

Holly's expression was puzzled as she looked from Serianni to Luke and back.

Luke took the box, dropping to one knee. The studio went dark with only a follow spot illuminating the couple in a circle of light. Holly's hands went to her face, covering it in disbelief. A hush blanketed the room as Luke spoke.

"When heaven opens and drops an angel into your life, a man would have to be a fool to ever let her escape."

Tears poured down Holly's cheeks, as she blinked her eyes and curled her lips inward. Her knees felt too weak to support her body, and knots in her stomach tossed about like a volley ball on an Olympic court.

"That event took place in my life fourteen weeks ago. I'm many things, some not so good, but I'm not a fool. Holly Dawson, will you bestow on me the honor of accepting this ring and agreeing to become my wife and dancing partner for life?"

Holly thought she would choke. She could hardly breathe, much less speak. Seeking to convey a response, her head bobbed vigorously up and down, propelling tears through the spotlight beam as the camera moved in for a close-up of her mascara-streaked face.

Luke rose, removed the ring from the box, and took her hand. Sliding the diamonds on her finger, he then captured her in his arms, kissing her tenderly. Their medals tangled as they attempted to separate.

Colorful, fountain-styled bursts of pyrotechnics cascaded at the rear of the performance area, while streamers fell from the top of the studio. The audience went totally wild as the general lighting returned. The cast immediately converged on the couple with hugs and hearty pats on the back.

"Thank goodness she accepted," Serianni quipped to the camera. "Our producers would have hated a waste of the special effects—and—what a spectacular way to close the season!"

CHAPTER FORTY-SIX

It took several minutes after cameras stopped broadcasting for the commotion to wane. As the din diminished, Holly tugged on Luke's arm, beckoning him closer. He leaned over.

Shielding her mouth with her hand, she spoke softly into his ear. "When did you decide to do this?"

The corners of his mouth turned up. "Thanksgiving. Seeing you in your native element, I knew I was not only insanely attracted to you but also respected and admired the total woman you are."

His words filled her with a warm glow. She paused, gazing at him for a second. "What would you have done if we lost?"

He grabbed her, hugging her so tight he nearly cracked a rib. "The same thing, minus a million witnesses."

As the crowd began to disburse, Andrei Rodchenko came up and slapped Luke on the back. "Congratulations, English. Well done."

"Thanks. You're a hell of a dancer and made it damned tough. Sorry you had to lose."

"No, how is it the Americans say? No sweat. For me, there's always the next season, but tell me we aren't losing our new pro champ?"

"Not on my account," Luke said. "But, you guys better remember she's spoken for, and I'll be around a lot." He smiled and gave the Russian a high-five.

As a few members of the cast and crew lingered on the floor, Holly glanced around the room and saw Mary Lou and Les standing all alone at the front of the audience seating. She poked Luke and pointed. "My parents. I forgot about them." She then swept across the room, arms open wide. Luke withdrew from the remaining group and trailed after her.

"Mom, Dad, I'm so sorry I've neglected you." She threw her arms around each in turn, hugging them with all her might. "I'm *so* glad you were here."

"We understand, honey. You were caught up in an avalanche." Mary Lou embraced Holly, giving her a kiss on the cheek.

"Congratulations, baby," Les said. "We're so proud of you." He turned to Luke and thrust out his hand. "Welcome to the family, Luke."

Mary Lou put her arms around Luke, gave him a slightly stiff hug, and turned to Holly. "Let me see that ring. I could see it sparkling from our seats."

Holly held up her hand.

"My goodness—gorgeous. Did you suspect Luke was going to propose?"

Holly shook her head. "Not a clue." Although to an observer Mary Lou appeared happy, Holly sensed a glimmer of reserve. *She's playing gracious, southern lady, but I know her. She's not thrilled with this engagement.*

Standing behind Holly, Luke addressed her father. "I apologize for not asking your permission ahead of time. I hope you'll give us your blessings."

"Absolutely. Not that it would do any good to object, given the expression on my daughter's face."

Holly beamed. "You are both welcome to attend the after-party on the top floor. After we change, Luke and I will be up."

Mary Lou took Holly's hand. "No, no. We'll head back to the hotel. You'll be busy with your obligations. We would be in the way." She turned to her husband. "Les, don't you agree that's best?"

"I do. It's been a long day for the old folks. We'll get together tomorrow."

"Are you sure?" Luke asked.

"Absolutely," Les said.

Holly spoke up. "There is a talk show tomorrow morning, but we should be through by lunch. Why don't we plan to be at the hotel around one?"

Before either parent could answer, Luke put his hand on Holly's shoulder. "You're forgetting, love. I meet with the brass of my new series at one-thirty. But the three of you can have some quality, family time." He directed his attention to the Dawsons. "Plan on dinner at my flat tomorrow night. I'll send a car to pick you up at six."

The after-party was a haze of questions from the media, additional congratulatory remarks from cast and crew, and a little more wine than Holly usually drank. Kat Kenley was the most enthusiastic of all.

Greeting them at the door, Kat almost threw Holly off balance with a bear hug. "I told you he was a winner, girl. The expression on Cantrell's face when you pulled off that spectacular lift last week was worth a million bucks." She pointed to Luke. "And you—you rascal. Whipping a proposal out of left field. What the devil would you have done if she rejected you?"

"Felt pretty damned awkward, but thank God, she accepted."

Kat socked him playfully on the shoulder and then raised her wine glass in the air. "Here, here—to the champs and their engagement!"

Sam pushed his way through the crowd to give Luke a hearty handshake and then turned to Holly. "Did I not call it right?"

She threw her arms around him and hugged him tight. "You have been awesome."

During the following two hours, clamor over the proposal and the win temporarily blotted out Holly's concern about the stalker. Only twice did it cross her mind, causing her to instinctively look around for Lisa. The first time, the dancer was engaged in conversation with a reporter; the second time, Holly did not see her. Neither time did she spot the celebrity chef.

It was near midnight when Holly and Luke made it to their car and driver. She was half-wired on the wine she had consumed and half on the coffee she drank, attempting to regain a clear head. As soon as she was nestled in the curve of his arm, Luke whispered, "Your mum is not happy about our engagement."

She pulled away and faced him. "Why would you say that?"

"My dear, I'm a dumb actor, but even I can tell the difference between socially correct responses and sincere enthusiasm."

"But—"

"No buts." He pulled her back under his arm. "It's okay. I don't blame her. Hell, I wouldn't want my daughter marrying me."

"Luke! That's a terrible thing to say."

"The more important question is does her attitude affect you?"

"It doesn't." *Almost true.*

The next day, as Jimmy drove Holly to the Hilton, her stomach was in knots, caused by the shadow of the unknown stalker and Mary Lou's attitude toward the pending marriage. She had attempted to speak with Detective Montgomery earlier, but he was out in the field. She continued to debate the issue of telling her parents about the harassment.

I do not want to hear negative comments about the engagement. Les had appeared onboard the night before, but Holly feared Mary Lou spent the evening convincing him it was a bad idea. On the bright side, Chris had called to enthusiastically congratulate her, and before Holly had rung off with him, a call from Dana had beeped on her cell with another from Gabi close behind

"I can't believe it!" Dana shouted. "My best friend is marrying Luke Damian! I better be in the wedding party, or I'll never speak to you again."

"Who else would be my matron of honor?"

After the short exchange with Dana, Holly returned Gabi's call.

"I am so happy for you," Gabi said.

"You saw the show? I thought you were still on tour."

"I've been home since Sunday and so glad that I got to see that proposal."

"I want you in the wedding. Think it can happen?"

"I'll do everything in my power to make it happen."

When the SUV stopped under the hotel portico, Jimmy got out and opened the door for Holly. It was then reality struck. She would have to tell her parents the truth. Otherwise, how could she explain why a tall, solemn man in a black suit with a lump bulging under his coat was shadowing her?

"What's the procedure when we get to my parents' room? Do you go in with me?" she asked as the elevator took them to the fifth floor.

"No, ma'am. I'll be in the hallway where I can observe the entry to the room you'll be in. Should food service be ordered, notify me on my cell."

Why did I ever think I could keep this secret?

When Holly knocked on the door, her mother answered, wearing a huge smile, and threw her arms around her daughter. "Oh, honey. I am so proud of you."

Didn't say she was happy for me.

Her dad was sitting on one of the two sumptuous sofas, watching a TV program, but got up and came over to hug Holly. "You were beautiful last night, princess. You and Luke outshone them all."

"Thanks, Dad. Spoken like a true father."

"Would you like something to drink, honey?" Mary Lou asked. "This suite has about anything you could want, and the view is fabulous, even from the bathroom."

Holly glanced through the wall of glass on the opposite side of the room at the Hollywood skyline. "I can see."

"I must tell Luke how much we're enjoying the luxury."

"He will be happy to hear you're comfortable."

Les broke in. "Tell you what. You gals need time for girl talk. I'll go in the bedroom and watch TV—might even take a short nap—if the two of you don't mind."

Holly smiled and gave him a hug as he passed by. "See you later." Turning to her mother, she said, "I'll take a Coke, Mom."

"The ring is spectacular," Mary Lou said, walking over to the mini-bar. "But, I did want a chance to chat."

Here it comes.

Holly sat down on a chair at the circular dining table near the terrace. Mary Lou brought her the soft drink and sat in an adjacent chair.

"I don't want you to take this the wrong way, sweetheart." She put a hand on the table close to Holly's. "Dad said I shouldn't say anything, but I just have to."

Holly looked at her mother, debating whether to listen or leave.

"I'm concerned for you. Do you know what you're doing?"

"What do you mean? Do I know what I'm doing?" Holly made a face.

"Honey, marrying an actor is asking for heartbreak, especially Luke Damian. You've only known him for a short time."

"Are you going to be a Debbie Downer? If so, I don't want to hear it. Last night was one of, if not *the,* happiest nights of my life."

"I know, and I'm sorry. I'm thrilled you and Luke won the competition, and I like Luke. Honestly, I do. He's a nice man. But, Holly, step back and look at the big picture. He's got two ex-wives; he's famous; he's incredibly handsome; he was an international heartthrob. *You* had a puppy-love crush on him."

"So, you believe those are reasons I shouldn't marry him?"

"Exactly. Don't you know? Women throw themselves at his feet. How long do you think it will be before he is seduced by some younger, prettier starlet or fan and you become a nuisance to dispose of? Even if that isn't true, how can you be sure you're *really* in love with the man and not just infatuated by the persona. You're probably still on the rebound from Don?"

"Most of what you just said is not true. You don't know him. As for Don? I won't even dignify that absurd idea." Her eyes shot daggers at Mary Lou. "I'll admit that I considered some of your negative thoughts. But, I'm willing to take a chance." Holly lowered her voice. "As far as cheating . . . where is there an insurance policy against that? A lot of men in your world jump into that pool—Dr. Carrington, Mr. Sinclair, Professor Simon. Look around you. Count your friends who have been victims of adultery."

Mary Lou pulled her hand back. "I said I *like* him. I just don't want to see you hurt, honey. I understand the attraction. If I were younger, I would find him attractive. But, he's not the kind of man you marry. Have an affair—live with him."

"Mother!"

"I'm serious. Be engaged for a while. Sleep with him. Get it out of your system."

"I can't believe you're saying that."

"Just don't rush into marriage. It's a lot more than sex and romance. What if you have children, and it falls apart? He's not an American citizen. He could take my grandchildren to England."

Holly stood, fighting to contain a combination of hurt and anger. "I think I need to go. We'll start over tonight—pretend we didn't have this conversation. But I've got to warn you; if you carry this on, it won't be a pleasant evening." She pushed the drink aside, leaned over, and gave her mother a stiff hug and then started for the door. "Tell Dad, I'll see him tonight."

"I've said all I'm going to say, Holly. Just be careful."

When Holly exited the room, Jimmy rose from the chair where he sat on guard.

"Take me home."

"Yes, ma'am."

At least, I escaped telling them about the stalker. Tears pooled in her eyes as they rode down in the elevator.

CHAPTER FORTY-SEVEN

The ride from the Hilton back to Luke's through a second day of rain did nothing to improve Holly's mood.

I won't let her destroy my happiness—not today. She wiped the trace of a tear from her cheek. *But, what if she's right? Is the chemistry masking my common sense?* She closed her eyes and mentally replaced her mother's image with Luke's—the way he looked down on his knee the night before. *Will he break my heart?*

When they arrived, Jimmy walked her to the door and stood while she let herself in.

"You know where I am," he said as she started in.

"Thanks."

As she passed through the entry hall on her way to the bedroom, something in the living room moved, catching her eye. Her hands turned to ice, her knees to mush, and her heart stopped.

"Oh, my gosh!" She took a deep breath, collecting her faculties. "You nearly gave me a heart attack. Why are you home?"

Luke sat motionless on the sofa with Gigi curled up in his lap and a smug grin on his face.

"And what are you doing with Gigi?"

"Answer number one—meeting canceled. Carl had an emergency on the set of another series. Answer number two—she jumped up when I sat down and won't let me move."

Holly's mood changed instantly, a huge smile crossing her face. "Luke! You're six-two. She weighs less than six pounds. Put her on the floor."

"No way. I'm not pissing off the queen. This is the first time she has granted me petting privileges. She generally treats me like an invisible footman, even when I feed her."

Holly dropped her purse on a chair, went over to him, and kissed him. "I knew there was a reason I fell in love with you. For the record, Don hated Gigi. He accused me of loving her more than I loved him."

"Don was a fool in many ways. I *know* you love her more, but I'm fine with it because she can't take my place where it counts most." He tipped his chin with a flirtatious gleam in his eye.

Holly started to pick Gigi up. Luke pushed her hand away.

"Do not interfere. We're bonding. I've been explaining this is the new forever home, and she's been giving me her list of rules and requirements."

"Well, pardon me for intruding." She flopped down next to him and started scratching the cat's head.

"How was the meeting with your parents? You're back earlier than I expected."

Without taking her attention away from Gigi, Holly said, "In a word—disgusting."

"I take it they hate the idea of our marriage."

"Not they—Mom. But I don't think that's the right way to put it. She insists she likes you, but—"

"But?"

"She has reservations . . . and that's all I'm going to say."

"Should I wear Kevlar tonight?"

Holly grinned and punched his arm. "Have no fear. Mary Lou Dawson will be the epitome of grace and manners. Otherwise, ancestors would pop out of cemeteries across three states."

"Coming from an empire filled with ghosts, that is a chilling image."

Holly stood and Gigi jumped off Luke's lap. "Changing the subject. I'm going to take a power nap. Are we taking them out for dinner or ordering in?"

"Neither."

"Excuse me."

"We're cooking."

Holly's brow wrinkled. "We're cooking? Why are we cooking?" She sat back down.

"The way I see it, your mum thinks of me as some celebrity version of a toff—shallow, spoiled, and self-absorbed. Why wouldn't she? She's seen me only on TV and in a formal, guest mode for what? Two days? Tonight's my opportunity to show her and your dad who I really am—my terms, my territory."

Her face relaxed. "Where was my head? I should have known you had a plan."

At six-thirty, the gate guard called to announce the Dawsons had arrived. Holly took a deep breath, crossed herself, and stood as Luke went to the door.

"What a lovely apartment, Luke," Mary Lou said, gazing around the spacious living room.

"It's a condo, Mom," Holly said.

"Excuse me—condo."

"They all look alike," Luke said, shaking Les Dawson's hand. "What can I get the two of you to drink? Wine? Cocktail?"

"Do you by any chance have a beer?" Les asked.

"You bet I do, and I'll join you."

"White wine for me," Mary Lou said.

After small talk about the show, the California weather, and Holly's engagement ring, Luke excused himself to check on dinner.

Holly stood, intending to go with him.

"Sit down, honey. I'll help," Mary Lou said, rising to follow him. "I know you want a chance to talk with your dad, and I want to get to know Luke better."

Holly eyed her mother. *I just bet you do.*

"I'd enjoy your company, Mary Lou."

Inhaling a deep breath as she neared the kitchen, Mary Lou said, "Something smells wonderful."

As Luke and Mary Lou exited, Les turned to Holly. "Mind if I take a look at the NFL game?"

"Sure." Holly took the remote out of a wooden box on the coffee table and flicked on a TV that was nestled in an elegant wall unit. "Make yourself comfortable. I'm going to the kitchen to be sure Mom doesn't poison Luke." She rose to leave.

Les chuckled. "She'll be all right, princess. Just let her get used to the idea. You are her baby, and she was counting on your moving home in the near future."

Holly paused for a second, contemplating his statement. "And marrying Luke means I won't be coming back to Jacksonville. . . . I hadn't thought of it that way." She walked over and gave him a hug before going to the kitchen.

As Holly took a seat on a kitchen barstool, Mary Lou turned. "I thought you and Dad would have a chat, honey."

"He's watching football."

Mary Lou shook her head from side to side in mock disgust. "The first thing he'll want to know when he gets to heaven is where is the TV?"

Luke laughed. "We men never grow up. Hope you don't mind British cuisine, Mary Lou." He took an apron off the counter, tied it around his neck, and then opened the oven.

"You did the cooking?"

"That depends." His eyes twinkled. "If you like it, I did. If you don't, I'll blame it on Holly. In either case, she gets credit for the dessert."

"You'll like it. He's a great cook. You should taste his spinach-stuffed pancakes."

Mary Lou smiled. "I admit I'm surprised. I would *not* have pictured you wearing an apron. I expected you to have a personal chef."

"Nope. We . . . I prefer to cook. I've been in the kitchen since I was ten." He grabbed a pair of pot holders and transferred the casserole to a heating tray. "Because Mum worked two jobs, I was cooking before I knew multiplication tables."

"Really? I don't think Holly knew how to scramble an egg when she left home for New York."

"She's does well enough, now."

Holly spoke up. "The cottage pie is an authentic British recipe—

his mom's."

"I'm looking forward to it," Mary Lou said.

Luke stopped what he was doing and looked at her. "Mary Lou, I sense you're less than thrilled with Holly marrying me—"

Luke don't!

Mary Lou's face turned pink. "No . . . yes, Luke—"

"Hear me out. I don't blame you. I absolutely don't deserve her. I told Holly I wouldn't be happy with a daughter of mine—ours—marrying a man like me." He reached across and took Mary Lou's hand. "What I want to say is, on my mother's grave, I swear to you I will do my best to make her happy," His eyes flashed with determination. "My goal is to contribute as much to her life as she already has to mine."

The older woman stood frozen for a couple of seconds. "I believe you mean that, but you *have* been married twice before. I'm sure in the beginning you thought you loved both of your wives."

"Mom. . . ." *Let it go!* Holly's eyes had a desperate look.

Luke nodded toward Mary Lou, holding his hand up toward Holly, signaling her not to interfere. "I understand your concern. Holly is dear to you as she is to me." He looked his future mother-in-law firmly in the eye. "You are entitled to an explanation." He took a deep breath. "In a nutshell, I attended a wedding at twenty-one in which there was a bad case of mistaken identity. My lovely, nineteen-year-old bride thought she was marrying Alexander Holmes. Luke Damian was a dismal disappoint—"

Mary Lou said, "You don't have to—"

He interrupted. "I think I do. My second marriage was made in Hollywood—starlet and successful actor. All we lacked was a reality show. When I went from asset to liability in three easy film flops, the wings fell off the plane. I'm not defending myself. I wasn't perfect, but I was faithful." He glanced at Holly and back. "Here's the deal. If you ever believe I'm not being a good husband, call me out on it."

Mary Lou stood silent for several seconds and then looked at Holly.

"Don't look at me. This is between the two of you." Holly pointed back and forth to each.

Facing Luke, Mary Lou removed her hand from his grasp and then took his, squeezing it with both hands before letting go. "Thank you for that."

Luke wrapped an arm around her in a quick hug. "Now, that's out of the way, let's get this dinner on the table." He glanced over Mary Lou's shoulder and winked at Holly. She gave him a smile and a subtle, thumbs-up.

He charmed her. I hope it's not the wine.

Holly turned her attention to her mother. "I made bread pudding for dessert—your recipe."

"That will make your dad happy."

Holly glanced back at Luke. *It's probably not over, but you won this round.*

Later, as the group finished dessert, Holly's cell rang. She jumped. "Who is calling now?"

"Why don't you let it go?" Luke said, but she was already up and headed to the credenza for her phone.

Picking it up, Holly froze when she read the caller ID. Adrenalin rushed through her veins. "Oh, my gosh." She covered her mouth with one hand while color drained from her cheeks.

All eyes were on her.

CHAPTER FORTY-EIGHT

Luke reacted instantly, quickly moving to her side as she pressed the talk button.

Holly's hand trembled. Her finger hovered over the speaker button. She wanted him to listen but was afraid for her parents to hear. Her voice shook as she spoke. "Hello."

With grave concern written on his face, Luke put a reassuring arm around her shoulder.

The call was brief, with Holly saying nothing until shortly before hanging up. "We'll be there." She turned, still grasping the phone in her hand.

"Who *was* that, Holly?" Mary Lou asked.

Ignoring her mother, Holly's eyes connected with Luke's. "Detective Montgomery." She tried to say more but her heart was beating so fast it took her breath away.

"What did he say, angel?"

It took her several more seconds to take control. "They made an arrest."

His expression lightened as he pulled her tight against his chest. "Thank God."

Mary Lou and Les looked at one another, confused and concerned. Mary Lou stood, attempting to go to her daughter, but Les put a hand out to hold her back.

Mary Lou persisted. "Holly, what do you mean an arrest?"

Neither Holly nor Luke acknowledged her.

"Did he say anything else?" Luke asked. "Did he say who?"

She didn't answer, looking around at her parents and then back to Luke.

"Holly, please tell me what are you and Luke are talking about," Mary Lou said.

"I'll . . . I'll tell you in a minute, Mom. Let me catch my breath."

Luke took the phone from her hand and guided her back to the table. "Is it someone we know?"

Holly nodded silently.

"Lisa Cantrell?"

"No. . . . It *wasn't*."

Mary Lou clutched her husband's arm. Neither took their eyes off Holly.

Staring into her eyes, Luke stroked her hand as she paused, still trying to absorb the information the detective conveyed.

"It was Theo—Theo Svendsen. Lisa's partner."

Luke's face registered surprise. "The pretty-boy chef? What the—? Is he deranged?"

"I don't know anything else."

"Montgomery didn't give you any details?"

"No. He called tonight to let me know before it hits the media. He wants us to come in tomorrow morning, and he'll tell us more. I said we would."

"Of course, we will."

Her breathing slowed as she began to relax. "You can cancel the Perrington guards."

"In due time, love. Not yet."

Mary Lou reached across the table for her daughter's hand. "Holly, you're killing your father and me. What is going on? What are Perringtons?"

Holly forced a smile, hoping to calm her mother. "It's a long story, Mom, but I think the nightmare is over."

Luke spoke up. "Holly's been harassed by a stalker for several weeks. She didn't want to worry you. If I'm understanding correctly, that was the detective in charge of the investigation with news the stalker has been arrested."

"Oh, my Lord, no. Les—" The older woman covered her mouth,

her eyes popping open even wider than before. "Did you hear that? My God, honey, you've been in danger? Who is this person?"

"A celebrity on the show," Luke said.

"He is the blond, Swedish guy who came in third," Holly said.

"One of the celebrities? That's insane." Desperation was in Mary Lou's voice and body language. "And again, *what* are Perringtons?"

Les reached for his wife's hand. "Honey, let Holly tell us the story. You haven't given her a chance."

Luke tenderly brushed the top of Holly's head. "Take your time, love."

Holly shook her head in frustration. "Perringtons are private investigators—security guards. Luke hired them to protect me. There's one outside now. As for why Theo did this, I have no idea."

"This is overwhelming." Mary Lou's hands shook. "What did he do? Why was he threatening you?"

"I wish I knew more. Montgomery caught me off guard. I was too stunned to think or ask questions. Theo Svendsen?" She made a face. He was always pleasant, not that I interacted much with him. I can't imagine *why* he would do something like this. Lisa, I could understand. She's been the queen of the ballroom, but why would Theo?"

"I'm sure we'll learn more tomorrow," Luke said. "The important thing is they have him."

Holly turned toward her mother. "I'm not sure where to start."

It took her a little over five minutes to describe the events leading up to Svendsen's arrest. Careful to avoid revealing the role Joy Ambrose played, she omitted mentioning the initial contacts that included inferences about a baby.

"You need to get out of this business and come home," Mary Lou said when Holly finished. "You planned to do that before you and Don broke up. There's no reason you can't still do it. Dad and I will set you up in a studio of your own."

"*Mother.* . . . There's a very good reason I'm not going to do that. Have you forgotten what happened last night?"

Luke smiled but did not comment.

"My life is here. Luke and I both work here—or from here."

"How will you continue working after you're married? Your careers will take you in different directions. You're going on tour next month, aren't you?"

Holly looked at Luke. "I'm supposed to."

He nodded. "You are, love. We'll sort out the wrinkles."

Refocusing on her mother, Holly said, "We've only been engaged twenty-four hours. I'm sure we have a lot to work on."

"Luke, are you okay with your fiancée dancing off in skimpy costumes with a troupe of shirtless men?"

"Mother!" *I knew it wasn't over.*

Luke broke out in a large grin, shaking his head. "Hell, no. But, I've got to be a big boy and suck it up. Plus, I know I can trust her."

Holly's face softened as she gazed at him with affection.

"Mary Lou, I think it's time we went back to the hotel." Les spoke with a soft but firm tone. "The young people will work out their careers without your help."

"Thank you, Dad."

Mary Lou frowned. "I can't leave Luke with all these dirty dishes."

Luke reached over and took Mary Lou's hand. "For that, I *do* have people. You and Les go along and have a good night's rest. I've arranged for the two of you and Holly to have a tour of celebrity homes tomorrow afternoon. In the evening, we'll all go out for a fancy Hollywood dinner."

"I'll call you after we leave the police station," Holly said.

It was clear from her demeanor Mary Lou recognized she was out numbered. "I apologize if I've offended either of you." She glanced at Les. "I guess we should go, but I'd like to powder my nose before we leave."

"Sure." Holly pointed the way to the guest bath.

When Mary Lou was out of earshot, Les walked over and hugged Holly. He then turned and shook Luke's hand. "Don't let 'she who must be obeyed,' to coin a *Rumpole* term, upset you. She's panicked over the thought of losing her little girl. She'll be fine."

"Dad's right. She had my life programmed. Mom was more upset about Don and me breaking up than I was."

Les chuckled. "She and Sally Barrett were already shopping for grand-baby clothes."

Holly turned to Luke. "Sally is Don's mother. She and Mom have been friends since we were kids."

"That's tough competition," Luke said, smiling.

Les patted Luke on the shoulder. "No contest, son. You have the devotion of the one who counts." He nodded toward Holly. "Mary Lou will simmer down, once she gets used to the idea."

A few minutes later, as she closed the door behind her parents, Holly turned to Luke. "Can the nightmare be over?"

He wrapped her in his arms. "Sounds like it is, but we'll know more tomorrow."

She stood very still, clinging to him for several minutes. Pulling back, she wiped moisture from her eyes and then smiled. "Well, Mr. Damian, you *are* a magician. I was impressed with the fairy dust you sprinkled on Mom. Even though she's still resistant, I think you made progress toward winning her over. Thank you."

"I hope so. I know her doubts cast a shadow over you."

"I'm not letting that happen." Holly hesitated. "You know, she didn't even ask if I am living here. She must have suspected after you nearly let the cat out of the bag in the kitchen."

He tickled her ribs. "Oh, so you're admitting you live here now?"

Fighting him off, she said. "I meant, staying here."

"You better rethink that. Gigi put in her change of address. We'd both hate to see you leave."

CHAPTER FORTY-NINE

Friday morning, Luke and Holly were in the squad room at eight-thirty. As they took two seats, Luke spoke. "I understand you arrested Theo Svendsen. Can you fill us in on the details?"

Montgomery opened a folder on his desk. "Certainly. I believe I mentioned before Mr. Svendsen had come across our radar, but I couldn't elaborate at the time."

Luke and Holly both nodded.

"As you know, we were not able to identify the person breaking into to Ms. Dawson's apartment from the initial surveillance tapes. However, our canvas produced tapes from other cameras on the block. Two captured the unsub—unidentified suspect—exiting and entering a van. Running the plate, we were able to ID the van as registered to Mr. Svendsen's restaurant chain."

Holly had to grasp one hand with the other to keep them from shaking. "Theo Svendsen broke in my apartment?"

"Not Svendsen. One of his drivers."

"If the driver broke in, how did you connect Svendsen?" Luke asked.

"We brought the kid in for questioning. He was terrified and folded within ten minutes. Said Svendsen paid him to do the job."

"Why?"

"The chef is bankrupt—unpaid vendors cutting him off. The doors are barely open."

Luke shook his head. "What did that have to do with Holly?"

"Prize money. Think Tonya Harding-Nancy Kerrigan. Take out the competition and take home the prize. Svendsen desperately needed the money a win would give him."

"He needed money badly enough to break laws and make my life hell?" Holly reached for Luke's hand. Montgomery nodded.

"Svendsen was in more than financial trouble. He overextended expansion of his business and made the mistake of borrowing from a loan shark. When he failed to make timely payments, his restaurants and personal safety went on the line."

"How did you find out about that?" Holly asked.

"We pulled bank and credit card statements when we ID'd the van. With what the driver told us, we got a warrant for Svendsen's arrest. I think he was relieved when we picked him up." Montgomery smiled as though proud of himself. "Confronted with the evidence, he asked for a deal and then gave up the whole story."

"If he hadn't confessed, would you have had enough for a conviction?" Luke asked.

"Shaky, but once we had him in custody and fingerprinted, we matched both his prints to a couple of latent partials found on the last note and his DNA to some found on the envelope. He got either sloppy or overconfident."

"Are you sure Lisa Cantrell wasn't in on it with him?" Holly asked. "She acted so funny around me."

"There was nothing to indicate she was involved. Ms. Cantrell cooperated fully, even volunteered for a polygraph. She admitted telling Svendsen about the incident when Ms. Ambrose invaded your rehearsal."

"Which she must have heard from Art Jameson," Holly said.

He nodded. "I think that was the name—one of the executives on the show."

"But, why me? There were other contenders in the competition."

"He couldn't take them all on, and Ms. Cantrell was most afraid you would win, plus Svendsen considered you the easiest mark."

"What now? Does he stay in jail?" Luke asked.

Montgomery smiled again. "The man has no desire to leave lockup. He played with some bad dudes and knows he's a lot safer in our house."

"What will happen to him?" Holly asked.

"To avoid prosecution, Svendsen will testify against the loan shark and accept voluntary deportation back to Sweden. The man is ready to get out of Dodge."

"He certainly screwed up his career," Luke said.

The detective chuckled. "I expect we'll see a chain of restaurants up for sale pretty soon."

Enjoying his own humor, Montgomery started to rise when a clerk stepped over to his desk and handed him a note. Simultaneously, a text came through on Luke's cell.

The expressions on both faces changed.

Puzzled, Holly said, "What's wrong?"

Luke scowled. "Paparazzi."

"I'm sorry, Mr. Damian. Unfortunately, this building has leaks we can't always plug. Apparently, someone let it out that you're here." He picked up the telephone receiver on his desk and punched a button. "I'm going to need an escort team." Shielding the instrument with his hand, the detective turned to Luke. "How did you and Ms. Dawson come here?"

"Driver. He just texted me that he spotted cameras," Luke responded.

Returning attention to the phone, the detective said, "Have them meet us at the back entrance." As he hung up, he looked back at Luke and Holly. "Sorry about this, but we'll get you out of here without a hassle. Tell your driver to come to the other side of the building. I'll notify the guard to let him through."

CHAPTER FIFTY

Other than thanking Montgomery, Holly was quiet until they were in the car.

As if sensing she expected a comment from him, he leaned toward her, gave her a kiss and then said, "It has been a roller coaster."

"It certainly has."

Patting the top of her hand, he said, "I think we can put trouble in the past tense. How do you feel?"

"Relieved. Let down. A little sad. As much as I hate what Theo Svendsen put me through, I feel a little sorry for him. What a mess he got himself into."

"You're too forgiving. I don't think he would have done anything violent, but you can never be sure." He leaned forward to speak to Jimmy. "How about stopping at a convenience store? I could use a bottle of water or soft drink." Glancing back at Holly, he asked, "How about you, angel?"

She nodded. "A Diet Pepsi would be great."

When they reached Luke's condo, there were several vehicles on the street that Jimmy instantly sized up as paparazzi. "Do you want to rush the gate, Luke?"

"Circle the block to give us a second to consider." Turning to Holly, he said, "Your call."

"How did they know where you live?" Her eyes were huge as she looked at the three SUVs and two passenger automobiles lined up with drivers at each wheel.

"They know every unlisted address in the city. They'll likely camp out until they get a comment and at least a few photos."

"You've been through this before?" She looked at him quizzically.

"I have, but not for a while. What I learned is they don't give up until you throw them a bone. If you want time to prepare, we'll push through. We also have the option of letting Jeff contact a reputable reporter and volunteer to give a statement."

"Let's do that. I don't think I can handle questions yet."

Jimmy spoke up. "Probably be a good idea for me to call for a couple more guys, just to be sure I can get you through your gate without company."

When Luke and Holly got into the condo, Holly plopped down on the sofa. "I've got to call Mom and Dad. I promised to fill them in."

Luke turned, nodding. "Before you do, I'm thinking it might not be a good idea for you to go on the home tour with them."

"I thought the same. And we probably shouldn't go out for dinner."

"Agreed. Either they can dine at a restaurant without us, or I'll have a dinner catered here."

While she called her parents to relay the details of their meeting, Luke called his agent. He finished first and went to the kitchen to make sandwiches.

Returning to the living room with a tray, he put it down on the coffee table and took a seat next to Holly as she hung up.

"How did they take the news?"

"I think they're as relieved as I am."

"What about the change of plans?"

"No problem. Mom liked the idea of dinner at home." She took a half of a turkey sandwich from the tray. "Thanks. I am hungry. What did Jeff say?"

"He's going to set it up for his office at five-thirty with three TV reporters and two print lads. He said his phone has been ringing off all morning with media calling to the point he started to unplug everything."

"Being a celebrity has its down side."

"Most definitely. Do you have any doubts about living with it?"

She straightened the dishes on the tray. "None. But—"

"But what?"

"Are our careers going to be a problem?"

He shook his head. "No way. We won't let them."

"Are you thinking I'll give up mine?"

"Absolutely not. You've worked your whole life to master your art. I would never interfere. The only thing I might do is try to find a way to combine our work to keep us in the same hemisphere. Do you recall the day I signed the contract for the new series?"

"I remember, but nothing specific."

"I had contingencies the producers accommodated. One was they had to offer you a role on the show."

She almost dropped her drink. "Are you kidding? I'm not an actress."

"You act every second you're performing. All you need to add is the audio. You're far ahead of where I was when I started. To test the waters, it would be a small role, maybe an under five—five lines. It's entirely up to you. I've heard you say your career has a shelf life. This would be the introduction to the next phase. It's completely up to you."

Holly listened intently.

He continued, studying her face as he spoke. "It's there if you want it. We're going to be married for the rest of our lives, with problems along the way. If we can work together, at least some of the time, it might help solve one."

She smiled. "I'll think about it."

When they finished lunch, Holly took the tray back to the kitchen. Luke kicked his loafers off, propped his feet on the table, and turned on the TV. As she came back into the living room, he patted the sofa next to him. "Come relax with me. I feel like we've hardly had time to come down from Wednesday night."

She accepted his invitation and cuddled up under his arm. "The drama's really over, we won, and we're engaged. What a week!"

"Good things come in threes, I've heard." He stroked her arm with the hand that was around her shoulders. "Are you happy?"

She leaned her head against his chest. "Delirious. Happier than I think I've ever been in my life. Mom even sounded more positive on the phone—said she and Dad had a long talk last night. They agreed you're a special guy. I'm not dreaming, am I? But, I do have one question."

"Fire away."

"What made you sure I was the one you wanted to spend the rest of your life with?"

He took his time responding, gazing into her eyes. "I think I knew the day I first met you."

She shook her head. "Come on. You couldn't. You didn't even know me then."

"Not consciously, but something clicked in my subconscious. The night of our first meeting, I came back here and was overcome with a sudden urge to call Mum."

Holly turned her head, absorbing his words. His expression was pensive as if he were transported back to that moment in their history.

"I didn't realize at the time what it meant and actually forgot it happened. But, I wanted to call Mum—tell her I had just met the most intriguing woman." He smiled. "I *never* had that feeling before."

"But in those first weeks, you never came on to me or gave me any reason to believe you were interested."

"Believe me. It was a battle. I fought hard. . . . First, because Joy was still clinging; second, I didn't want to jeopardize our professional relationship; and third, I didn't *want* to fall in love. Not with my track record."

"What changed your mind?"

"You. Watching you day after day. Feeling myself insanely attracted to you. But, more than that, developing more admiration and respect for you than I have ever felt."

She made a face.

He tickled her ribs. "Don't give me that look. I saw your work ethic, your skill, your incredible drive and determination. You pushed me past my potential, refusing to let me take a shortcut or cop out. You would accept nothing less than my best. Most of all, I saw your gentleness, your sensitivity, and your integrity." He took her hand and pulled her around so she straddled his lap. "And that beautiful face and sexy, irresistible body were just icing on the cake." He began unfastening the buttons on her blouse.

"That's all hard to believe. I'm not that special."

He put an index finger across her lips. "Let me be the judge of that. I can't promise you I won't make mistakes or that we won't disagree. But, I can promise I will never lie to you, leave you, or be unfaithful. Now, let's stop talking and permit me to demonstrate how much I love you."

Acknowledgements

My lifelong love of dance is the inspiration for this first in a series of novels set in different dance genres. I am phenomenally grateful to all who supported and contributed to The Ballroom, beginning with my daughter, Allison Erwin Norton, Artistic Director of Dance Theatre of Bradenton, who served as my consultant and the choreographer/director of the video trailer.

In addition, I thank my brilliant editor, Julie Delegal, for her careful attention to detail and her astute suggestions. In addition, thank you to my equally brilliant literary consultant, John C. Boles and my beta readers: Marcella Beeching, Michael Heubeck, and Keith Gockenbach.

Every writer needs a team for moral support. I am blessed with the following: Perry, Bill, Allison, Lynda, Marshall, Judson, Trevor, Brooks, Sarah, Caroline, Amelia, and Nancy. They all put up with reading and hearing about the lives of Holly and Luke for many months.

I also want to thank the talented dancers performing in the video trailer, Mattison Bedinghaus and Xander Chawi, and the Online Binding team, Cheyenne, Darius, and Carrie, for making all my books beautiful.

Last, but by no means least, I thank my faithful readers who continue to inspire and encourage me.

JUDITH ERWIN was born in Atlanta, Georgia and currently lives in Jacksonville, Florida. She is a graduate of Jacksonville University and the University of Florida, College of Law. The Ballroom is her fourth novel.

www.juditherwinofficialwebsite.com

www.ingramcontent.com/pod-product-compliance
Lightning Source LLC
Chambersburg PA
CBHW020257120726
47904CB00001B/243